A KOPEK
in the
DUST

A KOPEK
in the
DUST

ARNOLD D. PICKAR

iUniverse, Inc.
Bloomington

A Kopek in the Dust

iUniverse books may be ordered through booksellers or by contacting:

iUniverse
1663 Liberty Drive
Bloomington, IN 47403
www.iuniverse.com
1-800-Authors (1-800-288-4677)

Cover image supplied by the author.

ISBN: 978-1-4697-8972-9 (sc)
ISBN: 978-1-4697-8974-3 (hc)
ISBN: 978-1-4697-8973-6 (ebk)

Printed in the United States of America

iUniverse rev. date: 03/20/2012

Contents

Dedication

Dedicated to the memory of
Abraham Ira Pickar, D.D.S.
1892-1963

Introduction and Acknowledgements

The origin of this book lies in an effort of mine, following the completion of some family memoirs, to reconstruct, from imagination, some incidents from my father's early life. I had long thought that my father's spiritual journey segued neatly into my own. Thus I came to realize that a broader story could be told that encompassed more than just boyhood events. However, I caution that this is neither biography nor autobiography. It is primarily a work of fiction, albeit informed by experiences in the life of my father and that of my own. At one level it is an immigrant tale, but I would hope it can be viewed largely as the story of one scientist's spiritual journey.

I am thankful for the presence in places I have lived of communities of thoughtful, liberal-minded persons that have sustained me in my own life journey. I also want to acknowledge the influence of a number of my teachers over the years, in the sciences and otherwise. Unitarian-Universalist minister, Rev. Preston Moore, supplied the spark that ignited my desire to turn to this writing. My appreciation extends to my good friend, Kenneth H. Bailey, for sharing some painful memories. I want to thank my son, David I. Pickar, for his careful and critical reading of the original manuscript; his insightful comments on both style and content have been invaluable. Finally, I acknowledge the patient support of my wife, Ann, who cheerfully ceded to me the necessary periods of quiet reflection on woodland trails and the private time for writing.

Arnold D. Pickar
Portland, Oregon
January 2012

PROLOGUE

This is the story of Abel Roth, born Abram Rutkiewicz in 1892 in Wizna, Poland, told from his point of view. His family saw no reason to note the exact date of his birth, but they remembered that it took place on one of those longest nights of the year around the time of the Feast of Lights. Abel, accompanying his mother and siblings, followed his father to America at the turn of the century, settling eventually in the Brownsville section of Brooklyn.

The village into which Abel was born was one of hundreds of shtetls scattered throughout the Pale of Resettlement, the regions of the Russian Empire in which, beginning with Catherine the Great, Jews were permitted to live ostensibly free from the requirement that they convert to Christianity. Eventually the Pale came to include, besides the eastern half of Poland ceded to Russia in the partitions of that country at the end of the eighteenth century, parts of western Russia, Lithuania, and Ukraine. Over the centuries, the Jewish residents, in their cultural isolation, developed Yiddish, a language rooted in medieval-German. Jews had lived in Poland since the fourteenth century, escaping largely from persecution in lands to the west. They prospered for a considerable time under the protection of the nobility, who saw their value as an easily controlled but literate class of managers, craftsman, and tradesmen. Not being nobility, clergy, or serfs, they filled a role that in Western Europe became the province of a developing middle class. The Jews of the shtetls consorted with their Polish neighbors only out of economic necessity, but shared, for the most part, the same burdens of poverty.

The America, to which Abel's family came, was in rapid ascendancy as a world power following the Spanish-American

1

War. Economic growth was in full flower, as it had been, with the exception of occasional downturns, since the Civil War. With the expansion of industry and population, the nation's thirst for new immigrants to power this vitality was unquenchable. The year 1900 was near the cusp of a spring tide of immigration that ended with the First World War. That year almost a half million newcomers made their way to U.S. shores, more than three quarters entering by ship through the port of New York. They were almost entirely Europeans, but unlike earlier waves of immigration, half of these new potential citizens arrived from Southern and Eastern Europe. They came especially from Italy and the Russian Empire, in approximately equal numbers. From the ports, immigrants dispersed throughout the country, often locating where earlier newcomers had established a familiar cultural base. Formerly rural people increasingly found new homes in urban environments. For large numbers of Jews and Italians that meant the teeming slums of New York.

Meanwhile, in the shtetls of Eastern Europe, the lives of the Jewish residents were growing increasingly perilous. The concentration of Jews in the Pale made them an easy target for pogroms and anti-Jewish riots, often government encouraged. Thousands were killed and their properties destroyed or commandeered. Public education was restricted as well. Even in the imperial cities, like Moscow and Kiev, the Jewish quota for higher education was only three percent. To Abel's family, the need to undertake the arduous journey across the sea was apparent enough. For those who chose to remain, the worst was still to come.

CHAPTER 1

Wizna in the Pale

1900

There it was. It was a bright spark in the road leading from the synagogue through the village. Or was it a trick of the eye? Perhaps it was from a shard of broken glass that caught the morning sun on a bright Sabbath day in October.

Why not a piece of glass? The men who stream from the tavern late Friday afternoons when it closes before sundown are not known for their steadiness or for always remembering to leave their beer mugs at the table. I can almost picture one of them. He is a robust man who tends his cheeses from early morning each day except the Sabbath. He stubs his toe. He goes flying into the path. The mug shatters. His companions help him up. They all laugh and help him gather the broken pieces of glass; he will pay the tavern keeper for the mug when he can. For now the man must dust himself off and hurry home. There he will hug each of the children in turn starting with youngest, then give his red faced wife a little squeeze. He will wash his hands and face and comb his beard before hurrying off to the synagogue for Friday evening prayers. But in the path in front of the tavern he will leave that shard of glass that was sparkling in the morning sunshine.

But perhaps it had been otherwise. I am seven years old—going on eight—and curious. And I don't accept easy explanations. I was on my way home from the synagogue but I stopped to examine the place where the glint of light had caught my eye. Looking closely, I saw something metallic protruding from the dust. Pushing aside the

3

dirt with my toe, it was revealed. A shiny kopek! So that is what that loutish man spilling in the dust had left behind.

With this treasure in my pocket the possibilities would be endless. Mr. Shafransky's store has a box of new pencils each costing a kopek, painted all yellow with a pink eraser fastened with a metal band to the top—like the tsar's bald head in his crown. Wouldn't that be a prize possession at the school! Vastly superior to those little stubby pencils that Shafransky the grocer gives us boys when they become too short to rest above his ear.

Father, before he left home to find us a new place to live, said I was much too curious. But I guess that is okay because he also said that I am studious. At least he always seemed to mention that when there was a visitor at our house. Perhaps this is all true. But at the moment on that Saturday morning I was mostly hungry. And it made me think about the grocer—the same man who grudgingly gives us the grimy pencil stubs. He also had a fresh supply of halvah of two kinds. There was a plain variety the color of heavy cream that sparkled with sugary dew when the light hit it just so. He also had a new kind with streaks of chocolate running through it, making it like the marble altar I had seen when I and the other boys peeped into the church window that the Polish people used on the other end of the town. And a kopek? A kopek would buy enough halvah for a nice treat after school with enough left over for a bedtime snack as well.

But this was only a tempting dream of a store-bought treat which Mother provided only on very special occasions. I could imagine the sweet taste of halvah, the texture of the flaky surface melting on the tongue, but there was a central problem. My dilemma was that on the Sabbath it is strictly forbidden to handle money. Even a kopek. It could not be spent. It could not be received. In fact, it could not be touched. Even a kopek! Who had made such a rule? Perhaps it was God. Perhaps some grand rabbi somewhere in Warsaw had made that rule. If it were a matter of life or death I would have hoped that this grand rabbi might have allowed an exception. But here in Wizna, far from the notice of the great rabbi but always under the gaze of God, to touch that coin in the dust would have been a sin.

Especially on this Saturday morning in October sin was not far from mind. My older brother Duv—he was, for the time being the "man" of the family—had brought me to the synagogue for the morning. The men and most of the boys assembled all day in the sanctuary, a room even bigger than our schoolroom. On a small balcony above us some of the older women and a few of the girls crowded together. A great flood of light poured through the windows but it was chilly, being too early in the season to hire Mr. Kowalski to light a fire in the stove. The older men stood bobbing and swaying and reading from the prayer books. They recited in Hebrew, a foreign language that made me wonder how much the men understood of what they were saying. The younger boys sat and stood with the men and often daydreamed. Only when the Holy Ark was opened and the scrolls appeared, and the men kissed the fringes of their prayer shawls and transferred their blessings to the "book", did we pay attention. The scrolls appeared from the hiding place like royalty emerging from their palace—adorned in embroidered velvet and silver jewelry. It was like God was let into the room.

But apart from this interlude of the weekly reading from the Torah scrolls, it is only when the rabbi gathers the young boys during an interlude in the prayers that Saturday mornings come alive. While the men take their tea at the samovar that bubbles in the vestibule just outside the sanctuary the rabbi often tells us stories from the Holy Book. Often they are about obedience to God. Today we heard again how the serpent tempted Eve—how Eve forgot about the rules and brought shame and pain to all of us. He told us how it was not for us to question the rules that were laid down, nor to blame the "serpent." We were to honor God and God would honor us. Why didn't Eve know this? The ladies I knew understood the rules better than anyone.

I was daydreaming about Eve and the serpent—about whether Eve wore at least a babushka and whether the serpent was like the black snake that my friend Jacob and I once captured in a bucket down by river—when Duv reminded me that it was nearly noontime. It was the time that most of us young boys are dismissed to go home and help our mothers.

And soon I was facing a "serpent" of my own, that tempting kopek in the dust! It would be gone by the evening. It could not remain for long in the road covered only with a thin layer of dirt. Everyone and anyone could claim it. But the rule remained: money must not be handled on the Sabbath. I nudged the kopek with the toe of my shoe. Surely this was not handling the coin. I gave it a little kick. The coin rolled and tumbled a short way down the path A few more kicks and the coin was in the road beside the baker's shop.

That was when Jacob caught up with me. Jacob is my classmate whose little house is next to ours. I put my foot down on the coin and stood there waiting for him to come up to me. He had not seen my prize. Jacob is shorter than me and a little chubby. He is like a coiled spring. I often noticed how he clenched and unclenched his hands or shifted from one foot to the other.

He presented me with his irrepressible grin. "Race you home," he said.

"No," I replied. "No games allowed on the Shabbas. You know that."

"Racing is not a game." Jacob maintained his friendly grin despite his remonstrations. "Games are only for fun. Getting home is allowed—unless it's on the back of Kowalski's wagon—and the sooner the better."

I was not sure whether perhaps Jacob was right. But I was obstinate. "Someone always wins a race," I said. "It's a game."

We stood there for some little while, each the arbiter of our own position. I resisted the thought that perhaps Jacob had the better case. But surely two boys racing through the village on a Sabbath morning was more likely to raise eyebrows than would a small boy scuffling up the dust on his way home from the synagogue. Eventually Jacob, with his baffling knack for simultaneous exasperation and good cheer, moved on, leaving me still standing on my secret.

It was obvious that Jacob was in a hurry to get home and pretty soon he was almost out of sight. I continued my arduous journey, blocking out the thought that perhaps kicking along a coin was kind of a game. God was busy listening to the men in the synagogue and, besides, I was breaking no rules. Or perhaps God was testing me to see if I could capitalize on my good fortune without desecrating the Holy Day.

After a few minutes the coin and I turned off the main road down towards the river among the Jewish houses. Now the going was more difficult. The dust lay more softly than in the main street where it was packed firmly by the coming and going of carts delivering goods to the shops, or by the wagons bringing in the peasants and their produce on market days. Here and there in front the houses lining the back street were knots of children, still young enough to be allowed to play outside on the Sabbath. Not wanting to arouse their curiosity, I took to the alleyways.

The houses in our part of the village are hardly like the large and handsome ones clustered near the church close to the market square. Here, a few of the houses are separated from the street by small yards hemmed in by rough fences of unpainted boards. It seemed to me as if these fences were held upright as if more by the will of God than by any visible support. But the boards might keep a wandering chicken from scratching up the beans planted alongside the front walls in the springtime. Now the brown and yellow remnants of the beanstalks quivered on the strings that tethered them to the windowsills. But most of the houses reach right to the road, just as does our own. Were it not for an old bed sheet that Mother has hung over the front window any passerby could see into our front room where all of the children sleep, except little Sari.

Alongside an alleyway I noticed that the lady of one of the houses had used flour sacking for curtains in the windows that faced the path. This caught my interest and momentarily I turned my attention from the coin in the middle of the path. The building was neither better nor worse than our own house. On the wall facing the street the seams between the boards were hidden by ochre colored stucco, but the back walls were rough, unpainted and weathered boards laid horizontally in uneven rows. If this part of the house was like ours, it is where the cook stove is located and where the family gathers, especially on cold evenings, to eat and pray. It would also be where the mother and father sleep. At our house Mother has already begun to patch for the winter some of the cracks between the boards where some of the wads of paper or cloth have fallen out. The owner of this other house had begun laying down a store of firewood—old tree branches and unwanted scraps from the sawmill just upstream on the river. An iron bathing tub had been moved to the back steps to make room for this wood.

I resumed my mission. Just before I reached our own house, I stopped at the one that belonged to the family of Jacob's older cousin Ruchel. Her house lay near where the river bends away from the town. A copse of trees separates the buildings from the flourmill on the water's edge. Ruchel's father, Jacob's uncle Gorodetsky works at the mill. I see him now and then delivering sacks of flour to the bakery and to Shafransky's store. I looked for the place on the wall where the bear had paid them a visit last fall. Sure enough, on a back wall a new board had been nailed into place higher than I can reach. It was a crooked piece of wood but just the right shape to fill the space among the other boards. Mr. Gorodetsky must have found it among the discarded wood alongside the sawmill.

The incident of the bear occurred after I had gone to bed, but I recall that I was wakened briefly by shouting and noise at the time. The next afternoon my brother Duv and my older sister Celia were fairly bursting with the story Ruchel had told them at school. The Gorodetskys were in the main room of their house preparing to go to bed when they heard an awful sound on the wall where Ruchel's mother was laying out bedclothes on the pallet where the parents slept. Ruchel said the wall was shaking and there was a loud scratching sound. Then there was a snorting and grunting and when they looked up the snout of the bear was poking through a hole in the wall above the bed. Mrs. Gorodetsky screamed at the beast but it only poked its nose further and further through the opening between the boards. It was not until Ruchel threw the iron stew pot at it that the bear decided it was time to leave in a hurry.

Just last month I heard Mother discussing this event with Jacob's mother, Yetta.

"So why did this bear decide to visit the Gorodetskys?" Mother asked. "It's been a long time since I heard of a bear crossing from the other side of the river." The two women were sitting in the sun just outside the kitchen door. Mother was peeling potatoes for the *latkes* she had promised me she would make for dinner. Jacob and I were kneeling in the dirt a short distance away pretending to be concentrating on a game of marbles.

"Who knows?" Yetta replied. She sipped from the glass of hot tea Mother had brought to her. Small beads of sweat formed on her forehead. "But this was a big, bold one, I can tell you," she went on. "I can hardly reach the place where it poked its ugly nose in. I suppose it was looking to make a den in the woods just across from the house. It didn't help that my sister had cooked up big pot of chicken stew for the Shabbas. The smell of that coming from the hole in the wall would be enough to interest any bear."

"So how come Gorodetsky had a big hole in the wall?" Mother wanted to know. "Above the bed yet!"

"No need to tell me about it. My sister has told that *schlemiel* of a husband to do something about it more times than I know. In the winter sometimes the rags she pushes into the hole fall out and she has to shake off the snow from the quilt in the morning. But thanks to Ruchel that bear learned a good lesson. It made such a noise when she hit its nose with the stew pot. You know some of the men came out with the constable and his gun the next day to look for the beast, but it must have gone back across the river."

Mother stood up holding the pot of potatoes in front of her on her way into the kitchen. "That Ruchel! Some strong girl! Did you ever see her toss bags of flour from the wagon for her father? And what about him? What was Gorodetsky doing during this commotion?"

Yetta looked up. "As far I know he was praying. It was as if he didn't notice that the bear was tearing down the house."

"Praying that the bear would go away, maybe?"

Yetta pursed her lips as she thought about it. "I'm not sure, but knowing him I suppose he was again thanking God to be among His Chosen People."

Mother bent down to look directly at Yetta's face. She lowered her voice and said, "I don't know about that, but I can tell you this. That night Gorodetsky was among the bear's chosen people!"

I grinned to myself at the recollection as I continued to move my kopek down the alleyway. Shortly the coin reached our doorstep and was finally slid beneath the doormat and out of sight. And there it remained hidden until the shops reopened on Monday.

I purchased the halvah just after school, and while it was true to its promise of heavenly sweetness, a certain unease of heart came with it. The rabbi had told us of the manna that came from heaven and fed the children of Israel. He read from "the book" that it was "like coriander seed, white; and the taste of it was like wafers made with honey." But, as the rabbi cautioned us, the people of Israel remained discomforted. Somewhere out there lay the Promised Land and the people had yet to prove themselves deserving.

CHAPTER 2

Leaving

1901

We are now well on our journey to a new home in America and I am thinking about how it all began. It seems so long ago that we left the village, but brother Duv has reminded me that it has been not even two days. It began in the dark, early morning on a cold spring day much like today.

For days neighbor ladies had come to call, one by one, to say goodbye. Mother would make a pot of tea and they would talk for a while. Most of the time Mother would have a gift for the neighbor, familiar things that she said we could not take with us. Sometimes she held each of these things—pots and pans, a feather duster, clothes or shoes, an oil lamp—and looked at it a long time before she carefully put the item in the corner of the room awaiting the visit. Once I saw her eyes water as she laid down a little blue blanket that I remember was my favorite when I was very small.

It was a cold spring morning on the day before we left that Jacob's mother Yetta came. Yetta is a cheerful and energetic, red-faced woman. She is taller than most of the village women, but she is not stout. Celia says she is younger than Mother, but not much. I like it when Aunt Yetta, as I call her, visits.

"So, have you heard from Jake again?" she asked. Jake is my father, Jacob Rutkiewicz. He left the village more than a year ago to find a new place for us to live. He explained that there were a lot of troubles going on and it was time to leave for some place that was "safer." I did not ask about the "troubles" or what he meant by "safer." I did not want to know. Meanwhile brother Duv has helped Mother as much as he can.

"Not since the last letter," Mother answered. "You can never tell, maybe he sent something else. There are thieves in that post office. They see something coming from America and immediately they think it has money in it. The last letter from Jake—for safekeeping it was sent to my father who has higher up friends in his village—in fact had a little money in it. Goodness, but it will be useful on this trip."

"So it's the same plan then? The 'organization' will get you on the way to the ship. And then you will meet up with Jake in New York. Don't worry. It will work out. So many have already done it. We even think about it sometimes." Aunt Yetta put down the glass of tea and grasped Mother's hands. "Don't worry," she repeated.

Mother did not reply. She had a thoughtful but worried look. She rose from her seat and, drying her hands on her apron, went to the corner of the room. There, wrapped in a cloth were two brass candlesticks. "Please take these, Yetta. To remember. There is just so much we can take with us."

"Are you sure?" Yetta said. "These are from your wedding, no?"

"Now it's for you not to worry. There are two more that I am taking with us, even if they weigh a ton. Also to remember. The other big wedding gift, the samovar—I know you have one—I had to sell. Jablonski, the Pole landowner up in the village, has it. At least he gave me a fair price, not like what he was willing to pay for this place." Mother looked around at the room. She looked a little sad. "My guess is he will tear this down and plant potatoes. Who knows? It was the best I could do."

Before leaving, Aunt Yetta went around the room hugging and kissing all the children. We had been pretending to be doing other things, but we were listening to the conversation. Yetta's good cheer almost made the slight fear in the pit of my stomach disappear. At the door she and mother embraced for a long time. I wondered if I would ever see Aunt Yetta again.

The next morning, while it was still very dark, Mother came around to each of us and shook us awake. Mother brought out some warm milk that she had kept under straw during the night. We dressed by the light of the remaining oil lamp. Duv and I carried the suitcases out into the alleyway, large ones for him and Celia and a smaller cardboard one for me. In the dim light we could see Shapiro in his milk wagon approaching. As he stopped near the door, Mother came out carrying a large cloth satchel. Celia followed with Sari.

Mr. Shapiro didn't say much, though as he clambered into the cart and pushed his milk cans tightly together, he mentioned that we were lucky that he didn't have a lot of milk to sell that day in Bialystok. Duv handed our belongings to him, and when he had pushed them into the rear of the cart he motioned for the rest of us to climb in from the front of the wagon, just behind his horse. I was first; then Celia came in beside me. Shapiro held the baby as Mother, pulling her skirts above her ankles, pulled herself in just behind the driver's seat. He handed Sari to Mother and jumped up into his seat. Finally as Duv took the seat next to him, Mr. Shapiro made a little nickering sound. The horse started up hesitantly, as if surprised and resentful of our added weight. I snuggled in next to Celia under the shawl Mother had laid over us. Before long I was asleep.

As I awoke the sun was just rising behind the buildings in Bialystok. I had been here once before, accompanying Father as he brought in his piecework tailoring and bought more cloth. So I pretended to Celia that the city was not a great novelty. But secretly I felt a mix of awe and dread as we made our way past the big stone buildings, through streets already choked with noisy carts and dray wagons. From under the shawl I looked around the cart. Mr. Shapiro, the fringe of his tallith moving in the breeze where it fell out from beneath his coat, was concentrating on his horse as it made its way along the crowded street. Duv turned around and looked in the back to see if anyone was awake. I looked too. Mother was sitting upright, smoothing her hair with her hand and checking where she had tied it in a bun behind her head. Celia, beside me, was struggling to open her eyes. Sari had crawled over to her, pulling her hair and giggling.

Suddenly the cart lurched to a stop, and Mr. Shapiro turned around. He had a squat oblong face. His neck and jaw were covered by dark gray stubble. His black cap was pulled down low just above his eyes. "Railroad station. All off," he said. "Unless any of you boys want to go to the cheese factory with me," he added. Then he broke into a grin, the first time I had ever seen him smile. It was as if he wanted to ease our anxieties. He helped us unload our belongings. Before leaving he reached down from his seat and shook mother's hand.

We were on the edge of a square. In front of us was the station, a long wooden building with a high-pitched red roof. It was not easy making our way inside with people coming and going, almost knocking us over. Duv, Celia, and I carried our suitcases. Mother struggled to carry her heavy satchel while holding tightly to Sari who toddled beside her. Finally we reached a bench in the center of a great room that was open on one side, giving a full view of the tracks and trains parked alongside. There we sat while Mother went to purchase our tickets. Eventually she returned with four round hard rolls. They were like the ones Father sometimes brought home from Bialystok, with a big dimple in the center filled with sweet, moist, baked onion. She gave Duv some money, and Celia and I went with him carrying some jars to a kiosk alongside one of the walls. There a lady wearing a babushka filled our jars with hot sweet tea from a samovar. While we ate our breakfast in silence Mother explained that we were to meet some strangers under the station clock before noon. From time to time she glanced at the clock nervously.

While we waited Duv took me by the hand and the two of us made our way closer to one of the huge locomotives alongside the station. I could not disguise my excitement in the presence of this wonder. I envied the men sitting high above me, mustaches drooping as if to emphasize their nonchalance. These men had the power to bring this huge, hissing, steaming thing to life. They could somehow order the gleaming wheels to turn, each of the wheels almost higher than I stood, and with that to set the massive engine and its string of cars into motion. As we watched, the locomotive slowly began to move. The cranks and rods fastened to the wheels shuttled back and forth, sliding in and out of a big, hot black box at the front end of the machine. And above that like an iron tower laid on its side was what Duv called the boiler, because it was where the fire turned water into steam. When he and I returned to our bench my head swam with an ill formed sense of a new world appearing, a world of mysterious power inhabited by strangers. It seemed odd that Mother and the girls did not seem especially curious about the big engines.

Just before noon Mother led us all to the part of the station under the clock where we joined a group of people who had also been waiting nearby. There were several families and a couple of young men who appeared to be traveling alone. Not long after that we all climbed up into one of the railroad carriages that was standing alongside the station. Again I pretended that this was a matter of course, meanwhile hiding the dreadful uncertainties of being inside this big machine. We had seen the trains moving in the distance across the horizon from edge of our village, but only Duv, Mother and I had ever before been up close to the huge, black, noisy body of a railway train. We found a place for all of us to sit down on two wooden benches facing one another. Duv put our suitcases on a rack above the seats but Mother kept her satchel at her feet. Soon, accompanied by three deafening shrieks of the train whistle, there was a shuddering of the railway car and slowly we began to move.

Fields and farms slid by. None of us had ever moved so fast. This was not like bouncing along in a milk cart. We children pressed their noses up against the windows. I imagined myself flying low across the field and muddy tracks as they swept by. The train stopped once at a town where some passengers descended to the platform while others came on board. A man in a white apron came down the aisle, a basket strapped in front of him. From him Mother bought some rolls. Then, when the train began to move again she brought out a jar of herring from her satchel. We were famished. Sitting at a window, eating the late lunch, I watched an unfamiliar world rapidly slide by. The afternoon hours likewise slid by and it did not seem long before Mother announced that we would be leaving the train the next time it stopped, along with the others that had boarded with us.

Now, out of the window as far I could see there were buildings, many of them large stone ones like we had seen earlier in the day in Bialystok. As we moved along other railroad tracks seemed to sweep into our path or sweep out to other places. Here there were other trains to be seen. Soon we slowed down to a stop alongside a long roofed platform. We gathered our belongings and stepping down onto the platform we made our way into a huge building. It had a marvelous roof of glass that allowed in an orange glow from the late afternoon sun. It was higher than any of the buildings I had ever seen. We were in Warsaw. So this is where the great rabbi lives, I thought.

This time Mother told us we must hurry. Tugging along Sari with her free arm she instructed the rest of us to join hands and follow her. This is where our real journey was to begin. We would be traveling with some others who were gathering outside the ticket seller's office. There seemed to be a handful of people clustered there already, and along with those of us who had come from Bialystok, we moved into the fringes of the group.

It was here that I first saw Boris. He was the biggest man I had ever seen. He towered above Mother and even above the men with whom we were traveling. He wore a dark frock coat buttoned almost to the top. The light coming down from the glass roof glinted off his bald scalp. Rising above them it did not seem at first at first that he was part of the gathering of people around him. But I saw him bend his head down to speak to one of the women. He spoke softly and I could not make out what he was saying. But I noticed his huge mustaches move as the older people moved in closer to listen carefully.

When time came to board another train the light in the sky was growing dim. A skinny man in a blue uniform made his way along the platform lighting tall gas lamps. Following Boris our group made its way to the last car in the train and climbed aboard. Boris stood by the side of the door helping the ladies and handing up children. Effortlessly he lifted up both Sari and Mother's satchel from the platform. Boris came aboard just as the fearsome blast of the train whistle signaled that we were about to move. Until then he stood on the outside just beside the door, looking down the platform as if he expected another one of us to show up. Before he took his own seat he went down the aisle stopping occasionally to whisper instructions to people in our group.

Again, Mother brought out some food from her satchel. This time she had a small loaf of rye bread and cheese. She divided a half-sour pickle among us. There was only a jar of water to drink, but she surprised us with pieces of mandel bread, firm and chewy and rich with raisins, nuts, and spice. Yetta had given these to us when she said goodbye. As we sat with our supper it began to grow dark. Dimly lit villages went by. In between them was blackness and an occasional light streaked by like a shooting star. When we finally were starting to become drowsy, Boris came down the aisle waking up the children and helping the ladies move luggage from the racks above us. Again there were whispered instructions.

The train slowed down. Another town with gas lamps in the street and a few lit windows came into view. With a lurch and a screech the train stopped, and our entire group descended to the station platform. Gathering in the chill behind the station Boris cautioned us not to speak and to make as little noise as possible. He implored mothers to try to keep babies from crying. Then he led the way down a dark road away from the town. A tall thin young man with a scraggly beard who was traveling alone was asked to stay at the back to shepherd along stragglers. The young man's dour expression brightened with the new responsibility.

We passed some farmhouses. Patches of snow lay in the fields. Somewhere a dog barked and then appeared to go back to sleep. In the distance the town clock struck one. From time to time Boris halted our group and listened. Silence. After some time we once again halted. I had never felt so tired, so I was glad to be able briefly to sit down on my little suitcase. But Boris told us we must now be prepared to move quickly. Then he raised his head to the wind and made a noise like an owl. Three hoots—a pause—then two more hoots. A moment later in the distance from behind a rise in

17

the road just barely visible in the dim light came an answer: three hoots—two hoots.

I have never seen an owl, but I had heard one. It lived in the woods behind our old village. I had also seen a picture of an owl. It seems like a friendly bird and comes out at night and catches mice in the fields. But this owl call in the distance in this strange place far from home caused me to shudder. Again Boris imitated an owl. This time two hoots followed by one hoot. Once again in the distance was the answering call. And now Boris in an urgent whisper instructed us to pick up our belongings and follow him to the rise in the road. There we found a small shack and outside a portly man in a fur hat and a huge coat. Light from his lantern glinted off the brass buttons running down the front of his coat. This was a policeman or soldier. He motioned for us to move ahead and as we passed I could see that Boris put something into his hand. No words were spoken.

Now we could see that we were approaching another town. Boris spoke to us in much louder tones. In this place, he assured us, we need not worry about the Tsar and the Cossacks. I had thought that the Tsar was in charge of the whole world, but in this place, it was a people Boris called the Prussians who made the rules. I could only think that if these Prussians would let me sit down somewhere and rest, I would be grateful, even to someone who made the rules for me.

My wishes were granted in time. In this new town, at the railway station, as the sky began to lighten, we were once more on a train. Again the five of us found a pair of benches facing each other alongside a window. This time Boris remained on the platform after the train began to move. He stood there facing the train, his collar turned up, framing his bald head. His hands were thrust into the pockets of his long black coat. He did not smile or wave as the train began to move. He looked, perhaps, a little like the rabbi did when Duv had read the Haftarah at his Bar Mitzvah last year—serious and pleased. I watched from the window until he vanished far behind the train. I leaned against sister Celia and closed my eyes.

There is nothing more to remember of this trip until a gentle shaking and Mother's voice asking if I would like a little lunch. Sun is streaming through the windows of the railway car. The countryside sliding past looks not so different from our old home, but I know that Wizna is now very far behind.

CHAPTER 3

A World Between

1901

The ship is rolling and pitching gently today and to my delight I am not seasick. Waking up this morning below deck in our cramped compartment reeking with odors of sweat and vomit, I actually found myself wondering about what the cook might have for breakfast. Duv took Celia and me to the "dining room" very early, even before Sari and Mother were stirring, so the three of us were able to ascend to the open deck and find room to sit down with our filled lunch pails. We knew that later on the deck would be a crowded jumble of people vying for space out in the fresh air. When I am outside I must be with Celia or Duv, but I refuse to hold on to them. I am now an expert in riding with the motion, flexing my knees with the rhythm of the ship, like I used to do standing in the back of Shapiro's wagon bounding along the road in Wizna. But many of the older people, when they try their turn on the deck, zigzag from one spot to another, like some drunk just out of the tavern. Mostly they try to find a spot to sit amidst the tangle of machinery and pipes. Otherwise I see them clutching a railing or hugging a post.

Now I can look back and remember where we have been since we left Wizna: the train ride, our stay with Aunt Esther and Uncle Max in Antwerp, and of course the first several days on this little world of a ship in the middle of the ocean. Each of these places was like a world of its own—each now beginning to fade as might a dream world. This last world has been a kind of nightmare, especially the

20

seasickness. At first I was often was so nauseous that I would curl up on my mattress in the corner of the room where they put our family. The first day I vomited at least six times into the big tin mother had been given by one of the cooks. I could eat nothing, but the matron who came around each day made me drink water. It was slightly warm and tasted slightly of salt, which made me feel even more ill. But at least there was something to get out of my stomach when I had to ask for the tin again. Most of us were sick. Only Sari didn't seem to mind. It was as if she enjoyed the rocking motion, fighting to keep upright and giggling whenever the ship made her tumble.

In a couple of days, after Mother had talked me into eating a bit of bread and cheese she had brought from the lunch line, I began to feel a little better. Celia took me up the stairs to the open deck where the fresh air seemed to clean some of the sickness away. There was a strong wind and I pulled my scarf around my neck and tucked it inside the wool coat Aunt Esther had given me in Antwerp. For the first time I began to look with interest at the sea. My legs were wobbly but I made my way to the rail and peered down at the water. I had not known that water could be blue—bluer than the sky above the ship. Bluer even than the velvet that covered the Torah scrolls in the synagogue in Wizna. The water stretched out in all directions, meeting the line all around us where the sky came down to touch it. There was nothing else in this world but our ship, the sea and the sky—no bird, no house, no other ship, and no marker to tell us where we were or where America was.

But today all seems well again. The open deck has quickly filled rail-to-rail with passengers and a few of the sailors—a collection of strangers back to back and sleeve-to-sleeve. Some sit silently with their thoughts, or else they are talking one on one, hands always in motion, in languages beyond my recognition. When it gets too crowded I may retreat below deck to our stateroom.

But despite all the crowding our family is fortunate, as Mother has reminded us. Because of Uncle Max and Aunt Esther's help we are able to travel third class. This is a lot better than the regular steerage passengers, who are in huge rooms with fifty or sixty other people. Three other Jewish families are sharing a room with us. It is an iron box with rough wooden floors that smell disagreeably, although I have seen them mopped at least once. Iron railings fastened to the walls hold up narrow metal bunks for us to sleep on, one on top of the other almost to the ceiling. There are some hooks on the wall next to the doorway, but most of our belongings are crammed in beside us in our bunks. We are lucky because Sari, being so small but entitled to her own berth, has extra room there for some of our other baggage. There is also a little space under the lowest bunk, the one that belongs to Mother, to keep some suitcases.

There is no window or porthole in our room. In order to let in some extra air and light the doorway is almost always open to the passageway. Sometimes when a male passenger or a seaman lingered at the doorway, Mother or one of the other ladies made it clear that he was to move on. A little fresh air constantly blows in from a pipe at the ceiling, but hardly enough to push away the smell of people and throw-up. Especially at mealtimes the smell of food, much like cabbage soup, permeates the nauseating mix of odors stealing in through the door.

The ship is filled with mysteries. Unexplained machinery here and there and everywhere tangles of pipes of various sizes. But the most captivating thing on the ship is the electric light in the center of our ceiling. From the first time I saw an electric light as we made our way along the corridor that leads to our room, I have thought about this wonder. Even in Aunt Esther's house in Antwerp I had not seen such a thing—a lamp that goes on or off instantly with the twist of a little handle, a lamp that does not need kerosene or gas, and does not burn away like a candle. I wonder if I would ever understand the secret of the glowing curly wire inside the glass bulb.

Now that I feel well I can think again about our journey and about our visit with Aunt Esther and Uncle Max in Antwerp. I remember that not long after we left the station where we left Boris we stopped again in the darkness at a place out in the country. Outside there were only a couple of small houses. After a while three men who looked like soldiers came through our car, stopping at each bench and looking at papers that passengers showed them.

They spoke strangely, but close enough to Yiddish that I could mostly tell what they were saying. One of them looked at Mother's papers very quickly, and then looked at each of us in turn before handing the papers back. Something about these tall, serious men in their stiff, high-necked uniforms decorated with gold braid made me nervous. I huddled close to Celia until they had left our car and the train began moving again.

The rest of the night passed in a fitful sleep, interrupted several times by brief stops of the train alongside dimly lit stations. But in the morning, as light once again filled the railroad car, my good cheer returned. Mother bought several big sweet pastries from a stout lady in light blue smock pushing her tea cart down the aisle. It was a splendid little breakfast to celebrate our imminent arrival in Antwerp.

Soon again we were entering a great city. As the train slowed, up and down the railroad car everyone prepared to leave. Down from the racks above us and scooped from beneath the seats, Duv and I gathered all our belongings. When finally we descended to the platform we gathered in a tight little cluster. As soon as she was sure we were all together, Mother began to look around hoping to see her sister.

In fact, I was the first to see, at the far end of the platform, an elegant lady in an enormous hat, looking at us intently. She rapidly approached us, followed closely behind by a young man in a plain dark suit. Upon reaching us her face broke into an enormous smile and without a word she threw open her arms and grasped Mother in a tight embrace. "Gittle, Gittle, Gittle," she exclaimed. It had been a while since we had heard anyone call Mother by that name. As the women hugged, we children looked on, not knowing what to expect. Both of them had tears in their eyes.

This is how we met Aunt Esther. She looked very much like Mother, although I didn't see the resemblance right away. Perhaps it was because of the way she was dressed. She looked unlike any woman I had known before. Her dress was pinched in tight at the waist and reached almost to the ground. She had a collar that was decorated in lace all around and her huge hat held down by enormous pins made her seem much taller than Mother. I shrunk back at first but soon she put us all at ease. Mother and Aunt Esther turned towards the rest of us.

"Duvid, my oldest," Mother said, turning to Duv. Aunt Esther extended her hand. Duv shook her hand politely.

"When I last saw you," Aunt Esther said, "you were just so high." She flattened her hand and lowered it to about half my height. Duv grinned sheepishly. "But of course you wouldn't remember." She then turned her gaze to the rest of us. In turn, Mother introduced us; first Celia, then me, and finally Sari, who was pressed against Celia's skirt as she held her hand. In turn Aunt Esther bent down and gave Celia and me a little hug and a kiss on the cheek. But Sari, much to her astonishment, was swept up in Aunt Esther's arms to receive her allotted kiss.

"Mm-mm!" Aunt Esther said emphatically through pursed lips. "Such a sweetie!" Then she planted a kiss on Sari's cheek before lowering her to the floor.

"But come. You must all be so tired. Maybe hungry too." She turned her head and nodded towards the young man in the dark suit. "Jan here will drive us home. Uncle Max is sure to be there for lunch when we arrive. And we have so much to talk about." She turned directly to Jan and said something to him I could not understand. Though she spoke with us in Yiddish, she spoke to Jan in a language I later learned was Flemish. Jan picked up several of our heavier bags. Then Aunt Esther led the way into the main hall of the station. It was even more magnificent than the one in Warsaw.

We followed her out onto the street and up to a fine carriage. A plainly dressed young woman stood in front holding the reins of the horse. I had seen a few carriages like this in Bialystok, and I had caught sight of others as the train had passed through larger towns, but I had hardly dreamt of being able to ride in one. Jan helped us up into the covered cab, Aunt Esther, mother and Sari on one seat, the rest of us facing them on the other seat. Before Jan closed the door, Aunt Esther motioned to the plainly dressed woman holding the horse. "This is Els," she said. "My other right arm, I call her."

Then Jan climbed to the driver's seat out in the front of the carriage. When Els had taken her place beside him, Aunt Esther signaled to them with a wave of her hand and we moved smartly down the street.

And what a ride it was! We sat on soft cushions, and there was only a little shaking. This was not Shapiro's milk wagon indeed. Outside there were endless rows of shops and behind their big windows there was everything I might ever think of needing: men's coats, ladies dresses, shoes, bottles, tools. In front of some stores lay crates of apples, cabbages, oranges, and strange, long, yellow fruits. Here and there little round tables covered by white cloths were on the sidewalks, with elegant gentlemen and ladies sitting at them, sipping from fine cups. Carriages and wagons were everywhere on the avenue and coming out of the side streets. People crowded the side of the road, sometimes darting across the road in front of the carriage. They all seemed in a hurry. It was a wonder that they did not collide with one another.

Eventually we came to a wide street lined on both sides with tall trees, their branches arching over the roadway like a great leafy roof. Rows of tall, red brick houses stood back from the road, each of them fronted by a set of gleaming white stone steps. In time we stopped in front of one of these houses. Emerging from the big front door was a bearded man in a very fine black suit. This, Aunt Esther told us, was her husband, our Uncle Max. He hurried down the steps and opened the door of the carriage even before Jan could come down from the driver's seat. As we stepped out he engaged us one by one—for Mother a long and close hug, and for each of the older children a smile and a polite handshake. Finally he helped Aunt Esther down from the cab and, after kissing her cheek, the two of them, arm in arm, led us up the steps and into the house.

The house in Antwerp is the best of the dream worlds that I carry in my memory from our journey. We lived there only a few days but in that world we walked on carpets and slept in feather beds. At mealtimes we ate from white chinaware and there was always enough. Aunt Esther or her helper, Els, drew warm water into a big stone tub for our baths, and there were books everywhere.

Company came for dinner one evening soon after we arrived. In the dining room we children were introduced briefly and then we were off to the kitchen for our own supper, but for a few minutes I lingered in the hallway furtively looking in on the party. Aunt Esther and Uncle Max spoke with the guests in French, leaving Mother silent and looking a little embarrassed. But in the kitchen Duv, Celia, Sari, and I had a nice little party of our own with Els and Jan joining us between their chores. Els was able to speak a little Yiddish and Jan sang us a Flemish song. For dessert there were cream tarts with berries.

At breakfast time one morning Uncle Max had just finished his coffee and was leaving for his business when the rest of us came to the table. Aunt Esther was there and for the first time we spoke about our leaving again. She began with a little quiz. "Who knows where you will be going in a few days?" She turned to little Sari who was leaning close to Mother while a piece of toast was being buttered for her. "I'll bet Sari knows."

"'merica," Sari shot back, not removing her gaze from the piece of toast.

"Very good," Aunt Esther said, giving a couple of little claps with her hands. "And what language will they be speaking there?" Celia and I were a little hesitant and Sari had lost interest in the conversation. But Duv was quick to reply.

"Eeng-lish," he said, making a great effort to pronounce the word as he supposed it would be in America. He had found a book on that language in the house and had been studying a little.

"Very good again," said Aunt Esther. "Now for a hard question. Which direction must you go to get to America?" she asked. She was now pouring hot cocoa from a pitcher for each of the children. Mother had her usual steaming glass of tea in front of her. There was a small platter of white and yellow slices of cheese in the center of the table. Els appeared with a plate of fresh toast. Aunt Esther restrained her gently by the arm and said something to her in Flemish, before Els left the room. Aunt Esther again looked around at us.

"Out that way," I burst out, feeling a little silly and pointed toward the front door. Mother had a disapproving look and Celia was suppressing a giggle. I had my eyes on the cheese and toast, but becoming more serious I thought about the fact that during most of our trip so far we had generally been moving away from the morning sun.

"That way?" I asked, pointing towards the study that adjoined the dining room. The morning sunlight was streaming in through the dining room windows in the direction of the study. "Yes, that way," I affirmed.

Just then Els emerged from the study wheeling a large globe of the world. Duv and I had discovered it while we were exploring the house the morning after we arrived. I had resolved to come back and examine it at a later time. Its garish colors caught in the morning sun, and I thought it was one of the most beautiful things I had ever seen. It deserved its ornate wood cradle atop the wheeled pedestal carved into three lion claws.

"Very good answer, Abe," Aunt Esther said. "Yes, that way. Towards the west." She spun the globe around until her finger stopped it at the edge of a big light blue patch that ran down the side of the sphere from top to bottom. "This is where you are right now," she said, tapping her finger next to the big blue patch. "And in a few days you will be floating out over the water in a big boat, further towards the west, out over the ocean." Her finger moved out over the blue patch as she slowly turned the globe. "The Atlantic Ocean. The most water you have ever seen."

Now she had even Sari's attention. "And then on the other side—." She turned the globe a little more. Now she tapped a big green patch. "On the other side, the New World, America."

"Father!" Sari exclaimed.

"Yes. Your father, Jake, is there. That's where his letters come from. It's a long way, but you have already come a long way." Now she spun the globe back and pointed out a big orange patch. "From Poland, all across Europe—." Her finger moved to the left towards the blue water patch. "The Old World," she added.

After breakfast I studied Aunt Esther's globe. It seemed we had traveled so far from the orange patch of Poland, across the whole of Europe, but the blue patch of the Atlantic Ocean dwarfed the whole of the Old World we had crossed to bring us to Antwerp. And beyond that, around the bend in the globe, was the huge green patch that will be our new country. It was as big as the ocean we had yet to float across. I was excited and a little frightened as I spun the globe and thought of how much there is still to see and do.

Since that day with Aunt Esther I have thought about Father. I cannot remember him clearly. He is like a person out of a book, or out of a Bible story—a name without an image attached. Mother had shown us a picture of him, taken together with her when they were married. In that picture he is young—too young to be my father—a sallow sad-faced young man, skullcap on his head, a short scraggly beard beneath his chin. Soon we are to see him again, and I am not sure what I will have to say to him.

And now, standing at the railing of this little tossing and rolling world between the old and the new, I am looking out at the ocean and trying to imagine what lies hidden from view below the limb of the earth in the distance. I picture Father on the shore waving as our ship approaches the land, but I know that it won't be that way. And behind Father, in that expanse colored green on Aunt Esther's globe, what? Cities, farms, woods, and little towns like there are in Europe?

I am also thinking of more than that. Somehow this whole, huge sphere beneath my feet, shaped like the globe in the study in Aunt Esther's house, floats among the stars suspended between the sun and the moon. The rabbi told us it was God's will, though I cannot see the reason for that. But, the rabbi added, "God saw that it was good." And today, looking out in wonder at the vast sea and sky, I would agree.

CHAPTER 4

Promises

1901

Great excitement erupted late yesterday. The passageway outside our room echoed with a jumble of languages and hurried footsteps. America was in sight! On the deck there was pushing and shoving to get a place at the railing. I squeezed between the skirts of two ladies and looked out across the water. It was a nice spring day and the sea was very calm. The ship was moving slowly, gently pitching up and down with the swells. On the horizon low hills framed a gap leading into a bay. Beyond that I could make out a hazy form in the distance looking like a tall slender tree rising from the water. Some people excitedly pointed to it and I heard one of them explain that this was the famous Statue of Liberty.

Slowly the ship moved between two spits of land and into the harbor. I could see buildings on the shore—buildings not too different from those we had left behind in Europe. And so many ships! There were boats small enough that four of them could line up in a row alongside our ship, and large clumsy vessels flying sails among the smokestacks. Ferryboats darted in many directions, trailing smoke from their short black funnels. I was reminded of the smoky chimney by the sawmill at the river in Wizna. There were also a few big ugly steamships like ours, railings crowded with passengers. We stared at these people and most certainly they were staring at us. Then, as we moved closer, all eyes turned to the great statue. Passing by her, it was as if we were gathered under her gigantic outstretched arm holding the big torch. For some moments I was speechless, while shouts and cheers came from the crowd. One lady was crying. I thought about the story of the Israelites entering the Promised Land. Of course we had not wandered for forty years, but it seemed to me we had traveled for a long time. And this great queen with her spiked crown stood there welcoming us to America.

I felt Duv's hand pulling on my arm. He drew me away from the railing and motioned towards the doorway that led below. "Enough already, Abe. Mother needs us in the stateroom."

I went reluctantly. Just beyond the Statue of Liberty another little island had come into view. On the edge of that island was a grand castle. It was larger than the huge train stations we had seen in Warsaw. It was mostly red, but around the many windows and at the corners were great blocks of white colored stone. The central part stood well above all the rest and was fronted by huge windows filled with many panes of glass rising into stone arches reaching almost to the roof. And above the bright red roof were four tall identical towers, one at each corner of the central portion of the building. They rose up white layer upon red layer upon white layer. I was reminded of the fancy cake Aunt Esther had produced for our dinner the day before we left Antwerp. On each tower sat a dome topped by a thin tapered pole. This had to be the palace of the king of America, I thought. I stopped and craned my neck to have a better look.

Duv, who had me by the hand, had stopped as well. "Ellis Island," he said. "That's where we'll have to go to see if they'll let us stay."

I was stunned. "Let us stay?" This is first time I had heard any doubts about us going to America to be with Father, or perhaps I had not paid attention. Duv immediately recognized my alarm.

"Come along," he said. He tugged on my hand and pulled me towards one of the deckhouses. When we had reached the bulkhead near the door that led down to our sleeping quarters he stopped and turned me around to face him. He took my other hand and looking me directly in the face he said, "I'm sorry, Abe. I shouldn't have scared you. We won't have to go back. I've been talking with the Hebrew cook. He said it happens sometimes, but not very often.

Usually it's someone who tried to cheat in the first place and tries to hide some sickness, or maybe somebody who develops something on the ship. Father's here. He got to America. None of us is sick. We'll be okay. Right?"

I cast my eyes downwards. I thought about the long trip, the days on the train, the seasickness. "I guess so, Duv," I replied. "Maybe I'm a little scared. I don't know what to expect. I don't even know whether I'll know Father. I don't know what to say or do."

"Just stick close to me, little brother. I've been keeping my ears open. There'll be men in uniforms, but the cook says they're usually nice to the people. And there'll be a doctor for a quick checkup, but another doctor gave us all an okay before we got onto the ship, so there won't be any trouble."

I wasn't sure he totally believed what he was saying, but I was determined to be brave like him. Duv put a finger under my chin and pulled my face up meet his gaze. I tried a weak smile, trying to regain the euphoric sense I had as we sailed into the harbor. Duv pulled me again towards the door in the deckhouse. But then he stopped and looked at me again.

"One more thing, Abe. No more *Duv*. From now on it's *Dave*—it's the American way. *Dave*, as in *David*." He seemed to have a little trouble saying the name, then repeated it. "*David*—that's how they say it here. So it's Dave from now on. Can you say it?"

"Sure, Dave. It's not too hard. But maybe I'll forget, but I'll try. Am I still Abe?"

Dave laughed. "Abe is Abe. You're lucky. But Mother may not say Dave. The older people don't change easily, and that's okay with me. Now let's go."

As we entered the doorway and climbed down the stairs to where we had stayed for two weeks, I was once again assaulted by the stench of food and sweat and vomit that hung in the air. For a moment I found myself thinking of whether there was a way to describe this smell as a single smell, like calling a certain paint purple instead of blue mixed with red. The smell was a little fainter than usual. The ship's crew had come through the corridors the day before mopping all the decks—or perhaps I had become accustomed to the odor.

But despite that, with the ship moving so slowly little air was being pushed down the air scoops on the deck. Down below it had grown even more warm and stuffy.

In our stateroom Mother and Celia and ladies from the other families were collecting their belongings. Cloth bags and valises lay about. A few of the ladies exchanged hugs. With our help, Mother quickly assembled most of our baggage in a neat pile in the corner of the room, then she and Dave went up to the open deck to receive instructions, leaving the younger children in charge of our possessions. One of the other ladies made us a present of a blue and white rubber ball she had carried all the way from Odessa in Russia. It had belonged to her son, she explained, and she carried it to remind her of him. But he was in America already, and she would see him again soon. Her eyes glistened as she told us this. Soon Celia, Sari, and I were having a grand game of catch.

Dave was right. It was not too bad in the red and white palace on Ellis Island. Early this morning we carried our belongings up the stairs and onto the deck. The ship was sitting in the middle of the harbor in sight of the buildings and towers of New York. Soon we were in a line of passengers descending onto a ferryboat that took us to the island. Inside the big palace there were more lines of people. Each of us, even little Sari, received a tag with a big number on it that hung around our necks. Men in uniform were in charge, but I remembered what Dave had told me—that they were there only to help. At a high desk one of the uniformed men, a tired looking grandpa with a small gray mustache asked Mother a lot of questions about our family, about Father, and about where we had been and where we were going. A kindly looking lady with a tall collar and puffy sleeves translated his questions into Yiddish and the answers back into English. I realized that I could recognize some of the English words already.

Finally we came to the doctors. The only other time I had been seen by a doctor was in Antwerp while we were waiting to board our ship. In Wizna the nearest real doctor was in Byalystok. If anyone was sick the rabbi's wife might visit, but to visit a real doctor meant a long bumpy ride. Here men and boys went to one side of a long partition; girls and women went on the other side. My doctor was a young man with thin-rimmed glasses and a large forehead. He motioned for me to undo the top button of my shirt and thumped a few times on either side of my chest and listened to my breathing through a couple of tubes attached to a device he pressed against my back. The next doctor was a very tall, skinny, military looking man in shiny black boots. I had watched nervously as he examined men who stood ahead of me in the line. When it was my turn he had me turn my face towards the ceiling. Then, with one hand he held back my head, and with the other he pulled up the top of an eyelid with a little hooked instrument. I could swear he was using a buttonhook like the one I had seen Aunt Esther use to put on her fancy high shoes. Just as quickly, and before I could resist, he pulled up the other lid with the hook, and then gently pushed me along. Dave was waiting for me rubbing the tears from his eyes. But he grinned and signaled me with a "thumbs-up." This was the famous trachoma examination. "Fail that," he told me later, "and you are back on the boat."

Outside the examination room Dave and I rejoined Mother and the girls and took seats along with hundreds of other people. I recognized some who had been with us on our ship, and many more who must have arrived on other ships. Some of them were in hushed conversation, but mostly they sat in silence as if they were dreaming about what lay ahead for them in America. There we sat. From time to time, a group of people got up and went to a high desk at the end of the hall as their names were called out. It was the middle of the afternoon and none of us had had much to eat since leaving the ship in the morning. But until now I had not noticed how hungry I was. From her handbag Mother produced a little bread and cheese. Then she sent Dave and me to a little shop at the end of the hall to buy a treat of chocolate for each of us. And we continued to sit and wait. Mother was unusually quiet.

I leaned against Celia and dozed. I dreamed that the young, bearded man in Mother's wedding picture was sitting with us in the big hall. He seemed to know everyone there. A couple of times he got up and went over to shake hands with another waiting family.

He went up to the official at the desk at the front of the hall and slapped him on the back. Then he came back to where we were waiting and began to put his arm around my shoulder. I awoke to find Dave shaking me. Our family name had finally been called.

At the high desk was a puffy-faced man in a uniform who reminded me of the official who had looked over our family papers when we boarded the ship in Antwerp. As we stood before this official there were more questions for Mother. He made some marks on papers he had before him. Then, with some flourish, he brought down on the papers a large rubber stamp. Handing these papers to mother, he said, "Welcome to America," and pointed to a stairway at the end of the hall. As we turned to leave he reached beneath the desk and pulled out a couple of little red, white, and blue flags, which he handed to Sari and me. Our first American presents!

At the bottom of the stairs was a long, wide, dimly lit corridor. I could make out knots of people at the far end, clustered at windows much like those at the ticket booths and sweet shops in the railroad stations. Closer to the foot of the stairs benches lined each wall. Women and children sat there in several clusters looking much like our own family. At a large, square post centered between the benches we were met by a imposing, matronly lady to whom mother handed our papers. Raising the spectacles that hung about her neck to the tip of her nose, this lady quickly looked over the papers. She motioned us to a space on a bench to the right side of the corridor. Mother sat down stiffly with her large purse in her lap. She stared quietly across the corridor, her eyes fixed on the double doors through which the matronly lady had gone after examining our papers. Again I was feeling drowsy. Sari was already asleep with her head in Celia's lap. I leaned against Dave and closed my eyes. Half dreaming, I pictured Mother and Father in their wedding picture.

There was a murmur of voices. Celia and Dave were saying something to one another. Mother was now standing. Across the corridor just outside the double doors the young man from wedding picture was facing us. As my reverie evaporated and the sounds of the busy place rose in my ears, the young man transformed before me. His hair receded exposing a broad forehead beneath the black skullcap. Little creases appeared around his eyes, and flecks of gray showed in his neatly trimmed beard. And just visible beneath his suit coat a gold chain hung in loop from a vest pocket. He was different, but he was the man in the picture. At last Father was with us again.

Father stood facing us for what seemed like a very long time. I saw him close his eyes for a moment and open them again, as if he was assuring himself that this was real, that the family was together. Then with a broad smile he came to meet us. Taking Mother's hands he drew close to her. She kissed him on the cheek and whispered something in his ear. Just then, Celia released her grip on Sari's hand and ran to Father, throwing her arms around his waist shouting, "Papa, Papa!" Father bent down and kissed her. Meanwhile Sari stood there rubbing her eyes and looking bewildered until Father scooped her up in his arms and kissed her on the cheek. Finally, putting Sari down he came over to Dave and me.

"Duv, do you remember your old papa?" he said with a twinkle in his eye. "Mother wrote that you have been quite the man of the family. No?" He grasped Dave's hand and shook it. "And how big you are! I almost cannot believe it!" He looked him up and down.

"I only did what I promised, Papa." Dave looked slightly embarrassed.

"Now who is this boy next to you? Does he know me? Can you introduce us?" He squatted down to meet my gaze at eye level. It seemed to me that his eyes were moist.

"This is Abe, Papa. He remembers you. He has grown a lot too."

Father laughed, and then gave me a hug. "Well, we all have to get acquainted again," he said. All at once I felt a tension within me begin to dissipate. A gentle draft of air was blowing through the corridor, bringing with it hints of the sea suffused with the odors of forest greenery. At the end of the hall a large door was open and I noticed for the first time that day the spring sunshine and the screech of gulls whirling about at the water's edge. Father stood up and said, "And now let's go home. America. A new home." He took

Mother's satchel in one arm and after looking around once more at all of us led us out into the daylight. Mother took his other arm.

While we waited for the ferry that would take us from Ellis Island to New York, Father told us about America. No one is hungry, he promised, because there is always a way to earn money. Then he was apologetic. He could not afford to pay for a very large place for us to live. It will be crowded—just two rooms. But I do not remember that we had more than two rooms in our house in Wizna. And he has plans. Before school begins at the end of the summer he thinks we will be able to move to a new place, to Brownsville, on the other side of the river from New York. There are trees there and some open places to play. He has friends from the shul who moved there, and maybe they will know of a job for him.

I wanted to know about school. "School is free," he told us. "All the children go to school. In fact all the children have to go to school."

"Even the girls? What do they learn? Cooking?" I was grinning. There were no girls in the *yeshiva*.

"Don't be silly, Abe!" Dave snapped. "Of course girls go to school." Then he thought for a moment. "Of course back in Wizna some of the Polish kids—especially girls—didn't go to school."

Father interceded. "Like I said, all the children go to school. Jews, Gentiles, everyone." He looked down at Sari, who was sitting on his knee. "Of course maybe not Sari; not for a couple of years." Then he turned to Dave. "But Duv—how old are you now? Fourteen? Almost fifteen? You'll get an after school job, too. We'll find something."

"I want to start right away," Dave said.

"We'll find something," Father repeated. He looked at me. "Maybe even Abe can find a little something to do. A delivery boy? We'll find something. But remember, Abe. You still have to go to Talmud Torah—regular school or no. You'll have a good bar mitzvah, I promise."

Now, finally on the ferry to New York, Dave, Celia, Sari, and I are lined up at the railing peering at the buildings and towers across the water in the distance. The sun is almost ready to set, casting the city in an orange glow. I can just make out a few lights along the shore and in some of the higher windows. All around us people are milling about and crowding the railing. A few of the children are waving their little American flags. Behind us Mother and Father sit on a bench with our belongings. They are talking, seemingly oblivious to the commotion.

We are getting closer and closer to our promised land. Its towers are bathed in a golden glow. Maybe it is really the *goldene medina*, the golden land. It seems also to be a land of promises. A real school. A way to earn some money. And right now, maybe something to eat. Father paid his landlady, who has been making all his meals, to make something extra today so that we can all have dinner together when we arrive at our new little home. He promised.

CHAPTER 5

Flying into the Century

1908

I will not easily forget what happened at the school assembly this morning. Ten of us eighth grade boys, our school's soccer-football team, received our medals for winning the elementary school championship for the entire city.

As usual, the weekly assembly began at 11 o'clock, with all grades attending. Mrs. Walsh sat down at the piano with her back to the auditorium to accompany the singing of the Star Spangled Banner. We all know that this is an occasion that calls for solemnity. But the sight of Mrs. Walsh's backside bouncing vigorously on the piano bench seems always to provoke barely suppressed guffaws from a certain group of the bigger boys in our class. There was no evident breaking of rules and no intended disrespect to the flag, but the smirks among the older boys garnered looks of steely disapproval from the teachers. We all knew that our measure was being taken, yet self-control seemed out of reach for some of my schoolmates.

The principal, Mr. Abramovitch, stepped to the podium to introduce Dr. Boykin, who, he told us in an unctuous, reverential voice, was the assistant superintendent for athletics for all of the public schools of Greater New York. Dr. Boykin stood in sharp contrast to the short and slightly dumpy Mr. Abramovitch. Tall and straight, with slicked back hair and thin-rimmed glasses, he rose energetically from his chair. Casting forth a smile that evoked a sense of his beneficence, he stepped forward. He called out the names of our team members and asked us to join him on the stage. This, he reminded us, is a day we will always remember.

"This occasion is the result of hard work, discipline, teamwork, and good sportsmanship," Mr. Boykin went on. It seems that there were several other virtues in his list, but up on the stage I was hardly listening.

Instead, I was thinking of how proud my sisters would be of me, especially Sari, whom I spotted grinning at me among the other fourth graders near the front of the auditorium. Brother Dave would be eager to see my medal, but I was sure that Mother and Father would not be able to relate to this. For them it mattered only that my school grades were good. It was important that I was learning something that some day would help me to make a living. By contrast, on the winter's day a couple of years ago when I did my bar mitzvah their pride was overflowing.

On that special occasion Father had put on his brown wool suit and his bowler hat and walked with me to the synagogue. He wanted me to be seen with him for the remainder of the service. Now I would come of age within the congregation of the faithful. On that day Dave and I nodded and swayed along with the older men. The Hebrew emerged beneath my breath, automatically, rhythmically, with little thought of the meaning. I felt a great presence, as I often did on Saturday mornings in the shul, and yet my mind wandered. Even on that special day, my bar mitzvah day, I actually found myself thinking about the coming spring soccer practice, wondering whether Saturday matches would now become a larger problem for me.

In the late afternoon, after the bar mitzvah, Father bought home from the shul three of the older men. Dave calls them Father's cronies. From the shelf in the hall closet he brought out a bottle of schnapps he kept for special occasions. We all drank a toast though Mother insisted that my drink be cut with water. "*L'chaim!*" Father said.

"*L'chaim!*" we repeated. To life! I was now accepted into their company, but I felt a confusing sense of separation. I noticed that even the Yiddish that was being spoken was becoming less transparent.

All day long my thinking was in English, not in Yiddish. When it began to grow dark and lighting the burner on the kitchen range was again permitted, Mother set a kettle to boil for tea. She brought out a tray of mandel bread, our favorite kind, full of cinnamon, nuts and raisins. The men took their tea in steaming glasses, with a lump of sugar tucked inside the cheek. Everything was familiar, yet foreign.

But today, a year later, there would be no family celebration. After school I came straight home and put away my medal until Dave and Celia came back from their afternoon jobs. Schoolwork could wait until the evening. It was hard to concentrate. I went out to the street expecting perhaps to see my school friends, yet hoping not to see the two of them who gave up soccer last fall because their parents would not allow Saturday games. I know that there had been some negotiation by our coach, Mr. McGinnis, with the other coaches about whether games would be held on Saturdays, and he assured the boys that he had kept these to a minimum. Father did not seem to care about this. He spent his own Saturdays at the synagogue with his cronies, even when there was plenty of piecework available at his shop. My soccer games were part of this new world that he didn't fathom. In this world there is no grand rabbi in Warsaw to decide whether soccer-football is work or play, or whether play is prohibited. Or for whom it is prohibited.

Often, on afternoons like this, when there are no odd jobs available at the corner grocery, and no stickball games going on in the neighborhood, I pay a visit to the library. I discovered the library as soon as I learned to read well. At that time it was in the Hebrew Educational Society's building on Pitkin Avenue, and a couple of years ago it became the Brownsville Branch of the Brooklyn Public Library. Now, in a new building, it has so many books that surely I could never have time to read them all. Frequently, I pick out one or two books for Saturday night reading, and sometimes I head for the corner where they keep the newspapers and magazines. I make sure I look at the latest issue of *Harpers'* magazine. And once a month, Miss Tuthill, the librarian, wagging a curled finger, beckons me to her desk. Then she reaches behind her and brings out the latest copy of *Scientific American Magazine* for me to read.

But this afternoon I was too excited to sit in the library and read. And I was not feeling especially sociable. I decided to wander over to the big open field near Dumont Street where there are some trees and a little creek. I set off down Stone Avenue. When I was little, there were trees nearby, but now there are block after block of tall tenements instead. I passed a gaggle of the younger kids noisily playing stoopball. In this game, a rubber ball is thrown against the steep steps that in most of the buildings are built over the cellar entrances. The object is to make it as hard as possible for the other kids to field the ball as it rebounds from the steps. I stopped and watched for a while, but I resisted the temptation to stop and give them some pointers.

After a few blocks I crossed Belmont Avenue, lined from curb to curb with pushcarts of every description. I had liked going with Mother to shop at the stalls when I was small. Everything you might want was here somewhere, but you had to find the right pushcart. A few of the grizzled old men or the ladies in their babushkas stocked their carts with more than one kind of ware: kosher soap and shoelaces side by side, or barrels of pickles and sauerkraut hiding behind a row of salamis dangling from strings along the front of the rain cover. One lady sold corsets. Mother always hurried me past that cart.

I turned left onto Sutter Avenue. On every block there were older, wooden tenements. These were much like the building our family was living in, but they seemed even more worn. Scabs of peeling paint clung to the bare, gray exteriors. Some of the buildings had open porches facing the street, one upon the other, with lines of laundry strung between the corner posts. From the hallways came a damp moldy smell. It reminded me of the basement of our building where I went with Mother to carry up baskets of clothes she had washed in the stone tub. Some women were sitting in the sunshine on the front steps peeling carrots and potatoes.

Here and there between the rows of old tenement houses newer brick buildings with stores on the street level appeared. Not far from

Stone Avenue a druggist had opened for business. Glass urns filled with rose, amber, and blue fluids hung like giant jewels from chains in the front window. Here I stopped for a while, peering under my cupped hand pressed against the glass to watch the pharmacist at work. A skinny, balding man moved among the rows of little drawers and shelves, eventually bringing out a jar from which he counted out pills into a brown envelope. He licked the flap closed and wrote something down on the envelope. It didn't seem particularly interesting. I wondered about the contents of the hanging urns.

An odious whiff from the dairy barns near the corner of Hopkinson Avenue came to me as I passed the blackened windows of the Sutter Pool Parlor a full block away. Finally, turning left into a side street I caught sight of a grove of low trees interrupting the roadway several blocks away. Rising just above the trees more rooftops were visible and framing the entire view was a low, gray line where an elevated railway cut across the horizon out beyond the town.

When I reached the vacant blocks where the trees grew I was reminded that this was hardly a stately park. For several blocks in either direction adjacent empty lots served a variety of uses for anyone who needed some unclaimed open space. There was a decaying rusty horse cart alongside the street on one end. Here and there some builder had discarded a load of broken or misshapen bricks, giving a lumpy surface beneath the growth of grasses and low bushes. But there were also some level patches covered in coarse grass, hemmed in by a few trees of various heights. Perhaps these groves once marked the edges of farm fields laid out by early Dutch settlers. As if inspired by the ghost of one of those farmers, a few neighboring families had laid out little vegetable gardens back from the street, surrounding them with rough boards.

I knew that if I made my way through the tangle of underbrush beneath the trees in the direction of a pair of willow trees I would find a little clear stream, narrow enough for me to easily leap across. Life had found a home here. Small green crayfish could be seen on the bottom if you looked closely, and on the surface, gatherings of water striders skated effortlessly back and forth. What explained how these creatures stayed on top of the water?

I climbed to the top of one of the higher piles of rubble and sat on the ground. Down on some flat, open ground nearby someone had improvised a baseball diamond, marking the bases with paving stones. A band of noisy boys had commandeered the field for a game. I sat down to watch. They were a ragtag bunch in their patched knickers and tattered sweaters. Just as I turned to watch, one of the boys connected powerfully with the ball, sending it into a high fly above the heads of all the fielders who now craned their heads watching it helplessly. The sound of the hit reached my ears not as a solid "pop," but as a kind of crackle that meant to me that the bat probably had a split in it. Maybe one of the boys had found the bat in the discarded trash after a Dodgers' game at the stadium downtown. The flying ball soared up and out beyond the boundary of the cleared space before landing in a jumble of weeds and scrub near a tree.

On the sidelines the batter's teammates shouted and cheered with loud enthusiasm, waving their caps in the air or beating them against their thighs. I made out some of their words of encouragement: "You show 'em, Hymie!" and "Yea! You're our boy!" All American language from this bunch of immigrant kids, I thought. Some of them may have only recently arrived here. Could I remember when I had begun to speak English? It seems to me as if I had always spoken English outside the home. Of course there was a time when English was a foreign language to me, but now and as far back as I could remember all my thinking and all remembered conversations, at least those in school, were in English.

As I sat on the rubble pile watching these kids, I remembered an incident when I was in the second grade, around six years ago. Miss Estes was our teacher that year. On that particular day, as I arrived in the classroom just before nine in the morning, she was in her usual place at the window with her back to the room. She was looking down at the front gate watching the late arriving children scurrying into the school entrance. In her hand was a wooden yardstick she carried most of the day. I sat down, anticipating the first act in

Miss Estes' daily school routine. Indeed, as the sound of the school bell rang down the hall, in one choreographed motion she slowly turned around and stepping to her desk brought the flat side of the stick down on her desktop. The noise was like a pistol shot, sure to quickly bring up the head of any dozing student. Then she closed the door to the hallway and immediately began the lessons. My own tribulations began twenty minutes later.

Morris Gevurtz sat at the desk next to mine that year. He was older and considerably bigger than I was. He had only arrived from Lithuania a year or two before. Although he had not been through the entire first grade, because of his age he was being pushed along above his grade level. He had acquired a basic use of English, but occasionally gave a bewildered look when spoken to. This was one those times. Miss Estes had just given the class some instructions. I cannot now remember what she wanted or even the subject at hand, but I do remember Morris turning towards me looking completely helpless. Taking pity on him, I whispered the Yiddish translation to him behind my cupped hand. Miss Estes broke off whatever she was saying in mid-sentence. She turned slowly in my direction.

"Did you say something, Abe?" she asked.

I hesitated. "Yes," I stammered.

"Yes what?"

I was sinking deeper. "Yes, m'am."

She didn't look entirely satisfied, but continued. "And do you care to share what you have to say with the rest of us?" All eyes were on me. Morris was nonplussed. I was mortified.

"Yiddish . . . your instructions . . . Morris . . . ." I was at a loss.

"You understand that we speak English here?" She obviously didn't expect an answer. "*Only* English." She laid a heavy emphasis on "only." "Please step up to my desk. Now."

I don't ordinarily think much about the rest of the incident. As instructed, I bent down and placed my hands on the edge of Miss Estes' desk. The blow on my backside from her yardstick was swift and well placed, but the physical pain was minimal. What hurt was the embarrassment. My face was burning, and I fought back tears. As I marched back to my own desk all eyes were still on me. In the back of the classroom I could see that some of the bigger boys were grinning. Morris looked solemn and downcast.

As I thought about that afternoon I began to recall some other details. I was aware that for the rest of that school day my mind was in a fog. I also recalled that when I explained my somber mood later that evening, my father's only reaction was to say that if I was punished I surely had done something bad. But now a more positive detail leaped to mind. As I filed out of Miss Estes' classroom that afternoon it seemed to me that she smiled at me, if ever so slightly. After that and for the rest of the year it seemed to me that she was especially nice to me. I think we understood each other.

When I think back on it, once the little incident in the second grade had faded into the past, I rather liked Miss Estes. I remember being pleased about being in her class when she reappeared as our teacher in the fourth grade. She was as stern as before, but now she only occasionally picked up the yardstick. When she did, it was usually to point at the blackboard, but sometimes when she was waiting impassively for a student to deliver an answer she would slap the ruler rhythmically into the palm of her free hand. That year she never saw the need to raise her weapon against a student. Maybe her reputation had cowed all of us into submission. Maybe it was because some of the fourth grade boys were nearly as big as she.

Towards the end of that school year Miss Estes assigned us a project, which was to write a composition about some "wonder" of the twentieth century. Norma, who lived downstairs, wanted to tell about typewriters, which she had seen at the lawyer's office where she helped out on Monday afternoons. Typewriters didn't seem that inspiring, belonging in dingy offices and were strictly for girls. Besides that, it wasn't exactly a "wonder"—a lot of little levers pushing this way and that. It was easy to see how it worked.

For my part I remembered reading a newspaper article around Christmas time about two brothers who had built a flying machine. These men could get into their contraption, start the motor, and fly over the trees then turn it around and come back. A flying machine! Now *that* was a real wonder. Sometimes some of the boys and I would build paper gliders, but they soon come crashing down. I tried

45

to imagine somehow pushing oneself from the ground and sailing around over our neighborhood, circling around over our street and looking down from the sky. The newspaper said the "aeroplane" had a gasoline motor. That seemed strange. Once in a while a motorcar would come through the neighborhood, but if it tried to go up the hill toward the "heights" it slowed down and sometimes stopped altogether. There was always some smart aleck who would call out "Get a horse!"

In the library, with Miss Tuthill's help, I found a report in the January 1904 issue of *Harper's Weekly* reporting that one of the inventors was able to fly three miles at sixty feet in the air and safely return to the starting point. It described the machine as similar to a big box kite with rudders and propellers pushing it along. By adding some things I knew about kites I was able to make a composition long enough to satisfy Miss Estes. I called my composition "The Flying Machine." She asked me to read it in front of the class.

This afternoon, sitting on a grass covered rubble pile four years later I was thinking again about the new century stretching out ahead of me. A few months ago I read again about flying machines in the *Scientific American Magazine*. Now there are other inventors from all over the world vying to build practical aeroplanes. So far none of these attempts measure up to the Wright brothers' flights beginning with the ones I wrote about in the fourth grade. The brothers have flown at a speed over 40 miles per hour. Imagine! I figure that at such a speed one could get from here to New York in less than 20 minutes. The clouds I watched drifting in from the west can do no better than that. Who knows how fast, how high, and how far people will be able to fly at the international competition scheduled for this coming summer?

Almost every day I hear of amazing things. Messages can be sent across the ocean without using wires. There is talk of building a subway that would connect our neighborhood with New York. Yet there is still so much to understand. No one knows how the sun can keep burning forever. Are there really canals on Mars and Martians who build them? And sometimes when I'm in the synagogue with Father I wonder where God is in all this wonder. We're told that there is no answer to that question; that God is beyond understanding. I suppose so, but I have the urge to learn what I can know, to discover what I can discover. And if I cannot understand God then I will at least respect Him and wonder about Him.

The clouds caught my attention. I imagined being up with them, maybe in an aeroplane, looking down on our neighborhood, seeing the little creek behind the trees, the roof tops, the pushcarts on Belmont Street. And beyond that? The farms beyond the town, and the ocean stretching away towards Europe.

Next year I will begin high school. I will have a job in Mr. Bluestein's shoe store for the summer, and maybe a promise of a part time job after that. A whole century ahead! I have little idea where that will lead, but I am ready to begin.

CHAPTER 6

The Light of Reason

1910

The clatter in the kitchen woke me this morning as it often did. It was still dark outside. Mother had put the kettle on the gas burner to make Father his morning tea and was putting out breakfast. Today would be much the same as other days. There would be heavy rye bread. and butter and cheese from the cupboard. Sometimes there would be bowls of oatmeal and on Saturday mornings some eggs boiled the day before. At the moment any desire for food was totally missing. Maybe later—I needed more sleep. But I was wide-awake.

From the corner of the kitchen just out of view came the murmuring that meant that Father had already laid on the tefillin and was in the midst of his davenning. By the light from the kitchen I could make out the time on my bedside clock—my precious find at the flea market on Pitkin Avenue. It was six o'clock—almost time to get up anyway. Across the room, Dave was sitting up at the side of his bed with his elbows stretched out in the middle of a protracted yawn.

"Hey Abe. Why are you awake?" he asked.

"I wish I wasn't," I managed to reply. I turned to face the wall, trying to fall asleep again. Instead I lay there thinking about what I had to do today. Mother usually let me sleep until six-thirty before she came to shake me awake. Reluctantly I swung my legs out from under the covers. The floor was ice cold.

Now, half way through my second year at Boys High School, the morning routine has become very familiar. Father is the first to leave in the morning. His work nearby as a finish tailor begins at seven. While he eats his breakfast Mother is busy making bologna or salmon sandwiches for our lunches. If there is enough money she tucks in a piece of pickle wrapped in waxed paper, or a banana. By seven o'clock Dave leaves home, allowing him enough time to travel by streetcar and subway train to be at his morning classes at the pharmacy school in New York. Celia, whose bed is in a corner of the kitchen, somehow manages to sleep through most of this. Her job at the butcher shop doesn't begin until nine, but she is usually busy helping Mother by the time I sit down for breakfast. Then she helps Sari, who shares the bedroom with Mother and Father, get ready. After the rest of us have left the flat Celia walks Sari to the elementary school on her way to her shop on Sutter Avenue.

Today I was early, so when Dave brought out his tefillin I decided to join him in the ritual. Every morning Father expects us to fulfill our religious duties. By now the routine has become mostly automatic and the prayers almost a reflex. The leather straps are wound around my right arm and head as prescribed The black cubes containing the parchment scrolls lie snug against my forearm and forehead. Inside are excerpts from the Torah. One declares the mitzvah of laying on the tefillin. The inscribed words of Moses I know in translation:

> And these words, which I command thee this day, shall
> be in thine heart, and thou shalt bind them for a sign
> upon thine hand, and they shall be as frontlets between
> thine eyes.

I can recite by heart the Hebrew blessings but it is discomforting that I do not often pay attention to what I am saying. I go through the ritual largely to please Father, though if I neglected this duty, he might not say much about it. I know that it is something to remind me daily of who I am, and of the oneness and power of God. Yet I argue with the notion that binding God's commandments close to my skin somehow binds them to my heart. It is mystical and informs me little. Nevertheless I lay on tefillin every morning before school and hurry as much as I think decency might permit. Then I speed through breakfast and often run to get the trolley in order to reach the high school for classes beginning at eight o'clock.

Boys High School sits at the intersection of Marcy and Putnam Avenues, about halfway to downtown Brooklyn. Viewed from the outside it's like a European palace or, with its splendid round corner tower, like a castle from a fairy tale. The soaring cone atop the tower reminds me of a giant dunce cap. But dunces never stay past the first year. They disappear into the city as errand boys or to the sweatshops alongside their fathers. And as if to make the point that excellence is demanded, the rest of the building is just as imposing. There are six towering gables, each set with a different style of decorative window, surmounting façades filled with rows of arched windows. At the far corner the round tower is complemented by an even taller square tower reminding me of a gigantic campanile looming over an Italian piazza.

I remember how intimidated I felt entering this imperious place for the first time. Now, most of the time, I am eager to commit myself there every weekday morning. It's like entering a lively new world far from the drab tenements, sweatshops, and familiar crowds. I am invigorated by surprising ideas and challenges. The kids are different too—Irish boys from Greenpoint, Italians from Canarsie, Poles from Williamsburg.

My classes cover a broad range of subjects. Mrs. Rose's history class is not my favorite—pointless battles, dead kings, and dates to memorize. Memorization is also a big factor in Latin class but somehow I am not bothered by it. Perhaps this because of the musicality of the spoken Latin, or the stories, or maybe the intriguing puzzles of Latin grammar. Mr. Rabinowitz, a short dark man with a bushy mustache, teaches biology. He speaks with great authority about the importance of biology, especially if we wish to study medicine. And he exudes a discernable smugness if any of us is squeamish about dissection. Fortunately I don't mind dissection, but I don't consider it much fun. English class, on the other hand, is almost always fun. I am thinking especially of play acting scenes from Shakespeare. But my favorite subject this year is geometry, taught by Miss McNab.

Miss McNab reminds me of the scrawny chickens running about in the tenement yard next door. She is bony and shorter than I am. Her hair, pulled up in a tight little bun behind her head, accentuates her pinched face. But when she speaks—and she does quite a lot—the space around her is alive with sound. And it seems as if she is everywhere at once. Yet Miss McNab is my favorite teacher.

I remember early in the school year when I came to her class for the first time. She stood off to the side of the room and looked at each one of us as we filed in. I took a seat in the middle of the room and watched her. At the sound of the bell she closed the door and began to speak. Just then the door opened partly and Maurice Fensterman eased his way in and began to head for the back of the room.

Miss McNab quickly blocked his path. Fists against her bony hips and arms akimbo, she looked up at him and demanded, "Just where do think you're going, big boy?" No reply. "Do you know what class this is?"

Maurice is one of the biggest boys in the school but it was clear he was nonplussed. "Geometry?" he ventured. "I got lost."

"Well you got the first part right, big boy," Miss McNab replied. She raised an arm and waggled a finger in the direction of an empty seat in the back of the room. "Let's not get lost in this class. You understand?"

"Yes'm," he replied sheepishly as he moved to his seat. Then Miss McNab turned to the rest of us.

"Getting lost in geometry is *not* a good idea, class. So keep your ears clean. Pay attention. No shenanigans. You do it right, and I'll do it right." She looked around the room. Then she added. "And I'll promise this. Geometry can be fun—for some of you, at least."

I would guess that not many of us believed that promise. Several times during freshman year some older kid had tried to frighten one of us about how hard geometry was going to be, as if exulting in his superiority for having gotten a passing grade in it. And Miss

McNab's encounter with Maurice certainly did nothing to take the edge off our anxieties.

Some of that first meeting was spent distributing textbooks and going over the roll. Miss McNab rearranged seating, smaller boys in the front, tallest boys at the back. Everyone should be able to see the board, she explained. "No hiding. I want to know what you're up to," she added. There is no question that we were all intimidated that first day in her class, but I soon recognized her genuine interest in seeing us learn. Even Maurice eventually warmed up to her.

Towards the end of the hour she drew a pretty diagram in chalk on the black board using a big wooden compass. Centering on a point on the periphery of a big circle that she had drawn on the board she drew a circular arc of the same radius that intersected two points on the circle. From these intersections she drew more arcs that intersected the original circle. She continued this way until finally a six-pointed flower-like figure emerged inside the original circle.

She passed out individual compasses and coached us in reproducing the six-petal "rosette," as she called it, in our notebooks. Then she called the class to order and challenged us with a question

"Why are there six petals?" She waited for a few moments, looking about the room at each of us, and then continued. "Why not five? Or five and a half? That's for you to think about and I'll give a hint. Think about what you should already know from your first year math class about triangles." She leaned with both hands on the edge of her desk and looked sternly at us. "But I suppose you haven't been thinking much about triangles—so we will begin to review that tomorrow. Meanwhile, remember—'triangles'. Here's a little mystery for you, so be a detective."

I did think about the mystery afterwards, caught up by the simplicity of the drawing scheme and the elegance of the resulting "rosette." Why indeed exactly six petals? Could there be a world in which the circle divides into more or less than six parts, or perhaps not an even number of parts? The explanation occurred to me after a couple of days. Drawing straight lines between the center of the rosette and the tips of two adjacent petals and another straight line between these two tips produces an equal-sided triangle. And we had learned the year before that the angle at any corner of such an "equilateral" triangle is a sixth of the total angle that it takes to fill a full circle. So exactly six of these triangles fit into the circle.

When we finally discussed the explanation in class days later, she posed the next big question, which was how can we be sure that the angles in an equilateral triangle are in fact a sixth of a full circle. In first year math we had been taught a lot of ideas as facts to be memorized—the number of degrees inside a triangle, Pythagoras' theorem, ways to solve simple equations—interesting enough, especially when applied to "word problems." But now Miss McNab was questioning assertions. She was suggesting that there might be some kind of underlying reasons for the mathematical facts.

She paused at this point and looked around the room. She wanted everyone's attention. Some of the boys averted their eyes as her gaze fell upon them. There was some squirming. After a few moments she resumed. "The way we will do that is the way we will solve a lot of puzzles in geometry class—by moving step by step from facts we know to a fact we hadn't yet thought about, until we find the explanation. Like a detective—think about what you know for sure, then use your head." She tapped her forehead with an index finger a couple of times. More silence. "Of course triangles aren't the only pretty figures in plane geometry," she went on. "But look around. They pop up everywhere." Just then, the hall bell rang signaling the end of the hour.

Miss McNab's class was at the end of the school day. Most days I have an afternoon job at Bluestein's Shoe Store. What I can earn pays for my trolley fares with something left over for the family. But that was a day I had the afternoon off, so instead of taking the trolley on Fulton Street I walked home—almost three miles. I was thinking again about Miss McNab's class. About a block from the school I turned around and looked back at the palace-like building. High above each façade the end of the roof terminates in an equilateral triangle. Four equilateral triangles lean together on the soaring north tower to form a pyramid. None of this seems especially remarkable; roofs lean at an angle to run off the rainwater and the edges of course form a triangle of some kind. As I walked on I noticed the crisscrossed steel bars in the girders beneath the el on Fulton Street forming innumerable triangles. I supposed there was a good engineering reason for this arrangement.

Walking down Fulton Street I gradually stopped thinking about Miss McNab and triangles until I saw the first indication that I was getting close to our neighborhood. It was Krinsky's butcher shop. And there in the window above the Hebrew letters spelling *kosher bosher*—kosher meat—was the *Mogen David*, the Star of David, the Jewish star. Two overlapping equilateral triangles give rise to a six-pointed star. The tips of the two triangles formed six smaller equilateral triangles, each perched on one edge of a hexagon. I quickly realized that if straight lines are drawn between alternate tips on Miss McNab's rosette the result is a Jewish star.

I thought about the Mogen David almost for the first time. What meaning might it have aside from being a symbol for the Jews? It was everywhere in my neighborhood—in the synagogue, on the windows of the butcher shops, on the velvet covers over the Torah scrolls. Was there some deeper meaning? Why did King David choose it for a symbol, as I supposed he had? Surely it was not simply because it was easy to draw or because it seemed to be a pretty shape. Maybe it was like the mysterious pyramid and the eye shining out of a triangle on the back of the dollar bill—not simply a distinctive symbol, but something with a hidden meaning. It was intriguing, yet somehow unsettling.

But early in the school year it was neither the ubiquity nor the practicality of geometry that intrigued me. It was the pleasure of discovery, of a way to dig out explanations for the observations I can make at every turn. And eventually I discovered that the fun of the math puzzles was especially satisfying when they involved the tangible and the visual—the shapes and figures that are the stuff of geometry. I was aware of the mild anxiety I harbor regarding of the darkly mystical—the *dybbuks* of the older people, the weird séances described in the popular magazines, magic in general. But most important, I recognized how these negative feelings can be put aside in the light of neatly reasoned explanation.

Brother Dave is studying to be a pharmacist and also has a part-time job with a florist in downtown Brooklyn. When Dave is at work I sometimes look at his textbooks. I admire Dave for how hard he is working toward a useful profession, but most of what he is studying does not seem particularly exciting. In the books there are a lot of "chemical reactions" represented by chemical symbols laid out like equations. But unlike mathematics equations it does not appear that there are necessarily logical connections among them. It seems as if they are presented as facts to be memorized.

However, there are some things in Dave's books that I find interesting—in particular, instruments and gadgets for measuring and preparing the pharmaceuticals. Recently I came across an illustration that especially caught my attention because it reminded me of a picture I saw in a library book when I was about ten years old. The library book, on various industrial arts, showed how workmen could tell whether two parts of a house were level with one another, even if the two locations were hidden from one another by part of the building. A hollow tube, filled with water, is put around the house from one of these places to the other. At each end of the tube is a glass funnel, such that the levels of the water at each end of the tube can be observed. Since the height of the water in the funnel on one side of the house will be the same as the height of the water on the other side, the workmen can tell if the two parts of the house are at the same level. The first time I thought about this idea it seemed mystical. How did the water level showing in one funnel "know" the height of water in the other funnel? Now it seems entirely reasonable, even if I can't make a mathematical argument for it. The water level on the two ends of the tube would be at the same height for the same reason that the surface of a pond is everywhere at the same height. The shape of the bottom of the pond connecting different places doesn't matter; the connection could even be like a tube. Nothing weird here at all.

After almost two years of high school I am very aware that the world abounds in mysteries. But they are not necessarily beyond rational understanding. I think of Miss McNab at the beginning of the year tapping her head with her forefinger. "Think about what you know for sure, then use your head," she said. "It can be fun."

CHAPTER 7

Bluestein's Offer

1913

It has been more than four years since I first began working at Mr. Bluestein's shoe store. At first it was part-time work doing odd jobs but eventually the boss gave me full-time work during summer vacations. Then, a couple of years ago, he began to have me wait on customers. But there is always all kinds of extra work for me. At the end of a busy day Mr. Bluestein insists that everything be put in order—paper is to be picked up, the floor swept, chairs rearranged, and most important, unsold shoes put back in their proper place. On this he is emphatic. "The customer is not to wait while we look," he repeats.

Since I graduated from high school in June Mr. Bluestein has given me a regular full-time job and more responsibility. I like to suppose he considers me a colleague, despite the difference in our ages. Business has been growing. More and more people are moving to Brownsville and the surrounding neighborhoods. Boatloads of immigrants continue to arrive in New York. Lower Manhattan still has big Italian and Jewish neighborhoods, and a Chinatown. But early arriving immigrants are moving out and many are coming to Brooklyn. Even my friend Jacob and his family, whom I had known as a young kid back in Wizna, recently came to the neighborhood and settled not too far from us.

But most of the men still work in New York. The coming of the subway to downtown Brooklyn and better trolley connections make this feasible. Besides, the small cutting and sewing shops around here are closing down. And better transportation makes it possible for people from outside the neighborhood—gentiles from Flatbush and New Lots and especially Italians from Bushwick—to come to Pitkin and Sutter and Belmont Avenues to shop.

The store on Pitkin Avenue is not far from our flat. Mr. Bluestein likes to point out that this is a good location to have a shoe store and emphasizes this by adding with a little nodding of his head. "And I know from shoes." He tells me this in his old country accent accompanied by a look of great satisfaction. "In this country," he lectures, "all things are possible." He came to America about the same time as I did, and from the same general region of Poland. Sometimes I imagine that he is one of the men in the group of people we met in Byalystok when we sneaked over the border into Prussia. But I only recall that time vaguely. Besides, Mr. Bluestein would have said something if he thought that this was a possibility. Nevertheless, when he is in a jolly mood, he sometimes calls me *landsman*.

Despite these connections between us I also sense a great separation. Mr. Bluestein is 49 years old, older even by several years than my father. But unlike Father his use of English is very good, even if he speaks with an accent. He will use Yiddish with some of the older men and women, but with me and with everyone else he prides himself on using English exclusively. This is just as well as my command of Yiddish has been gradually slipping. I cannot even remember when I did not think in English.

Mr. Bluestein prides himself as well on his knowledge of the shoe business. In the old country he tells me he made shoes. When he came to America he discovered that shoes were made in factories. But he was not about to be a slave to a machine. Besides he wanted to be his own boss. So with a little money he borrowed from a distant relative he opened his own business repairing shoes, first in the back bedroom of his apartment, then in a little shop on Sutter Avenue. Some years ago he began to sell new shoes in his shop and eventually stopped repairing shoes and concentrated on selling them. But even when he is selling, it is obvious that he does understand shoes. He speaks of stitching, and lasts, and arches, and heel counters, and various kinds of leather. Few of his customers seem interested when he goes on like that, but it is clear to them that they are dealing with an expert.

Mr. Bluestein is a married man and has two daughters. One of these daughters is married. "To a dentist, yet!" he says with emphasis. The younger daughter is single, but she has a "boy friend." When he mentions this he seems to roll his eyes and gives a hint of a shrug. I have never met his wife, but Becky the younger daughter often comes to the shop to help when I am about to leave for the evening. She gives her father a big kiss on the cheek and gives me a polite little handshake. Apart from being a family man, I see many differences from my father. This is especially clear to me when I come to work on Saturdays. Mr. Bluestein seems to respect the fact that I feel I owe it to my father to spend a few hours with him in the *shul* in the morning, but he himself disregards the synagogue altogether except on the high holy days. His shop opens at nine in the morning on Saturdays almost without exception. He likes to tell me that he thinks he is a good man, and that God will understand that he must do the best for his family in America.

Unlike Father Mr. Bluestein seems to have no "cronies," but he is friendly with everyone who comes by—with the Jewish customers, and with the Italian ladies, and even with the occasional Negro person who stops by. He has an especially cheery greeting for the Irish policeman who comes down the street several times a day swinging his billy club. Sometimes I see the two of them chatting just outside the store when the weather is nice. I have no idea what they talk about, but the conversation is usually brief and ends with a little tip of the policemen's helmet. One time, I saw Mr. Bluestein hand something to him that the cop quickly pocketed in his brass-buttoned coat. But I have no reason to doubt the basic decency of Mr. Bluestein. He describes how, in the old country, the storekeepers would be expected to haggle with customers. "Over the price of a herring, yet!" he adds. But in his store the stated price is always the correct and fixed price—it avoids a lot of fuss and worry. "*Tsooris,*" is the word he prefers. And besides it brings the customers back. And if a good customer cannot pay until the next payday, the tab is put into the account book, no questions asked.

I regularly wait on customers now. With gentle coaching from Mr. Bluestein over the years I am getting pretty good at this, but I am still a little uncomfortable advising on shoe styles. Somehow style doesn't seem too important to me. I can judge pretty well when the fit of a shoe is right, but it seems that for some customers, especially the young ladies, being up-to-date is paramount. They say they want to be "in fashion." Once in a while I ask Celia or Sari for their opinions on style, but I don't fret about it much anymore. In fact, a young woman coming in the door of the shop always turns my head. If she is young and pretty I always hope I can beat out Bluestein to wait on her.

But this eagerness to wait on the ladies was not always the case. I especially remember a busy Saturday several years ago. I was just over seventeen. It was a warm day in spring and three young ladies sauntered in the front door. After looking around, they sat down in a row in the center of the room. I watched them whispering among themselves out of the corner of my eye while I reshelved boxes of shoes that had become scattered. I was tempted to study them directly but dreaded approaching them. Meanwhile Mr. Bluestein had his hands full with a stout lady and her two squirming, whiny boys. Momentarily catching my attention he motioned in the young ladies' direction with a sideways waggle of his head. I summoned my courage and approached them.

"Can I help you?" I asked.

"Sure can, sonny," the young lady on the left end answered. She was the tallest of the three—rather plain but with a nice figure. She stopped chewing gum for a moment while she spoke for the group. "You sell shoes, right?" She bore an enigmatic smile, but I know now she was teasing me.

"Yes, miss," I stammered.

"Well see if you can sell her some." She nodded towards the middle lady. The one sitting on the right end of the trio silently looked on with mild amusement. I pulled up a shoe fitting stool in front of the middle one, crouched down, and looked up at her. She was about twenty years old and the prettiest of the three. She wore a light beige-colored dress with a low neckline trimmed in lace.

"You have some nice brown pumps?" the pretty one asked. "Maybe you need to check my size." Without waiting for a reply she reached down and pulled up the hem of her dress. In bending over she revealed a lovely bit of bosom just above her neckline. I don't know whether she saw my glance ascend irresistibly from her dainty little feet. But I like to think that as she raised her face to me to tell me what kind of shoe she wanted, she gave me a playful little wink. I was flushed and befuddled, but in the end the sale went well. As the three young ladies left the store they were giggling among themselves about something, but I cannot be sure.

The evening after that encounter four years ago, we had the usual meal of cold leftovers from Friday night dinner. The Sabbath is a day of rest and there was to be no work, including cooking, on that Saturday. Sometimes I told Mother that it is not like the old country where it was really work to gather wood and light the fire in the cook stove, but that striking a single match and turning on a gas burner is not work. But compromises on matters of what she perceives as her sacred duties are not in her nature. That day she had sat in the women's part of the shul all morning, leaving Celia at home with Sari. After dinner I found it hard to concentrate on my homework. I thought about the morning in the synagogue among father's cronies who chanted the prayers in well practiced ritual, about the various customers who came to the store, about Mr. Bluestein's casual attitude about the Sabbath, and about the young lady to whom I had sold a pair of brown pumps. I thought of those dainty little feet and that lovely bosom with a mixture of confusion and pleasure. It had been a difficult day.

But there have been great changes since then—in the business and in the job. The neighborhood folks do not come to the shop in great numbers on Saturday, but the "outside" people like to come on weekends. Now Mr. Bluestein has also opened his shop on Sunday for them, when so many shops in their own neighborhoods are closed. Last year he began leasing the space next door that had been used by the barber and had a doorway put in between the two shops. He has put me in charge of the whole expanded shop on Sundays, but he lets me take off Friday nights and most of the day on Saturdays. I have grown a little mustache, hoping it might make me appear a little older than twenty. These days girls don't giggle among themselves after I wait on them.

Being in charge is a lot of responsibility, but Mr. Bluestein has confidence in me. Yet I was quite startled when he posed an intriguing proposition the other day. He asked me to consider going into partnership with him eventually. He explained that he was sure that neither of his girls had any intention of being anything but housewives in the long run. For the time being Becky works as a stenographer, and is studying to be a court reporter. Mr. Bluestein was sure that her older sister would quit her job as soon as she becomes pregnant. "God willing," he added. In any event neither of them have much interest in running the business. But he would like to see the enterprise he created continue when the time comes for him to step away from it. To become part owner is a captivating idea. It was an honor to be asked. But I have reservations. I told Mr. Bluestein that I would think about it.

When I graduated from Boys High School last June I had some thoughts about going to college I came up with this idea, probably when I was a junior. I could work full-time for a year following high school and save my money. Then I would find part-time work while attending college. It all seemed quite feasible. Father and Mother had little concept of why or how I would do this, even though Dave was almost finished putting himself through pharmacy school. To them it made sense for Dave to do this because in the end, he would have a well paying profession. But neither they, nor I, for that matter, could quite picture what would justify going to college besides preparing for a well defined career. Of course Mother and Father admire learned men—the judges and prophets of the Book and the great rabbis. But here in America, success has a more practical twist to it. Of course, if learning is part of that, so much the better.

Recently I have pondered my future, but it is still not clear. Only what I would not like to do is lucid. Many of the boys I knew in school had definite ideas about their directions in life, the commonality among them being earning a good living. That doesn't seem to me to be enough. My friend Irv showed me what his father wrote in his autograph album when we graduated from Boys High. It was not that he was proud of Irv, or that he hoped for his health and happiness. Instead he wrote, "Go get a job!" Irv seemed a little amused by the old man's directness. In fact he had plans to work his way through law school. Personally, I do not feel inspired by this particular plan, though admittedly I am only vaguely aware of what lawyers do. As for some other professions—medicine, dentistry, podiatry—the intimacy in those lines of work makes me uncomfortable.

For a while I thought about being an engineer. So many exciting things are happening. Even in grade school I tried to learn as much as I could about some of the marvels going on everywhere—airplanes, the Brooklyn Bridge, the Panama Canal, telephones, and most amazing of all—wireless telegraphy. And I know I like to do things with my hands—though apart from a shop course in grade school, my only experience with this is when some small repair was needed in the store.

During my senior year I visited Mr. Rabinowitz, who had been my biology teacher and was now assigned to be my guidance counselor. I wanted to talk with him about engineering. Since I had been in his biology class I had had little contact with him, but I would see him from time to time in the hallways. He was easy to spot, with his bushy mustache and a hairline receding to the crown of his head. He was never seen without a stiff, white collar and a bow tie selected from an apparently extensive collection. On the day I visited, it was a navy blue tie with small white polka dots. I didn't count him among my favorite teachers. But I respected his ability as a teacher and liked him well enough.

During one of his advising hours I made my way to his office tucked away on the fourth floor in the round tower at the corner of the building. The door was open as I approached and I could see Mr. Rabinowitz, red pencil in hand, looking over some papers on his desk. It was an odd little room with curved walls and very big windows looking out at the intersection of Marcy and Putnam

Avenues. Under each window he had a shelf lined with a curious collection of plants—an assortment of cacti, a small bushy begonia covered in clusters of miniature red flowers, and some kind of drooping tropical plant with enormous deeply serrated leaves. On the floor alongside the plants were neat piles of papers and pamphlets. I knocked gently on the doorjamb.

He looked up from his work and removed a pair of reading glasses that I had not seen him wear before. He studied me for a moment, perhaps trying to recall my name. Then he beckoned me in with his free hand, and almost to my surprise he smiled weakly. "Abe—Abe Rutkiewicz—isn't it?" he asked. "Yes, come in. Have a seat." Putting down his red pencil on the pile of papers, he folded his hands in his lap. He swiveled in his squeaky desk chair to face me. "What's on your mind, Abe?"

I explained that I had begun to think about the future and wondered about the possibility of studying engineering. He listened patiently as I explained how I had always taken an interest in how and why things work. He nodded occasionally to signal his understanding. When I had finished speaking, he stood up and began rummaging through a file cabinet that stood alongside the desk. He withdrew some papers and laid them on his desk. Then, reseating himself, he turned again to me. There was a serious look on his face.

"I understand perfectly what you're saying, Abe. Engineering is interesting work. But . . . . ." He paused in mid-sentence, as if trying to think of the best way to frame the thought. "But, to be perfectly frank, this is not a thing for a Jewish boy."

"What do you mean?" I half-stammered.

"I want you to think realistically, Abe. Engineering is a fine thing. I even thought about it myself at one time. But you'd be working for a corporation in all likelihood. And the fact is, as such you will always be the last to be hired, and the first to be fired." He shook his head slightly from side to side. as if shaking off the thought. Then he picked up the file he had laid on his desk and riffled through it while I absorbed what he had said.

Before I knew how to respond, Mr. Rabinowitz spoke again. "I'm looking at your record here and as I expected you have done nicely in most subjects—not only in science and math, but even in English and Latin. There's no question in my mind that you would enjoy going to college. I know that suggesting you work towards a college degree doesn't answer the question of how you would earn a living in the long run but there are a lot of possibilities."

I couldn't dispute what he had said. The only reply I could manage was "I have to help the family."

"Yes. Yes. I understand," he said. "But I want you to think about it. It might take a little longer to find a way to earn a living but in the end, you'll find something. You might think about majoring in one of the sciences." He looked wistful. "Maybe you could teach. In the meantime I know you would enjoy the learning." He pulled out a watch from his vest pocket and looked at it. "I have a class to meet soon."

We talked briefly about some of the other professions as he gathered some papers and books, but I was readjusting my thinking. I told Mr. Rabinowitz I would consider what he had to say. As he closed his office door behind us he said, "Don't worry Abe. Whatever you finally choose I'm sure you'll do well. There's a world of possibilities out there."

That conversation was more than a year ago. These days I am at the shoe store most of the time and I have been saving money in case I do go to college. I help out Mother and Father with the rent and the food, but I think that soon I will have enough to pay the tuition for the first year at one of the local colleges. I have copies of the course catalogs at home and look at them from time to time. The range of subjects has opened my eyes—European literature, Middle East history, philosophy, psychology, calculus, anthropology, electrodynamics. The course descriptions are intriguing, but at the moment I can only dream of immersing myself in such things.

Meanwhile, I have not forgotten Bluestein's offer to go into business with him. I would have to pay him something to buy into the business. Over the years my share of the business would grow until perhaps I would be able to take over completely. The details are yet to be worked out. So even if I choose not to go to college, the money I am putting into the bank would be useful. I have mentioned all this to brother Dave on the few occasions I have seen him lately. He thinks I should seriously consider Bluestein's offer. But sister Celia is not so sure. "Follow your heart," she tells me. "Do what feels right." Her advice is deeply sincere, but vague. She is a sentimental young woman and perhaps doesn't have a good concept of my choices.

On Saturday mornings I go to shul with Father and Dave, but the dilemma of my future is not left behind. In the synagogue a sense of awe comes to me as I connect with the history in my blood and with the great mystery beyond understanding. There is a comfortable bonding with my elders. Yet there seems to be nothing that leaves me with any increased wisdom. The chanting of the cantor, the swaying and dovening of the men, the reading from the Torah—it is all familiar, but my mind wanders. The Hebrew requires great concentration to extract meaning. But praise and faith in the Almighty somehow lifts me from the mundane, and momentarily I am pulled out of myself. But time after time I find my thoughts are far away, on something else entirely different.

Usually I take my leave of the shul at midday. I feel I have fulfilled my obligations. Now that Mr. Bluestein has put me in charge of the store on Sundays he usually lets me take Saturdays off. Sometimes I go to the library, a treasure house of books I never found time for in high school. Sometimes I meet my friend Jacob. When the weather permits, we take long walks as we had done occasionally in the past. Often we go out beyond the houses in New Lots to where there are still farms raising vegetables for the markets in New York There we find Italian farms, with row after row of big red tomatoes in the summer, and ripening grape vines in the fall. Neither of us has lived in the countryside since we left the old country with our parents and there is something evocative about the open spaces and the trees.

On one walk we went in the opposite direction and reached Prospect Park. Despite all of the trees, the feeling contrasted with that evoked by the open countryside. In the Park, people were ubiquitous—ladies pushing baby carriages or walking their dogs, men hurrying by discussing business, old guys on benches feeding the pigeons. All around in the distance were the tall buildings of the surrounding neighborhoods and the sound of clattering carts, or of the Coney Island streetcar. Out beyond New Lots, on the other hand, the sky stretches from horizon to horizon. Sometimes there is no one in sight. And most marvelous of all, the birds are there in such profusion and variety of coloration and size—breaking the silence with singing and chattering as they go about their daily needs. I sometimes imagine that they are expressing their praise for the gift of life. It seems odd, but sometimes it reminds me of the synagogue chants of praise.

I am almost always at our flat by six o'clock in the evening. On Saturdays, after a long day at the synagogue Father and Dave reward themselves with little glasses of schnapps. Then Dave generally excuses himself. He is now working and has taken a room in the Y.M.H.A. in Manhattan. He and his friends always seem to have a party or a dance to go to. He cuts quite a dashing figure when he is dressed up in his suit and tie, and a bowler hat tipped rakishly over one eye.

The rest of us have dinner together after Dave leaves. If the sun is still up this must be restricted to cold leftovers, but in the wintertime when it is permissible for Mother to light the stove we enjoy a hot meal. On most Saturday nights one of Celia's friends stops by, and they go out for a while to meet with some of the young men from the neighborhood. Sometimes I wish I felt as free as Dave or Celia to go out, but for the time being I have resolved to work and save as much as I can. And, I have to be up early to open the shoe store for Sunday business.

CHAPTER 8

Going with the Muse

1914

Perhaps it was late last year, during one of the long walks into the countryside that I took with Jacob, that my thinking about college began to coalesce. It was a cold but clear and sunny Saturday afternoon. There was hardly any wind and as we walked briskly along we hardly felt the cold. At such times our talk ranged widely. I remain amazed at how interesting our conversations often could be. In so many ways we are very different. He arrived in New York almost seven years later than I and speaks with a Yiddish accent like my brother Dave. It is an accent I find easy to imitate, yet a hard one for the speaker to overcome. Particularly difficult are the flat "a" and the whispering "w" of English. Shabbas falls on "Settiday" and "when" comes out "venn." Like Dave, he had to make up a lot of lost time because he was not in American schools in the early grades. He is not scholarly, but there is a keen intelligence behind his comments. He quickly grasps the kernel of the matter while groping for the evidence or the language to frame it. And he knows how to ask questions; not to put me on the spot, but with an eagerness to learn—or maybe to challenge me to find an answer.

That particular day we were still out in the country after it had become dark. There was no moon and the stars were out in a dazzling display in the sky extending from the eastern and southern horizons to where the faint glow from the town and lingering twilight obscured them in the west. It was a sight whose magnificence I had witnessed only on rare occasions. Jacob may have been less startled.

After all, he was nearly fifteen when he left the shtetl in Poland where stars never failed to fill the sky whenever it was clear and dark. I shuddered just a bit as I momentarily relived the night so long ago walking on a dark road near the German border on our way to America.

"I wonder how many stars are up there," Jacob said. His remarks did not necessarily require a factual response, at least when he suspected I might not have an answer.

"I think no one knows for sure," I replied. "Every time they build a better telescope they find more of them."

"I wouldn't want to have a job counting them," he commented.

I was quiet for a while, craning my head to take in the display above. From articles in the *Times* and the *Herald* that I had been reading at the library, I knew that all the stars I could see were part of a gigantic cluster of stars. The bulk of these we see as a luminous band across the night sky—the Milky Way. Recently astronomers had discovered similar large groups of stars, the spiral nebulae, and there was some evidence that these formations lie far beyond the Milky Way. Indeed, I thought, would there be any point in counting them? "I wonder if you realize that each of those stars is kind of a sun. Maybe there are planets like the Earth revolving around them," I finally said.

"How can anyone know that?" he asked. It was a very good question, and I didn't have an answer. "Can you imagine?" he said, "Maybe there are people on those planets looking at us." He chuckled. It was a light-hearted exchange, but at the same time it brought up a well of thoughts about where I fit in all this, about what my life meant in this cosmic reality. It was a strange juxtaposition of serious thought embedded in the glow of a friendship that reminded me not to take myself too seriously.

I looked up again and thought about those hypothetical beings looking down at me. Then it occurred to me that to them, I am looking *down* and they are looking *up* at me! Suddenly my place in the cosmos was transformed. Now I was hanging by my feet, pinned by gravity to the surface of our globe, looking down into endless space at these other worlds. I felt a surge of vertigo. With some effort I turned the universe around again, and I was safely on the ground. But the sense of the magnificence of this spectacle of the night sky did not leave me until we again were walking among the gas lamps on the streets of Brownsville.

On Saturday afternoons I would often visit the library where, besides finding books to read, I liked to catch up with the daily newspapers. In the spring the headlines were fairly screaming about the rivalries among the imperialist powers of Europe. There were troubles between the U.S. and Mexico. President Wilson was having difficulties with Congress. All of it fascinating and troubling news. Nevertheless, especially since that chilly walk in the country with Jacob, I found myself especially drawn to reports about science.

I especially remember coming across a story about a group of astronomers planning an expedition to the Crimea in southern Russia to test an idea of the physicist Albert Einstein. I knew that he was famous for his Theory of Relativity, but I had to admit that I had only a hazy concept of what this relativity idea was about. Some of the boys in the high school liked to say that only two people understood Einstein's theory. This struck me as a silly rumor likely to spread among kids who are embarrassed about their ignorance. Clearly one of the two people who understood must have been Einstein, and these kids could never name the other person.

Myself? I did know that relativity had to do with the speed of light and the relationship between space and time. As I understood it, one conclusion is that if you are moving rapidly with respect to another person, and use a yardstick you are carrying to check the length of an identical yardstick the other person is carrying, you will find that his stick is shorter than yours. This would not be a mere illusion but the result of careful, honest measurements. Oddly, he would find your yardstick to be shorter than his. As if that is not mysterious enough, Einstein showed you would observe that the clock you might carry would be ticking at a different rate than the clock the other person carried.

Could I ever totally grasp these concepts? Or some of the newer ideas Einstein had developed? Perhaps not. Yet the thought of an expedition to test these things stirred my imagination. In the expedition that was being planned, the idea being tested was that light can be deflected by gravity. As the newspapers described it, scientists will observe the positions of stars whose light passes close to the edge of the sun during a solar eclipse. If Einstein is right, the observed positions of the stars will be altered by the gravitation of the sun. In my mind's eye I saw telescopes and other instruments, meticulously built to the scientists' design. The researchers would be a group of mutually respected colleagues joined in a common adventure. I pictured them engaged in long, spirited conversations about the science and how the experiments should be carried out. Most alluring of all for them, might be the satisfaction of witnessing something about the nature of the universe for the first time. For a short time at least, they alone could have the privilege of knowing a truth long held secretly by nature, and thereby sharing an intimacy with an ultimate reality.

I pondered this last thought from time to time all through the winter. The idea of being at the forefront of understanding, of uncovering some secret of nature known only to oneself at the moment, was tantalizing yet disturbing. Surely, at the outset of his discovery, only Einstein knew about relativity. But did Einstein, at that moment, feel arrogance in his uniqueness, his superiority? Or did he instead feel privileged, or even humbled in the presence of truths beyond himself? Perhaps he felt somewhat as I have, humbled before the starry night sky among the farms in New Lots, or as the old men feel standing each Saturday before the Holy Ark.

But early Sunday mornings at the shoe store I was always much too busy for cosmic thoughts. Sunday afternoons can see a huge crush of customers. The cash till must be prepared and the books checked. Shelves have to be carefully organized. The work was not unpleasant. Occasionally one of the ladies would give me a seductive smile that at once would embarrass and daze me. I was in charge and of importance. Bluestein had given me complete authority, except for granting credit. For this, I must tell customers, to check directly with the boss. In fact Bluestein would often pay a brief visit in the mid-morning to check on any problems. I especially enjoyed training the two schoolboys who come to assist. Earlier on

Bluestein's younger daughter Becky used to come in on Sundays to help out, but she eventually married and lives in the Bronx. That was one of the reasons Bluestein now took Sundays off, so that he can make long trips with his wife to see his daughters and their families.

By most measures I had been doing well. I was helping out Mother and Father and still banking much of my salary. And I had the prospect of earning a good living in the future if I would choose to take up Bluestein's offer of partnership. Once in a while, when I had an evening off during a slow period, I would treat my sister, Celia, to an evening in the big city to see a performance at the Metropolitan Opera. We would sit in the inexpensive balcony seats, looking down at the swells in their tuxedos and evening gowns in the orchestra seats. It didn't matter to us that we weren't rich; the opulence was infectious and the spectacle and the music transporting. Celia has often said that I should find a girlfriend to go out with but I don't feel quite ready to have a love interest. Despite how smoothly life had been going, I sensed a persistent unease, as if all of it was not enough.

The final break in my thinking came in early summer. The Austrian Archduke and his wife had been assassinated in the Balkans in June. It was a spark in a powder keg. A flurry of threats, demands, and ultimatums arose in Europe. Armies were being mobilized. It seemed as if Europe was unraveling. Even the great expedition to test Einstein's theories during the eclipse had been called off. These squabbles, which often elude my understanding, now dominated the news. Mankind, it would seem, was not noticing the magnificence of the sky or the tranquil beauty of the countryside. There began a perceptible shift in my perspective. Despite its tangible rewards, I saw the selling of shoes as less important in the scheme of things.

I took out my college catalogs again, and last month I submitted an application to Gallatin College in lower Manhattan for admission to the class starting at the end of September. I have been accepted. Mr. Bluestein was not entirely surprised when I let him know of my decision. He never let on, but I sense that he knew my choice before I did. Perhaps he believed that were he in my position he would do much the same as I. Mother and Father were less certain, but they seemed to be pleased to think of me as an educated person. Bluestein's only request was that I continue to take over the store on Sundays, and that I spend summers at the store so that he could indulge in this American thing, the "vacation."

With some trepidation I showed up early this week at an imposing Gothic building just off Washington Square to register for classes. This is an unfamiliar part of New York. Upscale brownstone homes fronted by large leafy sycamores lie in rows along the side streets. On the main thoroughfares small restaurants mingle with other businesses—bookstores, smoke shops, small hotels. I was struck by the youthfulness of the passers-by. The scene on the street stood in sharp contrast to Brownsville's pushcarts and food stores spilling aromas and produce out onto the sidewalks.

Entering the lobby of the building along with a stream of other young people a phalanx of tables confronted us. At these barriers was a cadre of steely-eyed women, reminding me of certain of my grade school teachers. These ladies were clearly the gatekeepers to our future. Before being permitted to move on they were to be satisfied that we had been properly admitted and were prepared to come forth with the balance of our tuition. No coddling and no pity—cash on the barrelhead.

I cleared the first hurdle with some relief and was directed into the main part of the building. The scene inside brought forth in me a dim recollection of the great hall on Ellis Island. It was a massive space that I supposed was normally used as a gymnasium. The din made by hundreds of young men and women echoed off the roof high above. It was like a large train station but instead of train gates around the edges there was a perimeter of tables, each labeled with a sign proclaiming one of the disciplines—Philosophy, Music, Mathematics, and others. An updated collection of the Muses. In a corner near the main entrance there were two tables labeled 'Advising'. A queue had formed at each table. I took my place at the rear of the shorter line.

In time I came face to face with a bored looking young man in a tight fitting tweed suit. A wide, thin mustache creased his pinkish face. He was no older than I was. I took him to be one of the teaching assistants. "What class are you in?" he asked as soon as he had briefly looked me over. He was direct. No niceties.

"I'm just starting," I answered.

"A freshman then. Getting started a little late, aren't you?" He appeared to disdain looking me in the eye. And he seemed not to expect an answer. "Do you have a major in mind?"

"Not yet," I said. "Probably one of the sciences. I have been thinking about physics."

"Physics," he repeated to himself. "Hmm-m." He reached for a small sheaf of papers fastened to clipboard. "Let's see." After finding an appropriate page he went on. "I suppose you've had high school math?" This time he looked up at me.

"Yes. Algebra, geometry, and trigonometry. I did pretty well."

"Hmm-m." He studied the paper briefly before replying. "This is pretty clear," he said, wagging a finger at the sheet of paper. "You'll want to start with a year each of college mathematics and chemistry, and the required course in English literature and composition." He reached for a blank weekly course schedule and wrote down some course numbers at the top. Then, almost as an afterthought, he added, "You should also take some non-science elective to round this out."

He shoved a college catalog in front of me. I had a number of non-science courses in mind already. While I thumbed through the catalog the tweedy assistant buffed his nails on his lapels. Finally, I turned to the Philosophy Department page. "How about this one?" I said. "Survey of Western Philosophy. Philosophy 200."

He didn't reply. He added the course number to the list and handed the blank schedule to me. "You can get on the class lists out there." He gestured towards the tables ringing the room.

I cursorily thanked the young man, hoping he was not in a science or the math department. At the departmental tables I was relieved to find his type was not the norm. Most of the professors and teaching assistants proved genuinely helpful in working out a conflict-free class schedule.

The commute I will be taking every day will prove arduous. The streetcar in Brownsville will connect with the Fulton Street el downtown. The train from there will cross the Brooklyn Bridge and meet up with the Broadway subway, which will take me to the Eighth Street stop in Greenwich Village. I hope to use the travel time for study. I cannot suppress my unease, but the burden of indecision has been lifted and I am in high spirits. Classes begin next Monday.

CHAPTER 9

World Enlarged

1915

Summer again! A full college year is now behind me. Again I am at work with Bluestein full-time, but life is far easier than it had been during the last ten months. College has been fulfilling but I need this summer break. Bluestein gives me all of Friday and Saturday mornings off. As usual I take care of the store on the ever-busy Sundays. I am at home among the aisles of the shop, with the smell of fresh leather, the neat rows of boxes in the storeroom, the young ladies coming occasionally with a fiancée in tow. Nothing is especially exhilarating but it is comfortable. I am replenishing my bank account.

Brother Dave sent me a note early in the week suggesting that we meet for lunch on Friday in the city. We do not see Dave often, as he still lives at the Y.M.H.A. in Manhattan. He tries to visit the family occasionally, but this particular proposal was unusual. "We haven't had much of a chance to talk lately," he wrote. "I'd like you to meet a friend of mine." There was a postscript. "P.S. This is my treat. You know the food at the Excelsior. So go light on breakfast." I agreed by the next post. Actually, after the non-stop routine of the school year, I almost feel guilty about having an uncommitted Friday. But I suppressed any misgivings. I really looked forward to spending some time with Dave.

Today at noon I showed up at the Excelsior Kosher Restaurant on Houston Street. It was going to be one of those typical humid summer days in New York. Already the feel in the air suggested the heat that would descend later in the day, but there was a nice breeze coming from the harbor. As I came in the door and began to approach a burly waiter in a low slung apron and rolled up sleeves, I felt a tap on my shoulder. It was Dave. On his arm was a smiling young lady, short and full-faced. She looked directly into my eyes. Dave and I gave one another a brief hug, then he turned to his friend. "This is Dolly."

Dolly extended her hand. "Pleased to meet you," she said as I shook her small hand. It was warm and moist. I sensed that I would come to like her. I cannot be sure, but there was hint of an accent in her voice, though hardly as pronounced as Dave's. Before I could respond, the waiter was ushering us to a table near the front window. Dave mentioned that he usually brings in a sandwich for lunch at his new job in the pharmacy department at the hospital, but he had managed to get a long lunch break today. He wanted me to meet Dolly.

The Excelsior is an authentic lower East Side kosher eatery. I wondered when it was that I had last been there. Perhaps it was several years ago when Dave graduated from pharmacy school, and he, Celia, and I chipped in to take the family out for a celebration. After so many years in her own kitchen it was clear that Mother was uncomfortable eating among strangers and perhaps suspicious of this place's fidelity to the dietary laws. But she knew that it was indeed an occasion for special celebration.

After we had taken our seats, Dave quietly placed an order with the waiter. The chicken noodle soup was soon at the table in steaming metal cups. It was obvious that Dave had ordered an old country Jewish dinner. An assistant placed a large bowl of "soup—nuts"—little egg-pastry nuggets—in the center of the table, while the waiter tipped each cup of soup into our bowls. A hot day was in the offing, but this steaming amber liquid with a flotilla of soup-nuts floating before each of us somehow seemed fitting. And I was famished.

As the conversation began, it was clear that Dolly already knew a great deal about our family. She seemed eager to hear my version of family news—the usual things—everyone's health, how sister Sari was doing in high school, whether Celia was seeing anyone "special." The news was quite ordinary but Dolly was warmly engaged with it.

When the main course appeared at the table, the conversation had turned to my situation. The food was familiar Sabbath eve fare. Portions of roasted chicken were set before us, and in the center of the table, a hot, savory bowl of *tzimmis*—plump prunes stewed with sweet potatoes.

"Your brother tells me that not only have you been taking classes but also doing part-time work," Dolly began. "And it's a long trip each day—isn't it?"

"I didn't get a lot of sleep this year," was about all I could think of saying immediately. She had sounded concerned. "But I managed fine." I added.

"Have you decided on a major?" Dave asked. "Math maybe?"

I had been holding to the idea of choosing physics, despite not yet having taken a college course in the subject. I was aware of my long time fascination with natural phenomena and technology, but I was still undecided about what that implied. "I don't think it will be mathematics," I said.

"How so?" Dave wanted to know. "I didn't think you would have any trouble with math."

"No. No, that isn't it. I got A's both semesters. The work was a little intense, certainly compared with high school. But I can't get enthusiastic about it like I once did."

Dolly listened attentively but didn't comment. Dave thought about my answer for a few moments before he said, "Well I guess I never had that enthusiasm at all—I remember more or less a slog." I recalled how Dave seemed exasperated at times in high school.

I considered further clarifying my feelings about high school math. About the fun of working through a geometrical proof by deduction from simple premises, but also the delight of thinking about problems in the context of spatial relations, ideas that I could image as well as make abstract arguments about. Instead I tried to explain my reaction to the college math course in terms I thought might be better understood. "Maybe it was the teaching," I said. "The prof was a pretty dull type. He was impressive enough at manipulating the symbols, but as for the applications, he didn't seem particularly interested—or even aware."

Both Dave and Dolly nodded. Then I added, "I admit there is a certain beauty in mathematics—maybe it's the cleverness of it, or the precision, or the conciseness. I'm not sure. Sometimes I think maybe it's the sureness of it that sets it apart—none of the 'on one hand this, on the other hand that'." I wondered if I was making too much of the subject but I wanted to finish the thought. "However, for some reason, it's only when I can relate the math to the real world, when the abstractions are not the only focus, that it really catches my interest."

Dolly gave me a tender look. "I picture you as a scientist, Abe. Maybe you should concentrate on the chemistry."

"I do like the lab work," I responded. I wanted to turn the conversation away from me. Besides chemistry is at the heart of Dave's profession and I was afraid I might inadvertently denigrate it. "A useful subject, all right. It's a possibility," I said finally.

My response had been cursory. Chemistry is indeed a science, but I would have had to admit to Dave that I felt put off by the amount of rote memory that was required. I had done well enough in chemistry, but I mostly liked those parts of the course where we had to think about physical explanations lying behind the phenomena. I momentarily recalled an experiment on the effect of pressure on boiling points of liquids. The course did not go into great detail in explaining the phenomena, but did provide a simplified model involving forces of interaction among atoms and molecules. There were subtleties and still unanswered questions in the theory, but even that cursory brush with the mysterious unseen world of atoms evoked a kind of delight.

"Enough about me," I finally said. There was a lot more I could have said about the grueling, but exhilarating past year. A lot more. It had not been entirely about science. There were some new friends and many new ideas. From time to time I had been reflecting on my philosophy course, especially our discussions of Spinoza. The idea of God has always been a struggle. So the thinking of this Jewish philosopher and pantheism—God as Nature—had caught my attention. I would have liked to talk about that with someone. But Dave was not the person, and certainly this was not the time.

When our plates had finally been cleared from the table a large dish of mandel bread was set before us. The hard slices of cake, copious with raisins and nuts and running with sugary cinnamon, reminded me of Mother's baking, but these were not warm from the oven as at home. I supposed that Dave missed home cooking. I watched him reach eagerly for a piece as soon as the waiter had poured the tea.

I changed the subject. "You two seem like very good friends." I was indeed curious about the relationship but didn't want to appear to be a busybody.

Dave and Dolly turned and looked at one another. I could only guess what they communicated in their looks. Dave again turned towards me, and placing his hands palms down on the table, he leaned closer to me. "We are thinking of getting engaged," he said.

I had been reading their body language, so I was not entirely unprepared. But this was probably the first time anyone I knew as closely as Dave had taken this step. People of my parent's generation in the old country typically were married off when they were considerably younger than any of us. But here in America my group of friends was generally focused on finding practical futures and not so willing to be tied down by marriage. Our image of marriage, modeled by our parents, implied burdensome responsibilities: children, endless work—and deferring adventure. For the time being, at least, many of us are wary. But for Dave—secure in his new profession, looking mature with his hairline beginning to recede, and especially with this appealing girl at his side—it made abundant sense.

"Gosh—that's wonderful news! Mazel tov! Mazel tov!" I blurted out. Then I hesitated. "You say you're *thinking* about being engaged? You're not sure?"

"Actually we've decided, but we are trying to find the right time to make it official. Especially we're not sure when to tell the old folks." For the first time Dave was looking as if he needed advice from me, the younger brother. That was a new concept, added to the new concept of having an addition to the family. "You know that in the old country marriages were pretty much arranged. I wouldn't be surprised if the old man has talked with his cronies about whether their own daughters were looking around." As usual Dave spoke of Father and his friends in language that was at once both dismissive and affectionate. I was glad he didn't use his newfound word for Father and his generation: *geezer*. "To his credit the old man hasn't suggested to us to have him intercede, but I suppose he and Mom worry about whom all of us will end up with," he added.

"I'm sure they'll be pleased as punch with Dolly," I said. I looked at Dolly and grinned. She was beaming as well. I had not known her very long, but I felt I had taken her measure: bright, not terribly sophisticated—but warm and loving. Not exactly my type, but I knew I would like her. "If you want I'll drop a few hints around the house."

"Yes do. You can tell Sis—Celia, I mean. And thanks," he said. Then he pulled out his pocket watch, the one the family had scraped up money to buy as a graduation present. Instinctively he put it to his ear to make sure he had not forgotten to wind it before flicking open the case and checking the time. "I have to get Dolly back pretty soon to her desk at the law firm. And I have a big date with my pills."

Dave paid the bill. The burly waiter opened the door for us, and we said our goodbyes on the sidewalk. Dave and I shook hands. I turned to Dolly. But instead of putting out her hand she reached up and gave me a little hug and a peck on the cheek. "I'm so glad to meet you," she said. "We all ought to get together again soon. There is a lot to talk about." I nodded, feeling a little flushed, but very pleased. Then, almost as if she wished to bring our new relationship back to a neutral level, she added, "Maybe you should think about cutting back a little on course work next term."

"That's what Celia tells me," I responded.

A new phase of our family life was beginning. I was pleased and excited with the news from Dave and Dolly. As for myself, I was still very much on my journey. For the rest of the afternoon I had planned to stop by at the library and in the evening I would go with Father to the shul. It was my compromise for not spending the whole day with him on Saturday.

At the library I intended to catch up on the news of the war in Europe and some of the general science journals. But the conversation with Dave had also stirred me to reflect again on this past year in college.

I found myself thinking once more about the philosophy course. I sensed my ambivalence about the subject. It was intriguing material for the most part. Yet sometimes I questioned the value of the course. Even the organization of the course reinforced my discomfort. In sequence there were the various philosophers: the ancients—Epicurus, Democritus, Plato, and others. Later on—Leibniz, Hegel, Kant, Burke. It was almost like the Bible—words of truth being handed down from sages and prophets. I saw the contrast with my chemistry text in which the discoverers are incidental and the story proceeds according to ideas—acids and bases, metals, chemical equilibrium, organic compounds. The reference points are in Nature rather than in human authority.

However the discussions on Spinoza strongly caught my attention. And it is not just his ideas but also his personal story that intrigued me. Baruch de Spinoza, born into the seventeenth century Jewish community in Amsterdam, was excommunicated from the synagogue for "abominable heresies" when he was not much older than I. I had never heard of such a thing! Some Jews I know drift away and even weird ideas are tolerated if there is no disruptive behavior. But nobody now ever talks of excommunication or heresy in Judaism. And his banishment was complete with no possibility of reprieve or return. He never converted to any other faith but lived as a seventeenth century anomaly—a person with no formal religious community.

Professor Vogel, who lectured the course, supposes that the severity of Spinoza's punishment had more to do with fear than with unorthodox ideas. The Jews of the Low Countries were not far removed in time from when they were Spanish and Portuguese *Marranos,* hiding their Jewish practices behind a public profession of Catholicism—daily risking incineration in the pyres of the Inquisition. There was no way that they could allow their Christian neighbors, no matter how tolerant, to view them as godless deviants. Whatever it took to prove incontrovertibly their devotion to holy belief was necessary to avoid incitement of the wider community.

But the most astonishing thing is that the ideas that probably moved the Jewish establishment to curse and shun Spinoza irrevocably seem so reasonable and so harmless to me. Of course nobody really knows what blasphemies this brash young guy was mouthing all around because he hadn't yet published. But we can assume they were more or less the ideas for which he ultimately became famous. His underlying principle was that God and Nature are two names for the same thing, in fact the only thing. Everything else he wrote—about ethics, politics, immortality—followed logically from that reality. It seems to me that much of my life I have wondered about the essence of God—though hardly to the point of distraction. Where is God? Surely not only in the visible heavens. Should we stand in awe of God? No more so perhaps than we stand in awe of the spectacle of the night sky. Does the love of God move us to righteousness? Perhaps in the same way that contemplation of nature moves us to humility. Of course Spinoza's God doesn't hand out rewards and punishments, but I have never seriously thought I should ask God for special favors. I don't think I am ready to reframe my life on the basis of one philosopher's ruminations, but this Dutch Jew's point of view seems so reasonable. At least it is consistent with how I have come to view the world.

I will be with Father this evening and much of tomorrow. The ritual is familiar. The sense of awe in the presence of this ill defined—no, undefined—deity is familiar. But who—or what—is this God we spend the Sabbath praising and obeying? It seems real enough—but it is mysterious. I am aware that the sense of awe—and humility—that comes with worship is often akin to my feelings about the physical universe. Of course contemplation in the presence of the Holy Ark is a different practice than exploring the natural world. Worship is tenuous and almost dismissive of my rational side, whereas science offers a methodology for deepening my understanding of the ultimate reality—and my sense of being at one with it. But they are not inconsistent. And for the time being I am at home with both.

CHAPTER 10

Professor Connor's Lab

1916

Just after the start of the Christmas recess there was a snowstorm that coated the Brownsville neighborhood in almost a foot of glistening white. The noise of traffic, the little traffic that was able to move, was muffled. The houses and streets took on an unaccustomed beauty. For a while country and city appeared to have merged.

Bluestein had asked me to help during the holiday season every weekday morning and all day Sunday. There are not many displays of Christmas in our neighborhood, but Bluestein has made a small effort with the addition of a couple of paper wreaths and some tinsel in the storefront, along with winter shoes and boots. He refuses to put up a Christmas tree.

My decision in the fall to concentrate on physics has not been disappointing. Even the fundamentals of the subject pose interesting challenges. Bedrock ideas like Newton's laws of motion in all their elegant simplicity can be deceptive. Applying these ideas correctly and efficiently sometimes requires ingenuity and imagination. And as in high school geometry, there is a peculiar sense of satisfaction in solving mathematical puzzles. Sometimes the feeling is not unlike scoring a goal in eighth grade soccer.

I'm in the first semester of my third college year, but I'm not sure how long it will be before I can complete my degree. The problem is that I have reduced my course load a bit in order to put in some more time at the store. Yet in general I am pleased with my program. I have even rediscovered beauty in the mathematics. And the liberal arts courses are almost like challenging recreation, especially the literature courses. Mostly, however, I have become very devoted to my major in physics. At the suggestion of my faculty advisor I registered for undergraduate research credit, and have been helping in Professor Connor's research lab.

Right now the College is in Christmas recess, but in many of the research labs work will go on right until the actual holidays. Today at midday, as I do three times a week, I traveled to the College to help out. The mounds of snow had hardened into blackened irregular heaps along the gutters. At the end of Bluestein's block there was a little lake of gray water and slush blocking the sidewalk. Someone had stomped a temporary footpath over the nearest piles of snow. The kids scampered across this little mountain path, but the old folks moved with trepidation. In the old country snow did not become black and hard like that.

Emerging from the subway station in Manhattan it was a different world. The major streets were largely bare of snow. Holly wreaths and colored lights and hovering angels adorned the shop windows. And a merry band of Santa Clauses seemed to have taken up residence alongside the merchandise. Often sharing the window space were holiday trees festooned with shiny colored balls, tinsel, and glass stars. It seemed somehow foreign and pagan, but I welcomed this cheerfulness at such a dark time of the year. Perhaps, however, it was merely the release from the pressure of daily classes and assignments that buoyed my spirits.

I made my way to the science building a few blocks from the subway station and descended immediately to the basement floor. Physics labs are often placed low down where the imperceptible swaying and vibrating of a building is least likely to interfere with delicate instruments. During the holiday recess the barely lit halls are hollow and mostly quiet. Muffled voices coming from the end of the corridor grew more distinct as I approached Professor Connor's lab. As I walked into the umbrella of light coming from the open door I heard Russell, one of the graduate students saying, "I think Abe's coming."

The windowless space beyond the threshold was lit by two bright bare light bulbs hanging by wires from a very high ceiling crisscrossed by a maze of pipes. Along one wall were a long low workbench and some hand tools hanging haphazardly from a rack. An assortment of objects lay strewn about on the bench top, conveying not so much carelessness as industriousness. Among these items: a glass blower's torch, spools of wire, and a bottle of some kind of solvent. In the background one could hear the continuous gurgling of a mechanical fore-pump and the faint smell of pump oil hung in the air. In the center of the room, among racks of glassware and gauges, was the focus of our attention, a skeletal structure about six feet high holding a silvery "Dewar" flask. The Dewar, essentially a very large Thermos bottle, enveloped the very cold metal sample whose electrical properties we would be measuring. It insulated the sample from the intrusion of heat from the surrounding room.

As I stepped through the door Russell spoke again, "Hey, just in time, Abe. Butch and I need a little help." Russell is a little younger than me, of medium build, with a pleasant face topped by a head of sandy, thick, unkempt hair. He was wearing a heavy, black hand-knitted sweater, and protective goggles covered his eyes. He was perched on a wooden step stool, pouring liquid nitrogen into the Dewar. Butch, the other graduate student, a tall, gangly fellow who always needs a shave and makes me think of a circus roustabout, was half hidden behind a rack of glassware.

Liquid nitrogen, or "liquid air," is an extremely cold but generally harmless substance. I had been introduced to its properties the first day I reported to the lab in the fall. The graduate students liked to demonstrate its unconventional behavior as kind of a ritual to impress the novices. The show usually began with some liquid air being poured over a lab bench. Riding off across the tabletop as little colorless balls of liquid suspended by the boiling vapor beneath each drop, the liquid quickly disappeared in puffs of white vapor. Next some flexible rubber tubing was plunged into a flask of liquid nitrogen. When the bubbling and boiling ceased and the tube is lifted out, it shattered like glass under the blow of a hammer. This little show-and-tell usually came to a musical finale by showing how a lead bell, which normally would produce a dull thud when struck, could emit a merry tinkle when it was cooled to the temperature of liquid nitrogen. But always embedded in these amusements were cautionary lessons for the novice: don't stick your finger in liquid air, avoid wetting clothing with it, and above all protect your eyes.

The research underway in the lab has to do with "superconductivity," a phenomenon that was discovered in Holland about five years ago. It concerns the way metals conduct electricity when cooled to very low temperatures. It is to be expected that when electricity streams though a wire there would be some kind of "friction" interfering with the flow. This is usually explained in terms of tiny electrical particles, "electrons," encountering metal atoms as they move along the wire. This idea accounts for the resistance of metals to the flow of electrical current in most cases. But for some metals, when cooled to temperatures hundreds of degrees below room temperature, this resistance completely vanishes. It is not simply that the resistance to electrical flow becomes very small; it apparently disappears completely. For instance, as far as anyone knows, as long as the temperature remains sufficiently low an electrical current circulating in a ring made of a superconducting metal would continue flowing indefinitely without the help of a battery. Or perhaps it is *almost* indefinitely—that is still an open question. Adding to the mystery of this surprising quirk of nature is the fact that all of the ordinarily very excellent carriers of electricity like copper, gold, or silver, no matter how cold we have been able to make them, do not exhibit this odd property.

There is no explanation for this phenomenon, but not for want of trying. An understanding of this will probably require more observations. We are part of that effort. What metals show this behavior? How are the phenomena affected by the presence of magnets? It is as if there is an unexplored land across an ocean and only a few are able to cross that ocean and look around. And we can make the voyage. In the bottom of the Dewar flask this afternoon was a coil of aluminum wire. First it was cooled to the temperature of liquid nitrogen. The crucial next step was to lower the temperature far lower by submerging the wire in liquid helium. Then we would be truly across the ocean. Very few laboratories have access to liquid helium, an exotic substance in its own right. But Professor Connor has ties to the research group uptown at Columbia University that is able to supply us with some from time to time.

Shortly after I arrived this afternoon Dr. Connor appeared. He is a clean-shaven, cheerful looking man in his mid-thirties. The stiff rounded collar and blue bow tie under his white lab coat accentuated his angular jaw and receding hairline. He greeted us with a smile and asked if everything was set up for a "helium transfer." Then the feeling in the room intensified.

The transfer operation is a delicate dance, carefully choreographed in the past. The two graduate students knew their roles. The Professor was in charge but also took part in handling the equipment. For the time being the formal hierarchy of academia was removed. There was an easy relationship between professor and student that is often absent in the classroom.

Liquid helium cannot be simply poured from container to container like liquid nitrogen. Its temperature is less than eight Fahrenheit degrees above the absolute zero of temperature—far, far colder than anything known on earth or, as far as we know, anywhere else. Upon contact with the room air it would instantly vaporize. So it has to be forced from its container into our Dewar through a delicate, vacuum insulated, U-shaped glass "transfer siphon."

Russell and Butch, each holding one side of the siphon, carefully lowered one end into the Dewar and the other end into the container of liquid helium. When the professor gave his okay, Butch slowly opened the stopcock that admitted the helium gas that pushed the liquid helium into the Dewar. Very few words were exchanged. The tension was palpable. No one wanted to waste valuable resources on a failed transfer. But soon, to our relief, we could see through a small transparent section of the Dewar, a spattering of drops of a colorless fluid. At first, as these specks of liquid helium came into contact with the relatively warm Dewar walls, they immediately flashed into vapor and disappeared. But eventually, as cooling took place, a puddle of bubbling clear liquid helium began to form.

When Professor Connor, who had been observing the level of the accumulating liquid helium, gave the signal, Russell quickly shut off the flow of gas that had been forcing liquid from the storage vessel. "Very nice!" the professor said, making an entry in his notebook. He has participated in this procedure dozens of times, but there is a sense that he is awed in the presence of this unearthly substance. Yet to a casual observer, it might seem merely like some fizzy soda water in a very large Thermos bottle.

"Ready, Butch?" Professor Connor asked. Very gently Butch and Russell, again holding opposite ends of the delicate, glass transfer siphon, lifted it up and out of the Dewar flask and the storage container. At this point I had climbed up on a step stool. Taking the siphon by its middle section I hung it on some hooks on the wall.

The goal of today's experiment was to see how the electrical resistance of our coil of wire changed when its temperature was made as low we could. The temperature just after the transfer was that of liquid helium as it comes from its container. But by reducing the pressure in the Dewar we could lower it even further. This effect is similar to that which causes water to boil at a lower temperature high up in the mountains, where atmospheric pressure is low. But if a person were to mistake our flask of bubbling helium for boiling water, he would be surprised to witness an even more curious phenomenon.

Next, Butch opened a valve connecting the Dewar to the mechanical fore-pump, thereby lowering the pressure in it. The pump noise now became louder and the bubbling and boiling in the liquid became more vigorous. The temperature of the liquid was gradually dropping. Then, without any hint that anything astonishing was about to happen, the bubbling suddenly ceased completely. The surface of the liquid helium could still be seen, but only with difficulty because instead of the surface being the place where rising bubbles break free, it was as placid as a lake on windless day. Evaporation of helium was still taking place, evidenced by the fact that the pump noise was just as loud and the level of the liquid was very slowly declining. But no bubbles were rising from within the body of the liquid. Apparently nobody has any understanding of why this transition to a different type of liquid occurs. Totally unexpected, I can hardly imagine the feelings of the original discoverers as they observed this state of matter that never, anywhere ever existed before—a liquid that cannot boil.

My main assignment during these procedures was to take and record measurements of the electrical resistance of the aluminum sample in the Dewar. By the time the last data were recorded it was nearly six in the evening. Enough information had been accumulated for the time being. The feeling is one of mild exultation. The experiment was carried out without any major crises and although the data still needed careful analysis, we thought that we saw signs of a transition to superconductivity. This was especially interesting as aluminum's ability to conduct electricity rivals that of "good" conductors like copper, which do not appear to make such a transition.

In less than a week it will be Christmas. There are no more experiments scheduled until after the New Year's holiday as there is little chance that Columbia will have any liquid helium to spare before then. Besides Professor Connor is undoubtedly immersed in Christmas preparations with his young family. I almost envy the opportunity they will have to abandon the day-to-day routines of life and surrender to what appear to be a festive round of activities. I am not sure how to deal with this Christmas spirit. But for the time being the break from regular classes at the College is sufficient to put me in a cheerful mood.

As Dr. Connor left the lab I wished him "Merry Christmas." My words seemed awkward. Yet they were heart-felt, moved by a sense of respect and admiration for the young professor. I wonder if he was conscious of my discomfort.

"And you have a nice holiday too, Abe," he replied.

Outside a light fog had enveloped the city. The shops were still open, the lights in their windows silhouetting the office workers as they scurried by on their way to the subway station. I slid into the stream of silent bodies, each of us in a slightly different trajectory. I imagined us, almost like the electrons in the wire, moving under the influence of similar forces yet giving rise to an often surprising whole. By the time the train had moved up onto the bridge, I was finally able to lift my mind from the special world of atoms and unfamiliar phenomena in which I had been immersed most of the day. I looked out on the twinkling little universe spanning the river that was this amazing city at night. Among the lights were clusters of green and blue and red. I began to think of what lay ahead of me this week.

Tomorrow will be another big day. Again in the afternoon, after spending the morning at Bluestein's, I will again travel into the City. But tomorrow I plan to spend my time at the college library. But it's not only scholarly dedication that drives my enthusiasm.

Since the fall I have spent Thursday afternoons at the library, and I usually meet up with Rosie, whom I met last year in our calculus class. We are both working on term papers over the Christmas break and I hope nothing keeps her away tomorrow because the library will be closed next week until after New Year's Day. Actually, I don't know a great deal about Rosie, except that her real name is Rosalyn Dubrow, that she lives uptown in Harlem, and that she hopes to become a teacher. I also know that her term paper is on the poetry of Elizabeth Barrett Browning.

Last Thursday Rosie and I, during our four o'clock coffee break, laughed about the contrast between her term paper topic and my ponderous paper on Wilhelm Friedrich Nietzsche. "I'm afraid he didn't see much hope or lightness in the world," I had remarked. I was responding to Rosie's description of her poet's celebration of life and love.

"Frowning Fred and sunny Liz," she said, with a chuckle.

"Not a good combination for a blind date," I added.

But Rosie is not all lightness and fluff. In fact what drew my attention from the first day was how she stood out, the only woman in a mathematics class otherwise made up entirely of men. I know I will miss meeting with her during the rest of the holiday break.

It has been an eventful day. Time for bed. As I fall asleep I am drifting on a cool, fog-shrouded lake. The lake is liquid helium.

CHAPTER 11

War

1917

For months the headlines had been fairly screaming about war. Now it is upon us. It is *the* topic of conversation in the College lunchroom. Judging by the conversations, loyalties are entirely with the Allied cause. If there are German sympathizers, they would be wise to keep their opinions to themselves. Dissidents cannot be identified by their names; many Jewish and German family names are the same. But anyone with a home in the Yorkville neighborhood, where so many German families have settled, might feel under suspicion.

Congress is about to pass a conscription act, and it is clear that unmarried men in their twenties will have to register to be drafted. I am ambivalent about this. On one hand I am anxious about how long it is taking me to earn a college degree; on the other hand I am not immune to patriotic zeal. Surely war is not as romantic as some recruiters or firebrands like Teddy Roosevelt would have us believe. But if it came to serving in uniform, I would volunteer for the Navy. Maybe it is my sense that the Navy so connected to science and technology. Perhaps I am persuaded by the popular argument that the Navy is the bulwark of our democracy against foreign aggressions. The other day I overheard one of the louder students, a self-assured history major, declaiming on the subject. "A nation with a strong army, but a weak navy can strike hard but not far," he said. "A nation with a strong navy but a weak army could strike far but not hard. But if Germany wins this war, and that is a possibility, it would be able to strike hard *and* far," he told his circle of friends.

It is in this milieu that I am ruminating on a conversation I had this afternoon with Professor Connor. During the regular school year I have scheduled several afternoons each week to assist with his research. Occasionally he has asked me to help in the lab when an experiment was to take place on a Sunday because of the sudden availability of liquid helium. He never has asked me to be available on a Saturday. Today, he asked me to come to his office just after noon. I found him behind his desk, almost hidden by some piles of paper. He appeared to be working on a manuscript. Beside his chair several physics journals were lying face down on the floor presumably open to some significant article. As usual, he was neatly dressed in a white shirt with a well-starched collar. He wore a bright red bow tie that accentuated the lower part of his face by drawing one's eyes down from his receding hairline. He had removed his coat. His shirtsleeves were partly rolled up.

"Ah, Abe. Good to see you. Got some data here which need some work," he said as he pushed his chair back and began to rise.

As much as I like the action and comradeship that goes with lab work, I find fascination in working over data that come out of the lab experiments. It is solitary work, and on the face of it, tedious. But as the results emerge from the raw data, I have this sense of being drawn closer to some deeper understanding. Put into graphical or tabular form and compared with expectations from theory or from related research, patterns emerge that challenge one's powers of explanation. What are these numbers telling us about the reality buried deep inside the atoms of lead or zinc at the bottom of the Dewar? Perhaps it is just a grand game—us against nature—but it is a game where our respect for the opponent is always deepens.

"The weekend run went swimmingly," Professor Collins said, as he made his way around to the side of the desk and turned his attention to a pile of notebooks at one corner. "Ah yes. Here it is. "He pulled out a hardbound notebook with a black and white marble design cover, like a schoolboy's composition book. Opening it to the last few pages, he scanned the columns of figures as if gazing at some piece of artwork, before closing it and handing it to me. "We need the manometer readings reduced to absolute temperature. Also, I'd like you to calculate the resistivities of the sample."

When I was about to leave with the notebook, and Dr. Connor was making his way back behind his desk, he turned again to me. Indicating a chair beside the desk he said, "While you're here I'd like to ask you about something else. Here, have a seat." He picked up a pile of folders from the chair and placed them on top of a similar pile on the desk as he settled into his swivel desk chair.

He leaned back slightly and placed his clasped hands over his belly. "Abe, am I right to assume you are a citizen?" I was a little surprised, because the professor had never before asked me any personal questions. Yet, given his generally friendly demeanor, the question seemed entirely in character.

"Why, yes sir. For several years," I replied with slight hesitation. "I applied for naturalization soon after my eighteenth birthday". Then, with perhaps a hint of sheepishness, I continued, "Well maybe that's not exactly accurate. In the old country people weren't too careful about keeping records. All I really know is that I was born in the dead of winter, so I declared that my birthday was the thirty-first of December. I guess that seemed like an easy date to remember, and it always comes during a school holiday. Later I realized that there is always likely to be a party. Anyway I went down and applied on the first workday afterwards, January second." As an afterthought I added, "That was the same day I petitioned to officially change my name to Roth."

Dr. Connor seemed interested and amused. "It's probably not a unique story. Lots of people coming to this country take the opportunity to reinvent themselves to one degree or another. My grandpa decided when he came through immigration to drop the O' in front of his name. I guess he felt that now that he was in America he would be a little less Irish."

Now he became more serious and he leaned forward. "I hope you didn't mind me asking a personal question, Abe. But I wanted to be sure you're a citizen before I brought up another matter that could be of interest to you." He picked up an official looking envelope from the side of his desk and placed it in front of him. "I heard yesterday from a friend of mine with whom I've maintained contact ever since we went through graduate school together at Columbia. Dr. Barry is a physicist at the Naval Defense Laboratory in Washington. He wrote that rumors about a staff increase have been swirling about for months, but now that we're officially in this war he has the go-ahead to look for new personnel. He asked me if I had people to recommend."

I shifted nervously in my seat. He continued. "Of course these are not regular civil service positions, just temporary positions, probably for the duration of the war. But the point is I could submit your name. That is, if you are willing." It took me a few moments to process this idea before I could respond.

"I haven't finished my degree yet. I was hoping that maybe I could wrap it up in another year—at least if I work extra hard and take some summer courses." I said.

"I know that," he said. "But in a way, that is the point. What Jim Barry is trying to recruit for his project are technician level people who know something about physics, or at least about laboratory technique. Naturally there is going to be a need for people with advanced degrees, but they'll be hired at another level, probably through the civil service system. Quite frankly, we'll miss your help in the lab, but having you leave is a lot better than losing you altogether, which is what might happen if you stayed around and ended up drafted into the Army. You'll be protected against that by doing war work for the Navy."

"I admit I have been thinking a bit about how I might serve, with mixed feelings. I hate the thought of interrupting my college work. On the other hand I really want to be part of the fight. It's dues I ought to pay. In fact, I even thought about volunteering for the Navy."

"Then this sounds perfect to me" he interjected. "Believe me, you'll be more of an asset to the war effort at N.D.L. than on a ship as an ordinary swabbie. It might delay your degree a while, but I'm afraid all of us will have to put up with some disruption. I wouldn't be surprised if our lab is asked to transition to war work in the near future."

"What will happen to Russell and Butch?" I asked.

"I think there won't be a problem for them. They should both complete their master's degrees soon. Butch is married and probably safe from the draft, at least for the time being. As for Russell, he has talked about volunteering for officer training, but more than likely the Army would use him in some kind of scientific work. Anyway, give some thought to what I've suggested and get back to me on it as soon as you can."

I thanked Dr. Connor and promised him I would have the calculations done by the morning and might even have a response to his suggestion. I found a quiet corner in the library and lined up the notebook and a slide rule and prepared to work over the data. But I was unfocused. My mind kept wandering to the proposal the professor had made. I was glad that I had not promised to finish the work by the end of the afternoon.

At four o'clock I was more than ready to take a break from the work and hurried off to the school cafeteria, hoping that I would meet Rosie for a coffee break. Since early January we had agreed that if we were able, we would take coffee breaks in the cafeteria at four in the afternoon. Most of the time we both showed up and had gotten to know each other much better. I was relieved to see her about to get in the line at the coffee urn. Smiling, she gave me a little waist-high wave acknowledging that she had seen me get into the line. We made our way to a table in the far corner and sat down opposite each other. She wore a light spring dress, blue, with a beige, wool shawl over her shoulders. As usual she had a cheerful look on her face. It was a look that I had now seen so often that I was certain that this was the authentic Rosie and not a façade put on in public to disguise a darker personality.

She leaned forward, her elbows on the table, her coffee mug cradled in both hands. "Why the furrowed brow today, Abe?" she asked. I didn't realize that my churning thoughts were showing. This was enough to break me out of my shell and I felt myself relax a bit. I wondered if she knew how pleased I was to be with her.

Then I told her about the conversation with Dr. Connor. She listened intently without interrupting me. "It's a hard decision," I said finally.

She replied without hesitation. "I don't think so." She had a nice smile, as if teasing me for not seeing the obvious. Then, looking more serious, she added, "Actually I understand why you're struggling with this. You're probably tied up in knots over balancing your job and school, feeling you're behind schedule, your patriotic instincts, an impending draft—all those things. But frankly, looking from the outside it seems pretty simple."

"You think you know what I should do?" I asked. For a moment I regretted saying this. It's easier having someone make your decisions, but I was only hoping for a discussion, not an immediate resolution.

Her reply put me at ease. "Well yes, I do have an opinion about what you should do. But it's not for me to say. It's entirely for you to decide. But I know you're concerned about how long it's taking to finish the degree. I will give you my opinion on that."

"Which is?"

"Let me quote my dad. He likes to say that to young people life seems long, but even then they are always impatient. Besides that, he has been saying for some time now that once the Americans get into it, the war is going to end pretty quickly."

"In other words a year or two one way or the other doesn't matter much," I said.

"That's one way to put it. Anyway, you really don't know whether you would be hired. There's certainly no harm in applying," she replied.

"You've shown your cards," I said. "I know your opinion now."

"Maybe. But you should think about it some more. It's for you to choose."

"Of course you're right. It *is* my decision." After some silence I turned the conversation toward the situation in Rosie's family. Her mother is relieved that brother Alec is too young to serve but worries about some relatives who have remained in Europe. Her father follows the news avidly and is wondering how he can be of use.

When we had finished our coffees and were about to gather our belongings, Rosie looked directly at me. "Abe . . . ." She hesitated, then dropped her eyes to where she was fidgeting with her empty mug before continuing. "Abe, I would miss seeing you, if you left." She hesitated once again and looked at me again. "Perhaps I shouldn't have said that lest it influence your decision one way or the other."

For the first time I touched Rosie. I cupped my hands around hers. She didn't flinch or withdraw, and any awkwardness I might have felt from this spontaneous gesture was removed. Under my grasp I felt the fine, smooth beauty of those expressive hands of hers that I had long thought of as one of her most attractive features. Words came effortlessly. "No, no. I can't tell you how pleased I am to have heard that. I must tell you that the feeling is mutual. And no. I will not let it influence my decision."

Rosie's flushed face was aglow with a barely contained smile. I tried to turn the conversation around. "Anyway your dad has it all figured out as a short disruption." I realized that Mr. Dubrow's opinion might just be brave optimism. Also neither of us knew what "short" meant. "Besides, Washington is not that far away."

As she adjusted her shawl and got up to leave, she reached over and squeezed my hand. "Let me know how you've decided."

I went back to the library and tried to work on the lab data. I was thinking of Rosie, but mostly I grappled with the matter of whether to volunteer my name for the Navy job. By the time I left for home I was almost sure that I would ask that my name be submitted. I began to feel comfortable with the idea. Even the impulse to "see some action" was swept aside by my suspicion that war research was not necessarily done in a protective cocoon.

At dinner I put on a cheerful face. I didn't want to reveal to Mother and Father that I had been struggling with a major decision. They didn't comprehend especially well the kind of work I did. But they had been following the war news in the Yiddish newspapers, and I could tell they were concerned and disappointed at the turn of events. In the old country they had seen wars and skirmishes. Kings and princes were replaced with other despots. And always, when it suited someone's purpose, the Jews were caught in between. America was a refuge from all of this, it had seemed. There was not much more I could do except reassure them that everything is OK.

Now it's two in the morning and I have finally finished the calculations. I will see Dr. Connor tomorrow and ask him to submit my name to Dr. Barry. I am hoping I will get the job. A new place, a new life. Perhaps adventure. But I will miss Rosie.

CHAPTER 12

Washington

1917

Rosie insisted on seeing me off on the train this morning. As we had agreed, she was next to the ticket booths in Pennsylvania Station at nine. It was one of those days that promised to be very warm, although at that time of the morning the cool scent of the night had not dissipated. Rosie wore a light, sleeveless, powder blue, cotton dress, as if anticipating the heat. Her familiar beige wool shawl was pulled about her shoulders, and she cradled several books against her bosom. We had an hour before the train was to leave, so we went to one of the little coffee shops near the gates.

"Big adventure, Abe," she said as I placed a couple of cups of coffee on our table.

"I guess it is," I responded. "But it's a bit ludicrous to have to admit that. What I mean is Washington's only a little over two hundred miles from here. When I was a kid I went with my mother almost all the way across Europe and then across the Atlantic Ocean. But since then I don't think I have been more than a dozen miles from here, so it does seem like kind of an adventure." I thought for a moment about the furthest from New York I had actually ever wandered. Maybe it was the time Jacob and I, on a lark, had taken the ferry to Staten Island. At the time it seemed exotic, although we were still within the city limits.

"Europe and Poland—that was another life. And you were just a little kid. You weren't totally incorporated into the place. Now I suppose you're a New Yorker through and through. Any other place is bound to be a little strange at first," she said.

"Not a New Yorker—a Brooklynite," I corrected her, feigning indignation.

"A real hick, then!" We both laughed. But in the back of my mind I knew that, in fact, there was at least some class distinction between us. She—native born, living a middle class life in a good upper Manhattan neighborhood—contrasted with my relatively poor immigrant roots in Brownsville. "But, Abe, I know another side of you. I think you feel a little caged in sometimes. You might like the countryside some day. But let me not begin to wax poetic. Instead let me give you this little going-away present."

She out pulled out a slim colorful package from among her schoolbooks. I was surprised. "Go on, unwrap it," she urged.

It was a book bound in dark leather. The title was set in gilt lettering above filigreed scrollwork of full-fruited grape vines: *RUBAIYAT OF OMAR KHAYYAM.* I hadn't yet looked through the book, but I sensed that this would be a treasure. Beautiful books have always had a special attraction for me. But the only other one I own is the ivory and brass decorated prayer book that father had bought for me as a Bar Mitzvah present.

I was a little bowled over by her thoughtfulness, and all I could think of saying was, "Thank you. Thank you. This is so special!"

"You must admit," she said, "your reading tends to be on the serious side. I thought you might like something for idle moments. It strikes some somber notes, but I think of the *Rubaiyat* as sort of a celebration of life. Maybe even a celebration of our connection to nature and through nature to the ultimate." She looked nonplussed at what she had said. "Sorry for sounding pedantic."

"Pedantic suits you. A good thing for a future teacher," I said. By now I was looking through the book, glancing at the colored prints facing every other page—lions standing in the doorway of an abandoned mosque, minarets rising to a starry sky, the couple beneath a banyan tree opposite the famous verse which begins: "Here with a Loaf of Bread beneath the Bough, A Flask of Wine . . . ."

"It's gorgeous. Thank you again, Rosie."

We walked to the train in silence. I took her hand and she squeezed my hand in response. I was pleased to know that my gesture was welcome. "I'll wait on the platform until the train leaves," she said.

"I'll write."

"Please do." With that she reached up and putting her hands on my shoulders pulled me down and kissed me on the cheek. It was a moment of awkwardness and delight. Her kiss was neither passionate nor casual. I stood there, a suitcase in one hand, her book in the other, cursing myself for my shyness. My heart was swelling.

"I'll write," I repeated. "As soon as I am settled." My impulse was to respond in a less ambiguous way, but I sensed that she knew that this was not the time to get too involved.

Later, as the train raced south across the flat, fertile, farmlands of New Jersey I was lost in a confusion of thoughts and feelings. There had been several chapters in my life already, but this new one seemed no less significant. This was the start of real adulthood. For the first time I would not be living in my parents' home. I would be earning a modest, but steady income. Enough income, I realized, that I might be able to finish my college work someday without needing a job on the side. I looked down at my new shoes, a parting gift from Bluestein. He had almost been a second father to me, I realized. I was happy that his new son-in-law had agreed to go into business with him after all.

In my valise were a couple of sandwiches Mother had insisted I take along. It was the most natural way she could express her maternal bond. She had seen so much separation in her life—her sister Esther leaving for Belgium, Father going off to England and then to America, her own separation from her parents. It must have seemed as if her whole familiar world pulled up its roots and spread across the earth. And in the past, the departures were permanent. For a few years letters might go back and forth, but ultimately contact would be lost. My temporary departure was not the most consequential of these separations, but she knew it signified permanent change.

I partially unwrapped one of the sandwiches. I was curious about what Mother had given me. Kosher salami in a Kaiser roll. I wondered if I would find the likes of that in Washington. I wondered whether the war makes much sense to Mother. We are fighting the Germans, yet it was the Germans who had allowed us safe passage on our way to America. She has said little about it, even keeping to herself her worries about whether her sister in Belgium is in peril. I supposed she was aware of the well-publicized atrocities by the Germans in that country,

Father, too, has had very little to say about the war, though I suspected he understood a great deal. He reads the *Jewish Daily Forward* and, as usual, spends a great deal of time with his cronies. Some of them have sons going into the Army. But his sympathies he has kept to himself. A primary hope of his, I was sure, is that the Jews will not catch the blame for what might happen.

As I looked out at the blossoming fields going by, I vaguely remembered the train ride so long ago that carried us out of Poland. That train had taken us to a new life. I sensed that again I was being swept to a new life. In my lap was Rosie's gift. What did that signify for the future now unfolding? I didn't put the book into my suitcase for some time but held on to it as if clinging to the past.

The train stopped in Philadelphia. Another city, but unlike the cities of that boyhood journey, there were no strange languages, no soldiers and border guards moving in and out of the cars. Beyond Philadelphia my mood changed. I felt I had crossed a divide and was ready to take on the new circumstances. The countryside was a little less developed. The track crossed creeks and rivers and ran alongside salt marshes. In Baltimore there were large neighborhoods unlike any I have seen, even in photographs. Street after street of identical attached houses were laid out near the tracks. Each house was built nearly to the sidewalk, and at the entrance to each was a little stoop of two or three uncovered brick or concrete steps. It was the hottest time of the afternoon and on the shady side of the street people congregated on the stoops, men smoking or drinking, women peeling vegetables, children playing jacks or bouncing balls off the steps. Most striking of all were entire neighborhoods in which everyone was a Negro. It was America, yet it seemed like a different world.

Finally the train pulled into Union Station in Washington, the end of the line. Over the next river is the South. In my imagination the South was an alien, even threatening, place. It was five in the afternoon as I descended to the platform. Inside the great colonnaded temple of a station it was relatively cool, but as soon as I stepped outside into the sunshine the muggy heat descended heavily on my entire body. I removed my coat and slung it over a shoulder as I looked out trying to get my bearings. In the distance, beyond the plaza, the Capitol dome shimmered in the sunlight. Several broad avenues radiated out from the station, but unlike New York there were few tall buildings. In front of the station a great number of people, among them many men in uniform, moved about in a purposeful way. There was little strolling or window shopping or loitering. There was great deal of activity, but on the wide avenues and in the open plaza noise was dissipated. It was surprisingly quiet compared with the din of a typical busy street at home.

In time, I found the streetcar line to Anacostia where the Naval Defense Laboratory had been established several years ago at the southeastern edge of the city. When we crossed the bridge over the Anacostia River it was almost a country scene. Here and there were clusters of homes, some entirely populated by Negro folk. All of the black people who got off at those stops came from the rear of the car. I was aware of Southern segregation, but I was surprised to find it in the nation's capital. It made me a little uneasy. In New York black people pretty much stayed apart, but here, even where they were a much larger part of the mix, their separation appeared more evident.

In time the streetcar reached the stop that the motorman informed me was nearest N.D.L. I set my suitcase next to me on the sidewalk and looked about. Small wooden homes, mostly unpainted, crowded upon one another along the street, which was laid out along the contours of the hillside. I took my bearings as I consulted a small map of the neighborhood that Dr. Barry had sent to me. Finally I made my way up a low bluff to the boarding house where I had arranged a room. I had been assured that it was within walking distance of the lab.

The house was a high, twin gabled, wooden structure, of some late Victorian style. I guessed it was thirty or forty years old and undoubtedly was built originally as a private residence. I noticed that most windows were opened wide and here and there the end of a curtain flapped out in the light warm breeze. I hoped that I would not be sleeping just under the gables. As I climbed the steps to the veranda that runs along the front and one side of the house I first noticed the broad sweep of the Potomac far below. On the far shore was Virginia and I thought I could make out some towns, their buildings backlit by the lowering sun. On the near shore was a cluster of large rectangular buildings that I guessed to be the Laboratory. A line of several small vessels was pulled up near these buildings at the river edge.

Nervously I twisted the ringer in the door. Eventually a scrawny woman of medium height in a dirty white apron opened it. She peered at me suspiciously over the top of her glasses. "Yes?" she asked.

"I'm Abel Roth. I wrote here about a room," I replied. I was not sure this place was the best choice. "Are you Mrs. Ambler?"

"Yeah, tha's right. Roth? Guessed you'd be here 'bout now," she said, still unsmiling. "Well let's not let the heat in." I stepped inside and closed the door behind me. "Got a room for you, second floor. Up to the right. We'll settle details later. Take your bag up and have a splash. Better hurry down if you want some supper."

At the dinner table there were a couple of men eating dessert and drinking coffee. They ate quietly without much conversation. But they did introduce themselves and explained that usually there were more men at the table. They mentioned that several who were working at the lab were off on a trip. "Hush-hush business, I guess," one of them volunteered.

A large Negro woman appeared from the kitchen with a steaming bowl of stew and a plate of bread. "Heated this up some for you. Good thing these fellas didn't finish up the whole pot," she said with a good-natured chuckle. "I sure hope you like puddin'. I'll dish some out for you in a minute." After my encounter with dour Mrs. Ambler and this pair of taciturn housemates, I was relieved by the lightness of spirit of this woman. I was also relieved that I had no qualms about this first meal at the boardinghouse. I had explained to Mother and Father that it would be nearly impossible to keep kosher in Washington, but that at least I would not eat pork or shellfish. Besides, they felt that exceptions were allowed in time of war.

After dinner Mrs. Ambler received my first week's rent in advance and went over the rules: breakfast and dinner every day except Sunday, six to eight in the morning and four-thirty to six-thirty in the evening, no noise, no guests, no pets, come and go as you please but always lock the door, and no smoking, or drinking—at least inside the house. When I assured her that this suited me just fine, she seemed to relax a little and I almost detected a smile.

So now, as I sit here on the front steps watching the sun sink over Alexandria on the Virginia side of the river, it is finally beginning to cool down. I am thinking that this has been one of the stranger days of my life. Just this morning I was saying goodbye to Mother and Father, and holding hands with Rosie. Now I am a world away, looking out across a river at what had been the head, if not the heart, of the old Confederacy. I am surrounded by strangers and about to embark on work the nature of which is yet to be revealed to me.

CHAPTER 13

The Naval Defense Lab

1917

The Naval Defense Laboratory is located in a group of boxy, three-story, gray buildings lined up on both sides of a grassy strip extending down to the Potomac River. It was created years ago to engage primarily in scientific research that might have long-range implications for the naval mission. Naturally, in this time of war the emphasis has shifted towards research of immediate use to the Navy.

I was at the gate to N.D.L. promptly at eight o'clock on the morning following my arrival in Washington. A beefy Marine guard, with a pistol holstered to his waist, stepped smartly out of his sentry shack. He blocked my way and firmly, but politely asked my business. He took my appointment letter and confirmed it with Dr. Barry by telephone before summoning one of the sailors who had been lounging inside the shack. The young sailor, who appeared to be no older than eighteen, was assigned to escort me inside the compound. He was very quiet and had little of what I had thought of as "military bearing." This changed abruptly when we passed a naval officer whose rank I was still unable to identify. The young sailor suddenly straightened up and threw out a snappy salute. The gesture seemed exaggerated, as if he was asserting his solidarity with the military side of the organization. By the time we reached our destination halfway to the river he was again sauntering along and looking about in a casual way.

On the third floor the sailor left me with Dr. Barry, who had come into the hallway from his office. He appeared to be a cheerful man, resembling Professor Connor in some ways. He extended his hand and greeted me warmly. "We've been looking forward to your joining us, Mr. Roth. I'm James Barry. Call me Jim. Welcome to our little empire." He gestured towards one end of the corridor. We shook hands.

"I'm pleased to meet you. I hope you'll call me Abe," I said.

"Of course, Abe. Richard—Professor Connor—has written to me about you. I'm sure you'll fit in well. Come on in." He stood aside and followed me into his office. It was a small, windowless room, perhaps ten by twelve feet. Another doorway opened onto what appeared to be a laboratory room whose windows looked out over the grassy mall bisecting N.D.L. Momentarily excusing himself, he soon reappeared rolling in an extra chair for me from the adjoining lab.

Before we sat down he asked if I'd like a cup of coffee. "Navy fuel," he said with a smile. Though I declined his offer, I realized that I might come to depend on the lab coffee pot in the future, having sampled Mrs. Ambler's boiled version earlier that morning. It had been very black and bitter and tasted vaguely of the eggshells she used to settle the grounds.

"I'll give you a little tour later on," he said as he set his own coffee mug at the side of his desk. "But for the moment perhaps we should get to know each other a bit." Jim asked about Dr. Connor and how the work was going at his lab. He told me a bit about how he had come to know him and about the work they had collaborated on at Columbia.

"New York's a different kind of place, and I'm always curious about the atmosphere up there. Of course right now everything's about the war down here. Actually I don't miss the big city much—this southern town has its charms as well." He asked me about my coursework at Gallatin, and whether I knew anything about radio technology or vacuum tubes. I had to confess that my direct experience in that area was very limited.

"No problem, Abe. From what Richard has told me, you'll catch on quickly. Of course you have to understand that a lot of what we do here involves instrumentation, though always from a physicist's perspective. But I know you're not shy about 'getting your hands dirty,' so to speak. We have serious work to do, but I think you'll find it fun as well."

The conversation was casual and almost leisurely. I could tell from the apparently unfinished calculations on the desk in front of him and dog-eared reports piled to the side that he was taking a break from a busy schedule of urgent work. But his manner remained calm and collected. Finally he announced that it was time to see his "empire."

"We'll discuss exactly what we are up to this afternoon. Meanwhile let's meet some people. Unfortunately most of the technicians are on a mission downriver but you'll be starting by working with Rick Thayer, and he's around today."

We found Rick in the next room at one of the lab benches, bending over some apparatus I couldn't identify, busily soldering some wires in place. He was a clean-cut young man, perhaps a little younger than me. We shook hands. "I know Rick can use some help right now." Rick nodded in agreement. "I expect you'll get back to him later. But for the moment let me show you around a little more." The lab had a couple of workbenches lined up in the middle of the room. Along the walls were some cabinets, a glass-blowing bench and a rack supporting a vacuum diffusion pump and gauges.

Jim led me into the adjoining lab room. The center of this space was dominated by what appeared to be an automobile-size tank of water with glass observing ports. Near the room's windows were several filing cabinets, a bookshelf, and a large desk, behind which was a middle-aged woman.

"Abe, please meet Mrs. Bloom—Gladys to us all." He turned to her. "This is Abel Roth. I know you've been expecting him." She rose enough to bend across the desk and extend her hand. She had a plain face, not pretty, but pleasant—even motherly. She was devoid of makeup of any kind and her large wire-rimmed glasses seemed exaggerated by their proximity to her closely bobbed hair. "Gladys is our girl Friday," Jim went on. "And Monday through Thursday, I should add. And she knows a lot about physics, never forget."

"You left out a lot of Saturdays and Sundays, Jim," she said. "And I can handle a soldering iron if I have to, remember."

"How can I forget, Gladys?" Then turning to me, he said, "But what we're most indebted to Gladys about is her political skills. Believe me, if you ever want to work your way with the Navy brass, leave it to our Gladys. And on that note, I'll excuse myself and put you in her hands. You still have some paperwork details to get out of the way. I'll see you early this afternoon."

After Jim left I sat down with Gladys while she helped me through a bewildering packet of documents to be filled in and signed—hiring agreement, emergency information, citizenship documentation, information on next-of-kin. I had a glimpse of her political skills when she phoned the immigration people downtown to verify my citizenship. It appeared that confronting the bureaucracy was a challenge she enjoyed. The final document was the oath of allegiance. Then she cautioned me about security. I was not to talk or write to anyone, not even people closest to me, about our work. I was not even to talk to my own colleagues about the work outside the work place. She reminded me of the war poster that was on the wall of the lab. It showed an evil-faced German in a spiked helmet with his hand cupped behind his ear. It read The Enemy is Listening. Finally Gladys accompanied me to another building and left me at the security office to have a temporary identification badge prepared.

While waiting I struck up some small talk with a thin and slightly grizzled middle-aged man sitting alongside me. It was he who initiated the conversation. He extended a bony hand.

"Elmer," he said. "You waitin' for a badge too?"

I explained that I had just arrived from New York the day before and expected to get to work as soon as possible. "N'York? Never been, but I reckon I'll pay a visit sometime." He seemed mildly interested.

As we waited I learned that Elmer was from the Deep South. "Ca'line, nigh 'bout Charleston," he explained. I could have guessed.

His accent was similar, though not identical, to that of some of the colored porters and janitors who worked at the College. Hearing him speak heightened my anticipation of the broadened world that lay before me.

"I'm going into the machine shop." He pointed out the window in the general direction of one of the factory-like buildings across the grassy mall. "Weldin' 'n rivetin's my game. Could'a had good pay in the shipyard. But then, I'm gittin' a little creaky for ladders and such." After a little pause he added, "Too old for the military, guess." He began to ask about my "game" but was called up to have his picture taken and a temporary badge prepared. I was next in line. As Elmer went out the door he grinned and tipped his cap.

Before returning to Jim's office I stopped off for a snack at the lunchroom as Gladys had suggested. The fare was little different from that in the college lunchroom I had sampled occasionally, except for a couple of Southern items—grits and collards. I remembered my promise to honor the kosher restrictions as best I could, so I ruled out the baked beans—this was more than likely to be pork and beans. An egg salad sandwich seemed to be a safe bet. As I ate I looked around at this slice of America. There was a sprinkling of sailors, their caps pulled rakishly down close to an eyebrow. Four thirty-ish ladies in basic, cotton business dresses huddled close at the end of a table. I imagined them to be secretaries sharing office gossip. There were several men in overalls and a couple of bespectacled older men I could have mistaken for college professors conferring over some document. All the Negroes in the room occupied a couple of tables at the far end, engaged for the most part in animated but indistinct conversation. From the look of their rumpled work clothes I took them to be groundskeepers or building maintenance workers.

When I returned to Jim's office he beckoned me inside and pulled up a chair for me facing him at his desk. "I suppose it's needless to say that a lot of the Navy is preoccupied with the submarine threat," he began. Indeed the problem of submarine warfare had been a staple of newspaper stories for several years. The *Lusitania* sinking in 1915 was the most dramatic incident, but the threat to the free coming and going of American shipping had been viewed with increasing alarm in the months leading up to our declaration of war. Moreover, it was no secret that the command of the sea by the British fleet was being rapidly undermined by German U-boats. This was also a grave concern. I had heard several animated discussions in the University lunchroom about how this country had been dependent on British naval power in protecting our interests all over the world.

"The Navy, long ago, learned how to fight on the surface," Jim continued. "You're too young to remember, but any doubt about America's naval power was probably dispelled by the Spanish American War." I recall being fascinated by the world tour of the Great White Fleet when I was a teenager. It had been big headline news. It occurred to me that, perhaps it was on that account, that I first developed the idea of volunteering for the Navy. "But this submarine warfare is a different kettle of fish," he went on. "Those little sea rats can pop up from anywhere, and at any time. We think we know how to destroy them. The problem is knowing where they are."

I had not thought much about this problem, but it was obvious once it was mentioned. I had hardly anything to add, so I listened carefully, nodding occasionally to signify my understanding. "There are two things we are trying to do. The most obvious is to listen for the sound made by the submarine's engines or by its screw propellers—'screws' we usually say. The second approach is what we call echo-ranging. That's where we send out a burst of sound underwater and listen for a return echo from an underwater object, such as a submarine hull. Seems simple, doesn't it?" he asked.

Perhaps the question was intended to be rhetorical, but Jim's easy-going manner led me to respond. "Well, I can think of at least one problem." He looked up as if to invite me to elaborate. "I wonder how you can distinguish between the sound of your own screw and that of the sub."

"Right. That's good thinking. As for that problem, of course you can turn off your own engines while listening. Not an especially good idea, I can tell you. You don't want to be dead in the water while there might be a Hun lurking out there somewhere with a loaded torpedo tube." I nodded. I had already thought of that problem.

"Once you begin to think about it there are a lot of problems, some less obvious than others. As for the listening issue," he continued, "you want to know the direction the sound is coming from. You also want to know whether the sound is coming from a friendly ship nearby. How do you detect very faint sounds? What are the best sound detectors to use underwater? There are a lot of questions."

"Echo-sounding," he continued, "has a whole lot of its own problems that need good answers. For instance, what sound frequencies are best to use underwater? How do you match the properties of a sound generator to the water medium in which it is immersed? How do you tell the difference between a submarine and a whale? How do you measure the time interval between the sending out of a sound burst and the receiving of the echo? And, of course, the Germans are listening to us! To repeat, there are lots of questions."

Despite this formidable list of challenges, I felt sure there were some others he hadn't mentioned. But Jim appeared not to be fazed. "Naturally we aren't the only people thinking about this. The Brits have programs of their own, though under the present conditions it's hard to keep in touch. There's some work taking place on the West coast and possibly at a university or two. We don't actually know the extent of it. Our main collaboration is with the folks down at the naval base in Norfolk. I can promise that you'll get to know some of them. But a general problem is that most engineers and probably all naval architects don't understand well the basic physics behind the technical difficulties. Which is where we come in."

It was all very interesting to me. I realized suddenly that tackling some of these problems actually seemed like fun, though I just as quickly reminded myself that the issue of ships and sailors being blown to bits should not be a matter of "fun." I was about to ask exactly what kind of work I would be helping with, when Jim changed the course of the conversation. It became obvious that he had other things to do before the day was over. "But right now the main thing is that we get you to work. For the time being I'll turn you over to Rick Thayer, whom you met this morning. He can use some help, and he'll be able to get you started."

It was clear that, for me at the moment, discussions of the big general questions Jim had posed were on hold. And almost as if to reinforce the point, the first thing Rick suggested I do was to hurry down to the storeroom to pick up a set of personal tools. He wrote out a list of small hand tools—screw drivers, pliers and diagonal cutters, files, a machinist's square—items familiar to me from my work at Dr. Connor's lab at the College. While he was doing this I found myself thinking of how, as I grew up, I was aware that many of the older folks considered manual skills not to be the highest achievement a boy could aspire to, even though many of the men were themselves craftsmen. In highest regard were the "learned professions"—law, medicine, teaching—and perhaps highest of all, the rabbinate. Somehow I could never subscribe to this prejudice. I suppose that it had to do with the differences between American culture and the sharp social distinctions of the old country.

When I returned from the storeroom, Rick had emptied some drawers and cleared space for me at one end of his workbench. Then he began to explain the specific project I would be working on with him. But throughout that discussion I was aware of a strange satisfaction in having a personal collection of tools for the first time. Perhaps it was a metaphor for my release from the old culture that had bounded me for so long. And I felt ready to move on.

CHAPTER 14

New Waters

1917

During these first months in Washington the incessant demands of work have kept me from dwelling on a nagging loneliness. Being very busy has been a way of life for me during the last few years as I balanced school, work, and long commutes. But now, increasingly, I miss family and familiar places and, most all, Rosie.

There are a few compensations. Most days I walk down the hill to the lab to arrive before seven in the morning. Below is the wide expanse of the Potomac River disappearing around a bend far to the south. To the north, on clear mornings, the Capitol dome stands out like a sentinel on the horizon. Ahead, stretching to the horizon is the broad Virginia countryside. Here and there, a glint of golden light is thrown off as the morning sun catches some church spire in its rays. Since the middle of September the weather has begun to cool noticeably and the first fall colors have appeared. Now they have deepened, and I am reminded of the enchantment I felt during occasional walks with Jacob in Prospect Park, surrounded by crimsoned maples and golden birches. But here the panorama of luminescent color stretching all around as far as the eye could see, and cut through with a ribbon of blue water, stirs even greater delight. At times, with the morning air feeling cool and fresh, I have asked myself why, with this magnificence here for the taking, hasn't mankind found a way to avoid bloody conflicts.

Sundays have been hardest to manage. Unless there is an emergency project or we are away doing field-tests, most of us have the day off. I have gotten to know Rick Thayer better, and occasionally we have spent a Sunday together. In many ways his situation is like my own. He comes from Brockton, Massachusetts and had been studying physics at Harvard before being recruited into Jim's group. He has some cousins living in Washington and knows the area from previous visits.

One Sunday in October Rick and I took the streetcar to the old colonial town of Georgetown, perched on a bluff alongside the Potomac not far from the center of the city. There we set out along the towpath of the old Chesapeake and Ohio Canal, a remnant of the days before the coming of railroads when the key to the West was thought to be a network of waterways. Here and there the canal had virtually disappeared, but the path was clear, passing at one spot close to the violent rapids of the Great Falls of the Potomac. It took us through groves of magnificent sycamores and, near the water's edge, huge drooping willows. Everywhere, in sight or sound, was bird life. Being accustomed to the confining, noisy, paved streets of New York, I had to marvel that this natural beauty could be so close at hand to the city

If possible, I set aside Sunday evenings to write letters. I keep in touch with Mother and Father at least once a week through Dave or Celia or Sari, with whom I exchange letters on a rotating basis. Dave's wife, Dolly, corresponds regularly. She seems to have appointed herself guardian of family history and lore. From her I have learned that my old friend Jacob volunteered for the Army before he was drafted. She thinks he sees that as a fast track to citizenship. Though Jacob and I have largely parted ways since high school, our mothers have remained close friends, as they had been back in Wizna. Jacob is still single and has been employed as a social worker at the settlement house near our home. Apparently, for some reason, he had never thought of applying for citizenship until now. This news of Jacob fills me with a little dread. I have resolved to see him if the opportunity arises.

Rosie and I exchange letters at least once a week. These letters are the hardest to write, at least for me. I want to pour out my heart, but I know the circumstances do not lend themselves to that. On the other hand I will not resort to trivia in order to fill up pages. I am prohibited from revealing much about my work, which after all, is my main preoccupation. In particular I cannot say much about our field excursions, though I have to explain the gaps in my correspondence. I say mostly that the fieldwork involves ships and there is no need to worry. However with time the writing has become easier, if only because Rosie's responses are so intelligent and insightful.

Washington
November 4, 1917

Dear Rosie,

Your letter was waiting when I returned from our field tests last evening. I was so delighted to find it on the hall table when I came back to the boarding house after almost a week away on our ship. It was next best thing to having you waiting at the dock when we pulled in. As usual I cannot give any details about what we had been doing. Suffice it to say that there was some success—enough to make up for the failures. We all work very hard, but I must confess that on the whole Mother Nature is smarter than we are. On that score she deserves all the respect I can give, but it is my belief that she challenges us to figure the world out for ourselves—like any good mother.

If all this sounds like aimless philosophizing, there may be a reason. During this past week in idle moments my ruminations have had a somewhat philosophical bent. This frame of mind—perhaps not the most appropriate frame of mind when one is crawling around in the bilges trying to get an experiment working—was triggered by a visit I made to town last Sunday with my friend Rick Thayer. I've mentioned Rick before. We work a lot together on our projects but occasionally we've had time for casual conversation. What has amazed me is how similar our thinking is despite the differences in our backgrounds. A couple of weeks ago he suggested that I would find a visit to the Unitarian Church really interesting. He was raised in a Unitarian family, though in recent years he hasn't participated much. Naturally I reacted with a great deal of trepidation. Just the word "church" sets off alarm bells in me. It isn't that I feel antagonism to gentiles of any faith—practically all of my heroes, except maybe for Einstein—are not Jewish—but I am innately suspicious of the religious side of the wider world.

Anyway, Rick assured me that he knew me well enough to be sure I would enjoy a visit to All Souls' Unitarian Church. I asked him "What on earth do they mean by 'soul'?" He grinned and said that "all souls'" was probably an old-fashioned way of saying "everyone's." After all, the church has been around for a hundred years. "You wouldn't expect them to call it 'Some Souls' Unitarian Church,' would you?" To make a long story short, I like and respect Rick enough that I agreed to meet him at the church last Sunday morning.

The church is a fine Georgian building up on a rise of land on 16th Avenue in the city's Northwest section, a few miles north of the White House. The first thing I noticed was the absence of any Christian crosses inside or outside. I shouldn't have been surprised. Rick had told me that the Unitarians are not Christians, though he added with a look of amusement, most of them think they are. He explained that although they will speak of Jesus, they do not assign any divinity to him. Rick maintains that if you won't assign the title Christ (Anointed) to this guy you shouldn't go around calling yourself a Christian. Rick thinks it's a bit of a pose that affirms the connection with the rest of the culture. At best the Unitarians regard Jesus as a teacher in his time, perhaps even a latter day Hebrew prophet. In any event he is not some sort of god. In fact he explained that there is not only no central figure, but no required doctrine. This is a startling idea—I thought all religions had to have a central required belief.

If anything, Rick certainly made me curious. So despite trepidations, I thought that checking out these people might be interesting. And interesting it was. I can't offhand remember every detail but a few things stick in mind. There was a short reading from the Bible—from the book of Amos—in which the prophet rails against false piety and mistreatment of the poor. I confess my ignorance of the Bible. To be sure, we read from the Torah every week in synagogue, but I can't pretend I follow the Hebrew. I'm not sure many of the old men can follow it either. Besides the Torah is only a small part of the Bible. I found myself thinking, "What about the rest of the writings that my ancestors thought to be worth preserving?"

The minister gave a sermon that more or less dealt with the difference between piety and righteousness. What most caught my attention was not his delivery or turn of phrase but the amount of scholarly content drawing upon history and even present day politics. No appeal to the supernatural or official dogma—rather an appeal to reason and common sense. It isn't so much that I took away a specific message that was stimulating, but the sense of getting some perspective on where all our ancient traditions and I fit in the world. Certainly food for thought.

Finally the congregation stood to sing a hymn. Naturally I stood with everyone else though I wasn't sure I would join in the singing. I remember the name of the hymn: "Praise to the Living God." The tune seemed familiar. Then I realized that it was the Yigdal that is sung in some synagogues. Anyway, you know me—I enjoy group singing, so I joined in. Afterwards Rick and I took a walk around the neighborhood and ended up having lunch at a bakery/café just by the streetcar turnaround in a neighborhood called Mount Pleasant. Pleasant indeed, and near Rock Creek. Also more upscale than I am accustomed to. Rick wondered what I thought about the morning service, and the best I could come up with was that I was glad there was no mumbo-jumbo superstitious talk. I guess I am still processing.

But this letter is getting a bit lengthy. I am sorry you have not heard from me for most of a week. After I left Rick I walked all the way home, which is quite a few miles. Then I had to catch up on writing to my brother and make a brief visit to the lab to ready some equipment for our departure down the river at the crack of dawn. So I didn't get to this letter until now. But to be honest I should say that I thought of you a lot while we were away and look forward to your next letter. Meanwhile I am hoping that I will be given a few days off during the latter part of December to visit New York. I hope we can meet.

Fondly,
Abe

It was not long before a reply from Rosie appeared on the hall table at the boarding house.

New York
November 7, 1917

Dear Abe,

Your letter arrived this afternoon and although I am up to my ears in midterms I am inspired to answer your letter right now. I can hardly say how pleased I am to know that with all your comings and goings and long hours I am not forgotten. Let me assure you that here in chilly New York you are not forgotten. I especially miss our four o'clock tête-à-têtes. But what must be done must be done. War is hell, as they say.

Your brush with the Unitarians intrigues me. I became aware of them during the course on American literature that I took last year. Not many people outside of New England seem to know them, but they actually have a big place in American cultural history. We were reading from the Transcendentalists—Emerson, Thoreau, Parker, and some others I can't recall offhand. They were writing in the decades before the Civil War and, partly due to their somewhat stiff 19th century style, they make a difficult read. They were almost all Unitarians or close to Unitarians. I admit I am still at a loss to succinctly define Transcendentalism, but I found myself fascinated by how these people connected their spiritual leanings with nature, reason, and individual freedom. I also found it interesting how involved most of them were with the social reform movements of the time—mainly anti-slavery and women's rights—kind of hotheads, I guess. Of course that was some generations back and there's no telling what these Unitarian folks are like now, but I wouldn't be surprised if they have a refreshing take on things, even today.

It is really good news that maybe you will be able to get away during our school break. If you are comfortable with it, I hope you would be willing to pay a visit to our home. We don't take holidays particularly seriously but Mama always makes a point of having a dinner in celebration of Hanukah. Maybe she thinks we need a little more ritual, or perhaps it's just something she can tell her friends about. I have mentioned you and Mama immediately made the suggestion about having you for dinner. If your time off—and I fully understand that it is not a sure thing—more or less coincides with the holiday, then I'm sure she would adjust her plan accordingly. Papa expresses little opinion on this, but that is his way. And brother Alec is just a teen-age brat who seems to care mostly that the food is good, though, as you know, that is more difficult these days. Of course you'll let me know what will work out for you.

But speaking of the war's effects, it is beginning to impact the student body here. Some of the boys have been called up and many are anticipating a call. Even certain faculty members have had to leave for some war post or other. So several classes have been canceled and others are very crowded. The rest of us do what we can. Going to pick fruit upstate, as you know I did at the end of the summer, seems like such a puny contribution. (And it was almost a vacation. There is something about the countryside—even with having to sleep in a tent and putting up with mosquitoes—that releases something primeval in this city-girl's heart.) I go with Mama a couple of evenings each week to make bandages and she has put in her name to be a volunteer in military hospitals when she is needed. Brave soul! I might have a difficult time doing that but I do worry about the boys. I am glad you are here in the states and likely to remain safe.

I do think about you. Or am I being repetitious? Now
back to the books! Please write as you are able.

Affectionately,
Rosie

P.S. I almost forgot. Good news! The dean has agreed
that I can do a math-English double major.

There is so much more I would like to tell Rosie, but cannot.
Mainly it is about our field excursions downriver. We have use of a
rusty old cutter that the Navy has taken over from the Coast Guard.
It is usually pulled up to the dock at the far end of the N.D.L.
compound. That is convenient as far as it goes. For checking on
the efficiencies of various configurations of sound producing or
detecting equipment that we can slap onto the side of the hull below
the waterline, it is quite okay to sail around in the calm waters of
the Potomac or Chesapeake Bay. But the real test is in open ocean
operations that we are conducting out of the Navy yard in Norfolk.
Here our little cutter transfers us in midstream to our "luxury liner,"
as we like to call it. In fact it is an ancient, coal burning fire-tube,
ex-merchant steamer that the Navy undoubtedly deems expendable.
But it serves the purpose whenever the admiral can round up a spare
submarine and an escort vessel for our open water tests.

Sailing for the first time out of Hampton Roads into the wide
waters at the mouth of the Bay, to my great surprise, evoked a sense
of nostalgia. At first I found it hard to identify. It was something to
do with the odors—an acrid combination of burning coal, grease,
and salt water. And the indistinct squeaks and groans, as the vessel
gently rolled in the protected waters of the estuary was also part of it.
Then I realized that somehow the memory of the Atlantic crossing
so long ago, when we came to America, still lingered within me. I
had always thought Marcel Proust's touting of the evocative power
of odor—the smell of the little cakes, madeleines—was a trivial idea,
but that instinct is also lodged in me. When we reached the open
ocean, even though it had been almost twenty years since my ocean

crossing, it all seemed astonishingly familiar—the startling blue of deep sea and, to my dismay, a touch of motion sickness.

But in these operations there is much work to be done. And, as I was soon to be reminded, an element of danger. Seasickness is quickly put aside and fortunately I have pretty much gotten over it. Beyond Cape Henry enemy submarines are on the prowl. They steer clear of a flotilla of well-armed Naval vessels coming out the Roads, but an old rust bucket like ours protected by one small escort is an easy target. Clearly there is no way for them to know that we aren't carrying cargo or troops. We may not be worth the waste of a torpedo, but their deck gun could do us in. Our best defense is to keep moving, especially in broad daylight, and hope that our escort sees them before they see us.

CHAPTER 15

The Dubrows

1918

Again we are at sea but I can't help thinking about my visit to Rosie's home at the end of December.

It was a short walk from the 125th Street subway station to Amsterdam Avenue where I found the Dubrow's apartment building at 3162. It was a very plain, gray-brick five-story building fronting directly on the sidewalk. In the lobby a uniformed Negro man sat in a corner eating some creamy delicacy from a bowl. When he saw me, he rose, putting the bowl on the radiator near his chair.

"Yes suh?" he asked.

"I'm looking for the Dubrows," I said, my attention momentarily fixed on the bowl warming on the radiator. "I think I'm expected."

"Yes suh. Miss Rosie mentioned that to me. I'll punch them a little ring, then I'll take you up." He searched for the appropriate doorbell button on a panel, pushed it briefly, and motioned towards the elevator. I glanced again at the bowl. "Ice cream soup," he said. He chuckled at his little joke. We rode to the fifth floor.

Rosie was in the corridor waiting when the elevator door opened. I hadn't seen her in more than four months. She was just as I remembered her. Her beauty is not of the kind that Mr. Ziegfeld might promote. She has a rare beauty that is hard to categorize. She is of medium build, trim, but not gaunt. Perhaps it is from her eyes, large eyes set in a slightly rounded face with a wonderful complexion that her beauty emanates. Her eyes somehow convey the cheerful, good nature that lies within.

"Thank you, George," she said to the Negro man, as she grasped my hand.

George tipped his hat slightly. "Have a nice evenin', miss."

She led me down the hall. "You found us okay. No trouble?"

"Not a problem," I replied. "3, 1, 6, 2. Square root of ten. Anyway, to the third decimal place."

She smiled. "Ah, Mr. Roth: master of the rational idea, admirer of the irrational number." I remembered that we had once had a little discussion about the mysteries of irrational and prime numbers. She released my hand as she pushed open the apartment door.

She took my coat and I handed her the bouquet of flowers I had been carrying. In the small living room her father put down his newspaper and rose from his chair to greet me. We shook hands. He reminded me of Mr. Bluestein, somewhat short and stocky, but not fat. His hairline had receded to the middle of his scalp, and his hair showed flecks of gray. His neatly trimmed mustache was entirely gray, so that it was hardly noticeable. Rosie disappeared into the kitchen with the bouquet. Mr. Dubrow and I made a bit of small talk. He had been in Washington once.

After some minutes Rosie and her mother appeared in the doorway. "Mama, this is my friend, Abe," she said. Mrs. Dubrow stepped forward, wiping her hands on her apron. She looked a bit flushed, an appearance my mother assumes when she has been hovering around a stove cooking a meal.

"Pleased to meet you." She extended her puffy, slightly damp hand. "The flowers are lovely, Mr. Roth," she said. Then "Rosie, they should go in the middle of the table, don't you think? Go fetch, please."

I immediately recognized the physical resemblance between Rosie and her mother. I also felt some of the same warmth but little of Rosie's sophistication. "You can call me Abe," I said.

"Here Abe. Sit, sit." Mrs. Dubrow motioned towards the sofa that just squeezed into the space between the opposite wall and the window. A large steam radiator was beneath the window. "That's the warm spot in the room. But please excuse, there's dinner on the stove. You like potato latkes, Abe?" When I made it clear that I liked almost everything, she retreated to the kitchen. I noticed Rosie placing the bouquet on the table in the small adjoining dining room. Then she came to the doorway and announced that she would be helping in the kitchen.

I wondered where the kid brother was, but assumed he was hiding out until called to the table. Mr. Dubrow and I were left alone. Rosie had told me a bit about her father. As a very young man he had emigrated from Kiev in the Ukraine sometime around 1890. His family explained that it was the Tsarist regime's restriction on advanced education for Jews that lay behind his decision to leave. A couple of his uncles were professors. But Rosie thinks it was his desire for adventure and independence that led him to leave family and friends and come to America. Fortunately, he was able to take enough money with him to open a small haberdashery on the upper Westside not long after he arrived. Rosie thinks those scholarly genes are still there, however. He learned English very quickly and was well read. In fact his only hobby was reading. There was an overflowing bookshelf next to his reading chair.

Mr. Dubrow got up and moved to a small liquor cabinet. He removed a cut glass decanter and raised it slightly." Maybe you would like a little schnapps, Abe?" I nodded affirmatively. As he set the brandies on the low table in front of the sofa, he looked down noticing my suit. "That's a nice suit, Abe," he said. "Very nice. Do you mind?" He leaned down and took the lapel, rubbing the cloth between his fingers. "Good goods. Very good."

"My father made it," I responded, not knowing whether I was exhibiting pride in father's workmanship, or admitting to his social inferiority.

"He does this? Very nice work. I should only sell suits like this."

"Actually he does piece work for a living. He can't compete with the factories. But he likes to keep in practice. Sometimes someone asks him to do a custom job," I explained.

Mr. Dubrow returned to his chair. He lifted his glass. "*L'chayim*—to life! Also to good health. Bon santé!" I didn't know whether that bit of French was meant to signify erudition or a subdued sense of fun. We drank together. The brandy warmed me from the inside. I felt more relaxed. He went on. "Hanukah. A nice little holiday. Do you know the story? The Jews had real heroes in those days. They were fierce people. But I can tell you I thank the Lord for Christmas. It's a gift to the haberdashery business. It's also a nice holiday—if you don't think too seriously about it. Very cheerful." He raised his glass again. He was warming to the subject.

He continued. "Of course the real holidays are the High Holy Days. I always go to shul then. We promise God we will be better. Not a bad sentiment, I think." I was amazed by this voluble side of Mr. Dubrow. Rosie had said he was often very quiet. "Self-contained," as she described it. She thought that perhaps he was busy thinking about some book or other he had been reading but felt he couldn't discuss. Once in a while he and Rosie would go for a walk and he would talk to her about his reading, but hardly ever at home. Rosie's mother was not especially interested in books. She had married not too long after arriving from Russia with her parents as a teenager. Rosie described her as good-natured and innately smart.

I remember a few things about the meal itself. Kid brother Alec appeared at the table when called, giving me a limp handshake when prompted. Before the dinner was served Mr. Dubrow lit the appropriate candles on the small brass menorah in the middle of the sideboard. It was a nice dinner of chicken and potato pancakes with spicy applesauce. There was a sponge cake with raspberry sauce and hot tea. Alec was noticeably quiet, concentrating mostly on his plate. Occasionally he looked suspiciously up at me, raising his eyes rather than his head. I felt as if I were intruding in his place as the younger male, but when I agreed after dinner to look at his stamp collection, he brightened considerably.

I especially recall my parting. Rosie had put a wool shawl about her shoulders and stood by quietly as I thanked her mother and father for a wonderful evening. Alec had disappeared. "I'll see

Abe down," Rosie announced. As we waited in the hallway for the elevator to appear she said "I hope the evening wasn't too difficult for you Abe."

"No. No, I enjoyed meeting your parents. And Alec . . . ."

"Alec will grow up," Rosie broke in.

"He's a good kid," I said.

"He'll grow up," Rosie repeated. "But I'm happy you seemed to like Mom and Pop. They're both sweeties in their own ways."

The elevator arrived. George pushed back the sliding gate and we stepped inside. Rosie smiled at him. "How's the evening been, George?" she asked.

"Nice and quiet, Miss Rosie. Peaceful-like." As we descended he added. "Sure good ice cream. The missus liked it too."

"Makes good soup," Rosie replied. Then to me, "George is the building character He has his own ways with things. And he's kind of the glue that holds everyone connected around here. We never forget him whenever we go out to get some ice cream."

"Yes'm. This is one fine young lady, Mr. Abe." Somehow he knew my name. When we reached the ground floor, Rosie told George that she was going outside with me just for a few minutes and would be back soon.

On the street in front of the building it was cold but calm and not as frigid as the usual evening in late December. "This is too cold for you," I said, looking at Rosie's light shawl.

"Then I'll just have to get closer." She put her arms lightly around my waist and looked up. My restraint evaporated. I put my hands behind her shoulders and kissed her. I can still taste that kiss.

"Perhaps that was a mistake," I said. "I have to be away for I don't know how much longer."

"But you're here now." Then she recited the lines from the *Rubaiyat* that go

> Lo! Some we loved, the loveliest and best
> That Time and Fate of all their Vintage pressed,

I finished the verse:

Have drunk their Cup a Round or two before,
And one by one crept silently to Rest.

"Maybe that's a somber refrain to depart on," I said. "But I'll take an optimistic interpretation. Indeed I must creep off to rest, but I will be back."

Rosie gave me a hug. Then she pushed me away to arm's length. I took her hands. "We are both going to be busy. I can wait. But meanwhile please be careful. For both of us." I promised to write when I returned to Washington and headed for the subway station. I was walking on air.

But for the time being I must put aside the reveries and focus on the here and now. The rumors are that we are making great progress against the German wolf packs but there are still improvements to be made. Great convoys of troop ships are making their way to France. There is still a sense of urgency about developing anti-submarine surveillance. But with important targets crossing the Atlantic we feel a little less threatened in our single rust bucket cruising off the coast. Yet we remain a target of opportunity, and our precautionary tactics, as feeble as they are, have not relaxed.

Here at sea I have some opportunity for reading and studying. There are so many courses in literature and history that I will have to put aside when I return to college and try to finish the physics major. So I always take a few of the classics with me. Right now *The Red Badge of Courage* and *Anna Karenina*. But I am also trying to get a leg up on some math and physics. I have almost worked my way through a textbook on vector analysis—elegance and practicality, all in one.

Out there in the dim light, in the darkness beneath the sea is our own submarine. He plays games with us. We are told where he may be, but then he eludes us for a while. Sometimes he surfaces, always at a prearranged place and time, usually in dim light. A skiff takes our skipper over to the sub and the captains plan their moves. At such times, moving slowly through the water, despite our puny escort moving about, despite the gunners standing by on the deck of the sub, there is a sense of vulnerability. The water is cold. How would it be to be blown off the deck into the ocean? I think of being in the water, thousands of feet between the bottom and me and I feel a familiar momentary surge of vertigo. Never mind, there is work to do.

Chapter 16

Jacob's Story

1918

The letter from Dave arrived unexpectedly. Apparently he had not yet received my last letter when he mailed this one.

> New York City
> September 15, 1918

Dear Abe,

I expect to hear from you soon but I want to give you a piece of news right away. I paid a visit to Mother and Father yesterday. By the way they are okay. The influenza does not seem to get to the older folks as much as to everyone else but I warn them of big crowds anyway. Mother's friend, Yetta, visited the other day and brought terrible news about her son, your friend, Jacob. He was wounded in the battle of the Marne. The good news is that he is alive and has been returned to the States. In fact he has been placed in the Walter Reed hospital, which I think is not too far from where you are. So I thought you would want to know about this as soon as possible. Maybe you could find a way to pay him a visit. I do not know many details. Mother seemed reluctant to talk about it.

As long as I am writing I should mention other things. About the influenza, as you know it is very bad and getting worse. At the hospital all that can be done is to treat symptoms and hope the body can fight it off. Too often it can't. We pharmacists feel helpless that we can't offer better remedies. The only thing that can be done is to caution about crowds, to avoid sneezing on people and also to wear a facemask in public. So please be careful, especially if you visit Jacob. Hospitals are easy places for diseases to spread.

I am pleased to report that Dolly and the twins are just fine, though I worry. This month they were able to go upstate for a couple of weeks with an old friend of Dolly's to pick vegetables and berries. I was glad to see them get away from the city crowds. Dolly and her friend took turns watching after the kids—and they take lots of watching. They are getting very fast on their feet.

There are no big things to report about Celia and Sari, but I'll fill you in next time I write. Please take care of yourself. Love from all of us—

Dave

On my first free Sunday I made my way to Walter Reed to visit Jacob. I approached the building in which he was housed with mounting apprehension. The pleasant appearance of neat brick buildings in a park-like setting did little to deflect my thoughts from the grim reality inside in the wards. I wasn't even sure I would recognize Jacob.

He was midway down a row of perhaps a dozen cots. At the far end of the ward a pair of visitors was gathered around one of the cots, but most of the men were lying or sitting silently on their beds. A couple of them had turned on their sides facing each other quietly talking. When I approached it was clear that it was indeed

Jacob, outstretched with his head and shoulders propped up on two large pillows. But he was noticeably different from when I had last seen him. He appeared so much older, especially his eyes, which, half squinting, looked as if he was trying to shut out the world. And he was noticeably thinner, even gaunt. When I was a couple of beds from him, he noticed me.

"Abe? Abe, is that you?" He broke into a smile, which while not the boyish, gleeful grin that I remembered, was still characteristically Jacob-like. I was hopeful that this was the same optimistic, cheerful person I had known all my life. I extended my hand, to which he raised his own in a tired way. He motioned for me to sit on the edge of the bed.

"How are you feeling, Jacob?" I asked.

"Okay, Abe. Okay. Right now there's still a lot of pain. They're cutting down on the pain pills they allow me, but the pain is going down too. I'll be okay. I haven't been killed—that's the bright side."

We exchanged news of family. He wanted to know what I had been doing. When I told him that I had been in the anti-submarine business, he responded enthusiastically. "You fellows are doing a great job, as far as I can see. On the way over, I can tell you, there was a lot of nervousness. Lookouts everywhere, navy guys talking about torpedo attacks. Some troop ships did get sunk, I hear. But on the transport back, it seemed a lot more relaxed. Maybe they figured there was not as much point in a sub attacking an almost empty ship. But the navy guys said the sub problem was almost under control. Of course there were precautions. At night, outside lights of any kind were out of the question."

Then Jacob changed the subject. He asked me to see if I could get a wheelchair so we could go outside on the grounds. I found a nurse, a great stocky, middle-aged woman, who accompanied the wheelchair and me back to Jacob's cot. "We're going to get this boy walking again," she announced in that soft northern Virginia accent so common in Washington. "This is one lucky boy, I'd say. That Jerry bullet jes' missed his vitals, you know." She grinned and half winked.

"She means vital organs," Jacob said. The nurse helped him swing around and lift himself into the chair, while I kept it steady. At this point I saw the enormous cast that covered the upper part of his leg and across part of his torso. It prevented Jacob from completely assuming a sitting position, so a pillow was placed behind him against which he partially reclined. "Yeah, lucky. They say I'll always have a limp with this shattered hip. Better than having a leg missing, I guess. The worst, I think, are the guys who got blinded."

The nurse shook her head sadly. "Lots of them," she said.

I wheeled Jacob out on the grounds. It was one of those pleasant early fall days, which, while still warm and mildly humid, was doubly welcome after a summer of the intolerable muggy Washington heat. I found a place in the shade of an enormous elm tree.

"So how was it, Jake?" I asked, adding "Or maybe you don't want to talk about it."

"No. It's okay. I can talk," he said. "You know, in some ways the hardest thing was the training and waiting until we got into action in France. I was the 'Jew-boy' in the company. I don't know whether it was supposed to be mean, but I didn't feel fully accepted. Fortunately I could easily keep up, better than the average, I would say. And all that stopped as soon as the bullets started flying. When I was hit, it was a big Irish guy in our company who dragged me back to cover."

"Once they get over that childish thing of starting fights with the Jewish kids, like they used to do in Brownsville, most of the Irish are very likeable," I interjected.

"Yes. I actually think of my company like brothers, in a way," Jacob said. "But the battlefield stuff is a sort of painful to think about. Another side of it was—maybe I could say—well, it was interesting." I felt as if I was beginning to see some of the old Jacob. "Sometimes I think of the French villages we went through. It's funny, but they reminded me of Wizna. Do you remember anything about Wizna?"

I practically never think about Wizna. "I was only eight when we left. It's all pretty vague," I responded. "I remember there was a village store . . . ."

"Shafransky's store," Jacob interrupted.

"Yes, that's it. Mr. Shafransky. Somehow, when I was a kid in Brownsville, every time I bought some school supplies I thought of Shafransky's store, but gradually I forgot the name. I wonder if it's still there."

"It burned down." Jacob looked wistful. "Maybe I should say it was burned down."

"When? Why?" I sensed I might be intruding in a sensitive place. "You never talked about Wizna before, Jake."

"I've had a lot of time to think. Maybe too much time," he responded. "When we were kids in Brownsville I guess I was a little fearful of thinking about the old times. But, you know, after some of the things that happened in France it's not that hard any more."

"You don't mind talking about Wizna any more? I admit, I'm kind of curious. Who burned Shafransky's store?" I hoped that my tone of voice made it clear that I was prepared to drop the subject at any moment.

"Have you ever seen the Cossacks?" he asked. "The Tsar's thugs."

"I heard of them as a kid, but I don't remember anything about them. We left when I was pretty little," I answered.

"I know. I also heard of bad things happening, but somehow I thought that was only for the older folks to worry about. They knew how to take care of things," he continued. "The early days were not bad at all, it seemed. My father was making a living. We didn't have a lot, but Wizna seemed like a nice place to be." I nodded in agreement.

He continued. "That is until maybe I was twelve years old and I realized things were not really so good after all. We heard of the pogroms, and the Tsar did nothing about it. I heard that the Bolsheviks shot him in the head this summer. I can't say it makes me sad to have heard that." I had never before seen this kind of bitterness in Jacob.

"So what happened in Wizna?"

"It was in the late afternoon. I remember because I had a little job helping old man Shapiro with his cows after school. I heard them come into town. There were three of them—Cossacks. Each had a horse and they rode into town as if they owned it, making a lot of noise, singing Russian songs. Generally causing commotion. I don't know if they were already a little drunk, but the first place they headed for was the tavern. Do you remember the tavern?"

"Sort of. It was in the middle of town, wasn't it?"

"Yes. And the shul was at the end of town where the Cossacks rode in. Nobody knows where they had been or where they were going. Further along was the tavern, and after that was Shafransky's store. We lived on a side alley, not too far from there. Later we all thought it was a good thing they didn't stop at the shul. But probably it showed them that this was a little Jewish shtetl and a place to take advantage of. Anyway, when they reached the tavern, they went in and sat down. They laid their pistols on the table. I guess nobody was going to stand in their way."

"Then what?" I asked.

"In small groups the village men left the place and walked away as fast as they could. I was watching from Shapiro's barn. There was shouting and laughing. As I understood it they helped themselves to the food and drank up what vodka they could find. I doubt if they paid for any of it. The tavern keeper was afraid to complain.

"After a while they spilled out on the street. Clearly they were drunk. One of them tripped over himself and pitched into the dust. There was a roar of laughter. The others hauled him to his feet. He didn't even brush himself off.

"That's when they headed for Shafransky's store, but it had closed for the day. Their Polish was pretty awful but it was clear they wanted more vodka. 'Open up!' they were shouting. Shafransky appeared from behind the store and tried to explain he was closed for the day, but they grabbed him by the collar and demanded he open up." Jacob paused, as if to pull his feelings together.

"The next thing they were loading Shafransky's supply of vodka into their saddlebags. He tried to object but they knocked him down and kicked him in the ribs a couple of times. Meanwhile the family escaped through the back door. We put them up in our shed after that." Jacob paused again.

"I had no idea," I said. "The old people keep things from kids. How did it end?"

"Fire," he said. "Two of those gorillas had managed to get back on their horses. Then the other one went back into the store. I saw a flicker of light inside, then some smoke. The Cossack came out grinning and climbed onto his horse. He was so drunk he could hardly make it. On the way out of the village he was leaning forward holding his arms around the horse's neck just to stay on. The other two were laughing. Maybe they were feeling righteous that they hadn't killed anyone.

"Shafransky and the neighbors tried to beat out the flames but it was useless. The whole place burnt up. Everything. All the merchandise. The living quarters. Everything." Again Jacob was silent. He looked around at the hospital grounds—stately trees, neat lawns. A sweet perfume from a nearby cluster of late blooming roses drifted by from time to time. I imagined that Jacob was thinking that even with his wounds that this was a far better place to be.

He went on. "That's about when we decided to leave Poland. Before the real pogroms came to Wizna. My father sold everything we had to one of the Polish families from the other side of town. It was enough to bribe our way out of the country and take us to America. It went pretty much the same way it was for you seven years before, at least according to my mother. You know. We met up with a group and a guide in Bialystok. It was an adventure."

"What happened to Shafransky and his family?" I asked. "What did they do?"

"That's sort of interesting. You know, they had nothing. Everything they owned was burnt up. But the guide—his name was Boris . . ."

I interrupted. "Boris? I seem to remember. A big man."

"That's right. A huge guy, with huge mustaches too. Slightly graying."

"I don't remember much in the way of details. But yes. A very big guy with mustaches. It must be the same one who took us over the border. But you were saying?"

"Boris offered to take the Shafranskys along free. He even paid their way to Berlin. They had relatives in Berlin, I think. But I don't know what happened to them after that. My mother said they talked of somehow getting to the Holy Land, but I really don't know what became of them."

"This Boris—do you know why he helped out the Shafranskys?" I asked.

"My father asked him that during the trip. All he said was that he understood persecution. That was his only explanation. But we don't know much about him except that he said he came from Rákow. That much stuck in mind even though I don't even know where Rákow is." He shrugged. "In any case he was probably taking a big chance."

"I always supposed that these guides did it for the money. Probably they did, but it makes you wonder if in some cases there was more to it."

We fell silent for a while. The sun was much lower in the sky and our shady spot under the great elm was now dappled in sunlight. Jacob looked tired. "What will you do when they let you out of here?" I asked.

"I can still have my job at the settlement house. Counseling, teaching English, that sort of thing. I expect there'll be a lot of people trying to come over here when things die down in Europe. Let's hope that comes soon. It's devastation over there." He looked thoughtful. "Anyway I like the work. I guess I won't be able to run up and down stairs, but I will manage, I'm sure. No more long walks in the country, Abe. I'll miss that."

As I wheeled Jacob back to his ward I assured him I would see him again when I could. And that I would keep up, long walks or not. The nurse helped me get him back on his cot. "One of these days, this soldier's gonna get outside all by his self," she said.

Since my visit with Jacob I have thought about his story about Wizna. I have tried to recall the village, but it's vague, mostly fragments. I have been in America twice as long as I lived in Poland. I do remember the little incident when I found a kopek on a Saturday morning in front of the tavern. I don't know why that little memory persists.

Now the end of the conflict appears to be in sight. The Germans have retreated to the Hindenburg line; Austria-Hungary has made a peace offer. But at the lab our work still goes on, although there are discussions of changing directions. There is no telling when my job will end, but increasingly I am thinking about post-war plans for myself.

CHAPTER 17

Resuming Course

1918

Professor Connor is in Washington for a few days conferring on some War Department research. While in town he also visited with his old friend, my boss Jim Barry. Jim let me know that the professor would also like to see me before leaving for home.

I arranged to meet him this morning for a late breakfast before he caught the Sunday afternoon train to New York. I chose a small friendly café on the edge of the Negro neighborhood that borders Union Station. The food has a Southern flare—eggs and grits, hush puppies, sausage patties. I thought he would enjoy the local touch. I have given up the idea of remaining strictly kosher but I still avoid pork meat or mixing dairy and meat. It is a compromise that I struggle with.

I had settled into a booth when the professor appeared at the entrance. I rose to meet him. "Abe. It's good to see you again," were his first words. He extended his hand. "How have you been? I suppose I need not ask. I get reports from Dr. Barry from time to time." He may not have been certain that we were on a first name basis in our research group. "Well, you are looking fit."

"You are looking well yourself, Dr. Connor," I said as I shook his hand and led him to our booth. He placed his small traveling bag on the seat beside him. I sat facing him. Then he took up the menu and scanned it very quickly before putting it down, satisfied that he knew what he wanted to order. He was as I remembered—friendly, decisive, dignified. I thought that his hairline had receded a bit, but it may only be the way he had combed his hair. It had been only fifteen months since I had last seen him, but it seemed like years.

A short, stocky waitress approached our booth with a pot of coffee. "Fill up, gen'lmen?" Dr. Connor nodded, turning his cup upward. I pushed mine forward.

"Southern hospitality," I said. "And they never let your cup run dry. It's unusual these days though, what with coffee being in short supply. Probably doctor it with chicory. Can you taste a difference?"

He took a sip and put the cup down. "It's good. Just what I needed." He looked directly at me. "My friend Jim has given me a positive report on your performance in his group." I may have looked a little embarrassed. He went on. "No war secrets, of course. Generalities, but very positive."

The waitress returned with an order pad and pencil in her hand. "Ready to order, gen'lmen?" As we ordered our breakfasts I tried to review the muddled thoughts I have had lately about the future of my college career.

I resumed our conversation. "It's been very interesting. Very busy. But interesting. It's good to know that Jim—er, Dr. Barry—is satisfied with my part of it." The professor didn't seem to take much notice of the ambiguity in how we referred to my boss.

"Have you been thinking about a return to college, Abe?" he asked. He looked directly at me. The question was not a matter of casual curiosity. "I looked at your record. You could probably graduate in a year if you worked hard."

"Well, yes," I replied. "I've been trying to do some reading and studying on the side, supposing it would help whenever I can get back. But up to now there's been a lot of pressure around here. I don't feel I can quit the work."

"Of course. But Jim tells me—you call him Jim, don't you?" I nodded. "Hang it, why don't you call me Richard? The war has broken down a lot of barriers. For the better, don't you think?" It was a rhetorical question. "Besides you're a grown man. We all know each other pretty well."

"Well, sure. I might make a slip out of habit, I suppose."

He smiled. "Whatever comes easiest, Abe. We won't get hung up on details." He took a sip from his coffee cup. "But to get back on track—Jim tells me that the pressure from the Navy is about to ease up. There may be a change in the direction of the work."

"I have that feeling as well," I said. "But it's only been in the last few weeks that it has become apparent. I haven't felt that quitting the job was a practical option until now. And now, unfortunately the semester has already begun at the college."

"That needn't be a problem—or least much of a problem. We've become pretty adaptable during this war. All sorts of special cases: returning veterans, temporary professors, self study credits—all sorts of odd arrangements. Anyway, if you don't delay too much longer, you could catch up on what you might have missed. You might have to do a few makeup credits in the summer, but you could probably do it all in a year."

I was listening with some eagerness now. The thought of returning to New York and finishing the degree had been kind of a dream that I had learned to dismiss. To do formal study and interact with the students, to broaden my horizons with a few more humanities courses—most of all perhaps, to be able to be with Rosie—I had learned to treat it all much like fantasy. It was for the future.

"At least the problem of money isn't an obstacle," I added. "I've been able to help out the folks this past year and still saved enough. I won't need to take a job on the side. But there is still a war."

"Yes there is, although if you believe the newspapers it looks like the Central Powers are crumbling." He grinned. "Naturally I don't get inside information from President Wilson, but I can tell you that I've talked to a few people here in Washington in the last several days. The guess is that it's just a matter of weeks."

The waitress reappeared with our breakfasts, seesawing the plates slightly while deciding which of them was for whom. She guessed correctly. I had a fleeting thought that maybe she decided that I wouldn't be the one that ordered ham. Without a word she picked up a pitcher of coffee from a side table and refilled our cups. "Enjoy, gen'lmen."

We began to eat. I asked Richard about his family and about the lab. Butch finished his master's degree recently and had an excellent thesis defense. Russell, as expected, is in the Army and Richard has lost track of him. Eventually he may return to finish his thesis. The lab has continued to operate with students who have not been conscripted. "There will always be work for earning some research credits, if you wish," he assured me.

While we finished our breakfast coffees, Richard's expression became more serious. "I wanted to ask you about something else, Abe. Have you ever thought about graduate study?"

"It has crossed my mind," I replied. "But frankly, just getting a bachelor's degree has been a big enough dream. Nobody I have known personally has ever gotten a college degree. Just some of my teachers. My brother finished pharmacy college."

"Actually it was exactly the same for me when I started college. My parents weren't sure what the point was to pass up getting a good job right out of high school—unless it was to become a priest." He smiled momentarily, adding "And they weren't too fond of that idea."

He went on. "But seriously, how do you feel about more years of study after you graduate? Of course it's a different kind of study—as you've observed. The emphasis is on individual research, especially at the doctoral level. Not that academics are absent."

"I like academics, and research as well. To tell the truth when I have thought about it, it has almost seemed like a far off and impossible dream. Unless I had some financial support like a teaching assistantship, I couldn't afford to go."

"I hope you realize that you would be first in line for an assistantship in our department and I would be more than pleased to have you in my research group. Or you could broaden out by working with one of the other professors. But I would be less than honest if I didn't advise you to aim straight for a doctoral degree if you took on graduate work. As you know for the time being we are restricted to offering master's degrees on our campus. You could, of course, shoot for an M.S., then transfer somewhere for the Ph.D., but you've already lost a lot of time. If the doctor's degree is what you want, if I were you I would go for it directly."

My response uncovered what heretofore was a suppressed concern. "I'm afraid I might not be admitted."

"I suspect you're thinking of quotas." I was relieved that it was he who used the actual word 'quota.' He looked thoughtful. "It's an unfortunate problem, Abe. It bothers some of us a lot. By and large it's not a popular system for most of the professors, especially in the sciences. It's mostly due to the influence of alumni. Many of the old boys have an out of date sentimental image of their college experience as it was in the good old days, when almost everyone was a WASP—especially in the Ivy League universities. So they have these quotas, especially for Jews—not to mention Catholics, Italians—name it. Negroes? You can almost forget about one of them being admitted. I have this hope though, that if any good things come out of the war it might be a relaxing of some of the old prejudices."

"It seems you think there's reason for hope—about admission, that is. I admit it's an exciting thought."

"Very few things are absolutely predictable, especially in the affairs of men. Nothing ventured, nothing gained. The main thing is it's not too early to be giving this serious consideration—that is if you can finish up the bachelor's degree in the next year. And you should be making up your mind on that very soon." He pulled out his pocket watch and checked the time. "I've got a train to catch. It's been very nice to see you. I hope I haven't rattled your brain, too much."

I reached for the check. "It's a rattling it needed. It's easy to become complacent. But let me cover the bill. I'm a working guy now—an overpaid government lackey, if you believe some of the politicians. You and Jim have been very good to me."

We walked to Union Station. On the way I told him that I would talk with Jim about the possibility of quitting and returning to school. "That's a capital idea—very appropriate for the location," he said, pointing at the Capitol dome directly ahead of us. "Seriously, I get the impression from Jim that with the end of the war imminent he expects there to be a bit of reorganization."

As we shook hands in front of the station, he reminded me of our discussion of graduate study. "If it has any appeal, you might look into the kinds of research that's being done at some of the major universities. Jim and I can share what we know. But above all do consider Columbia. I am always on the lookout for appropriate candidates for them. And I know that my recommendation carries a little weight with them. Jim's too."

I walked the four or five miles back to the boarding house lost in thought. The fall colors were past their prime. It was a clear sunny day, but cool. A persistent wind was blowing from the southwest, scattering the drifting leaves. Along the bluffs above the Potomac in Anacostia it felt downright nippy. From time to time V-formations of migrating geese sailed overhead, powering their way against the wind as they moved south with the river. In their goose-minds, which we cannot possibly comprehend, each of the birds knew what it must do. No thought of the arduous return migration in the spring. No hesitation about it, no weighing the odds. I almost envied them.

As I walked, I turned over in my mind my current career situation. Jim had spoken to me the other day about possible changes in the research mission of our group. The anti-submarine effort, of which our group had played a significant part, had been successful. Improvements were still to be made, but engineers working with the manufacturers would carry out much of that. Jim had learned that an area of research that the admirals working with the Bureau of Ships were eager to have investigated involved methods of communicating with our own submarines while they are submerged.

The ideas about which he had been in discussion involved radio transmissions that penetrate the surface of water. Normally, radio waves reflect from the surface of the sea, which acts like a mirror. This happens for the same reason that the silvered coating of an ordinary mirror reflects visible light waves. Radio waves are of the same nature as light waves but have a considerably longer wavelength. Thus, since silver and seawater both conduct electricity, they both respond in the same way to the electrical forces of incoming waves—by generating outgoing waves. These outgoing waves constitute the reflection. Of course there are details in this physics that are interesting in themselves. But the essential fact that has implications for the naval mission is that seawater, being a relatively poor conductor of electricity, does not reflect the radio waves at the very top of the sea surface. Instead the waves penetrate to some distance below the surface. The longer the wavelength, the greater the depth of penetration. One could even imagine a submarine receiving radio messages while cruising fifty or sixty feet below the surface of the sea.

I know by now that nature doesn't bend to our ideas very readily. So it came as no surprise, as Jim told me about this possible new direction in our research mission, that whereas the basic principle was straightforward enough, the practical challenges were very large. Very long wavelength radio waves require very long antennas to be practical. On the transmitter side of the communication link, land-based antennas could be made almost as long as one wished—even miles in length when strung between mountaintops. But on the submarine the antenna cannot be longer than the ship itself. What is needed is ways to detect very faint signals gathered by an antenna very much shorter than an ideal length. Those are the areas that need exploration.

As I thought about this, the nature of my discomfort became clear. On one hand technical challenges are appealing—like games requiring imagination and creativity. I sometimes wonder if, at heart, I am primarily a tinkerer delighting in solving practical problems. On the other hand I am strongly impelled to come to a deeper understanding of nature. There has been no problem working on the problems of submarine detection. I see that as being in the service of good cause—protecting our sailors and seamen, and achieving military victory. But helping our submarines do their killing work, despite an unabated sense of patriotism, doesn't stir in me the same enthusiasm.

Back in my room I sat down to write a letter to Rosie.

Washington, D.C.
Sunday evening
October 13, 1918

Dear Rosie,

I have to tell you about today—at least as much as I am able to reveal. Professor Connor (in private we are now on a first name basis—that will take getting used to) has been in Washington for a few days. Today we met for a late morning breakfast and a frank discussion of my future. Beneath the bow ties and dignified suits Richard (there, I said it) is the good egg I always suspected he is. I should add, as I have probably said in the past, a good teacher and an able mentor. If I were a professor, I would aspire to be the same.

Why do I even mention being a professor? It's a wild idea, a suppressed thought. I guess I have not even mentioned it to you, and we have shared so many thoughts. But Richard has put the notion of heading for a doctorate in the front of my mind. At the very least I am convinced that I must make some real plans right now about the immediate future. As for the distant future, even I were able to get a Ph.D., I know nothing is guaranteed beyond that. For all I know, I would have to go back to being a shoe salesman—an erudite salesman, for sure—reading copies of the *Physical Review* in the back room in the company of the shoeboxes. Even then, there is some appeal in the idea.

Of course, there are obstacles. There is still work to be done here and I would feel more comfortable about leaving if I had Jim's blessing. He has been good to me as well. Then I must still finish the undergraduate work—the sooner, the better. More uncertain is my chance of being accepted into a good graduate school with a paying assistantship. Finally—and this is the most difficult issue for me to raise—I don't know what four, five, maybe six more years as a poor student implies for our friendship.

In any event I do plan to speak with Jim tomorrow. It is clear things are bound to change at the lab. Thank goodness it looks as if the war may be over soon—and none too soon. I only wish I had more confidence in the leaders to make a just and lasting peace. The human toll is way out of proportion to the issues that needed to be settled. There is more than enough fault to go around on both sides in Europe. Maybe Wilson, with an American perspective, can bring some reason into the process.

I needed to share my ruminations with you. Apart from Rick Thayer there are not too many people here to bounce these thoughts off. I suspect he is toying with some of the same ideas. The notion of getting back to college is admittedly a delicious thought. If I were able to do this soon we might even graduate at the same time. Wouldn't that be something? Please give my regards to your parents. I think of you often.

As ever—affectionately,
Abe

CHAPTER 18

Celebration

1920

Yesterday Rosie and I graduated from Gallatin College. Following the ceremony our families gathered for a celebration that Dave had arranged at the Excelsior Kosher Restaurant. Mother and Father, the Dubrows, Dave and his Dolly, Celia and her new husband, Harold, were there. Young Alec Dubrow begged off from the celebration. He chose to spend the evening with his high school chums. The guests assembled in a private room just off the main dining area. On a large round table in the center of the room there were several spritz bottles of seltzer and baskets of Kaiser rolls. A starter course of fruit compote was at each setting. After some milling about, Dave called everyone to attention. He urged us to find our marked places and begin to eat, as we were all undoubtedly famished. Formalities and announcements would come in due course.

The meal was well underway when Sari, who had to miss the graduation ceremony, hurried in from her secretarial job. She appeared as cute as ever as she pulled off her gray cloche hat and smoothed her bobbed hair with the back of her hand. Looking about the room, she quickly spotted Rosie and me. She hurried over to us.

"Congratulations, you two!" Turning to Rosie she took her hand in both of hers. "It's great finally meeting you."

"Likewise," Rosie responded. Though they were approximately the same age, it was evident that Rosie's subdued good humor could not match Sari's ebullience. Rosie introduced Sari to her mother and father, who were sitting beside her. There was a brief exchange of pleasantries. Turning back to us, Sari suddenly gave me a peck on the cheek and before I could mount any defensive action, she playfully roughed up my hair.

"Good work, Abie!" Sari said, before bouncing off to her place. On the way she gave Mother and Father each a little kiss. For a moment all eyes were on her. I thought I noted mild disapproval in Mother's expression. Mr. Dubrow was amused. When the waiter brought in the main course, Sari still had not come down completely from her high spirits. "Ooh! Brisket and knaidlach!" she exclaimed.

Sari's mood was infectious. There was much lighthearted small talk. The older folks, breaking into Yiddish, spoke with one another of the old country—where they came from, how and when they arrived, where they had lived on the lower Eastside. The ladies commented on the food. Rosie was her usual warm engaging self. She spoke at length with Dave and Dolly. She asked about the two-year old twins, the situation at the hospital, where they were living, about whether Dolly missed working outside the home. For my part this was an opportunity to speak with Harold, whom I had met only occasionally during the past year while I was finishing the college work. Harold is a machinist and die-maker for the National Biscuit Company. It came as a surprise to him that I had any interest in or experience with machine tools. Harold held the common misconception about science that it is all equations, white lab coats, and test tubes. I tried to explain that science is often tinkering and inventing, crawling around apparatus and, as Butch liked to say in Professor Connor's lab, being "handy with the hands." Celia was obviously pleased that we had something in common.

As the main course was being cleared great steaming pots of tea appeared, along with two heaping plates of mandel bread. It looked and smelled as good as the mandel bread mother baked—hard, elongated slices revealing layers of tawny raisins and nuts glistening with a sugary cinnamon coating. Mother's expression did not reveal whether or not they had her approval. Finally Dave stood up. He tapped the edge of a glass with his spoon until he had everyone's attention. Raising a cup of tea, he spoke.

"Ladies and gentlemen. I must first of all apologize for our great national leaders, who in their wisdom have recently given us the eighteenth amendment to the Constitution, thereby depriving us of the opportunity of celebrating this occasion with a liquid more warming than hot tea. But, dear celebrants, we must do with what is left to us in the cause of the greater good."

Sari clapped. Harold grinned. Cups were filled with tea. Dave continued.

"Indeed, it is good. Here we will have a toast—with tea. And as our mothers have often reminded us when we have been less than what we should be with the whirly-tummy, tea and toast is the remedy for what ails us. Second best to chicken soup, admittedly, but far better than any potion we pharmacists have in our best formulary. So I raise my cup to the new graduates and good riddance to all that ails us!"

Everyone raised their cups and sipped their tea. "Speech, speech!" Sari exclaimed looking at Rosie and me. Mr. Dubrow beamed. Some of the English may have eluded Father, but he looked pleased and turned our way. Dave remained standing and continued.

"Not so fast, little sister. I have the floor for the time being. Now this young man we have here—I have kept my eye on him for a long time. And each time I think I know what to make of him he has always managed to surprise me. There was the time he played on the championship school soccer team—did you all know about that? Well, it was perfectly clear to me that he was destined to be a great athlete. A fast runner, I can tell you—and an outstanding stickball first baseman. But no—that was just a sideline, it appears.

"Then there was the time when I struggled with Shakespeare in high school and who came to my rescue? Little Abe, of course. He may have been a seventh grader at the time. This time I really had him pegged. A great orator, a teacher of the great classics—a great rabbi? No, again. That kind of stuff was just for fun, it seems. In pharmacy school I had it nailed down. Abe my math tutor would forever confound us mere mortals with talk of binomial theorems and other mathematical mumbo jumbo. Wrong again—our boy remains as down to earth as ever. Oh and did I mention that he is also a star shoe salesman? I make no more guesses about this brother of mine. He has found his path all by himself. As you know, in the fall Abe will begin a new career as a graduate student and teaching assistant at Columbia University. Joining that august institution is in itself worthy of our applause."

There was scattered applause. Everyone looked my way. I felt flushed and a little nervous. It occurred to me that a shot of schnapps would have been a big help. Mr. Dubrow may have been anticipating that more announcements were yet to come. I saw him signal a waiter. He whispered in his ear. The waiter left the room again. Dave went on.

"But dear guests, I cannot forget our other honoree. This lovely young lady, a friend of Abe's, and therefore a dear friend of all of us all, should make her ma and pa proud—very proud. I cannot say I know her as well as I know Abe. This is only the second time we have met, but I know a lot about her. Abe has been quite unable to keep her out of our conversations. Nobody needs to be told just how fine a young lady she is—just looking at her tells you that she is both smart and sweet. And accomplished—and not typical either. Now, the fact that she has graduated with a degree in mathematics is in itself enough to win the greatest admiration from a math klutz such as myself. But she combined that math major with a major in English—oh, shades of my old Shakespeare teacher! I fairly swoon with admiration."

Dave brought the back of his hand to his forehead in a dramatic gesture. Dave is normally a down to earth guy, but occasionally he can be a performer. There was some laughter. The waiter shortly reappeared, setting a tray of small whiskey glasses on a side table. He left again, closing the door behind himself.

"But, friends. There is more. In the fall, our dear Rosie, true to this age of the liberated woman—indeed soon to be the age of the fully emancipated woman—begins her own career in the public schools. And, at a school of her own choosing not far from her home. So we must salute her and also congratulate a number of lucky seventh and eighth graders!"

He raised his cup again. I looked at Rosie. Her eyes were cast down but she was beaming. Once again Sari said, "Speech, speech!"

Dave said, "Yes, we must hear from the graduates." Rosie turned to me, and putting one hand on my arm and another beneath my elbow, nudged me up. I rose and gathered my strength.

"Friends—family," I began. I looked around the table at each face. Rosie looked passive, knowing what was to come. Other eyes fastened on me. A superfluous thought occurred to me—that if I were to soon to begin as a teaching assistant I had better get used to being the focus of attention.

"Thank you all for being here. And I especially have to thank brother Dave for the very kind words—perhaps undeserved, except of course for what he has to say about Rosie. But I have other special thanks to give, as well. First of all, on behalf of Rosie and me—and we have talked about this—to the parents, for years of patience and support and, most of all, love. It is a great leap of faith to believe in the value of years of study. I'm reminded of what the father of a friend wrote in my friend's autograph album when we graduated from high school. Apparently all he could think of inscribing was, 'Congratulations. Go get a job.'"

There was some chuckling. Once having started, I felt more comfortable speaking to the gathering. I noticed that Mr. Dubrow, while keeping most of his attention fastened on me, had silently retrieved an object in a paper bag from the inner pocket of a light top coat that he had thrown over the back of a chair along the wall.

"Then too, I have to personally acknowledge the other people in my life who are here tonight. First of all, brother Dave, whom I have looked up to as long as I can remember—almost as I might emulate an uncle. He parted the waves for me, maybe for all of us in the family—when we arrived in America so long ago, when we kids began high school, when we found jobs. I know he was a rock to stand on for Mother and Father—our American guide, perhaps. And in him the inspiration to reach as far as we can. And he and

Dolly have made it possible, in fact, to become a proud uncle myself. So thank you both."

Everyone looked at Dave. He nodded in acknowledgement and put his arm around Dolly's shoulders.

"I cannot thank Celia enough for being the understanding big sister who always knew the right words to console or encourage. Those words, God knows, were needed from time to time. Harold, you have a gem here. Never forget that. And then there is Sari. Ah Sari—need I say anything? It should be obvious that you are the sparkle that lights our family's days and nights. The one that always sees the cheery side, the one who banishes gloom wherever you are."

Sari had her hands clasped in front of her. She hunched her shoulders as if to make herself as small as possible. She had a sheepish grin and her gaze roamed the table without hardly turning her head. I looked down at Rosie momentarily, and then continued.

"Of course, I have been speaking strictly for myself. Rosie feels blessed by all the support she has had all her life as well, but has asked me to do the public thanking. So from her and from me as well, to mom and pop Dubrow—thank you for years and years of love, support, and understanding. Finally I must thank Rosie herself. Sometimes study can be a lonely business, as I think you all know. But then there has been Rosie—even a half hour coffee break with her has made the difference for us both. Yet from here on we are on different paths—more study for me, a new career for Rosie."

Once again I felt a little nervous. This was a big moment. Mr. Dubrow had removed a whiskey flask from the paper bag. I drew a breath.

"Rosie and I have talked about this a lot. During this past school year we have learned how we feel about each other. Rosie and I have grown very close and now it is time to share our feelings with all of you. We have come to love one another and we want you to be the first to know of our intention to be married."

Rosie stood up, and putting her arm around my waste placed a kiss on my cheek. There were a few gasps and a scattering of applause. Sari came swiftly around the table and drew Rosie into an embrace. Celia gave me a hug and a kiss. Dave leaned over and said something to Mother before standing and clapping. Mother placed her hand over her breast and whispered something to Father who, in turn beamed with pride as he locked his thumbs behind his lapels. Mrs. Dubrow had walked around the table to Mother and Father, and placing a hand on Mother's shoulder was saying something to them. Meanwhile Mr. Dubrow, who had evidently anticipated my announcement, had begun filling the whiskey glasses on the sideboard. As he did so, he glanced occasionally at the door to the room. He rapped lightly on a water glass to call everyone's attention. Then he spoke.

"Friends, this is truly a blessed moment for all of us—especially for the new couple, Abe and our dear Rosie—and for the proud parents, Flossy and me, Jake and Gittle. In fact, to be able to celebrate the success of years of hard work by Abe and Rosie and receive such wonderful news at the same time—it's a doubly blessed moment. It requires a special toast."

Mrs. Dubrow had begun passing out the whiskeys around the table. Mr. Dubrow continued.

"First, though, I must speak of our Rosie. Her mother and I have watched her grow—from the impish little girl, who was always the first to reach me when I came through the door at night, to this lovely young woman who sits among us tonight. She is the apple of my eye, and although I am going to miss her in our home, I know she will be received with love from all of you. Flossy and I are thankful for that. I know she will find happiness with your Abe—and we are thankful for that as well. So—you have your glasses, yes? To the couple!"

He raised his glass. "L'chayim—to life!" Everyone raised glasses except Rosie and me. We held ours at table level. "L'chayim!" was heard around the table. Father said, "Gut gesund!"—to health. Everyone drank. Rosie and I touched glasses and sipped a bit of the whiskey. We kissed publicly for the first time.

There was a general hubbub—much shaking hands, back slaps, hugging. The ladies gathered around Rosie. Of course they wanted to know the wedding plans, to which she answered that there were no plans and might not be for quite a while. She tried to explain that she and I have a very trying year coming up with many uncertainties. She pointed out that I would still be a student with only a marginal income as a teaching assistant. She reminded them that she had still to work on her teaching credentials and had yet to face her first classroom of students. "Students of an awkward age," she added.

Later, as we all left on our separate ways, I walked with the Dubrows to the subway station. Rosie and I agreed to meet on Sunday for a walk in the park. I shook hands with Mr. Dubrow. For the first time I hugged Rosie's mother. Rosie and I kissed. As they made their way down the steps to the subway station, Rosie turned, and in a reasonable imitation of sister Sari, called back, "Good work, Abie!" She threw me a kiss.

On Monday both of us will embark on new adventures. Rosie will have a part-time summer job in the millinery shop near the Dubrow apartment and the following week will begin her first course at Columbia's Teacher's College. I am to meet with my tentative graduate advisor, Professor Tenley, at Columbia. He had been Richard Connor's advisor years before and has arranged a summer research assistantship for me in his lab. Usually such a job is available only to advanced graduate students working on theses, but the war had interrupted the normal flow of students. I will be living at the Y.M.H.A. I try to imagine the possibilities which lie ahead. But I try to reign in my imagination lest I be disappointed. And I cannot stop thinking of Rosie.

CHAPTER 19

Reaching for the Patch of Blue

1922

It was only 9:30 in the evening when Rosie and I arrived back at our apartment after attending the Passover Seder at Father and Mother's flat in Brownsville. Our apartment is small but we are fortunate to have found it just as we had begun our married life together. It is a third floor walkup in a pre-war brick building on a side street just off Amsterdam Avenue. From there it is an easy walk to Columbia and to Rosie's school, and not far from the Dubrows' apartment. On good evenings we can take walks in Central Park or along the bluffs above the Hudson in Morningside Heights.

A narrow dark vestibule leads from the entrance to a small kitchen-dining area at the back of the apartment. This room looks out on a dim courtyard, strewn with bits of rubble and undistinguished except for a small sumac tree that miraculously has taken root in one corner. A doorway in the hall opens on a narrow living room, which is lit by a single window that gives access to a fire escape. This room is almost completely taken up by a pair of old desks placed back to back. Once in a while, I look up from my books to find that Rosie has interrupted her grading or lesson planning and is looking back at me. I can escape such distractions by retreating to an old threadbare easy chair beside the window behind Rosie's chair. There is a tiny bedroom off the vestibule next to the living room. In good weather we place our bed against the window and try to ignore the occasional street noise. In cooler weather we move the bed away from the window, despite the fact that the doorway is then partly obstructed. Soon it will be time to move the bed back to the window.

When we entered the apartment following the Seder, we went directly to the kitchen area. I took a seat at the little table in the corner next to the kitchen window, while Rosie put a kettle on to boil. I was watching her, wondering whether she would be the first to speak. Finally I ventured, "Well Rosie, what do you think?"

She was obviously lost in thought until I spoke. "Think about what?" she asked.

"About the Seder, about the family. I know you're thinking about something." "You're right. I was thinking about the Seder." She hesitated. "Abe, is it always that way?"

"That's an open question. Do you mean how my father's stuck in tradition?" We have been married over a year and engaged for a year and a half before that, but this was the first time Rosie had been at Father's Seder. While we were engaged, each of us had been at our own family's Seder. Last year the Dubrows had us to their apartment for the Seder. Stressed as I was while preparing for my first qualifying exams I welcomed not having to travel back to Brooklyn. Mr. Dubrow has modified the ritual somewhat. He uses a shorter Haggadah and includes passages in English. The Seder is supposed to be a teaching experience and he makes some attempt at that.

"I suppose that's some of what I'm thinking. The value of this rigid devotion—I have mixed feelings about it. It *is* somewhat endearing when your nephews ask the *vier fragen*—the four questions."

"*Ma mish tanah ha'laeila hazeh, m'cal ha'leilos?*" I intoned. "Sorry—habit," I said in feigned apology.

"Which means?".

"How is this night different from all other nights?"

"And the answer?" Rosie had poured tea into our cups. She brought them to the table and sat down.

"It's obvious. 'Tonight we eat only unleavened bread, whereas on other nights we eat leavened and unleavened bread.'" I spoke with mock solemnity.

"You shouldn't ridicule it, Abe. There must be a reason the *vier fragen* have been asked for thousands of years."

"Actually it's a tradition that probably goes back only to the Middle Ages, although the Seder itself is ancient. Seriously, the reason is to get the children engaged. The Seder is all about reminding everyone of their debt to God, and especially to teach the next generations about this." I took a sip of the tea. "But I can't help feeling that it is trivializing the meaning. It seems almost demeaning to think kids can't be engaged at a deeper level. I mean the answer is like giving the reasons for a disease by describing the symptoms. It's like a tautology. Oops—there's the academic talking."

Rosie put her hand on mine. "You are what you are."

"I am what I am. And to paraphrase Descartes, 'I am therefore I think.' A troublesome habit perhaps."

"Perhaps. But frankly, Abe, in this case I'm thinking about more than the *vier fragen*. I guess I felt a little troubled by almost everyone's behavior."

"You mean that not a lot of attention was paid to what Father was reciting?" Rosie's look affirmed this. "Well, it has bothered me all my life. The Seder is full of amazing symbolism, the outcome of a tradition building for probably more than three thousand years. Somehow it has survived all that time. It's really amazing. And yet I feel like it's disintegrating before our eyes. Will it survive? Should it survive?"

Rosie contemplated this remark for a few moments before replying. "Perhaps it is because people don't quite comprehend what is being said. Or maybe people take it lightly because the Seder's also meant to be a time of relaxing. My dad says at the Seder we're supposed to feel like princes and kings for a short while."

"Maybe some of us can feel like royalty, but as you can see my mother is like a slave getting ready for the holiday. All that food for all those people. She even makes the wine. Anyway there was only a little participation by the family—besides Dave's twins asking the four questions, I mean."

Rosie thought about that. "We all drank the wine at the appropriate times," she said with a little chuckle. "But yes, the hiding of the *afikomen* got some attention. And leaving the door open for Elijah."

"Those are quaint rituals. They do get people's attention. Perhaps this is a way of reaffirming their identity. Maybe it explains the resilience of the Jews—to persist in the face of all the persecutions. But I am a little suspicious of all this tribalism. What is the point?" I found myself answering my own question. "It's like an instinct. Binds people together into cohesive groups. Gives them collective power."

"To what end?"

"To beat out the other groups, perhaps. Survival of the fittest. Maybe we should look to Darwin."

"You're a cynic Abe," Rosie said. "We're talking about *Pesach*. What is the special message that accounts for this amazing survival?"

"I'm not sure," I said. "The message is supposed to be redemption. Redemption from slavery. Redemption and freedom and choice." I looked down through the window next to me into the darkened courtyard behind the building. The sumac tree was barely visible in the light from someone's kitchen window. Somehow it grew in this place surrounded on all sides by buildings. The sun practically never found its way into this dark well, yet the tree was budding out. "Survival and freedom," I finally added.

"Freedom and duty," Rosie reminded me.

"Well yes. A covenant of the Chosen People with God to proclaim His supremacy. I admit that there is something in that. Maybe we are the original—or at least, the oldest—surviving monotheistic religious group. It is interesting to me—this idea of a universal God—a power beyond ourselves that feeds us a huge dose of humility," I said. I was surprised at the gravity of my words.

"It seems to me the Chosen People have gotten a pretty rotten deal for the most part. But personally, we are very lucky—should I say blessed?" Rosie was trying to lighten the mood. "But you're right about the power of the idea of a universal God. Do good. Love God. Love your neighbor. The rest will take of itself." Rosie's tone changed. "So Abe, what really troubles you?"

"In my case, at least, it's confusion about my father. He goes on and on every Passover chanting from the Haggadah, going through the rituals. He seems oblivious to the fact that very few people in the family are paying much attention. Of course it's all in Hebrew. Maybe even in Aramaic for all I know. I wonder how much he himself understands of the words. He seems satisfied that he is fulfilling his duty—yet it's supposed to be a teaching experience."

"Actually, I was thinking much the same thing," Rosie responded. "In the old country all this tradition clearly had a value. Something that somehow gave meaning to life. My dad used to tell me how they lived in the old country—something had to get them up in the morning and make it all seem worthwhile. The trouble for you is the disconnect with your father."

"Never mind," I said. "Indeed, there is the freedom—I'll come to grips with my confusions in my own way, in my own time. Meanwhile, I'm here with you." I took Rosie's hand. "You're the best friend I ever had and I love you so much."

She squeezed my hand. Then she looked at the kitchen clock. "It's late," she said.

Rosie and I were up early the next morning. We both had a busy day ahead of us, but echoes of last night's conversation continue to run through my mind. God, as I suppose most people understand Him, is never clear in His messages. Was the story meaningful that God should deliver a people into slavery, only to make with them a covenant grounded in thankfulness upon their release? It sounded like a torturer who is praised and thanked by his victim when he ends the torture. Yet the God concept is a universal idea. It must have a survival value. I wrested myself from these thoughts and forced myself to think of the research I was getting underway this year. But here too, I realized, were parallel dilemmas. God, if understood in the Spinozan sense as the grand totality of natural law, holds tightly onto His secrets.

My advisor had suggested I look into some of the details of the photoelectric effect, which is the ejection of electrons from solid surfaces by beams of light. I have been reading the papers of Robert Millikan and Arthur Compton coming out of the University of

Chicago, and also preparing a laboratory setup for experiments that I hoped could begin in the summertime.

The basic idea of the photoelectric effect can be traced, like so much else, to Einstein in his miracle year of 1905 when he published three absolutely ground-breaking and unrelated papers. In an uncanny leap of faith he suggested that a light beam under some circumstances could be better described as a rain of particles rather than as a sea of waves. Ever since the days of Isaac Newton the description of light in terms of undulating waves had been undisputed. Light bends around corners to some degree. It can be made to interact with other beams of light to produce patterns of alternating cancellation and reinforcement, so-called interference patterns. Even electromagnetic theory shows that vibrating electric particles generate light waves. Nonetheless several lines of experimental evidence are inexplicable without the strange idea of Einstein's light quanta—not only the photoelectric and electron scattering experiments of Millikan and Compton, but also the detailed characteristics of radiation given off by hot objects. This wave-particle duality in nature is difficult to wrap one's mind around.

In the morning I was again thinking about this apparent dilemma. It was like the grand old God of the ancients—evident, yet ultimately mysterious—beyond the ability of the human mind to fully comprehend, yet manifest in the world. One can only marvel and accept.

Before we left for the day, Rosie made up some matzo *brei,* egg soaked matzo lightly fried in butter. We sat again with our coffees at the kitchen window. Up above the courtyard the visible patch of sky was unusually blue. Below, the courtyard sumac tree was putting forth leaves. Reaching for those light quanta, I thought. This year it even was showing evidence of the coming of its fuzzy flowers, like clumps of little red pompoms. When we emerged on the street the sun was just rising above some of the buildings. It was to be a glorious spring day. We walked together to the spot where our paths diverged.

As Rosie turned to go in her direction, I gathered her in my free arm and kissed her lightly just beneath her ear. "Love you," I whispered. I felt the warmth of her body and felt an urge to linger.

"Must go, Abe," she said. She squeezed my arm. "See you in the evening." She turned to go. After a few steps, she turned her head. Putting her fingers to her lips, she tossed me a kiss.

CHAPTER 20

Wolf Mountain

1925

Susan B. Anthony State College is located in the town of West Goshen in the northwestern part of Massachusetts. West Goshen is, for the most part, friendly and self-contained. What it cannot offer in the way of entertainment is provided by lively cultural offerings on the growing campus. What is even more important for Rosie and me, are the mountains and lakes so easily reached, now that we have our first car. From the campus, formerly the location of Berkshire Normal School, one sees above the rooftops of the town, a line of rolling wooded hills framing the valley farmlands. On a clear day, Mt. Greylock, sitting on the northern horizon presides over this splendor.

With the ratification of the Amendment enfranchising women five years ago, the College was renamed in honor of the great suffragette who was born in the vicinity. The push to develop the college came from local politicians who, with rare insight, were responding to a post-war change in the local economy. Entrepreneurs, many from the Albany-Troy area across the New York state line, had found a hospitable place for small manufactures and food processing. The town was growing, with a solid middle class of business and professional people and skilled workers.

Now, in the midst of a hot summer, Rosie and I are almost surprised to realize that we have been in this place a full year. We have long since gotten over our initial doubts about living in a town the size of West Goshen. Almost every moment has been a small adventure. Of course we miss visiting with our families on a regular basis. But we are both fully engaged in our starting careers. Shortly after arriving last summer, Rosie was hired to teach in the new elementary school serving families in the expanding residential neighborhood on the west edge of town. Meanwhile, as a new assistant professor, my expectations have been largely borne out. Manny Gutierrez, the Dean of Science, when he came to Columbia to recruit faculty, described it as a place "in transition and on the rise." The challenges, to teach well and to build up a research program, have been formidable. But Manny has been supportive and the students receptive. I love the teaching and feel excited about playing a role in developing an important regional institution.

Today, at midday, I returned from the lab to have lunch with Rosie. I was indulging in a luxury rarely possible during this past school year. Her school is in summer recess. As I drove up, I spotted her in the backyard of our little rental house, digging up a patch of ground for a long planned garden. Just as I opened the car door she was alongside. I gave her a hug, then held her at arm's distance and looked her. She had a pink kerchief on her head and a smudge on her cheek. "Ah, Rosie, my little farm maid," I intoned.

"More accurately, Rosie, your little warm maid," she responded. She wiped her forehead with back of her hand. "But my, you seem in good spirits."

"Au contraire, ma chérie," I said. It was forced cheeriness and my expression undoubtedly changed as I thought about the morning. "To be honest, I'm kind of frustrated and befuddled."

"Poor dear! A little lunch will do you some good, I'm sure." She pushed open the frayed screen door leading to the mud room and kicked off her shoes. I followed her into our little kitchen. Inside, some of the morning coolness lingered. Rosie removed her kerchief and washed her hands and face at the sink, while I removed lunch makings from the icebox. I checked the ice compartment to see how the latest of ice was holding up against the summer heat.

I placed butter, a bowl of lettuce, Muenster cheese, and a jar of mustard at the center of the table. I fetched a package of sliced bread from the breadbox. I wished we could buy a good kosher rye bread somewhere. Then I sat down and looked around the room. Not bad, I thought. Light and airy. Nice glassed-in cupboards. Rosie had made some red and white checkered curtains for the windows. The white wainscoting had scuffmarks from the backs of the chairs. I made a mental note that the woodwork needed painting, remembering for a moment how painting bulkheads and decks was a constant preoccupation of the sailors on our ship down at N.D.L. I had never had to take care of home repairs before, but discovered that I rather enjoyed the challenge.

"Got to fix that screen door," I said, as Rosie came to the table with a couple of plates and utensils. "Big, ugly, black flies come through. Don't want them in my soup."

"But how much soup can a fly eat?" she said, mimicking the Yiddish accent used in the vaudeville joke. "Seriously, Abe, what's happening at the lab?"

"Oh the usual arguments with Mother Nature," I replied. "She doesn't let go of her secrets very easily. When one of us is clever enough to know where to look, she creates an obstacle course, just for fun."

"If it were easy you would know all the secrets by now," Rosie said.

"Not necessarily. I suspect there are mysteries ad infinitum. But I hope I don't sound as if I'm whining. Actually, I enjoy the obstacle course. Otherwise I wouldn't be an experimentalist, you know. But it is frustrating that just when you think you've got the experiment ready to go, some technical problem crops up."

"Let me guess," Rosie said. "The vacuum system again."

"Yes. We've tried everything we can think of to find the leak: varnishes, soap film tests, illuminating gas, spark discharges. Checked the seals. Checked the stopcocks. Swore at the apparatus a little bit."

"Does that do any good?"

"No, though sometimes it makes us feel better. But we'll find that leak. It's not magic. There's a reason somewhere. Funny thing is, some days things work; then some days you think you've gone through the exact same motions and things don't work. We like to say the stars are not aligned."

"Take the rest of the day off," Rosie said. I was startled. "You've been working very hard all year. Evenings and sometimes into the early hours preparing lectures. Going into the lab on weekends. Writing up your thesis results for publication. You need a break sometimes."

"We haven't solved the problem."

"You've got a student working at the lab?" she asked. I nodded. "I'll bet you didn't say whether or not you'll be back."

"He's got plenty to do without me. I do try to give the students a sense of independence."

"Abe, I would really like to do a hike. The weather is fine. The daylight lasts long this time of the year. Give the stars a chance to line up."

I thought quietly for a while before agreeing. Rosie needed a break as well. While she cleared the table I threw a few supplies into a backpack and put them in the back of the car. Our older model candy-red Studebaker roadster was our most prized possession. One of the retiring professors sold it to us before he left campus to move to New York.

It was about a half hour drive, half of it on a dirt track, before reaching the spot where the newly declared Appalachian Trail crossed the road. Here, the trail began its ascent to our destination, a high point on the ridge above the valley. I parked the car in a little clear spot at the side of road, nicely shaded on the west by a grove of box alder. I locked up and put on the backpack. Then we set off on the path with Rosie in the lead. I was beginning to relax already.

The trail climbed gently along the edge of the mountain for about a mile and a half, passing occasionally through ghostly stands of paper birch and fragrant balsam poplars. In a couple of places, probably the site of some grown-over earth slides, there were open spaces, glowing with goldenrod. Queen Ann's lace lined the trail. Then the trail rose sharply up the mountainside in a series of switchbacks before resuming a gentler grade following the contours of the landform. The air had become warmer, except in the densely shaded spots, which almost seemed chilly by contrast.

Suddenly Rosie froze in her tracks. As I caught up she grabbed my arm. She was looking straight up the trail. In a half whisper she said, "There was this animal! Did you see it?"

I looked up the trail. "No. What was it?"

"I'd swear it was a wolf, Abe," she said softly. Her voice displayed more curiosity and excitement than alarm.

"I don't think there's been a wolf in this area for a hundred years," I replied. As I spoke, a large dog-like creature appeared a hundred yards above us coming around a bend in the path. It paused and looked in our direction. Now I could make out the creature clearly. It certainly looked like a wolf. It had a full gray-brown coat. It was hard to make out at that distance, but its slanted eyes appeared to glint with a dull blue color. We stood still, studying the creature as it took our measure.

Presently a well-built young man appeared around the turn in the trail, descending in our direction. The "wolf" turned to join him and as it did so, began to wag its tail. The pair came down the trail side-by-side to meet us. I vaguely recognized the man as a student from the College. He had a small rucksack and carried a walking stick. We started up the trail again. He smiled as we met up and spoke first. "Good afternoon,

Professor. Nice day for a hike, isn't it?"

"It certainly is," I replied. "Beautiful dog. We took him for a wolf for a moment." I noticed that indeed, he had startling gray-blue eyes. His ears, however, I thought were larger than and not as pointy as a wolf's. Of course, the only wolves I had seen were in the zoo in New York.

"Wolf mix," he replied. "Lots of German Shepherd in him also. Smart—and gentle as a kitten. But I call him 'Fang'." Fang had come up, sniffing and taking stock of us, each in turn. "Are you going to the top?" We told him it was our intention. "Well it's the day to do it," he assured us. "Gorgeous view from up there. But apart from you, I haven't seen a soul all day."

After a few more pleasantries we resumed our hike. At a spot where the trail leveled out a small stream trickled out of the woods. Next to the path, where the water ran slack in a shallow pool of crystal clear water, was a large cluster of yellow and purple monkey flowers. "Mimulus," Rosie said with some authority as she squatted down to have a closer look. "Do you see the funny little face in each of them?" I thought this was a slight stretch of someone's imagination and I had not really noticed. But I was taken with this garish display of color that was like an exclamation of vitality in this quiet corner of the forest. Rosie had been taking nature walks with one of the other faculty wives on Saturdays when I was tied up in the lab. Her newfound enthusiasm for looking closely at the details of our natural surroundings was infectious.

We stopped for a few minutes and splashed our faces in the pool of water. Despite the elevation the air temperature was still quite warm, but in the shade it felt moist and deliciously comfortable. We scooped up some water in a tin cup and quenched our thirst. I reached down for Rosie's hand and pulled her to her feet. As she came up to me I gave her a little kiss before we both turned and started back up the trail. "Off to the top," I said. I took the lead now.

Shortly the path began to climb sharply, then more gently as it paralleled the ridgeline. In about half an hour we reached a broad summit. It was a rocky place. The vegetation was mostly low shrubs giving us a view in all directions. Shading our eyes from the lowering sun, the town could be seen indistinctly alongside the river in the folds of surrounding hills. To the northwest the gray and blue shapes of the Adirondacks in New York State were just barely visible. A panorama of rolling farmland and forest stretched eastward to the horizon.

We sat down on a large rock and looked around in silence. After a while Rosie spoke. "This is such a special place, Abe. Does it have a name?" I replied that as far as knew nothing of that sort appeared on the maps. "Well," she said, "I guess it's up to us to name it. What do you think?"

Without hesitation I blurted out the first thing that came to mind. "How about Wolf Mountain?"

"Wolf Mountain it is!" she exclaimed. "I'll drink to that." I had begun rummaging in my rucksack and had withdrawn a jar of fruit juice. "It's a little warm in the sun, though. Maybe we can find some shade."

On the edge of the clearing I could make out a very faint deer track in the high grasses. It led past a thicket of low sassafras trees into a grove of mixed deciduous trees bordering the summit on its eastern flank. I picked up the rucksack and Rosie and I followed the faint trail for about a hundred yards where it ended at an open grassy bench. I took out a light blanket and spread it out in the shade of a young white oak tree at the upper edge of the open spot. We sat down beside each other.

Poking around in the rucksack I pulled out a package of biscuits. I again found the jar of fruit juice. I filled a couple of tin cups and handed one to Rosie. Holding my cup in one hand I raised the biscuits with the other like an offering and recited:

> Here with a Loaf of Bread beneath the Bough,
> A Flask of Wine, a Book of Verse . . .

"Imagine the book of verse," I said.

"Also imagine the wine. But juice will do," Rosie said. We touched rims and had a sip. I continued:

> and Thou—
> Beside me singing in the Wilderness—

Rosie finished, improvising a tune that reminded me of *America the Beautiful:*

> And Wilderness is Paradise enow.

I thought about how lovely her voice was. We each had a biscuit and finished the juice. Lying on my back and looking up at the sky.

I felt as if I could see forever. Of course the physicist in me knew that I wasn't seeing beyond the blue light being Rayleigh-scattered in the atmosphere. 'Forget physics,' I reminded myself. Rosie lay next to me on her side. Presently I asked, "Happy?"

Her eyes were closed, but she answered me. "In paradise," she said. My eyelids grew heavy.

When I awoke the sky had lost much of its brightness. The moon had begun to rise above the treetops. I turned my head toward Rosie. Her head was propped up on her bent arm and she was looking at me. "I wonder how long we were asleep?" she asked softly. She answered herself. "No matter." She reached over and we grasped hands.

Then we made delicious love.

Afterwards, we lay quietly for long time in a light embrace, looking up at the sky and the moon. Finally Rosie spoke. "Abie, the sky creatures could see everything we did."

I was amused. "We were beneath a bough—remember?"

"But you know what?" she said. She was grinning "I don't care." She stood up and straightened her clothes. It was time to go. I folded the blanket and put away the provisions. Before we started off down the trail I drew her into my arms and kissed her lightly. My love was overflowing.

The trail was easily seen in the twilight. We paused briefly at the spring and drank from its cool sweetness. Out in the darkness, the high-pitched throaty *woot-witt* of a whippoorwill repeated three times in succession. The daylight was gone when we reached the car. Driving home, the moon followed along beside us, sliding sometimes behind the trees and casting a white sheen over all.

1926

Nine months after our excursion to Wolf Mountain, almost to the day, Rosie gave birth to a strapping boy we named Jason.

When Rosie's water broke, we were already packed up and prepared for the drive to the hospital in Pittsfield. The weather had been looking threatening so we wasted no time. She sat in the seat beside me, resting her head on my shoulder. It was a cool spring day and I tucked a thick car rug around her. In the hospital the pains began in earnest. I sat beside her bed for a day and a night, holding her hands, breathing with her, trying to empathize with the agony of each spasm as if I could draw some of it into my own body. But when delivery was imminent the doctor and nurses expelled me, protesting, to a waiting room. I paced about with worry and fatigue, wondering why I could not be with Rosie. Did the doctor think I would be in the way or critical of his performance, or perhaps faint dead away on the floor of the delivery room?

The baby arrived vocal, alert, and wide-eyed. I knew that he was only beginning to process the curious images being sent to his newly awakened brain, yet I was swept up in imagining the power and potential of this new life I held in my arms. The sense of awe suffused with love that I felt caught me by surprise.

———

1929

Three years after Jason's birth, baby sister, Esther, arrived. She was named for her recently departed Belgian great-aunt. It seems that the medical people had become surprisingly enlightened. I was with Rosie throughout and witnessed my daughter's first breath and her first cry. I saw her swaddled for the first time and I gave over the tiny bundle into Rosie's arms for the first time.

When I think about those moments the word "miracle" rises to mind. Yet it is a word I normally renounce. Not a miracle I remind myself, but a manifestation of the great and marvelous mystery in which I am embedded. I am filled with gratitude and a sense of immense privilege.

CHAPTER 21

Vital Mystery

1930

On a weekday evening in March, just after I had tucked Esther in for the night and was getting ready to spend an evening preparing my lectures, I received a telephone call.

"Dr. Roth?" the caller asked. He had a mild baritone voice with a distinctly New England flavor.

"That's correct," I replied. Jason was galloping around the house, emitting war whoops, and stopping only momentarily to grab me around the knees. "Pardon me for a moment. There seems to be a wild Indian on the loose here," I explained. Rosie appeared from the kitchen and scooped Jason up and carried him away.

"This is Carl Becker. I think we met briefly at a town meeting last year. I'm the minister at the Unitarian church. Do you have a few minutes, Doctor?"

"Yes, yes, I remember. Of course I have a little time. But please call me Abe." I easily recalled meeting him. He was a pleasant looking fellow of about my age. I had been struck by his relative youth. My image of the clergy was undoubtedly colored by the appearance of rabbis I had known. Many tended to look grave and ripened beyond their actual years, especially the bearded among them. Even the Unitarian minister whose service I had attended in Washington, though clean-shaven, was an older, gray-headed gentleman.

"Yes, of course. And please call me Carl. I'm sorry to bother you in the midst of 'night riots', as we refer to them at our house. I hope you're well. I called to ask a favor of you."

"No trouble, Carl," I replied. "What can I do for you?"

"We have a social group here at the church. It generally meets on the first Wednesday of each month. There's a little lunch and a speaker and discussion before the group launches into a business session and various service projects for the afternoon. I hoped I might I interest you in being our speaker next month."

As he spoke I glanced quickly at the appointment calendar that was laid out on the hall table alongside the telephone. "Sure. I think I could arrange that. After all, it's part of the job description. Does the group have anything specific in mind?"

"I suppose I should add that there is no stipend. But, of course, lunch is on the house." Carl sounded a little embarrassed, and I hastened to reassure him.

"Really. I wouldn't think of any compensation. Consider it to be my pleasure. But again, what might I talk about?"

"Relativity." He said this with an inflection that straddled the line between declarative and interrogative. He appeared to be unsure whether this was an unreasonable suggestion. "The group tries to work some science into their programs along with literature and philosophy, among other topics." He chuckled slightly as he added, "They leave religion to me. Anyway, this time they seem to have elected relativity."

"I don't think there's a problem. Although in a limited amount of time I couldn't be expected to go deep. But perhaps I should first learn more about the group."

"They call themselves, The Alliance. Actually they trace themselves back almost a hundred years to a group of ladies who came out here from the Boston area with their families and decided a Unitarian church was needed in town. It was a pretty progressive movement that was blossoming in America at the time, particularly in New England. I don't know how much you known about Unitarians."

I explained that I had some familiarity with the Unitarians. I thought it best to explain that Rosie and I both came from Jewish backgrounds, but pretty much lived a secular life style. Carl responded by commenting that, in fact, Judaism and Unitarianism were remarkably compatible, but that this was besides the point with respect to talking to The Alliance.

"The original group was The Ladies' Sewing Circle, and they raised much of the money for our original building by selling needlework in the vicinity. Eventually they became The Women's Alliance. When the nineteenth amendment was ratified in 1920, the ladies admitted the men, who had, for the most part, been strong supporters of the suffrage movement. Of course, men rarely show up at the meetings. That is, until recently when so many of them are out of work or have only part-time jobs."

"That's interesting," I said. "But I should have a feel for the level at which to pitch a talk."

"Generally speaking, they're a pretty astute group of people. Many even have college degrees, though probably not in science and math. They're eclectic in their tastes. I quite enjoy meeting with them when I have time."

"Good. It's the kind of challenge I enjoy in teaching. Science, even relativity, doesn't necessarily have to be entirely technical. Besides, I would suppose I shouldn't do anything that would take much more than an hour, and that puts constraints on how much detail is possible." We ended the conversation settling on a date and time.

I met Carl just before noon on a gorgeous, though chilly, spring day in his cramped office at the back of the Unitarian church. The building was a pleasant wooden structure located just off the main street. It appeared to be of turn-of-the-century vintage, all white shiplap siding, with a modest steeple. There was no ornamentation, crosses, or other symbolism evident. It was New England severe, yet welcoming in appearance.

Before we went downstairs to the basement meeting hall, Carl explained that he would have to leave the meeting at some point to make a pastoral visit to an ill congregant, but would return by the end of the question period. He wanted to know if I might join him for coffee afterwards. My Wednesday schedule is usually flexible. So, motivated at least partly by curiosity, I accepted his invitation.

We went down a rear stairway, then through a couple of rooms that appeared to be classrooms for younger children, dimly lit by transom windows high on the walls. A pair of double doors led into a large, brightly lit open room supported here and there by iron pillars. Several ladies in aprons were arranging chairs around a cluster of bridge tables set in front of a podium. A portable blackboard had been put near the podium as I had requested. One lady was in the kitchen area at the back of the room stirring a huge kettle. The place smelt like the vegetable chicken soup Rosie liked to make on winter weekends. Carl left me to look over my notes while he went about the room speaking with the ladies and greeting new arrivals as they came through the main entrance to the room.

At about a quarter past twelve one of the ladies at the front table at which I was seated rose and called the meeting to order. There were perhaps thirty-five people, predominantly women. A few men were scattered among several tables towards the rear. Carl, seated next to me, rose to the podium and delivered a very simple grace honoring the blessings of food, companionship and love, and reminding us to not forget the needs of those in want. Several ladies appeared and served bowls of soup and distributed baskets of warm freshly baked bread. After a while Carl rose again to introduce me and then retreated to a seat at the back of the hall.

It was my intention to be as non-technical, yet as scientifically correct as I knew how. With respect to Einstein, I hoped to point out that his reputation for speaking out in favor of liberty, free expression and social progress was almost to be expected in view of the way he approached physics. His greatness was not due to his ability to think in old ways better than anyone else, but to challenge the old ways and to ask seemingly impertinent questions. Also I hoped to emphasize that his brilliance did not come from an unusual ability to manipulate complex mathematics. In fact the core of his thinking was hardly mathematical at all, but very physical—often couched in terms of what he termed *gedanken experimente,* thought experiments. I would try to avoid almost all mathematics in my talk.

I began by pointing out that, in fact, the idea of relativity is a very old principle recognized as far back as the days of Isaac Newton. If we to be in a sealed and quiet moving railway car, we shouldn't be able to tell by performing experiments whether we were at rest or in steady motion with respect to the world outside the car. If we dropped a marble inside the car, it would seem to drop straight down, for example, just as if we were on solid ground outside. The problem with relativity arises when we try to explain experiments with light, a phenomenon rooted in the physics of electricity and magnetism, rather than in mechanics. The laws governing such phenomena, formulated by Maxwell almost seventy years ago, predict that we could tell if we were in relative motion by doing optical experiments. That turns out never to have been shown by any experiment. Even the famous Michelson-Morley experiment, in which beams of light were observed at different times of the year, failed to show changes in the value of the speed of light. This is despite the fact that the earth is in rapid motion in various directions throughout the year. For experiments like that, the earth serves as our swiftly moving railway car.

I went on to explain that no attempt to fix the laws of electricity and magnetism could account for these results. Moreover many physicists were uncomfortable with the fantastical idea of a hypothetical medium through which light waves move, the *ether.* Mechanical arguments suggested that the ether would have to be at once as rigid as steel and as unsubstantial as a vacuum. Einstein's famous thought-experiment was to imagine what would be observed if we were to ride along with a beam of light. From this he realized that we have to be very careful about the fundamentals of measuring both time intervals and distances, that is, we must carefully reconsider how we use clocks and rulers. The notion of motion relative to some medium was unnecessary; the ether was superfluous.

Einstein reached surprising conclusions. A railroad car moving past us should be a tiny bit shorter when measured with our own "stationary" ruler than when measured with the same ruler carried aboard the train. Paradoxically observers in the "moving" train would determine that we and our surroundings seem to have shrunk. Moreover the clocks aboard the moving train would appear to tick more slowly compared to our own, but in turn the "moving" passengers would observe that our clocks are slower than theirs.

"Admittedly, this is hard to grasp," I was obliged to say. "Even seasoned physicists sometimes get turned around in thinking about the subject. But I need to add that there is nothing to the notion one sometimes hears, which is that hardly anyone understands the subject of relativity. Certainly, at the outset, only one person understood—Einstein himself—but as soon as he published his ideas many physicists understood. It was a case where a new idea suddenly laid a whole range of confusions to rest.

"A few die-hard, old-fashioned physicists had to admit their discomfort. A few never signed on. Oliver Lodge, a very influential British physicist, even built an enormous and expensive iron flywheel in a vain attempt to stir up and observe an 'ether wind.' It is interesting that Lodge also was an ardent believer in psychic phenomena. However, almost immediately, better physicists embraced Einstein's insights. It was like a fireball of illumination coming from a spark of one man's lucidity and inspiration."

Before opening the floor to questions I emphasized that these relativity effects are ordinarily very small but have profound implications in some areas. For example it is the basis for explaining where all the energy of the sun and stars come from.

Towards the end of the question and answer session I saw that Carl had slipped back into the room. Eventually the chairwoman took the podium to announce that there were a few more items on the agenda for the afternoon. Before Carl came forward to add a gracious note of thanks, I invited anyone who is interested to call or visit me at the College. Then Carl and I made our way up the back stairway to his office.

He motioned me to a deep comfortable chair in a corner beside the window and went to the opposite corner where he switched on the electric hot plate beneath a big blue enameled coffee pot. I looked around the room. Behind the desk the wall was covered by bookshelves almost to the ceiling. The room was not well lit so I could not easily make out many of the titles in Carl's library, but it did seem from the fine bindings and gilt lettering on some of the books that he had inherited part of the collection from his predecessors. Several piles of papers and some books lay on his desk. Beneath the window was an electric room heater. It appeared to be the only source of heat.

Carl went to a cupboard and took out a couple of plates of the apple crumble that the gathering had been eating while I gave my talk. While he did so he commented, "I don't suppose I ever mentioned that my undergraduate degree was in physics." He was watching my expression as he handed me a plate. "Does that surprise you?"

I briefly reflected on the question before replying. "Perhaps so. But then again it shouldn't surprise me. We like to think that physics is a good background for almost any profession. That is, it trains in critical thinking. And one could argue that physics is kind of a philosophical subject."

"Yes. That's how I think about it," he said. "I really enjoyed physics, but then I began to think I wanted to be more immersed in the day-to-day issues of people's lives. A short period of service in the army gave me time to think about my choices. After the war I returned to Harvard to finish up the degree before I went after a master's in philosophy. I ended up in divinity school."

"You studied physics at Harvard? Did you know Rick Thayer?" I asked.

Carl was retrieving a couple of coffee mugs from a shelf. He turned around. "Rick Thayer? You know Rick?" He seemed delighted. "I've wondered from time to time what became of him."

I explained how I had gotten to know Rick at the Naval Defense Lab. I told him about going to All Souls' Church with him. Carl commented that this was one of the more influential Unitarian congregations in the country. He was interested to learn that Rick decided to stay with the Navy work, finishing his degree on the side at George Washington University.

"I guess I'm not astounded. I always thought Rick was a "do-er"—sort of an adventurous spirit. Good company, too." Carl put down a mug of coffee by the side of his chair and brought out a can of condensed milk. It reminded me of the coffee "cream" aboard ship. "It's nice we have that connection, Abe," he said. "But to change the subject, I was wondering how the question and answer session went. I'm sorry I wasn't there for that."

"Altogether there were a number of good questions, mostly asking me to clarify some point or other I had made in my discussion. One the men wondered if there was a mistake in one of the diagrams. A lady told us how she had seen Einstein being cheered at the Metropolitan Opera in New York a few months ago. All in all I don't know if I was entirely convincing, but I think we all enjoyed the discussion." I paused for a while before I added, "There was one question, though, which I wasn't sure I could answer very well."

"And that was—?" Carl was now sitting opposite me, leaning back in his desk chair, his mug cupped in both hands.

"One lady asked me what the practical use of all this was. I suppose I could have offered a list of the marvels in the way of practical conveniences that physics and chemistry have already made possible. Perhaps, in the future, Einstein's insights might lead to new sources of energy, perhaps better materials. I alluded to all of that. But my answer really was about humility. About how, as we come closer to a deeper understanding of the great mysteries, our humanness is enhanced."

Carl looked thoughtful. He took a sip of coffee. Then he asked, "Tell me, Abe. As a physicist what would you say the greatest mystery is?"

"In idle moments I've asked myself that question," I replied. Then I hesitated, wondering whether my answer would be clear. "I think the greatest mystery is why there is something, rather than nothing."

"Do you mean empty space with nothing in it?" he asked.

"That would be a mystery also," I replied. "But I mean more than that. Why is there space—and time? The astronomers talk about an expanding universe. Extrapolating that back in time one might think that there was a zero time when there was nothing. No space, no time—just a point, a singularity." I was glad that I felt free to use some of the rarified vocabulary that physicists throw about.

"And nothing existed?"

"Well, nothing except perhaps the potential for something—an abstract potential," I answered.

I was feeling some unease in straying from the safe ground of verifiable science. But Carl seemed mildly delighted with my response. "We 'men of the cloth' might be tempted to call that God. But I'm curious; do you have anything better to offer than giving this a name, as we do?"

"If I had a good answer, I would be very famous," I replied. "The best I can offer is to say that somehow existence may be inevitable, like the rules of mathematics. It is hard to imagine that in another kind of universe two plus two would not be four. Maybe there could be a different kind of geometry, maybe more—or fewer—dimensions. But the mathematics would make sense to us. It's kind of a Platonic notion, I guess, that all is—or at least like—mathematics. The existence of the universe just cannot not be."

"That is where you diverge from the traditional notion of God. That God may be the potential for creation, but He is free to will—or not to will—creation. But I really like your answer to my presumptuous question. I'm making a mental note of it," he said with a twinkle. "Always on the lookout for sermon material."

"Yes," I said, warming to the pleasantness of the exchange. "This physicist's God, if you will, apparently does not have free will." I thought for a moment, my mood dampening a bit as I weighed whether the next comment I was tempted to make would sound conceited. But I went on. "I have to say that I often think that rather than God having created us, we have, in fact, created God."

"Or gods," Carl added. "But tell me, Abe, does that make God any less real?"

"I tend to tread lightly in the halls of philosophy, but I should be able to venture an answer from the standpoint of an experimental physicist. From that point of view God must be a testable hypothesis—testable by independent observers. And—" I continued with emphasis, "must remain a hypothesis subject always to the possibility of being disproved."

"What test might you suggest?" Carl asked.

"One test might be in the power of prayer. But I'm reminded of the recent news story of a little girl from a very Orthodox Jewish family who wandered into the woods. Her family looked for her the rest of the day and into the night calling her name repeatedly. When she was found the next morning she was asked why she didn't hear them calling. Her reply? 'I was so busy praying.' So much for the efficacy of prayer."

"So perhaps one could say that prayer may be a bad test for one kind of god, and a good test for another kind of god," Carl commented. "Tell me this. Do you believe in the reality of atoms?"

"Yes. I do. It's a hypothesis that has been tested over and over again."

"But a hypothesis. Subject to disproof—or modification," Carl added.

"That's right. No one can actually get their heads wrapped completely around the concept of atoms, but we have simplistic models of what we mean by them. It's all very useful." It was clear that Carl understood this, but I enjoyed keeping up the dialectic.

"Ah—'useful.' That's the key word," Carl added. "Do you have a useful concept of God, Abe?"

My hands were palm-to-palm, forefingers pressed against my lips. I pondered the question for a while. Finally I said, "I'm sure my father does. But frankly I can't quite conceptualize it. Some ineffable thing. Indescribable, beyond human understanding."

"But useful," Carl ventured.

"Yes, undoubtedly." I paused. "For him, and undoubtedly for his forebears."

"Therefore real—at least for them. I don't mean to be intrusive, Abe, but I'm curious." He repeated his question. "What about you? Answer or not as you wish."

"I'm working on it. For the time being I think of the great mystery I mentioned to that lady this afternoon who asked about the usefulness of knowing about relativity." I thought a bit. "Yes, it's what I had said to her. It's about humility. About having perspective. Humbleness. Awe. I'm not sure exactly how to put it."

"That's a real God, I would say." Carl was looking thoughtful. We sat in silence for a while. Then I looked at my watch and realized I was expected at home.

Carl thanked me again for meeting with the Alliance. He made it clear that I should feel free to call him if he could be of any use. I promised I would give his regards to Rick Thayer if I saw him at a physics meeting or elsewhere.

Outside the weather had turned mild. The promise of spring was evident in the small, pale green buds on the tips of the maple branches. Crocuses were showing in the sunnier parts of the flower bed surrounding the church.

CHAPTER 22

The Eternal Now

1933

The phone call had come in the middle of the night towards the end of June. It was the local operator connecting us with a call from New York. Brother Dave was on the line. Sleep evaporated into a kind of dread. Oddly, I found myself thinking of how remarkable it was that we could communicate so readily over these many miles of mountains and rivers that lay between us.

"Abe, how are you?" Dave hesitated. "No, no. That's inane. Obviously I wouldn't call at this hour just to find out how you were. It's about Father. I had thought about waiting until morning but I wanted to be sure to reach you." Actually I didn't know what time of night it was. I looked across the dimly lit living room. The mantle clock read 11:30. I saw Rosie in the opening to the dining room. She was barefoot in her nightie, leaning against the archway.

"It's O.K., Dave. What about Father?"

"I'm afraid he's gone, Abe. This evening. I found out about it a few hours ago. I came down to Brooklyn right away. The super in the building is letting me use his phone."

"What happened, Dave? Is Mother O.K.?" I asked. I sat down on the edge of the easy chair. A light early summer breeze came in through an open window. I felt chilled.

"Mother's all right. Celia and Sari are with her. Soon after Father returned from the synagogue he collapsed. Mother hurried down to the super's apartment and he called the doctor, but it was too late. The good part is that he didn't seem to have suffered."

It was hard to take in this news. I had never felt especially close to Father, but he had been a constant presence, even in his physical absence. I was like an amputee who looks down to see his hand and is amazed to find it gone.

"What can I do?" I asked. It was Friday night. Our plans for the coming week passed in quick review through my mind. There were a couple of students who needed to be started on their summer projects. A journal article had just arrived for peer review. Rosie was helping organize a summer day camp with some of the other women. She was just beginning summer classes in the School of Education.

Dave had thought out exactly what needed to be done. "The main thing is for you and Rosie to get down here by Sunday morning. I managed to find the rabbi. The funeral is scheduled for noon. It's a good thing tomorrow is shabbas—that gives you an extra day to get here. Do you think you'll bring the kids? We can squeeze you all in—at least temporarily. Celia has offered her place as well."

"I'll talk to Rosie about the kids." She had snuck off momentarily to the rear bedroom and was now putting a light blanket around my shoulders. She was drawing in the robe she had slipped into. I looked up at her and mouthed 'Father died.' I continued, "I'll phone you about our plans. Can you manage to be at your phone, say at noon tomorrow?"

After we hung up I recounted everything Dave had told me. Rosie agreed we would figure out the details of our trip in the morning. There was little point in trying to make decisions this late at night. We knew that we had plenty of time to get to New York the next day. But we had to think out whether or not Jason and Esther were up to the experience. And we had to let various people know that we would be out of town.

We turned off the light and went back to bed. We lay in each other's arms for a while in the darkness until I heard Rosie yawn. Then we lay side by side. I had supposed I would fall asleep thinking out whether the kids should go to the funeral and about the options for getting to New York. But I put those thoughts aside as I watched the moonlight creep across the foot of the bed. I remembered the time so long ago when I felt such awe at being told by Dave that the same moon, which was shining down on me, was also shining down on Father far, far away in that magical place called America. At the time I had only a vague recollection of Father, but I wondered if he also knew that that same moon was shining down on me. I never had an answer to that. Now I never would.

In the light of morning it became easy to decide that Jason, a bit over 7 years old, and Esther three years younger, should go with us, if for no other reason than for their grandma's sake. We took the car over to Albany. Then, if only to skirt a 150-mile battle with kids' carsickness, we boarded the train for the remainder of the trip. The train always delighted the children. In clouded memory I knew it had delighted me when I was Jason's age. By Saturday evening we were at Dave and Dolly's apartment in Manhattan. The young cousins quickly fell into play. It was hard to tell how they were conceptualizing their grandpa's death. For the time being, it seemed, it was an abstraction. But we were apprehensive about their reactions to the funeral.

Sunday morning Dave and I took the subway into Brooklyn to the funeral home to meet with the rabbi. Mother, Celia, and Sari were there. Rosie, Dolly, and the children were to follow later in Dave's car. Before burial, there was to be a brief service there. After conferring with Mother, Dave and I ordered that the casket be closed during the service.

A beefy young man fairly bursting out of his dark suit and exuding an air of self-importance ushered several of us into the viewing room before the lid was put down. Mother had never seemed so tired. She took my arm, leaning heavily on me. I realized how small she had become. None of us said a word. I looked at the face in the casket and thought against my will, 'This is not he.' Of course it was he. The cosmeticians, carrying out their mission to transform the deceased, obliterated the person in favor of a youthful caricature. I was appalled at myself when I realized that it was only this minor annoyance that had evoked a strong emotion—not his death, not the departure of a man who had taken my hand and showed me proudly to his friends at the synagogue. This man who, for my Bar Mitzvah, had scraped together spare change to buy me the most beautiful prayer book he could find—bound with brass edged covers, decorated sheets of ivory and gilded brass filigrees—was gone. The book remained dusty and unused on a high shelf at home. And yet, not a tear rose up in my eyes.

A half dozen of Father's cronies crowded into the little chapel with us for a short ceremony. Afterwards we wedged into the limousines forming a procession behind the hearse. As we moved into the neighborhoods beyond Brownsville, I thought about how long it had been since Jacob and I had made our expeditions into the farmland of New Lots and East New York. Here and there were some open fields, but mostly there were now row after row of homes crowded in upon one another, each with its small backyard, each with its brick stoop, and clusters of children in the side streets. The day was growing warm. Every window in our limousine was rolled down. It was a long way to the edge of Queens. Esther sat on my lap and Jason leaned against me; I told them stories about how Uncle Jacob, the one who had been hurt in the war, and I would wander the country roads here, reaching through the fencing to pick a tomato or stuffing our pockets with apples that had fallen on the roadside.

We emerged from the car in a dazzling patch of sun and retreated to the shade of a tree as the funeral party reassembled. Then, in groups of three or four, we all moved slowly up the roadway behind the hearse until we reached the gate of the cemetery plot reserved for the Young Friends Fraternal Alliance. I tried to imagine this group of elderly men when they were in their prime, fresh from the old country, meeting in the back room of some synagogue to found the Alliance. Very likely it had provided only the slimmest kind of security in the face of economic crisis, a function better assured in the long run by the ward bosses of New York. But now it was serving its ultimate purpose, to assure a final resting place in sanctified ground. We gathered around the grave, men to one side, women to the other. Mother, looking tiny but composed, stood with Celia and Sari.

When it came time to recite the Kaddish the rabbi placed himself between Dave and me. Perhaps he anticipated that I would need some prompting.

"Yisgadal, v'yiskadash, sh'may rabbor . . . ."

I knew that my rudimentary knowledge of Hebrew was not entirely useful in interpreting the words. This was Aramaic, the popular language of the time of the Second Temple. I had looked at the translation ahead of time: 'Extolled and hallowed be his great Name . . . .' Why was it in the vernacular, in fact the language of Jesus, not in the Hebrew of the Torah and the other prayers? I put aside these distracting thoughts, entranced instead by the somber lilt of the second paragraph.

"Yishborach, v'yishtabach, v'yispoar, v'yisromam, v'yisnasay,
v'yishador,
V'yishaleh, v'yishallal sh'may d'Kudshor, b'riech Hu . . . ."

'Blessed, praised and glorified, exalted, extolled and honored, adored and lauded be the name of the Holy One, blessed be He . . . .' It was an odd thing. The meaning of the words suddenly ceased to matter. Explanation was beside the point. This was not a prayer beseeching personal favors, nor promising personal goodness. It did not ask for intercession for the deceased. It seemed no more than an assertion of the greatest humility, a confession of awe in the face of the great mystery, a recognition of a power that surpassed understanding. And its only plea was peace for all Israel, and then only as an afterthought. 'There's been little peace for Israel,' I thought.

In the weeks that followed I found myself reflecting from time to time on the funeral. Did I need an ancient ritual to bolster a sense of humility? Did I need repetitive reading of ancient texts in alien languages to reinforce a sense of awe in the great mystery? Did I need tradition to come to grips with loss? I had no doubt that there was a spiritual side to my being—a desire to be in touch with the ultimate. I saw that in Rosie as well. But what I was pondering, I came to realize, was whether organized religion was required in all of this. I reached no conclusions, but through it all was the enveloping question: if religion had a role to play, need it be so defined, so prescribed, and most significantly, so ethnically bounded as that which I had inherited?

But actually, there was little time for such rumination during the summer. Almost weekly I traveled to Brooklyn to help settle Mother's situation. I was teaching in the summer program most mornings and spent afternoons in the lab. Rosie was busy with day camp and with her course work. Towards the end of August it was abundantly clear that we needed a break before the beginning of the fall semester. On a warm Saturday morning towards the end of the month we put the load of camping gear that had been accumulating near the front door into the trunk of the car, tucked Jason and Esther into the rear seat among an assortment of bags containing clothes, books, and groceries, and headed for the Adirondacks in upstate New York.

The road was familiar as far as Albany, and then turned northwest into terra incognita. At Schenectady the road paralleled the Mohawk River. Rosie found a copy of *The Last of the Mohicans* among our books and began to read to the children. Jason clung to every word; Esther soon became bored and nodded off to sleep. I was thankful that Rosie had no trouble reading in the jostling car. In mid-afternoon we found a grassy spot along the road. We opened a jar of lemonade and found the cookies. While Rosie played a threesome game of catch with the kids I had a little nap. Near Herkimer a smaller road turned north as a shortcut around the city of Utica. Then, near the village of Poland, we found a so-called motor-hotel—a row of tiny cabins, each furnished with two big beds, an electric hot plate for cooking, and a little attached bathroom. For the children this was high adventure. After supper we sat by the door of the cabin on the lawn facing the edge of the surrounding woods. Rosie read to the children. I allowed my mind to wander over the events of the summer. But my family was with me in this pretty place and the tension began to lift.

The next day, in the middle of the afternoon, we found a perfect campsite on the edge of Eighth Lake in the Fulton Chain of Lakes. We set up a couple of tents at the edge of the woods bordering the lake. In front of the tents was a fire pit with a cooking grate. We put up a folding card table to one side and brought out a couple of folding lawn chairs. I dragged over a short log for extra seating. Then Jason and I set out to look for firewood.

Supper was sumptuous: some small steaks done directly over hot coals, baked beans, and sliced tomatoes. Rosie had packed away a tin of cupcakes for desert. Afterwards, as the day cooled, we took a walk on a path to the end of the lake where a brook, flowing from Seventh Lake, entered. 'What a curious thing to give these lakes these unimaginative names,' I thought. But then again, I realized, it had never seemed curious to me that major streets in Manhattan are called by the ordinal numbers—or, for that matter, that we physicists had named the main components of radioactivity alpha, beta, and gamma. At a small cove not far from our camp, a cluster of mallards glided in close to shore. The metallic green head and bright yellow bill of the male was unmistakable in the subdued evening light. Esther was delighted and intrigued as they dabbled for food in the shallows, their heads emerging as dry as when they went under. At the end of the lake we found the stream we had been seeking. Then we hurriedly made our way back to camp after promising the children that we would return the next day to look for crawdads.

It was not yet dark on the following evening when the children, weary from an exciting day of swimming, splashing and exploring, were more than willing to crawl into their sleeping bags for the night. Rosie had finished putting the food back in the car for safekeeping and had pulled the chairs close to our small cooking fire when I emerged from the kids' tent. I had been reading to them another installment of *The Last of the Mohicans*. I was not certain whether Esther was taking in the story, but she seemed intrigued by the wilderness settings. Jason, on the other hand, had been intent on the plot until I saw his eyes flutter in weariness. Soon both of the kids were fast asleep.

Before taking a seat by the fire, I put a couple of small dry logs on the coals. As I sat down next to Rosie, she handed me a little cup of brandy. We sat quietly looking into the fire. The woods on the further shore formed a black silhouette against a faintly pink cloudless sky. We had both pulled on sweaters to guard against the evening chill that drifted in from the forest behind us. Rosie broke the silence. "I keep turning over in my mind all that has gone on this summer," she began. She said this in a detached tone of voice, her eyes never leaving the dancing firelight.

"I know. It has been hard to take it all in," I replied.

"My mind returns from time to time to the funeral." She paused for a few moments. "Abe, do you think about death?"

The question startled me. Rosie is normally such a cheery, upbeat person. "Naturally," I replied. "From time to time. But I don't think I dwell on it. Why? Is the idea bothering you?"

She reached out and put her hand on my arm reassuringly. "Not exactly. I can't say I'm afraid of death. But I haven't come to grips with the idea of nothingness."

"That's the downside of being rational. If you were a bit more gullible or maybe a committed Christian you would be relishing the thought of lolling about for eternity among the clouds playing on your harp." We both chuckled. "It's a nice idea if you can buy it."

"Some like to assert that religion has been invented because of our awareness of the inevitability of death. But I can't see, apart from naïve concepts of heaven and hell, exactly what role religion plays in that. I'm not even sure how Judaism approaches death."

"It's a bit foggy for me as well," I admitted. "I believe there is mention here and there in the old Jewish liturgy of a life to come. But it may simply refer to the life of generations to come. Otherwise I don't think much is made of it. Certainly no clouds or harps. I'm no expert of course, but I did pay some attention to the translation of the Kaddish before I had to recite it at the funeral. It says nothing whatsoever about an afterlife or the soul of the departed."

"Which doesn't help my thinking very much," Rosie said. "The best I can come up with is to not worry about it. Live a good life and if there is a heaven so much the better."

"I have to admit that I used to fret a bit about how to think about one's own death—this rushing towards the inevitable abyss. But recently I find myself very much at peace with the idea. No new revelation—just a different perspective." I felt a little self-conscious. "But it's a bit peculiar, perhaps."

"A different perspective. What do you mean, Abe? I'm curious."

I got up and stirred the fire. "As I said, it's peculiar. I'm not certain I can frame it in words very well. But I can at least say what kind of thinking led me to this perspective." As I sat down I added, "That is, if you're willing to put up with some quasi-physics talk."

"I did say I'm curious."

"Well," I began, taking a sip of brandy. "It was last year—I think it was when we were on that hike on the Appalachian Trail at the end of the summer. I was lollygagging in the rear of the group, just letting my mind wander."

"You do that, I've noticed. Having great thoughts I like to say."

"Well, not necessarily 'great'. More like free-form processing."

"I do that in the bath. Each one to his taste," Rosie said. "But I interrupt." She patted my arm.

"As I was saying, I was thinking about some of the things that have been happening in astronomy over the last dozen years or so. Actually the beginnings of the story probably go back to Slipher before the World War. The gist of the idea now is that the universe is expanding, getting bigger all the time. All the galaxies, and probably everything else scattered around among the galaxies are flying apart from each other at tremendous speeds." I saw Rosie instinctively raise her eyes to the heavens as if she could see this motion. Of course she knew that isn't possible.

I went on. "The most interesting thing about all of this is that if everything is flying apart, then at some time in the past all of the stuff in the universe must have been at one spot—a place of origin at the beginning of time. Even Einstein, who had long clung to the idea of an infinitely old, static universe, now admits that there probably was a beginning."

"A moment of creation. Just as in the Bible," Rosie added.

"Yes. Only in Genesis, God sets it all up. And it doesn't conjecture about what set God up in the first place—at a time before there was a universe. In the exploding universe scenario there is no 'before'. Time was created at the moment of its birth. But this is a digression. God is quite beside the point here.

"Anyway, what I was thinking about was what one might imagine will happen in the distant future. Each bit of matter in the universe is attracted to every other bit by gravity, so maybe this expansion will eventually stop and reverse—the universe will contract on itself until everything falls back to one point as it was originally. After that? Maybe the whole expansion thing would start over again there and then. Maybe the universe has been blowing up then crunching down an infinite number of times already.

"But I hasten to add that this is mostly unsuppressed, perhaps irresponsible, speculation. Freedom of the trail thinking. And I'm sure it's not original with me. And there is no evidence for any of it except the currently observed expansion."

I stopped speaking and looked towards Rosie to see if I was boring her. "Do go on, Abe" Rosie said.

"All of this brought me to think about what the world would be like during a great collapse of everything—or even during the next explosion of everything. Now comes the fanciful part. Maybe it would look exactly like it does now. Maybe we—you and me—have existed an infinite number of times. It's a crazy idea—but that's what you can get if you let your mind run out of control. And who's to say that it isn't true?"

"Do you mean everything would run backwards at some point?" Rosie interjected. "The smoke and flames here would be going down into the fire instead of rising up out of it?"

"That's the hard part to grasp. No. I don't think it could ever be that way," I responded. "The human mind could never perform its function if it perceived a result before the cause. The laws of thermodynamics would have to look the same—chaos arising from order, not the other way around. Of course it's easier to picture the world repeating during the next expansion—but even then there's nothing to say it would be exactly the same each time. But then again, who's to say it would not?

"The important point, I began to realize, is that however it might happen—assuming identical reincarnations of the universe—the beings inhabiting it would perceive each reincarnation as a one-time event. Even in a scenario of an imploding universe where, in a sense, we perceived time 'backwards'—." I held up a pair of fingers on each hand to simulate a pair of quotation marks. "Even then everything would seem to be simply the here and now—like the two of us sitting here in front of the campfire."

"So now I know what ethereal thoughts you're having back at the end of the line," Rosie said with a look both puzzled and amused. "I thought maybe you were thinking about how to get the back porch rebuilt."

"Yes—that too. A lot of mundane stuff, or the family, or politics, or—"

Rosie interrupted. "I'm sorry to have gotten you off track, Abe. You were talking about a perspective on life and death."

"Don't fret. I needed to be brought back down to earth." I paused to take in the moment. With my most precious loved ones in this circle of light within the dark forest. I felt utterly content.

"But do go on," Rosie said after a few moments.

I continued. "The main thing about all this is that now I find myself regarding my life not exactly as a singular occurrence in time—blinking into being at some point in the past and eventually totally winking out in the future—but as total organic entity, an entity with a kind of permanence in the fabric of being—sort of an 'eternal now'.

"Maybe another way to think about it is to regard life as an 'event'—or more precisely a 'trajectory of events'—embedded permanently within the fabric of space-time. Maybe this sounds a little weird unless you're a physicist used to throwing around terms like the 'four-dimensional space—time continuum', but it works for me at least. You and I—our trajectories intersect—thankfully—and all that surrounds us is, in a sense, our region in space-time."

I looked at Rosie. "Am I being confusing? I'm not sure how to make it clearer. Maybe we should change the subject."

Rosie had been sitting quietly staring into the fire, her cup of brandy cradled in her hands, just as she held her coffee when we had our afternoon breaks back in college. Then she turned to me and said, "No, no. I see what you're trying to describe. Life should not be viewed as a transitory thing—here today, gone tomorrow. Better, life is to be experienced, relished if possible, without regards to its finiteness. It's a permanent fixture in the cosmos."

"That says it as well as possible—though language may not be up to the task. Maybe our experience repeats endlessly—though that concept may be really bad physics—but if that were true, none of the experiences would be distinguishable from the others. They would each be as if they had a unique existence."

"We are embedded in this life," Rosie added. "We own it. We always will."

"Yes," I replied. "I don't worry about life's end, except for how I might make a difference on the world that transcends my existence. It's oddly comforting." I paused. "Thank you for being patient with my wild musings."

Rosie reached over and squeezed my hand. "Abe, listen to me. I don't easily tire talking with you."

We sat quietly for a long time and watched the campfire gradually burn down to a bed of glowing coals, a lick of flame occasionally leaping out from among the embers, and then quickly receding. Each of us was in our own thought world, worlds into which there was no need to intrude. A mellow glow began to rise in the sky behind the forest on the eastern end of the lake. As the night chill descended, Rosie excused herself. She nuzzled my neck from behind and then crawled into our tent. After securing the fire and looking into the kids' tent, I followed after her. By now the lake sparkled with moonlight.

CHAPTER 23

Raków

1936

I first met Nick Mahaley at the railroad station in early September. He was of slight but athletic build, medium height, clean-shaven, with straight sandy hair. I might easily have mistaken him for one of our graduate students. He emerged from the train, bearing two large suitcases and wearing a rather handsome Harris-tweed suit. I later learned that this air of prosperity was a thin veneer laid upon a person close to the edge of his resources. The suit was his only really good material possession, and except when delivering a formal lecture or at a reception at the President's home, he drew upon a collection of sweaters, a few of them wearing very thin at the elbows.

Nick was coming to Susan B. Anthony as a part-time visiting scholar under an arrangement with the Federal Writer's project, part of Roosevelt's WPA. His main job was to work on parts of the State Guide to Massachusetts, gathering oral histories in a part of the state rich in literary culture dating back to the mid-nineteenth century. In actuality Nick is a historian, specializing in the cultural history of Eastern Europe.

That the depression was eating at the fabric of academia had been evident for some years. Academic jobs were in short supply, not only because the size of faculties was not growing but because tenured professors have been reluctant or even unable to retire. Although the College had been elevated to the status of University several years ago, there was less money for supplies and support.

On one occasion the faculty had been asked to vote whether they would prefer to see their own salaries cut back or risk declaring financial exigency, with the possible loss of tenured positions. In the end the principle of tenure had been upheld but salaries remained stagnant. And regular faculty positions for younger scholars like Nick Mahaley have been a rarity.

The drive from the railroad station gave Nick an opportunity to size up his new surroundings. We passed several boarded up factories, prompting me to comment on the former prosperity of the town. I noted that although much of the skilled workforce had lost their jobs, many of those who stayed were eking out some sort of living in farming or forestry. A lot of the young men had joined the Civilian Conservation Corps, building trails in the mountains or working on small flood control projects. Nick commented that conditions here appeared less appalling than they did in the larger cities. I recalled the soup kitchens that we had seen when we visited New York City a year ago to attend the Bar Mitzvah of sister Celia's eldest boy. The city always had vagrants and beggars, but the number of men, and occasionally women, lying or sitting in doorways was startling. Nick made it clear that he considered himself fortunate to have work that might be an interesting exercise for a trained historian, despite it being peripheral to his major interests. Besides, a connection with the University might give him an opportunity in his spare time to continue some of the work he had been doing on Polish history.

When I spotted Nick at the faculty club last week I immediately sought him out. Rosie had asked me to make contact with him to invite him to spend Thanksgiving with us. Recently he had given one of a series of special lectures that the Provost had scheduled for Wednesday mornings throughout the year. This one was on the political partitioning of Poland in modern and medieval times, which I had made a special effort to attend. So I was especially pleased to see him when I dropped into the club for an afternoon coffee. When we saw one another he came directly over, a big, friendly smile on his face. This had been one of our few encounters since I dropped him off at his rooming house in September. He extended his hand.

"Professor Roth," he said, pumping my hand vigorously. "It's good to see you! How have you been?"

"Just fine, Nick. Just fine. But do call me Abe. I'm glad to see you looking hail and hearty. That was a good talk you gave Wednesday morning, by the way."

"Thanks. I spotted you in the lecture hall. I thought maybe I'd have a chance to say hello," he said.

"I apologize for that. I had to run off to give a lecture myself. But I have some time now, if you're not busy. I did want to ask you about a few things."

He eagerly accepted my invitation. We picked up cups of coffee and made our way to a sitting room at the back of the club. There were several large picture windows looking out on an expansive lawn. A gaudy patchwork of leaves drifting in from the woods bordering the campus lay upon the grass. We settled in a couple of comfortable chairs in a quiet corner of the room.

"It's not much of a faculty club as such things go," I began. "But I find it a pleasant retreat whenever I can break away." Nick had done his graduate work at Cornell, where I was sure the faculty club was an elegant retreat for Ivy League scholars. Here, the club was a couple of rooms set off from the student activities building. A coffee bar and tables for faculty to carry in their lunches were in the inner room. On occasion the place could become crowded and noisy, especially when there was some kind of a celebration. But today, at this time of the afternoon, there was not a lot of activity.

"Hey Abe, it's the only faculty club I've ever had privileges in. It's nice to have. Anyway, you liked my talk?" he asked.

"Indeed. I would venture that you kept everyone's attention. And I have a special curiosity about the subject." I explained how my family had escaped from eastern Poland at the turn of the century and that although I had very few memories of the old country, I have always wondered about the circumstances lying behind our situation there.

"Eastern European history is a pretty fascinating and often confusing tapestry of events. But for me there is also a personal connection." He proceeded to tell me that he is only a couple of generations removed from his own immigrant story. "They came from Belarus and became miners in Pennsylvania. I guess I have had my own kind of escape." He chuckled at the thought. "But anyway was there something that especially makes you curious?"

I thought for a moment. "I'm a little abashed to admit that I had not done any serious study of the subject. Let me start with a simple question. What do you know about Raków?"

"Raków? I thought only us pointy-headed specialists would think of mentioning Raków. Did your family have a connection there?"

I told him that I had once studied a map of Poland and determined that our village was some one hundred miles from Raków. However I knew that our flight from Poland had been facilitated by a guide named Boris who, according to the separate recounting by my boyhood friend Jacob, may have come from Raków. It seemed like a trivial piece of information, but for some reason it had stuck in my mind.

"I imagine that if you were to visit Raków today you would not think it was any more significant than dozens of other towns in that part of Europe. But for about a hundred years in the sixteenth and seventeenth centuries Raków was a principal center of learning and religious discussion. The press at Raków churned out books, especially about Socinianism, which were distributed all over Europe." He hesitated, obviously sensing my ignorance of religious history. "I think I'm getting ahead of the story," he said.

"I always thought of Poland as a Catholic country."

"Indeed it is, though if many Catholics knew about the tactics the Jesuits used to retake the country from the Protestants in the first part of the seventeenth century, it might temper some of their ardor about the nobility of the Church. Mind you, I'm a Catholic myself, but I take a liberal view of our religious history." He searched my face for signs of discomfort.

"I have a Jewish background," I told him.

"I might have guessed that from your immigrant story. The pogroms and dislocations at the turn of the century are dreadful reminders of just how far human beings have yet to go. But in fact, during the Reformation Poland was perhaps the leading country in terms of tolerance towards differing religious viewpoints. Protestants, Catholics, and Jews coexisted—perhaps uneasily—but there was a striking degree of religious freedom for a long period of time. In particular, from its founding, Raków was sort of a hate-free zone where different persuasions were welcomed."

"What about these Socinians?" I asked.

"Well, they no longer exist, but in their day I think it's fair to say that they were cousins to the Unitarians, perhaps one might say proto-Unitarians. I wonder if you are familiar with any of the Unitarians here in town."

I explained to Nick that I have had a fair amount of contact with the Unitarians, and had even enrolled our kids in the Sunday school at the Unitarian church. Of course, I approached it all with a Jewish perspective, but I found little among Unitarian core values that seemed incompatible with that. Moreover, as a scientist, the Unitarians' respect for reason was especially appealing.

"Of course the Socinians thought of themselves as Christians and held beliefs which might be foreign to twentieth century Unitarians, but there were important points of similarity too. They emphasized the monotheistic concept of there being one universal God. Jesus was a man, not a god—though not a mere man. He was to be venerated in order to achieve eternal life—he was a very special figure, literally a Christ. He was even prayed to. Hardly what you'd probably hear in the Unitarian church downtown. Yet some basic attitudes among the Socinians would seem familiar, such as freedom from creedal authority and toleration of differing opinions. Also a strong appeal to reason and service."

"And what happened to them?" I asked.

"Gone, exiled, dispersed." Nick flung apart his arms in emphasis. Then recovering his scholarly demeanor he explained. "They drew in a lot of people, especially among the educated classes. They even proselytized outside the country. And their main textbook, the so-called Racovian Catechism was in print for over two hundred years, long after they vanished from Poland. But especially when the Catholics began their efforts to reclaim Poland, the Socinians, as the smallest and most radical Protestant sect, was the first target. They were libeled in many ways—for instance, as followers of the Arian anti-trinitarian heresy. For many churchmen this was the most outrageous of heresies. They were confused with Anabaptists, whose mostly undeserved reputation stemmed from some sixteenth century rioting. They were also called Judaizers and confused with Sabbatarians."

Nick hesitated, realizing that he had lost me in arcane detail. He went on. "The upshot of it all is that by about 1660 they had been totally banished from Poland. At first they were kicked out of Raków, then by an act of the Polish Diet they were banished from everywhere else. Their press was removed but Socinian books continued to be published into the eighteenth century in Holland. The scholars and other followers dispersed to Prussia and Holland, and especially to Transylvania. Of course the other Protestants colluded in all of this, only to suffer the same fate in due course."

"And what about the Jews?"

"As you might guess, there were unspeakable atrocities and mindless riots from time to time. But interestingly, there was never a wholesale banishment. For one thing the Jews were never a threat to the power structure. They lived largely in their own enclaves, and as literate and generally skilled people they were seen by the nobles as being useful." He paused. "But all of this is perhaps a digression. Your original question had to do with Raków."

"I really don't know why I had remembered the name of the town," I said. I suspected that something deeper than idle curiosity lay behind my having asked Nick about Raków. "Perhaps it was that the guide, Boris, had somehow impressed me as a child, and any detail connected with him takes on special importance. What all this now brings to mind is another detail that my friend, Jacob, told me. He said that Boris had been especially generous to one of the families in the group that he was helping. Apparently when Jacob's father asked him about his motivation, Boris replied that he 'knew about persecution.'"

We were both quiet for a while. I had drawn to the edge of my chair. Nick unconsciously had reached for the tobacco pouch he kept in the side pocket of his sweater-vest. Perhaps we were having similar thoughts. "Do you think this Boris person could have been part of a remnant group of Socinians?" I finally asked.

It was obvious that Nick had decided on an answer to this question before I had verbalized it. "That's extremely unlikely," he said. "As I said the main body of Socinians was completely dispersed to various parts of Europe after the edict from the Diet. Interestingly, they gave them a grace period to settle their affairs. In Transylvania they merged with the Unitarians—many of them were, in fact, pretty much Unitarians anyway. The Transylvanian Unitarians exist there to this day—the only sizeable Unitarian presence outside of Britain and the U.S. It is true that there were scattered remnants in Poland for a while. But no record of them has turned up to document their presence more than a half dozen years after the expulsion, as far as I'm aware."

"Yet isn't it possible that a few stayed on living out their convictions in secrecy—perhaps like the Marranos in Spain who practiced Judaism undercover while living ostensibly as Catholics?"

"It's certainly a tantalizing idea," Nick admitted. "I dare say there are Catholics even now who keep their doubts to themselves. But with a conscious connection to a defined theology, such as Socinianism—?" Nick shrugged his shoulders. "If I were to make a bet I would put my money on Boris being mainly a mercenary who did his work for the money." He began filling a pipe with tobacco while he reflected further. Suddenly he looked up and said "Sorry to be absent-minded. I should ask if you mind me smoking."

I nodded my assent to his lighting up. Then Nick went on. "And yet—attitudes and behaviors linger on among people, even when they are not codified or enforced in a formal way. We see that a lot of that in society. Some groups have cultures of generosity, or respect for learning, or respect for the elderly, for instance. Of course there can be negative cultural markers too, like toleration of criminality, or abuse of women."

"Or there can be a combination of factors," I was compelled to add. Certainly few natural phenomena might be explained in detail in terms of a single physical concept. The task of the experimenter is often to exclude as many of the competing or superfluous ideas as possible.

"Yes," Nick agreed. "Maybe this Boris engaged in this risky business not only for profit, but also to act on some kind of a deep-seated altruism, which existed in cultural memory. Who knows?"

"To be sure," I responded. "I don't suppose we'll ever know. But it's fascinating to speculate."

Nick lit up his pipe. We sat in silence for a while and looked out at the lawn and the trees beyond. The wind had picked up somewhat and the sky had become gray. The smoke from Nick's pipe occasionally swirled in my direction, and although I do not smoke I found the odor pleasant—the incense of comfortable academia.

That night I had a dream.

> I was a boy walking with my friend Jacob in the countryside in New Lots back in Brooklyn. It was dark and we were alone. Across the fields here and there was the light from the window of a farmhouse. We didn't seem to be going anywhere in particular, just walking aimlessly along enjoying the silence and the mystery and the company of our friendship. Suddenly, we were in the company of other people and there was a general sense of alarm among them. I began to run. Jacob tried to keep up but he was having trouble running and he disappeared into a ditch. The people I was among had dispersed into the dark when, all of a sudden, my father scooped me up under his arm and carried me along at a run. I was sure it was my Father but he had very large mustaches.
>
> Eventually we reached a cottage set in a dark street and burst through the door. Inside, the walls were almost covered in bookshelves. I was now grown up and I was in the physics library that our department at the University had established over the years. My Father was no longer in the picture but the panic had subsided. The

light was dim, but eventually I became aware of at least
one other person present in the room. He was working
quietly at one of the reading tables. It was Carl Becker,
the minister of the Unitarian church in West Goshen.

Then I woke up. I lay in the dark for some minutes trying to
reconstruct the dream. Outside, illuminated by our porch light,
large flakes from a rare autumn snow shower were coming down in
profusion, slip-sliding slightly from side to side as they descended
vertically past the window pane. It was deathly still outside, except
for an occasional gentle thud as clumps of snow, accumulating on
the still plentiful leaves, dropped to the ground. I knew that this
snow would not lie long in the morning. Next to me Rosie lay on
her side, stretched out beneath the blanket, breathing gently. Perhaps
she was dreaming too, meeting me somewhere I cannot go.

CHAPTER 24

Coming of Age

1939

It may have been during the family camping trip we made in the summer of 1933, just after Father died, that we first discussed the matter of a Bar Mitzvah for Jason. Our religious commitments had for too long been an issue removed to the back burner. The kids had been enrolled in the Sunday school program at Carl Becker's church, and we had kept up a tenuous connection with the Unitarians. But now Jason was approaching his teen years and our families undoubtedly expected a Jewish ritual. We had from time to time made visits to synagogues in the towns and cities within reach of our home. These were mostly Conservative or Reform congregations. It is probably not entirely because of the Orthodox prohibition of driving on the Sabbath that make these congregations more prevalent. Rather, we think that beyond the large Jewish population centers like New York, Jews feel freer to shed old country ways.

What we found in those congregations was not completely unacceptable. For the most part the rabbis were interesting and we felt welcome. But we also felt some unease. We were uncomfortable with the kind of bland, incomplete Judaism we observed among the Jewish couples we met. The spiritual side of this ethnic Judaism was hard to identify. In time it became clear that Rosie's concern was not so much what religious path we followed personally, but how our religious practice impacted our wider family. She understood the disappointment that her parents and Mother would feel if Jason did not have a Bar Mitzvah. I had similar concerns. The older folks deserved everything we could do for them. But I recognized in myself a discomfort with, perhaps even a rejection of, the notion that we should simply go through the rituals of religious observance without a deeper commitment. I fought against the idea of being merely a "cultural Jew."

The matter came to a head on a summer evening in 1937, when Jason was 11 years old. It had been an especially hot day. We all sat in the backyard under the brooding birch tree that overhung the house. We were relishing an evening breeze that had come up. Later, when the house had cooled sufficiently, I carried Esther, who had fallen asleep in my lap, up to her room. Jason was fast asleep in the hammock which was strung between the back porch and the tree. When I returned, Rosie surprised me by bringing up the subject of the Bar Mitzvah.

"There's not quite two years for him to get ready," she reminded me.

I leaned back in my Adirondack chair, staring up into the branches of the birch tree as if there was wisdom to be found there. But that tree was a scolding presence that reminded me at various times of the year that its favors did not come free of charge. In exchange for shading the house in the summer and providing a convenient perch for songbirds visiting our feeder, it clogged the gutters with red catkins in the spring and later with its leaves until almost December.

The Bar Mitzvah was a subject that we had managed to avoid confronting seriously in the past. Now it was time.

"Yes, he needs to do that. Only . . . ."

"Only you don't have your heart in it," Rosie interrupted.

"You read me well. But what has my heart to do with it anyway?" I thought about this for a moment and continued. "I guess I'm not sure how to approach it. But this is for the grandparents, and for him. It's not really about me."

"Or maybe it's that need to understand. You don't like to do something simply because custom demands it. You want to know its purpose."

"In this case the purpose is to please the family," I replied. "And I'm sure it is meant to have a purpose beyond that—a rite of passage, I suppose. Welcoming a young man into the company of the elders. A tribal ritual conferring rights and privileges. Of course, that makes a lot of sense if life expectancy is thirty-five and everyone marries in their teens."

"I think your assumptions are a bit off, Abie dear." Rosie addressed me in the diminutive as a way of lightening the discussion. "Actually Bar Mitzvah took the form we recognize only in the mid-nineteenth century. Before that there's some mention in the Talmud as to the age at which a Jewish male is obligated to fulfill the commandments, but making it a public event outside of the immediate family had to wait for modern social conditions. It's not mandated from on high."

"You've been doing some research obviously," I replied. Rosie reached over and squeezed my hand. She probably regretted having sounded condescending. "Does that mean *the* Ten Commandments? I should hope that even a young boy would be expected to honor his mother and father, and hopefully would not covet his neighbor's wife." With a chuckle I added, "Like King David, maybe?"

"Frankly, I'm not sure how the religious part fits into the modern context—at least our own context," Rosie said. "For me, it's mostly a matter of honoring the child—like a super-birthday, but requiring something of the child at the same time. And I trust we'll do the same for Esther eventually."

"Ah, the Bat Mitzvah—an idea I didn't grow up with. But yes, it would only make sense." I looked over at Jason asleep in the hammock. The evening was becoming cool. I needed some time to think about these things. "I'll take Jason inside." I eased him to a sitting position and pulled him up. He was half asleep as I guided him, my arm around his shoulders towards the back door. "I'll be right back."

Inside Jason lay down on his bed. I pulled off his shoes and covered him with a light blanket. I wondered yet again at the marvel of this young life, with all its potential. I wanted him to have what I might have missed as I grew up. If we were to honor him, I wished it to be meaningful. If he were to affirm his heritage, he should understand it in his context, not as it might have been in medieval Europe or in the shtetls at the turn of the century. I looked around the room. Hanging by strings from the ceiling—a pair of rubber-band powered model airplanes Jason had built in the preceding year. There were a Stinson Reliant and a British Spitfire, its red and blue bulls-eye wing markings discernable even in the semi-darkness. A very faint odor of acetone from the glue he was using on his current model project hung in the air. A baseball bat and mitt had been flung in one corner. A collection of books had been pushed to the edge of the little desk where his balsa wood airplane was taking shape.

As I gathered a couple of sweaters to carry outside for Rosie and me I thought about how I was not much younger than Jason when I left the village in Poland. Very quickly I was an American kid. I had almost completely forgotten that other world, but I wondered how much of the shtetl was still within me. Nothing I could identify. Father had certainly done nothing to make his piety live in the American boy I had become. But neither had I turned my back on the premises of his devotion. I knew there had to be strength in this Jewish worldview that might explain its survival in the face of endless suppression and persecution. And I knew that at heart I had a strong spiritual impulse, but one that must be grounded in understanding rather than ritual. The Jewish view of God as that unfathomable, invisible, ineffable presence in the universe is consistent with all that I knew. And reverence for that God surely could not be reduced to blind tribalism.

I went outside and as I placed a sweater around Rosie's shoulders, she remarked that I had been gone longer than she expected. She reached up and laid her hand on mine as if to say that she was not complaining, merely being curious.

"Yes. I was thinking. About some of the things we were discussing."

"And have you concluded anything?" she asked.

"Well, one thing is that we must have a Bar Mitzvah for Jason. But I guess I had already agreed to that. I'm sure we can find someone in one of the Jewish congregations who would tutor him in the Haftarah reading and the rest of the ritual. He'll need to work on it maybe once a week and I'll drive him to his lesson, wherever that might be. He's a real brick. He'll do it, especially for the grandparents."

"Why not join one of the congregations, for all that?" Rosie asked. She knew what my likely response would be, but wanted a clear declaration of how I felt. Actually I suspected she felt much the same.

"You know how it is, Rosie. Most people we've gotten to know in those congregations don't seem to have gotten much beyond ritual. A lot of them—not even that far. They don't show up at the synagogue except to put in an appearance at Yom Kippur—and maybe to put on a Seder once a year. They're cultural Jews—tribalists in a way—but not particularly religious. I guess that's okay, as long as they're good people. And they are, by and large. Certainly better than being fanatics . . . ."

Rosie interrupted me. "Better than being nothing at all. I have to agree, Abe, that tribalism just for no good reason doesn't make sense—occasionally it's a vice. Think of all the senseless wars over trivial differences. It's like Lilliputians obsessing over which is the correct end of the egg to open. But—somehow along with this Jewish 'tribalism'—if you wish to call it that—a strain of openness and a progressive spirit seems to have been generated. I've been reading Margaret Sanger's autobiography. Apparently she searched long and hard to find a place to open her birth control clinic—the first one in America, you know."

"Yes, in Brownsville—just down the street from where we lived."

"She makes no bones about it. She wanted a Jewish landlord, and she knew that working-class Jews were receptive to new ideas—no hurled insults, no breaking of windows, she says. It's remarkable." Rosie shook her head slightly from side to side, almost as if she were saying "No" to threats and violence.

"I have to admit, it *is* remarkable. Maybe because it's a religion that, in principle, places proper living above proper belief. Or maybe—more important—emphasizes life over afterlife. But—" My voice trailed off as I pondered my dilemma.

"But you want understanding." Again Rosie anticipated my thoughts almost before I had formulated them. "You distrust the irrational. Perhaps that's to be expected for a physicist—though one does hear of so-called God-fearing, church-going scientists."

"Forgive them Father, for they know not what they are doing," I muttered.

"Now Abe, don't be cynical. Some people can make that dichotomy in their thinking—somehow. But you demand integrity, consistency—or call it sincerity. I'm really sympathetic with that. Actually it's sort of endearing."

"You make me blush. But really it's more than that. Yes, it's true that I don't want the kids to grow up feeling as ignorant of the deeper aspects of their faith as I was—or distrustful—" I paused momentarily in thought. "Maybe you had the right word: cynical, though I'm not sure of that. As I think about it, it's more than that. I see myself as a human being, not simply as a Jew. I would like to see more than just Jewish folks in my spiritual community. Oh, I know—I've had my share of rejection, of being excluded, and labeled, just on the basis of ethnicity. It's demeaning and unfair. But there are also good people out there, people who look for reason and good works and universality in their religious outlook"

"It sounds like you're talking about our Unitarian friends—most of them, anyway," Rosie said.

"Not necessarily. But you're right. I feel like I've come to understand more about my birth religion listening to Carl Becker at his church than I ever learned from my father or in the synagogue. Though making an official commitment is hard."

"I understand," Rosie responded. "I haven't gone down there on Sundays much, but I've gotten to know some of the ladies pretty well. And I've been surprised at how comfortable I feel with them. Perhaps it's their openness to diverse opinions. So often their thinking is compatible with my own—their receptiveness to progressive ideas. Also—." Rosie paused. "I get the sense that in general Judaism is respected, maybe even admired."

"It is interesting that a liberal outlook on religion seems to go hand in hand with progressive social thinking. I'm thinking of Einstein, for instance."

"But we digress," she reminded me. "This discussion actually had to do with the kids. So here's what I propose." With that, Rosie roughed out a plan.

In September I began driving Jason over to Albany every Tuesday evening where one of the men of the temple recommended by the rabbi, who is also a personal friend of Carl Becker, instructed him on the ritual of reading and chanting the Haftarah. That is the portion of the biblical Prophets that would come up for reading near his 13th birthday. On Sundays Jason and Esther continue to attend the religious education classes at the Unitarian church. Rosie and I alternately assisted in the classes and attended the services as we could.

Jason's Bar Mitzvah took place on a recent Saturday morning. It was a crisp early spring day. Most of the family came up to Albany on Friday morning. For Mother this was as far from the city as she had ever been since we arrived in America, excepting for one short stay at a Catskill summer hotel with Dave and Dolly. This time Sari and Mother shared a room at a hotel in Albany, while Celia and her family stayed in a larger adjoining room. Meanwhile Dave, Dolly, and the twins stayed at our house. The next morning we all assembled at the synagogue in Albany. The Dubrows chose to drive up from New York early Saturday morning. Of the immediate family, only Rosie's brother Alec, who had moved to Chicago, was not there.

The sanctuary was mostly filled with local congregants. I recognized a few of them. To my delight, towards the rear of the sanctuary, I spotted two familiar faces from West Goshen: Manny Gutierrez, the Dean of the College of Science, and Carl Becker, the Unitarian minister. They had driven over, as promised, for the ceremony.

Jason was understandably nervous. He had never before faced such a large audience. But Rabbi Berkowitz promised he would be right at his side and would help him out if it were necessary. "But

I bet I don't have to," the rabbi had told him. And indeed he did not have to. When the time came to recite from the scrolls, one of the men stood by his side, along with the rabbi, pointing to each line with a silver pointer. The first few lines came out haltingly, but then Jason recovered himself and he chanted flawlessly through the rest of the text. Only once did his voice crack, as it has a few times during the last months, as his soprano boy-voice has broken into the quasi-bass of adolescence.

In the social hall after the service several of the men came over to Jason and congratulated him on a good performance. Indeed, the ancient chant awakened in me a feeling of union with a line of descent that stretched back, perhaps even to some nomadic herders of prehistory. I thought about the miraculous survival of a cultural identity over such a long span of time—one so often threatened with obliteration. As usual, such ruminations did not speak to my intellect, but the liturgy did awaken a sense of humility in the presence of a greater power. I wondered whether that humility was different from the feelings of humility in the presence of the natural world or when confronting the riddles of science. But these were fleeting thoughts and not new—the occasion was principally about Jason and about family. I knew that the grandparents were not cerebrating about meaning or history. For them it was probably about an undefined joy and love—perhaps an unconscious expression of the biological impetus for survival of one's own genes. And I shared that joy.

Later on, Rosie and I hosted a festive lunch at a nearby restaurant. Manny and Carl joined the family in the celebration. Dave gave the toast from my side of the family. Looking directly at Mother he finished his toast in Yiddish. Mr. Dubrow toasted for Rosie's family, including greetings from his Uncle Alec. The last of the toasts was given by Carl Becker, speaking for all of our community in West Goshen. Carl reminded us that he had watched Jason grow up and how impressed he was with this young man. He told us that he had been at a number of Bar Mitzvahs and how Jason had done especially well-focused and competent. He kept the tone of his remarks light. He told the story, probably apocryphal, about one occasion in which the boy was so intensely focused on the gifts he anticipated, that instead of declaring to the guests the expected "Today I am a man!" he said instead "Today I am a fountain pen!"

But of course there were gifts. Dave joined Celia in buying Jason a fine beginner's microscope. Mother made sure that Jason had a set of t'fillin and a prayer shawl. I wonder if she thought about whether Jason would follow through with the daily binding of the arm and forehead. Indeed he had hardly any instruction in this and I had abandoned the practice when I left my parents' home. But the symbolism carried by these objects may have been all that she intended. Rosie and I gave him a huge Unabridged Webster's Dictionary. And, almost as if she had anticipated Carl's anecdote, Sari had brought a beautiful blue and gold Waterman fountain pen. Finally, Esther stepped forward with an album of family photographs she had assembled. On the cover, in multiple colors, she had printed **JASON'S**STORY**. Jason held it up for all to see.

This past Sunday at Carl's church in West Goshen, Jason and several other boys and girls were part of a Coming of Age ceremony. During the preceding year, the Sunday school program for this group of kids had focused on comparing religious beliefs. Each of them had worked with an adult mentor in the congregation to develop a statement of belief, a process it was hoped was the beginning of a lifetime of spiritual exploration. Also, they had each engaged in some sort of community service. Jason's belief statement, included in a pamphlet was entitled "I See God Everywhere." His service project was to work with me on improving a hiking trail north of the town. One by one each of the adult mentors rose to introduce each boy or girl. Mr. Crandall, who is also Jason's German teacher at the high school, characterized him as "always cheerful, always thinking." Rosie and I looked at each other. Crandall had got it right, while wisely leaving out Jason's occasional obstinate side.

Carl delivered a sermon titled "Does God Require Justice?" He pointed out that although the free faith of the Unitarians demands no special acts to certify the authenticity of an individual's faith, history shows that Unitarians have often been in the forefront of social action. It is a characteristic that has shown up time and time again, as a behavior somehow linked to the concepts of freedom, tolerance and reason that mark the appearance of the faith wherever it had sprung up. Social action is not unknown among other religious movements, but all too often, he pointed out, it is meted out preferentially. Correct belief, correct skin color, correct nationality have sometimes determined who is to benefit. However, in the context that honors a "single, universal, source of being," such tests of eligibility for justice do not suffice. He mentioned, as an example, the prominence of Unitarians in the abolitionist movement of the last century. Then he described an effort that is currently underway in Europe. One of Carl's ministerial colleagues, Rev. Waitstill Sharp and his wife Martha are now in Prague. There they are leading an effort to rescue endangered people who crowd the Czech capital in the wake of the Nazi onslaught. These refugees are mostly Jews, but also include a number of anti-Nazi Germans. The work is dangerous and daunting and he told the congregation that their support can make a difference.

As he described the work of the Sharps I could not help thinking, once again, about Boris, the mustachioed figure who led us out of Poland almost forty years ago. Boris had taken root as a vague but iconic figure in my early memories. Nick Mahaley had doubts that there was a Unitarian link involved in the story, but I like to imagine that there might be. Certainly there were parallels: a dangerous rescue mission selflessly done.

Instead of a closing prayer, the young people participating in the Coming of Age program came to the pulpit one by one to offer a short reading of their choosing. A couple of them had poems. One had a reading from scripture and one had a quotation from a speech of Franklin Roosevelt. Carl had encouraged Jason to offer part of the Haftarah that he had learned for his Bar Mitzvah. To our delight and mild surprise he agreed.

Jason stepped to the pulpit with little hesitation. A few months has made a difference in his bearing and his voice. After a moment's hesitation, he began the chant, His voice was that of a young adolescent, but it did not crack. The notes rising and falling in a cadence defined by centuries of tradition were not familiar in this setting, but the congregation was in rapt attention. I noticed that unconsciously and only slightly, Jason was shuckling, bending and swaying in imitation the devout men of the synagogue. The Haftarah was from the book of Micah. He followed with a translation:

> Wherewith shall I come before the Lord, and bow myself before God on high?
> Shall I come before Him with burnt offerings, with calves of a year old?
> Will the Lord be pleased with thousands of rams, with ten thousands of rivers of oil?
> Shall I give my first-born for my transgression, the fruit of my body for the sin of my soul?
> It hath been told thee, O man, what is good, and what the Lord doth require of thee:
> Only to do justly, and to love mercy, and to walk humbly with thy God.

Chapter 25

André

1946

André entered our lives more than five years ago on a ferry slip in New York. It was a chilly day in early 1941. He came towards us holding the hand of one of the ladies who had accompanied the refugee children on the voyage from Lisbon. He was about waist high—a shy, somewhat frightened little boy in a tight fitting, rough textured, woolen coat that almost reached his knee socks. On his head was a dark schoolboy cap that barely covered his straight, roughly-cut, auburn hair, which hung over his ears and the back of his neck. His head was tilted slightly downward, but his gaze was upwards, taking in the faces of yet another group of strangers.

Rosie, Esther, and I had come down to the city after receiving word from the Unitarian Service Committee. A ship carrying children that they had helped rescue from Vichy France was about to arrive. Our involvement in the program began soon after the Sunday of Jason's Coming of Age ceremony. Carl Becker had, at that time, mentioned in his sermon the European rescue operation being conducted by his colleague Waitstill Sharp and his wife. It was a few days later, while we were reflecting on that Sunday's events, that Rosie broached the idea of assisting the effort.

"Abe," she began, "I've been doing a lot of thinking about one of the things Carl had to say in his sermon—specifically about the rescue operation in Europe headed up by one of his minister friends. Now I'd prefer to do more than just think about it. We should do something, if we can."

"I don't suppose you mean you're ready to go to Europe to help."

"No, no," she replied quickly. "Even if I felt I was up to that, I'm sure it couldn't be done. Even if visas could be had, it undoubtedly would be an impossible, even dangerous job for an ethnic Jew to carry out. Anyway I don't think social work is my forte. But I feel we must try to do something."

"Such as—?" I was momentarily at a loss to think how we could be part of this overwhelming and unsettling tragedy that was unfolding in Europe.

Rosie continued. "I made a few inquiries. If the Sharps' operation manages to bring over some refugee children as they hope, they will need some foster parents to care for them." Rosie hesitated, then looking directly at me she said, "Perhaps I should have cleared this with you first, Abe, but I submitted our names."

"Impetuous you," I said lightly, momentarily postponing a serious reply. This required some thought.

"Of course I could withdraw our names, but to be honest, I would feel frustrated about it. After all, it's something we could do. Our own kids are teenagers and don't need continuous babysitting. We're reasonably well off—at least the depression hasn't devastated us as it has a lot of others. I think we have a pretty good record as parents—at least we're experienced. Anyway we're not talking about adopting a child—only standing in as human beings while God-knows-what is going on over there."

I felt a little like I did when I first learned that I was to be a father. I was gradually becoming confident in my role as a parent of teenagers. I had come to understand the challenges facing them—the lure of independence, the frightening bodily changes, the social adjustments. The constant care and attention needed by younger children, interesting and rewarding as that had been, was thankfully behind Rosie and me. To assume that kind of responsibility again was daunting. But in the end I knew Rosie was right. It was not just that in my childhood I had myself been rescued; it was correct thing to do.

When we picked up André in New York, we knew only that he was almost six years old, that his family name was Safron, and that he had lived in the south of France in Jewish family with his parents and two siblings. Rosie boned up on her high school French and I hoped that this, in addition to the rudimentary French I had learned for my doctoral work, would carry us through until he began to speak English. From my own experience I was sure that this would not take long. We would be everything a parent must be, we agreed, but we resolved that he would not forget that he had a biological family somewhere else.

On the pier the lady from the Service Committee gave us the documents certifying André's clearance by the immigration officials a few hours before. She turned over to us the little suitcase she had been carrying for him, then bent down and embraced him for a final goodbye. Her eyes glistened as she put his hand in Rosie's, then she returned to where some of the other children were waiting.

On the ride back to Massachusetts, André sat in the rear seat next to Esther. He would not relinquish the little backpack he had been wearing and held it in his lap. Presently, he retrieved from it a somewhat crushed shaggy Teddy bear and cuddled it to his chest, each of them peering over one another's shoulder at the sights and sounds of America—the confusion of cars and buses, the gigantic buildings, the river beside the Parkway. It was a different world from the one that greeted me forty years before, but to a child it surely stirred similar anxieties. We tried to engage him with our rudimentary French. He understood our questions but, his answers came only in single words, or nods of his head.

It was only when we stopped at a Howard Johnson's just outside the city that we saw a little spark of pleasure come alive in him. Undoubtedly he was famished, and he made clear that his heart's desire was *la glace.* The ice cream proved to be the magical potion. Afterwards, in the rear seat with Esther, he eventually curled up beneath her arm and fell asleep, Teddy clutched to his chest.

So began André's life with us. We did our best to make him part of the family, but we also made sure he understood that he was in our care temporarily—that he had a natural family in Europe and that he would see them again someday. During the first few months some letters arrived from his mother and father. Each of them contained notes from his teenage sister and brother. Then the letters stopped. There was no explanation. At the end of the year the United States entered the war and we knew that communication would end for the time being. In due course, we came to imagine the worst for the fate of the Safrons and tried to temper the hope that André may have harbored, that he would be reunited. It was a difficult role, knowing that there was a possibility that he would not have a family to return to, while keeping him prepared to leave us when the war was over.

Meanwhile, we grew increasingly fond of André. And he adapted to us. A month after he arrived we enrolled him in the kindergarten at Esther's school. By late spring he was beginning to master English. At that point, Rosie became determined that he would not lose a connection to the French language. Once a week he would have dinner with Mrs. Terwiliger, a French teacher at Rosie's school, spending the evening speaking the language with her. Much later, as he learned to read and write, Mamie Terwiliger would send him home with simple books in French for later discussion. She became as proud of him as she did of any of her regular students.

André's emotional state was difficult to fathom. For some months after we took him in, he would wake occasionally in the middle of the night quietly sobbing and calling for his *maman.* One of us would go and console him until, gradually emerging from his dream, he would come to grips with his reality and fall asleep again. He took a great liking to Esther, who would walk with him to their school every morning. In time he began to sleep through the night. Jason taught him baseball and sometimes the three of us would gather in the backyard and toss a ball around. By the time fall arrived he was nearly fluent in English in time for first grade.

In the course of the following year, he became increasingly part of the family. But there was always that unspoken understanding that we might not be together forever. At first he would tell us about the family vacations on the Cote d'Azure, swimming in the surf with his older sister and brother. Mostly he mentioned the sister,

Cecile—to him, almost a motherly figure. We guessed there was almost a ten-year difference in age. His brother, Robert, was more vague in his recollections. We surmised that although Robert was closer in age, he had spent most of this time with his own older friends. Oddly, André could not say much about his parents. Little by little over the following years they seemed to become icons of a mythical past, endearing figures for whom we had substituted. He was becoming an American kid, interested in sports and model airplanes. When he was nine he joined the Cub Scout den that Rosie had helped organize when Jason was younger.

With the Allied victory in Europe in the spring of last year our search for André's family began, but our efforts were frustrated at every turn. The Unitarian Service Committee was just beginning efforts to reestablish a presence in Europe. The Department of the Army could not help. Our congressman was able to find out that the military efforts on refugees and resettlement were piecemeal field operations. It was clear that in the spring and summer of 1945, the anticipated campaign in Japan was the Army's main preoccupation. The International Red Cross did respond to our letters, merely informing us that the situation in Europe was chaotic and that their own relief efforts were only just starting up. Zionist organizations had no information beyond some names of refugees who had managed to reach Palestine. Safron was not among them. No letters arrived from André's parents.

Then, in February of this year a phone call came from the Unitarian Service Committee office in Boston. They had been contacted regarding André's sister, Cecile, by a GI just returned from Europe. There was little other information and we were to wait for further details. With some trepidation we told André about this. What was the news about his sister? What about his parents and his brother? A few days later the telephone rang in the evening.

"Is this Dr. Roth?" a male voice asked.

When I identified myself, the caller continued. It was a young man with a New York accent. "This is Sol Greenberg calling from Fort Dix. I can't talk long. There aren't too many phones at the post here and all the other guys are lined up wanting to use them. The charges are big, too. So I'll try to be quick."

I assured him that he could reverse charges to us next time. Then he continued. "Me and Cecile, I mean Cecile Safron—well, we were hitched over in France by a chaplain before I left on the troopship. I'm at Dix now waiting until I'm discharged—any day now, they say. Anyway, the main point is that Cecile, as soon as she learned where her little brother is—she wants to see him."

"Where is Cecile, Mr. Greenberg?"

"Call me Sol," he replied. "But I guess it's Sergeant Greenberg, for the time being." He chuckled slightly.

"I'm Abe, Sol," I interrupted him. "Abe and Rosie. But please go on."

"Glad to know you, Abe. Anyway Cecile is still in France, but I expect there'll be some room on the ships for war brides in the next month or two. I can't wait until she gets here. I tell you she's some wonderful gal, my Cecile. She is anxious to see her brother—André? I want to see him too. And we talked about this. We hope he could live with us—do you think he'd be OK with that?"

It was a conversation I had been trying to imagine for years, but the implications were only now dawning on me. I had had no way of anticipating the questions that were being raised. We had been preparing André all along for the eventuality of being reunited with his family, but would he be willing and able to make the transition? Cecile was family but was there an obligation to return him to her rather than to his parents? In fact, had the parents survived the war? The news emerging from Europe made it seem less likely, so the appearance of Cecile was surprising. And assuming André was to join Cecile and Sol, what sort of care could they give him? What were they really like? What would their situation be like? The central question, apart from the legal issue, was what was in André's best interest. And at that moment I had no way of knowing.

Before hanging up I assured Sol that we would be speaking with André and looking forward to knowing more details. I was so confounded I almost forgot to congratulate him on his marriage and to welcome him back home. He seemed like a nice person, though a bit less than polished. But he had been living an army life for several years.

A call from Sol a week later answered some of our questions. Sol's parents lived in Queens. He had been drafted into the Army after finishing half a year of college and had been in combat infantry for most of the war. His plan was to resume studies at City College as early as the summer, and his parents had promised to subsidize him and his bride until he finished. They were now looking for an apartment for them near their home.

In mid-March a slightly battered Aerogramme, addressed in small, crisp handwriting to Master André Safron, arrived at the house. It was from Cecile and had an A.P.O. return address. In the late afternoon when Rosie returned from her teaching, André asked her to be with him when he opened the letter. It began in English.

> Paris
> 1 March 1946
>
> My dear little brother André,
>
> This is your loving sister Cecile writing to you after many years from Paris, where I wait until the official people here make it possible for me to travel to America. I think that you know that I met this wonderful American soldier by the name of Sol, and that we have become married. I will travel soon and then I will be able to see you again following so many years. Meanwhile I study with diligence the English and am becoming almost fluent. But it is difficult for me to write in the English, particularly the orthography. Therefore I hope you will permit me to complete the letter using the French. Perhaps you have forgotten our language but I am sure someone will help you to read what I want to tell you.

The letter continued in French, which André and Rosie were able to follow for the most part. Later, Mamie Terwiliger helped us with the finer points. In translation it went as follows:

I want you to understand first of all how much I have thought about you during these years of war and how affectionately I feel towards you, because some of the news I have is sad. You were only five years old when we had to separate, my little brother, but by now I am sure you are a strong little man and can be brave, even in the face of bad news. But first I must tell you a little about myself.

After Mother and Father took you to Marseilles to send you away to America they came home very sad. But at the same time they were sure you would be safe with the kind Dr. and Mrs. Roth, so the next thing they wanted to do was find a way to protect Robert and me. Eventually they were able to arrange for me to live with a very nice family in Lyons whom Father knew through his work and through false papers have me pretend that I was their niece. Life was difficult because of the shortages and constant fear of being found out, but thank God we were all able to stay safe. Also I was able to continue with school and even begin studies that will lead to my being a nurse someday. I am greatly indebted to this French family and I hope you will be able to meet them some day.

Now the bad news. I cannot tell you what happened after that to the rest of our family. Mother and Father tried to make arrangements for Robert but it was not easy. For a while I received letters from them and then that stopped. I have heard that the authorities in our part of France would manufacture reasons to take Jewish people into custody to please the German authorities who, after all, really were in control. Perhaps they were put in jail and deported. I have tried to find out, but there is no trace. I must assume that they are no longer living. I know this is as hard for you to hear as it is for me to say, but I must tell you about it. Please be brave for their sakes and for mine.

As for Robert, I can tell you even less. Even though he was just a boy he kept talking about joining the resistance. After Mother and Father were taken away, if that's what happened to them, Robert may have tried to join with underground forces, perhaps as a messenger. But I have no idea where he is. I keep hoping he will show up someday but so far I have had no word of him.

Rosie told me that as they read the letter André clenched his teeth as if choking back tears. At one point he lay his head down on folded arms on the kitchen table, but when he raised his head again, he asked to continue reading. The letter concluded by explaining that Cecile had traveled to Paris in the course of her search for the family. That is where she met Sol. She knew that André had been placed with a family through the Unitarian Service Committee and that is how Sol was able to find him. The letter concluded with these paragraphs:

I know from Sol that you have been happy living with the Roth family. He tells me that although he has not been able to see you he has spoken on the telephone with you. But I also want you to know that before I said goodbye to Mother and Father I promised them that no matter what happened to them I would try to keep our family together. Now it is only you and I, so I hope it would make you as happy as it would make me if you would come to live with Sol and me when I come to America. Life is still very difficult here and America is such a great friend. I look forward to being there and I know that the three of us could make a happy life as a family.

I do not know how to express enough thanks to Dr. and Mrs. Roth for taking care of you for so many years. They are surely the most wonderful people. I hope it is not too long before I can express for our parents and me the indebtedness that surely is due them. And not too long before I can see you again. I try to imagine how you look now—perhaps like our poor Robert did when we were last with him. To you I give all the affection I know.

Your sister,
Cecile

From the beginning the understanding had been that André was in our care only temporarily. Of course, in the beginning we could not have imagined the decimation of Europe's Jews that, to our horror, took place. We had naively supposed that eventually André's parents would emerge to reclaim him, so we were psychologically prepared to relinquish him to them. Now it appeared that the Safrons were themselves victims of that horror. Yet, from a legal standpoint we had no claim on him, nor were we willing to assert one. The claim of blood is usually the overriding consideration. André's feelings would have to decide whether we should even engage in a custody claim.

In the end, André settled the matter. His mindset was not a thing we could fathom, though we couldn't help but speculate about what persuaded him. He was a well-adjusted "American" boy, living in comparative comfort in a rural town, but he chose to be with two relative strangers in the big city. Perhaps it was his way of honoring the memory of his mother and father. Or perhaps it was an act of sacrificial love for his sister. Perhaps it even was a way to unburden us. Whatever the reasons, it was clear that this was not an easy decision for him. But once he had decided to join his sister he did not waver.

CHAPTER 26

Flame in the Chalice

1946

Finally the time came for us to let go of André and for him to let go of us. It was only the year before last that we had to learn to let go of Jason when he went to the Army.

After a short tour in Europe, Jason was now back in the States at Officer Candidate School. During Jason's brief furlough in June, Sol was also able to visit and the two young men bonded immediately. Sol had recently been discharged from the Army and was about to resume his studies in the summer program at City College. It was the first time we had met him face to face. Sol was a muscular young man of about 24, of medium height, with a broad, masculine face, and a strong jaw. His expansive smile easily distracted from the dark shadow of a beard that even early in the afternoon gave him a look of gentle power.

During the visit Sol and Jason easily took André into their company. The three made an overnight excursion to Jason's favorite fishing lake in southern Vermont. They returned late the next day, dirty, tired, happy and ravenous. We were left with no doubt about the fit between Sol and André.

In late July we heard from Sol that Cecile would be arriving within a few days. He wanted to know if they could visit as soon she had rested from her trip. Meanwhile they would be living with his parents, at least until he was able to locate a place of their own. A couple of weeks later, on a Saturday afternoon, a black 1939 Chevrolet coupe rolled into our driveway. We recognized the car

Sol had described as the one his father had put up on blocks at the beginning of the war. Sol leaned out of the driver side window and waved to André, who looked on from the living room window. The passenger door opened and a very slim auburn haired young woman emerged. She wore a light flowered print dress with sleeves just covering the elbows. She was squinting from the brightness beneath the brimmed straw hat that covered her shoulder length hair, the same color as André's.

Rosie went inside for André. Taking his hand she led him out onto the portico. For a few moments the sister and brother stood facing each other in silence. Then with a gentle push from Rosie, André ran to Cecile as she started forward. She knelt down to receive him. With his chin upon her shoulder they clasped each other in a tight embrace. They said nothing but for the first time since his early days in our home I saw tears roll down André's cheeks. Then Cecile stood up and taking him by the shoulders held him at arms length to look at him.

Cecile's first words to him were in French, but from then on she used English exclusively and without hesitation, even in those moments when the language eluded her. Grasping André's hand she walked towards us and extended her hand. Sol was now beside her and introduced her to us. She had the same fine features as André. But her sallow complexion and lean frame hinted at past privations.

On the back porch Rosie had set out a platter of cakes and pitchers of lemonade and iced tea. We gathered around the table. There was so much to talk about. We reported on André's progress in school, about hobbies, sports, Cub Scouts. Cecile told us briefly about the war years she had spent pretending to be someone else. She recounted how she had come to know Sol and having been married by an Army chaplain in a tiny wedding ceremony at the base chapel in Paris. Someday, she told us, they would repeat their vows at a big gathering here in America. But she was obviously hesitant to speak much about their parents or their lost brother, Robert, in the presence of André.

Eventually Sol took André out to the back yard to play catch. Only now did she begin to talk about the family.

"André, he doesn't have a lot of memories of that time before the war came, I think. He was five years old. I was almost fifteen and I remember it clearly. We will have much time to talk about it, but I know how he felt about our mother and father and I don't want him to feel sad—not today."

"You lived in Arles? That is close to Marseilles, I know," I began. "But we have never learned much about your family, just a few bare facts."

"Yes, Arles," she replied. Her eyes brightened as she thought of this. "Arles is very nice." She hesitated. "Arles was very nice, I should say. I do not know Arles today. There has been a lot of destruction in many parts of France."

"You lived well." I said this with a slight rising inflection. It was meant largely as a question.

"Yes. Yes, we were comfortable. Not rich but there was bread on the table and we were all close to one another. Father shared the ownership of a . . . how do you say it—dry goods?—store. Mother helped out there also."

"So the problem was being Jewish?" Rosie ventured.

Cecile looked thoughtful for a few moments before she responded. "Well, I don't too much remember problems until the war came," she said. "But yes—our main problem, for some authorities, was being Jewish. Actually, we were not very observant and we didn't make a big show of it. But we did not hide who we were. We got along with almost everyone."

"It sounds as if the French are tolerant. You know the word?" Rosie said.

Cecile smiled. "Ah, *oui*. The same as the French—*tolerant*." The word emerged only as the French can say it. "Mostly, I suppose. But actually I am not sure if there are not as many anti-Semites in France as in Germany. There was a Jewish community in Arles for centuries. And it suffered at times—especially at such times as the Black Plague—but mostly it was left in peace. The French, you know—they have an uneasy connection to religion. They may suspect Jews, but they also suspect the Pope. The Revolution was not about religion."

"So the family goes back a long way in Arles."

"On the contrary," she said. "My mother's family comes from Paris. It is not clear where or when they came there. But the family on my father's side came only at the beginning of the century to France. Most of what I know is through my father—I didn't think to question my grandfather before he died when I was small. The family was escaping the pogroms in Poland and was trying to make their way to Palestine. That's why they came originally to Marseilles. Some relatives had helped them get that far. Then grandfather went to work trying to save enough for the rest of the trip. He had once owned some kind of shop in Poland, but then he started over again loading and unloading goods for someone else's store in Marseilles. It was hard work—he was not a big man—but he was determined to earn a living doing whatever he could. Then came the first big war."

The revelation about being refugees from Poland piqued my interest, but I refrained from interrupting the story. Cecile looked at us as if to gauge our interest. "World War I," I interjected. "Please go on, Cecile."

"*Alors.* That was the end of the hope of further emigration. Father even entered the French army eventually—and he survived. But it earned him citizenship. When the war ended, a friend he had met in the Army offered to take him in as partner in a shop in Arles. And that is why we were there. Arles was very nice." She closed her eyes for a moment, remembering.

My curiosity could wait no longer. "Do you know from where in Poland your grandfather came?"

"I know very little, as I said. Father didn't talk about it much, and Grandfather spoke Yiddish at home mostly. It was in the east part, near a town—what is it again?—Bialystok, I think."

"Do you know the exact town? And the family name? I don't suppose it was originally Safron." I was afraid that perhaps she was feeling beleaguered by my questions.

"Yes, Safron is some kind of French adaptation. I'm not sure of the original," she said.

"It's a beautiful name, Cecile. And I hope you will pardon me if I am asking too many questions. I'll tell you why in a moment. But just one more. Is it possible that your grandfather's name was Shafransky?"

Cecile pursed her lips as she thought about this. Then she replied. "It does sound familiar, yes. But really Dr. Roth, I am not sure."

Rosie excused herself and went into the kitchen to make preparations for dinner. I briefly explained my own history in eastern Poland and what I knew from my old friend Jacob about the Shafransky family—the burning of their store and the escape from Poland. I apologized again. "I'm sorry for bringing my own story into this. I really want to hear about your story, and André's."

"No, no," she said. "It is an amazing thing. I'm glad you told me. All of these stories of escape and the kind actions of some people. It makes me feel connected—André and me." Seeing Sol and André returning from their game of catch, she paused. Then she added "Our story—that can wait a while. It is not easy to talk about."

We next saw Sol and Cecile about a month later. On a bright, late summer morning, Rosie and I drove down to the New York area with André to take him to his new home. During the trip, while he and Rosie were chatting and playing word games, I found my thoughts wandering once more to the story of André's family: How the parents had found safe havens for two of their children. How Robert had run away just as his parents were taken into custody. About Cecile's efforts to locate all of them. In the trunk of the car was a big box of André's choice possessions—his baseball mitt, two model airplanes, some favorite books. Most of his clothes had been sent ahead by Railway Express.

Finally we pulled up in front of a modest attached house in the Forest Hills section in the borough of Queens. I remembered that when I was growing up, perhaps three miles from here in Brownsville, this was terra incognita. At the time it was probably barely developed countryside. Now rows of low attached apartment blocks and neat stuccoed homes lay monotonously in every direction. Only Forest Park, barely visible on the other side of a busy parkway, stood in green contrast to the brick and asphalt of these housing blocks. Yet I felt a comfortable sense of the place as I reflected on the squalor of my boyhood home. On this particular street the brick-fronted homes were attached to one another in blocks of five or six. An internal alley ran the length of each block providing access to basement garages and small fenced-in backyards. Young sycamore trees, not yet fifteen feet in height, were planted down the street in the parking strips by the curb.

As we came to a stop, Cecile was already at the door. She was looking so much better than she had when we first met. There was color in her cheeks now. She had put on a little weight. Right away, André bolted out of the rear seat and ran to her. Sol was right behind Cecile and came out to the car. He shook my hand and hugged Rosie and Esther.

"It's not a lot, our new place," he said. "But I can tell you we are very lucky to have it. This street has one of the first building projects finished since the end of the war. Mom and Dad were keeping their eyes open for us for a long time." He came around to the trunk of the car with me and lifted out the box of André's belongings. "Let me show you around. And of course introduce André to his new room."

We went inside. The first floor was a single long narrow room lit by windows at either end. A half wall partitioned the living room area at the front from a kitchen area at the rear. Against the divider a card table covered in a checkered cloth was set for a meal. An attractive but slightly worn sofa divided this area from the rest of the room. Facing it was an equally worn deep easy chair. Against the wall between these pieces of furniture was a long bookcase made of painted boards supported by bricks. It was almost filled with what appeared to be textbooks, and the top held a record player and several framed photographs. A print of a Chagall stained glass window was on the wall. It showed a Jewish candelabrum from which a human figure appears to erupt and merge into licks of startling multicolored flames.

"Mom wanted some new furniture and we were more than happy to take the old pieces off my parent's hands," Sol remarked. "But let's get André settled in." He led me upstairs, with André and Esther following just behind. There were two bedrooms. In the larger one at the front of the house a double bed took up much of the floor space, leaving just enough room for a dresser and a makeshift desk made of a flush door panel in a corner next to the window. "My office," he commented as we passed by. "Cecile likes to work on the table near the kitchen."

André's room at the rear of the house had a window that looked down on the backyard and the alleyway. This would be a more confined personal space than he had in West Goshen, but I was certain he would quickly adjust. There was a bed covered in a blue striped quilt and a small desk and chair in the corner. On the wall was a large New York Yankees poster. Sunshine streamed through the window, casting the room in cheery light. Sol put the box of André's treasures on the floor. We left André and Esther behind and returned downstairs.

Cecile had laid out a small tray of hors d'oeuvres and some small glasses of cognac. "I have cooked something special for the occasion. I hope you are OK with the French custom of midday dinners. But this is a special time. Meanwhile we can talk, *non?*"

Sol raised a glass. "Love and family," he said. We raised our glasses in assent and sipped the cognac. It was awfully good. There was some general talk about plans for André's school, Cecile's plans for a nursing license, about Sol's studies. Presently Cecile rose and went to the closet near the front door.

"I have something for you." She brought a small cardboard box down from an upper shelf. "I could not bring much with me from France but I found something in Paris that I was able to put in my suitcase."

Within the box an object lay encased in tissue paper that Cecile carefully unwrapped. She lifted out a shallow silver goblet on a long stem. It had been carefully polished, casting reflections of the sunny room. She set it on the small coffee table in front of us. "There is no way that André or I can ever thank you enough for what you have done for us. But I wanted you to have something that will remind you that we will always be grateful for your kindness."

From the lower shelf of the bookcase she retrieved a round, flat candle and placed it in the cup. "When I went looking for something in Paris I knew that the symbol of the Unitarian Service Committee is a flame rising from a cup like this—they like to say chalice, like the French *calice*. I think it is something you could use and which also honors the people who helped rescue André and also reunited me with him. Also it has another meaning for me. It reminds me of the candle we would light each year on the anniversary of grandfather's death."

"A *yahrzeit* candle," I interjected.

"Yes, that it exactly what father had called it. The 'year-time' candle he explained. As a girl I would imagine how the air we were breathing was being sent to heaven by this candle—to grandfather somehow. It was very fanciful of me."

Rosie grasped Cecile's hands in her own. "It's a treasure, Cecile. It's beautiful and I feel attached to it already. Thank you."

"It's a perfect remembrance," I added. "We also light a *yahrzeit*—and we will use it. Thank you." There was a pause. Cecile looked pleased with our reactions, but also a little wistful. Almost reluctantly I went on. "In your family in Arles, did you carry on with the old traditions?"

"As I may have explained we were not too observant, but we did certain things. When grandfather was with us after grandmother died—I don't remember before that—he carried on most of his traditions." She paused in thought. "You know, Dr. Roth, I have been thinking about him and perhaps it is possible he did come from your village. But I don't know. I remember that whenever we learned news about Russia he would say some things about Cossacks. But I was young. I didn't pay much attention."

"What did you do with the traditions during the occupation?"

"Fortunately, the family that took me in was not very religious. I think Father considered that when he looked for arrangements. They were Catholics but rarely went to Mass. Of course on special occasions like Christmas or Easter they went to the village church with me—so as to not arouse suspicions with the authorities. They taught me enough about how to behave in the church but assured me that they would not let the priest talk me into anything."

"Weren't neighbors suspicious?" I asked.

"I think they believed the story that I was a niece escaping from the big city. And I didn't too much mind the times I had to go to the church. The religious part didn't mean much to me, but the music was nice. And I remember the candles. They reminded me of the menorah that Father lit at *Hanukah*. I tried to think about them like I had thought about the *yahrzeit* as a little girl; little flames reaching for heaven."

"Like the flames in your Chagall." I pointed to the print on the wall above the bookcase. "Candle flames are present in many religious traditions. It's interesting. They symbolize so many things we value—life, love, warmth, enlightenment, remembrance."

"Yes, especially remembrance. And Sol and I promise this—André will not forget about you."

"I am sure of that," Rosie responded. "Nor will we ever forget him."

Cecile rose from her seat and reached for the apron she had put aside. "But enough about me. You must be hungry after your drive and all this talk, *non*?"

I went upstairs with Sol to fetch André and Esther. I was indeed hungry and the heavenly odor of Cecile's yet-to-be-identified cooking served only to magnify that sensation. When we returned, a large steaming pot was on the table. We took our places.

Cecile began filling bowls as we passed them to her. "Today I have made a bouillabaisse like we made at home in the south of France, as best I can. We never used shellfish—only fish with fins—grandfather would never accept shellfish. But otherwise it is like they make in Marseilles. Of course, here the bread is different. Maybe some Frenchman will move nearby and make some baguettes. Who knows? Meanwhile we will have your delicious New York rye bread. We will combine the cultures." I was pleased to see how she was now smiling.

I had placed the chalice at the center of the table. After all the bowls were filled, Sol lit the candle at its center. "Love and remembrance," he said.

I looked around the table at the gathering, and especially at André. He looked at ease and happy. For the time being all seemed right with the world.

CHAPTER 27

A Letter from Poland

1948

When Jason re-upped a couple of years ago, the Army sent him to Officer Candidate School and nine months of intensive Russian language training. He is now permanently stationed in Berlin working on refugee resettlement and repatriation. A letter from him was waiting in the mailbox when I arrived home from the lab late this afternoon. I came in through the kitchen screen door a little breathlessly, waving the letter.

"News from the front," I exclaimed. Rosie turned around. She had been peeling potatoes at the sink. I put my free arm around her waist and gave her a little kiss.

"Good news, I hope," she said. She held her arms askew, avoiding wetting the letter or me. Wiping her hands on her apron she sat down at the kitchen table. She pushed aside the small pile of books and assignments she had brought home from her school while I seated myself opposite her. With a butter knife I slit open the envelope, unfolded the lengthy letter within, and then began to read aloud.

A.P.O. 967

10 September 1948

Dear Mom and Dad,

I am beginning this letter while on a brief assignment in Warsaw. I am sure Dad would be especially interested in the details of this latest adventure, so I decided to write some of it up before details slipped from mind. But first I should assure you that I am fine, at least in body. I have to say that some of the destruction and misery that we come across much of the time is heartbreaking and hard on the spirit. So I am glad that I can play some role in beginning the healing process. I am giving a lot of thought to plans for resuming college when I leave the Army, but more of that at another time.

Perhaps I have mentioned Vassili in a previous letter. He is my Russian liaison in Warsaw, whenever I am sent here for some kind of exchange or repatriation negotiation. He is in his mid-thirties and I find him a heck of a nice guy. Of course we never talk politics, but I suspect, if we were allowed to, we wouldn't disagree on many things. Before he was in the military he was teaching languages at Moscow State University, so his command of both English and Polish is superb. But he allows me to practice my Russian, except when I get stuck. (My German is also improving.)

But what I wanted to tell you about is a trip Vassili and I made into eastern Poland. I had mentioned to him that my father had emigrated from Poland when he was a kid. Without hesitation he declared that he would borrow a jeep from the Soviet motor pool and go on a trip to Wizna, if I were willing. I get the impression that he is well liked and respected among his Soviet comrades and easily wins favors. For my part I have a lot of flexibility when I am on one of these off-post assignments, so I eagerly accepted his invitation.

We set out in the morning and followed the main road running in a northeasterly direction from Warsaw to Bialystok. The destruction from the war is everywhere—wrecked buildings, burned out tanks and trucks, blast craters, some of them right in the middle of the road. In some respects this is not different from what I have been seeing in Germany. The big difference is that in Germany the repair and rebuilding is off to a good start, at least in the Western sectors. But in Poland it seems that not much is being done. Vassili says that the Russians are concentrating on the destruction in their own country, but I suspect they also harbor a basic distrust of the Poles. Where necessary, the locals have made makeshift repairs to the road, enough for a jeep or truck to get through. In one place they seem to have rolled boulders into a bomb crater and placed a large barn door over that to serve as a roadbed.

By early afternoon we came to the town of Zambrów where we stopped for a rest and a snack from the rations we had brought with us. We parked at the edge of a large square that was the site of a massacre that took place at the beginning of the war. The story is well known among the Russian troops and Vassili seemed eager to tell me about it. It seems that between the wars the town was the location of a major military barracks as well as a military school. In the course of the fighting against the German invasion in 1939, about four thousand Polish troops were taken captive in the area and cordoned off in the parade ground, which is where we were taking our break. The Germans surrounded the square with machine guns and at nightfall gave the order that no one would be allowed to rise from the ground for any reason. Some time during the night a large number of horses that had belonged to the local regiment were stampeded through the square, trampling the sleeping soldiers. When many of the Poles rose in panic the Germans opened fire, only stopping when some of their own men were wounded by stray bullets. Throughout the night, no further movement was allowed and no help was brought in despite the cries of the wounded and dying. I have to admit I lost my appetite hearing this, looking about and trying to imagine carnage taking place right where we were sitting. Vassili, having heard the story many times, seemed dispassionate.

I looked over at Rosie. She had a somber look. Her eyes were not focused on anything in particular and her head swiveled slightly from side to side as if she was saying, "No, no." As for myself, I felt ambivalent. Atrocity stories were nothing new. The Germans in Belgium in the First World War. The Japanese internment camps. And more recently the profusion of details about the extermination camps at Auschwitz and elsewhere. It was mind numbing. Besides I am ambivalent about the Poles. The old folks used to talk about the anti-Semitism and pogroms. I don't remember this personally, but there were many stories. I asked Rosie if I should continue reading. She nodded yes.

> After Zambrów, it was another 15 or 20 miles to the village of Rutki, where a side road turned north towards Wizna. (I am curious about the old family name Rutkiewicz. I suppose it means that some of our ancestors came from there. It appears to have been a significant crossroad town on the way to Bialystok, but it is a shambles now.) The north-running road is in even worse condition than the main road. In many places there are scars of heavy fighting that are only slowly fading. Eventually we joined another main road just a few miles east of Wizna.

> Entering the town after crossing a temporary bridge over the Narew River, I noticed off to the right a sign marking a footpath. Using my rudimentary Polish I decided it led to the Jewish cemetery. Turning south into the town we stopped at the Russian garrison, which is housed in the

rectory of the old Catholic church. By good fortune the commanding officer is a Russian captain who was a casual acquaintance of Vassili at Moscow State University.

Generally, the Russians are quite friendly and accommodating to Americans, despite the serious wrangling at high levels. (As you know the Berlin blockade continues, but we are kept well supplied by the airlift.) Captain Kirov is no exception. He gave us a room and a valet and we joined him and his second in command for supper. Nothing fancy-boiled meat of some kind, with potatoes and plenty of cabbage. Conversation at the dinner table was mostly casual and mostly in Russian, which I could pretty much follow—Vassili and Kirov swapping anecdotes about the University, news about the refugee situation, etc. I noticed that politics and the international situation were assiduously avoided.

After dinner Kirov led us on a walking tour of the town. We began at the Catholic church next to the garrison headquarters. The church is largely intact but in a state of disrepair. Religious devotion is strongly suspect under the present government, but a few of the older people who probably do not fear for their future prospects still attend and take care of the priest who lives in the basement. From here the main street, a rutted, muddy affair showing some evidence of a previous cobbling, passes by a collection of small, shabby, state-owned shops. We took a detour through some of the side streets off to the right that border the river. Here, Kirov explained, was the location of the Jewish quarter.

Naturally my curiosity was aroused at this point, but I chose not to break into Kirov's narrative, hoping to learn more in due course. The houses are small, single story stuccoed buildings, mostly ochre with shake roofs.

They are scattered about, separated in some cases by the charred remains of other houses. There doesn't seem to be much activity. Here and there some stocky woman looked at us from the doorway, often a scrawny child sitting on the doorstep at her feet. Some men were working in the occasional vegetable patch. Kirov did not offer much commentary except to say that no Jews lived here any more. He did offer that many of them abandoned the town during early part of the century and that about 700 lived here before the war, about a quarter of the total population.

I found myself a little surprised by the numbers. In my childhood memory I thought of the town as a much smaller place. Of course my world was confined to the Jewish quarter and the main street leading to the synagogue. I also remembered again having once or twice ventured with my friends to the Catholic church. It was strange to think of Jason being quartered next door to it. I resumed reading.

> We continued along the main street to the northern edge of the town where once again I saw the path leading to the old Jewish cemetery. Nearby was a ruined building site that Kirov told us was the location of the synagogue. Only a brick foundation wall and a shallow pit that had been a cellar remained. Most of the building debris had been removed, but it was evident that the synagogue had burned down at some point. While Kirov and Vassili stopped at a bench by the side of the road to have a smoke I wandered up the path leading to the cemetery. It was a narrow track in the woods behind some farmhouses. At the top of a low hill an iron gate guarding the entrance was still in place, but I had to look carefully to see that this was a burial site. Most of the stones had fallen or had been pushed over. It was obvious that no one had tended to the place in years and weeds and brush were

beginning to obscure the markers. I squatted in a corner of the enclosure looking about, trying to understand my feelings about this place. Here, I knew, were the resting places of some of my ancestors, mostly forgotten and desecrated. But it was a peaceful place in which nature was reasserting itself. The abundant bird life was oblivious to the meaning of the place. In the declining light a strange beauty coexisted there alongside a chilling reminder of a hateful past.

Rejoining Vassili and Kirov, we made our way back into town, stopping at a tavern on the main street. It appeared to be an old establishment now operated by the government and seemed to be the only place open for business at that time of the evening.

My mind flashed back to the fragments of childhood memory again. The dusty main street, the noisy men putting aside their toil at day's end, the kopek I had found in front of the tavern.

The main room just inside the door was filled with several groups of noisy Russian soldiers. At the sight of three officers the place grew quiet, most eyes turned warily on us as we made our way towards the back of the tavern. As we passed through Kirov made a gesture indicating that the men should carry on, sort of a wave with the back of his hand. We ordered dark Polish beer, just now starting to be produced at a restored brewery in Warsaw. Gathered around a little table in the corner, Kirov turned to me and said that I probably wondered what happened to the Jewish population of Wizna. He had guessed my Jewish roots. Perhaps it was our name. Perhaps it was my curiosity about the Jewish cemetery. What he told me I record with some trepidation. Perhaps you would rather not know, but you have brought me up to believe that truth withheld only serves error, so

I have written it down. But understandably you might want to skip reading the next few paragraphs.

I looked up at Rosie. Her face revealed her conflicted emotions: pride and delight in hearing from our son overlaid with sadness and dread. She still retains that certain kind of prettiness that I always thought revealed her essential sweetness. Her long hair was gathered in an ivory clip behind her neck and I noticed a few gray hairs that had lately appeared in the tresses. She murmured that I should continue.

Following the Russo-German invasion in 1939, the eastern part of Poland, including Wizna, was handed over to the Russians. Then, in 1941 the Nazis unleashed their Blitzkrieg in the East, overrunning the town once again. During the Soviet occupation the relationship between the town's Jews and their Christian neighbors had become tense. There had always been a latent anti-Semitism, but the fact that the Soviet occupiers overlooked this and provided opportunities for some of the more talented Jews sowed animosity, especially among the town's rabble. And this was despite the fact that Jews had participated in the celebrated defense of the town during the original German invasion. In fact, one of the most colorful anti-German partisans of the war, the author (and gangster) Ujrke Nachalnik, was a Jew from Wizna. Wherever the German army went, it was not averse to rounding up and murdering Jews whenever it suited their purposes. But whenever they could exploit local anti-Jewish feelings, they played the most cynical of games, by encouraging and supporting pogroms and atrocities. This way they could demonstrate that their racial policies were not just a German thing and therefore justifiable. In some cases by putting a lid on some more extreme behavior, they could even pose as "protectors" of Jews. It helped the scheme to have released from jail scores of Polish hooligans and degenerates.

In any event, when the Germans entered Wizna in June of 1941, they made their intentions clear by shooting several dozen Jewish men whom they accused of being Soviet "collaborators." Most of the Jewish quarter had been burned down during the air bombardment. The remaining Jews evacuated the village, most going north to the town of Jedwabne, trying to dodge Polish bandits along the way as best they could. It was in Jedwabne, about a month later, that the most unspeakable event took place. Early on a morning in July a group of Gestapo officers arrived in town to confer with local Polish authorities. The Germans, it is said, wanted to eliminate the Jews except for skilled craftsmen—tailors, cobblers, blacksmiths and the like—who could be of use to them. The Poles argued that no Jew should be spared. Meanwhile, groups of Polish peasants arrived from nearby villages as if there would be a fair, presumably poised to plunder any vacated houses.

Rosie was leaning forward with her elbows on the edge of the table. She held her head, hands cupped over her eyes in a posture of anguish. She did not signal for me to stop reading. I went on.

A short while later a group of Poles went about the town forcing every Jew out of their homes, including all the refugees from neighboring villages, including those from Wizna. According to witnesses, not a German was in sight. All the Jews were forced to the town square where, armed with a variety of makeshift weapons, the Poles ordered them at first to pull up the grass and weeds from among the cobblestones. Some young men were ordered to carry away a statue of Lenin that the Soviets had erected and bury it. The rumor has it that those men were shot and put in the pit along with the statue. Since the Poles presumably didn't have guns, if this rumor is true there must have been at least a few Germans involved. All day long the Jews were kept in the square under the sun without food or water, meanwhile being tormented by Polish hooligans. Finally they were herded in the direction of the Jewish cemetery. At the head of the procession was the rabbi of the town, forced to carry a red banner.

Next came the most horrifying phase of this event. The Jews were forced into a barn at the edge of town. Then the barn was doused with flammable liquid and set afire. Hardly anyone escaped. A local Pole stood at the door armed with an axe ready to cut into anyone who managed to come through. Estimates of those burned alive range between 600 and 900. By some accounts, even the Germans, who had indirectly set the whole affair into motion, were horrified by the bestiality of the Polish mob. Kirov said that there are many stories from witnesses which are horrifying in their detail, but decided that what he had told us was gruesome enough. An interesting thing is that, up to now, the official accounting of the Jedwabne pogrom issued by the Polish authorities claims that the whole episode was a massacre carried out entirely by the Germans. They like to argue that Poles rescued many Jews during the war and also that in most cases it was only criminal elements who were goaded into committing atrocities. But the evidence is so strong now that, in this particular case, the horror was carried out almost entirely by Poles who had lived side by side with the Jewish community for hundreds of years. Kirov claims to have investigated the matter himself, interviewing witnesses and other residents, and is thoroughly convinced of where the responsibility lies.

As I finished reading the page I saw that Jason's letter continued on a different kind of stationery and was dated a week later. Rosie had risen from her chair and had resumed working at the kitchen sink. She had not said anything. She was clearly deep in thought, but I guessed she was not eager to talk. "There's more of the letter. Shall I continue?" I asked. She replied that for the time being I should read it to myself. She would get to it later. Again I thought of Jason sitting in the same tavern that I had walked by as a child; an icon that remained fixed in earliest memories. I continued reading, this time in silence.

16 September 1948

I have returned to the headquarters in Berlin and I am able to continue the letter that I had begun to Poland. I realize that I stopped writing rather abruptly. Frankly I was not sure I could make any sensible commentary on what I had written. I only wanted to record the events before they faded from mind. Meanwhile, as I go about Army business I find myself pondering the events that I mentioned in the first part of this letter. What is it that drives people to act so horribly towards other human beings? What gives them this license? These are difficult questions that I know have been asked from time immemorial, and I'm sure many answers have been offered. But I feel I must find my own understanding. The Army is hardly a place for philosophical discussions, so I hope you don't mind my venting some of my feelings with you. After all, Esther and I have been encouraged to engage in our own spiritual journeys. Perhaps I know this will sound naïve, but let me try.

I think that at the heart of the matter is the error of idolatry. Perhaps some would label it sin. People create their own gods to worship. They may talk about "the" God and think that their loyalty is with this single entity, but it seems that when it suits their primitive instincts their loyalty is with a pantheon of gods. The chief god among these is the god of power who gives license to control, or even eliminate, any competing groups of humans. It is this god that permits his followers to dehumanize the "others," to categorize them as a threat that must be annihilated. Then there is the god of blood lust, a kind of brother to the god of power. Maybe this creation stems from the hunting instinct. Dominion over the world of nature for our own legitimate requirements perhaps is justified—but dominion, for its own sake or for thrill of seeing the hunted animal suffer, is another thing. I could also mention the god of material wealth who promises security and well being. It's a false promise, of course, but he gives permission to steal and plunder.

But I have to ask myself if there is a true god, and what does this god give us and what does he ask of us. To me, clearly he is not a great anthropomorphized being in the sky who floats on clouds and listens in on all of our prayers. I am not entirely sure of how to frame my feelings on this, but I think I had the beginnings of understanding in my Coming of Age piece when I was thirteen. I seem to recall I titled my presentation "I See God Everywhere" or something like that. Indeed, if one conceives of God as all-being, as a mystery of which we are a part and of which other humans and all nature are a part, it hard to see how we can be impelled to acts of needless destruction and cruelty. This then, is a god that is not out there or looking down, but a god that is indeed everywhere, and within us. Like the Hebrew God, this god is beyond understanding, beyond imagining, even beyond naming. Like the Hebrew God, He is constantly to be praised—which is to say, constantly kept in mind. What He gives us is a sense of place in the universe, a sense of being part of the eternal. And what He asks of

us is only, as it is put down in the book of Micah that
you may remember I read in my Bar Mitzvah Haftarah,
"but to do justice, and to love kindness, and to walk
humbly with thy God."

"His kopek is well spent," I found myself saying under my breath.
This odd thought had leapt to mind as I read Jason's ruminations
and I was startled to realize I had audibly voiced it. Like strange
juxtapositions encountered in dreams, I suppose it represents some
deeper tension in my life experience.

Rosie turned from the sink. "Did you say something?" she
asked. Her face had regained a measure of composure.

"It's nothing," I said. "Just an odd thought." I decided to put
it aside. "Let me know if I can help out with dinner." I resumed
reading the letter, which dealt with day-to-day concerns. He again
assured us of his health and inquired of ours. He wished Esther best
of luck as a new freshman at college. He looked forward to the end
of his tour of duty and resuming his college work next year. Finally,
he thanked us for being a sounding board for his musings.

While I set the table and tossed the dinner salad, Rosie read
the remainder of Jason's letter. For a short time, as we ate, we were
consumed in our own thoughts. It was not our usual pattern. I
was having difficulty making the reality of wartime Poland seem
congruent with my usual optimistic view of mankind. The fate
of the Jews of Wizna and the behavior of their neighbors was an
actuality that my mind accepted only with difficulty. Jason, on the
other hand, having come of age in a more expansive milieu, seemed
capable, for all its ugliness, to derive something from this history.

In time I asked Rosie what she was making of the letter. It was
clear her focus was on the implications for Jason of his experiences.
"It seems like a harsh dose of reality for a twenty-two year old to
deal with, especially when I contrast it with my own innocuous
growing up," she remarked.

"That's the story of war, I guess. Some very fast growing up
takes place."

"I know," she said. "And for those who survive, we can only hope some will be inspired to make the world a little better. And as for Jason, I somehow feel sure that whatever he decides to do in the future, it will be a wise choice."

Now, more than ever, I am eager to see him home and safe.

CHAPTER 28

For All that is our Life

1955

On a beautiful Sunday morning in August two years ago, while bathing, Rosie discovered a small lump in her breast. She was on her summer recess and I was involved only with research, free from teaching and committee obligations. We had planned to have lunch on the porch behind the house and then take a long afternoon walk. At lunchtime Rosie seemed unusually quiet. I suspected something was bothering her.

"You're a bit subdued, Rosie," I began.

"I'm sorry," she replied. She hesitated, and then continued. "I suppose I'm a little worried. It's probably nothing, but I think I found a lump in my breast."

"Are you sure?"

"Not absolutely, but it worries me a bit."

I tried to hide the small panic within myself. It had been just two years before that sister Celia had died as a result of breast cancer. This was an all too familiar story among Ashkenazi Jewish women. Younger women were cautioned to look for early signs in hopes that the cancer could be treated. I tried to sound upbeat and optimistic.

"Let's not panic yet," I replied. "These things can be benign cysts or some kind of mastitis. Or maybe nothing at all. But to be on the safe side I'll set up a visit to the doctor first thing in the morning." I went over to Rosie and gave her a long hug. "Meanwhile let's take advantage of this lovely day."

After lunch, Rosie and I walked down to the path that follows the river out into the countryside north of the town. Rosie brought along her bird glasses. The sun shone in a cloudless sky, but it hardly felt hot. A cooling breeze from the northwest raised ripples on the surface of the water. In mid-afternoon the bird life was not evident until, a couple of miles beyond the town, the stream broadened out considerably. Here a marshy area extended along the shoreline adjacent to the path. In this place the flow of the water was barely perceptible, but near the opposite bank I could see glints from faster moving water. We stopped and sat down on a log lying in the shade of a gigantic white poplar tree.

There hadn't been much conversation between us since the beginning of our walk. A few times, when the path was wide enough for us to walk side-by-side I took Rosie's hand in mine. She responded with a little squeeze but remained subdued.

"You're feeling worried, aren't you?" I tendered.

"Maybe. But, you know, out here somehow I feel quite okay. There's always something to worry about if you try. Perhaps there's not more to fret about than usual, and if there is, so be it. It can't spoil the moment. Look at this." She gestured towards the scene laid out before us.

I had been gazing about in a general way. Now I took in some details. For a moment I caught myself wondering what it was in the character of the reflected glints near the far-off shore that informed me that the water was flowing right to left rather than the opposite way. It was a physicist's kind of distraction, which seemed oddly out of place. A couple of hundred feet downstream, four ducks floated in the shallows. Occasionally one of them disappeared under the water, emerging with hardly a drop of water on its back. Even at a distance I could tell from the white bodies and green and chestnut colored heads that these were Common Mergansers. Just knowing that small fact somehow deepened the experience. It was through Rosie that I had mostly overcome the physicist's penchant for always favoring explanation over cataloging.

"Wait," Rosie whispered excitedly. She raised up her binoculars and trained them on the opposite bank. After a few moments she said, "A Green Heron. Just a juvenile. You'd mistake him for a rock if he hadn't moved." After studying the bird for a few moments she handed the field glasses to me, pointing out the location. I expected a stately bird but instead found a round medium sized hunchback directly at the water's edge—mottled brown and white below, chestnut cheeks, mostly brown above with a hint of green on his crown. He was indeed as still as a rock, only occasionally swiveling his head as he surveyed the water.

"Not much green about him," I remarked.

"Yes. But wait until he grows up. Meanwhile he does his thing—fishing for his dinner. I would venture he doesn't have a care in the world. Maybe there's a lesson in that for the rest of us. Play your part in the scheme of things. The future holds what the future holds."

"Are you saying that we are meant to be like the Green Heron?" I asked as I handed back the binoculars. "Fishing for our dinner?"

Rosie uttered a little chortle before responding. "Well, not really. We fit in the scheme of things a little differently. It's our nature to try to make the world conform to us, rather than the other way around, I guess." She thought for a moment. "But you know, we have our place in the scheme of things as well—maybe it's just to coexist with all of this." She stretched her hands apart as if to gather in the whole scene. "I feel privileged to be part of it."

"It is a privilege," I affirmed.

Rosie seemed lost in thought, then added. "It's more than that. Peaceful—happy. Let the future do its thing."

That was the way the greatest ordeal of our life together began. In the coming month examinations and tests confirmed a diagnosis of a cancerous tumor in the left breast. To be absolutely sure we drove to Albany and to New York for second opinions. Finally, in October, when the trees in the hills near our home were at the peak of their fall color, Rosie and I set out for the Cornell Medical Center in New York for a scheduled mastectomy. Esther, who was doing her practice teaching not far from Rosie's old home in New York, met us. It was a great comfort to be close to our families during the hospital stay, but Rosie longed to be home again. Jason, who at the time was in the middle of his history master's qualifying exams, phoned several times from Ithaca. Finally after ten days, Esther and I bundled Rosie into the car for the return trip. As we drove up the valley into town, Rosie's normal cheerfulness began to return.

Emerging from the car and grasping my arm, she stood for a while taking in the scene. The birch tree behind the rear porch shone like a golden halo over the eaves. A little distance beyond, on the low hills framing the neighborhood, maples and beeches flaunted their most extreme scarlets and oranges as if anticipating the late frosts and winds that would end their gaudy show. Rosie, withdrawing her arm from mine, asked that she make her own way into the house.

By January Rosie had resumed her teaching job at the middle school. She felt almost fully recovered. Our brush with the reality of mortality enhanced the joy we felt for the life we had built together. Nothing was to be taken for granted, and each day was a gift. Each new experience was to be celebrated. After we were introduced to the sport of Nordic skiing, we explored some of our favorite summer trails now shrouded in quiet white blankets of snow. Rosie resumed her bird watching hobby, discovering an altered world of wildlife brought about by the fall migration of species and the winter season's withdrawal of food sources. As spring came on we felt each change with an aroused sensitivity. In the woods, we perceived the smell in the air changing at first from a clean, sanitary crispness to the light vegetable scent of awakening greenery. Following soon came the mild perfume of blooming dogwood and rhododendron.

In June we went to New York for Esther's graduation with a Master's degree from Teacher's College at Columbia. There was a family celebration at The Excelsior Kosher Restaurant, where thirty-five years before, we had celebrated our own college graduations and where we had announced our engagement. Thinking of that time, I thought of the faces that were gone from the room now: Mother and Father, Mr. Dubrow, and especially Celia. But for the most part we were here again; even grandma Dubrow, somewhat shriveled and unsteady, but still showing that cheerful warmth that was so much like Rosie's. At the end of the evening, Esther delighted us with the news that she had found a position teaching biology at the high school in Pittsfield, not too far down the road from our home.

Then, only a few days later, the three of us drove over to Ithaca for Jason's graduation from Cornell's College of Arts and Sciences with a Master's degree in modern history. After the ceremony we walked down from cavernous Barton Hall to the lower campus. In Willard Straight Hall we bought some ice cream cones and then found a low stone wall to sit on behind the building while we ate them and enjoyed the sun. Off to the right in the valley Lake Cayuga glistened in the distance. Directly below us, across a handsome broad lawn, the rooftops of the town were visible. A series of low hills hid the other Finger Lakes lying west of there from view: Seneca, Keuka, Canandaigua. I thought about the family vacation in Ithaca when I was attending a meeting of the Physical Society. One of the children's car games was naming all of the lakes west to east, east to west, and alphabetically.

There, perched in a row on the wall, Jason told us of his plans for the future. It was one of those announcements that may catch one by surprise but, upon reflection, might have been expected. Jason revealed that he had been accepted at the Harvard Divinity School and intended to prepare for the Unitarian ministry. Like Rosie, Jason has the sweet disposition and composure one would want to see in someone who becomes involved in the lives of other people. But it is more than that. Over the years he had developed a kind of intellectual curiosity, which it seems to me informs his spirituality. I looked over at Rosie. She sat between Esther and Jason, and now as she expressed her approval of Jason's intentions, she placed an arm around both of them and drew them in. There was no mistaking her joy.

The summer was memorable. Rosie and I spent several weeks hiking sections of the Appalachian Trail running along the Blue Ridge of Virginia and North Carolina. Both Esther and Jason worked at summer camps not far from home and appeared at the doorstep from time to time, usually with a friend or two in tow. Rosie was in the best of health and in the fall plunged with enthusiasm into her teaching.

Even at the University the mood was increasingly upbeat. Requests for research grants were looked upon favorably in the federal agencies. Everywhere in academia student numbers were on the increase and administrators were aware that it would not be long before the postwar generation would come flooding into the colleges. All through 1954 we were caught up in this pervasive mood of hope and optimism.

But then, while taking one of our usual Sunday walks, Rosie noticed unusual back pains that refused to subside after several days. On Wednesday morning I drove her downtown to see Dr. Raskin, the young physician who had assumed the practice of our now retired family doctor. Raskin had first come to my attention some twenty years ago when he was a pre-med student. Over the years hundreds of students had gone through my courses, but only a few, for various reasons, lodged clearly in memory. Jon Raskin, who had a habit of following me to my office after a lecture asking challenging questions, was one of those few. Rarely did his questions have to do directly with the course material at hand. It was clear that he was having little trouble with the required work. At one point he was bothered with the concept of mass. Was it defined in terms of force by Newton's second law or was force defined by mass? Or was mass defined by Newton's gravitational law? Unlike a majority of students, who are content to work with the equations, Jon always sought deeper understanding. When he returned to town years later, after spending the war in the army as a field surgeon, I felt more than comfortable engaging him as our family physician. We were now on a first name basis.

After examining Rosie, we met with Jon in his office. He didn't look too much different from my memories of him from his student days—slight, athletic build, upturned nose, prominent chin. Only now his hairline had begun to recede, and he wore thin-rimmed glasses that barely obscured the crow's-feet alongside his eyes. He met us with a serious expression on his face.

"Let's not worry yet," he said to Rosie. "But you were right to come in. Most of the time back pain is just one of those prices of life—annoying, even debilitating—but sure to go away with rest and a few aspirin. But we can't be too cautious in your case."

"Could it be connected with the cancer?" I wanted to know.

"Well, as I said, Abe, it's too soon for major worry. But I would like to have Rosie go over to Albany for a series of X-rays. We'll know more then. You know, that's the problem with breast cancer—all cancers for that matter. We can take out the tumor and destroy lymph nodes, but the cancer can still sneak some malignant cells around the body. If they metastasize it can be a problem. For now let's just hope for the best."

On the drive home Rosie seemed subdued, but composed. Her first words after we pulled out onto the main road surprised me. "It's been a very nice year, Abe."

"I hope it continues this way," was all I could think of saying.

"Whether it does or not, it's been a very nice year. The future can never detract from this year—these years—we've had, Abe." She was silent for a minute. "For the moment, how about a nice lunch and a walk?"

We stopped at a favorite inn next to the river at the edge of town. Later we walked upstream on the riverside trail. Each of us was immersed in our own thoughts. I found myself thinking about the idea of gratitude. I have much to be grateful for. Yet, in moments of pain and crisis, should I be expected to utter prayers of thanks? I thought about the old Jews in the synagogues living in poverty, driven from their old homes, threatened with violence—chanting the Sabbath prayers:

> We give thanks unto Thee, for Thou art the Lord our
> God and the God of our fathers forever and ever.

I thought about some words we had sung at the Unitarian church:

> For all that is our life we give our thanks and praise . . .

I thought about the victims of the gas chambers. Did they utter prayers of gratitude as they choked on the Zyklon B fumes? Was there thankfulness in the minds of the terrified Jews of Wizna in the smoking hell of a burning barn in Jedwabne?

Rosie came up alongside me and took my arm. Silently she pointed across the stream. In a dappled glen about thirty feet beyond the river's edge there were three deer feeding in the brush—a doe and two yearling fawns. Patches of sunlight played on their backs. I thought that for them the moment was enough. Rosie's eyes shone with delight. I knew that though she worried about the future, for her the moment was precious. My dismal musings suddenly were gone. This, I thought, belongs to us forever.

Forever and ever . . .

I must have been smiling.

CHAPTER 29

Thou Source of Light Immortal

1956

We drove downtown to Jon Raskin's office early on a spring afternoon last year. It was one of those days when it seemed as if the winter was valiantly holding out against the coming of summer. All the trees when seen from a distance appeared as in a watercolor painting, bare limbs covered with a semi-transparent wash of pale green. In our front yard the dogwood was adorned in a profusion of white blossoms. Yet, with a chill wind blowing in from the northwest, I had pulled my mackinaw from back of the closet where I had thought it might stay until next year.

We hadn't been seated in the waiting room more than ten minutes when Jon appeared. This was unusual. Generally we would make our way into his office on our own. As usual, he was all smiles in greeting us. Both Rosie and I thought of him almost in a parental way, and we knew that his cheer upon seeing us reflected a mutual fondness. But I also felt that there was something ominous to be read into the spareness of his greetings and the fact that he had come out of his office to welcome us. He took Rosie's arm as we entered his office.

We sat down on the plain leather loveseat that faced the window. Jon pulled up a chair and sat opposite us. On this visit he skipped small talk. "How have you been feeling, Rosie?" he asked. "Pains, exhaustion, anything unusual?"

"I still feel the backaches," she replied. "They come and go and they don't seem to have much to do with how I'm moving. Sometimes I have this pain in the middle of the night."

Jon nodded his head. "I'm not surprised." He swiveled around, reaching for a file that was laid out on his desk. He opened it and turned to us. His expression was somewhat grave. "I'll come straight to the point. The results came in from Albany yesterday. I'm afraid there is a metastasis in the vicinity of the sternum and rib cage. It's not a nice situation, but there are still a few options."

Rosie had been holding my hand. Now she squeezed it harder as if clinging to the edge of a pit. Then she relaxed and replied. "I guess I've been anticipating this," she said finally. "Just let us know what must be done." Rosie's composure was not exactly a surprise. She was, after all, a realist in crisis situations. I realized that I had been living in a bubble, knowing intellectually what the possibilities are, but holding fast to the most optimistic scenarios.

"Well the first thing we must do is connect you with a good oncologist. It's not my specialty, of course, but I think the next steps will be radiation treatments. I don't know the odds of a cure, but hopefully the progress of the disease can be slowed and pain ameliorated. There are also hormone therapies, but I don't have a handle on that."

Jon gave us a list of several oncologists in Boston, Albany, and New York and asked us to let him know which of them he should get in touch with. Apart from that, he told us the best he could do at the moment was to prescribe a more powerful analgesic and a sedative.

As we were about to open the door to leave, he stopped us. "I don't know if you know that you two are special people in my practice." He seemed almost embarrassed. "Of course I try to do my best for all patients, but you two go back a long way. I guess I've told you that I was the first in my family to finish college, and when I look back at it Abe, it was you and a couple of other profs that inspired me to make the most of it."

"You were a special kind of student, Jon," I said.

"Kind of a pest, I sometimes think." He grinned. "But anyway, never hesitate to call if I can be of help."

The summer of 1955 went relatively smoothly. Twice weekly we drove over to Albany for Rosie's radiation treatments. Rosie busied herself in her garden, at least as much as her energy would permit. Jason and one of his girlfriends came in from Boston for a couple weeks. The four of us packed tents and other camping gear and set up a camp on Rainbow Lake, close to the terminus of the Appalachian Trail at Mount Katahdin. Rosie was no longer up to extensive backpacking, but we went for day-hikes and canoed on the lake. Jason has taken seriously to fly-fishing and surprised us a couple of times with a trout dinner done over the campfire. By the end of the summer Rosie was determined to return to her teaching job in September.

Soon our life settled into a satisfying routine of work and play. Each new day, more than ever, came as a gift. I had negotiated a reduced teaching schedule so I could be of more assistance to Rosie. Each weekday I would help her get to school, and if she did not have a ride home I would come and pick her up. Once a week we went to Albany for treatments and evaluation. Several evenings a week we would do something special: a dinner out, a movie, a concert. We made sure to take regular walks. If Rosie was not feeling well a drive in the country would take the place of a walk. We tried to focus on the positive. If Rosie sensed that I was about to lapse in a dismal "what if," she would quickly bring me around to "what is."

Sometimes Esther would come up for the weekend. She and Rosie would almost always end up in the kitchen trying a new recipe. This was my opportunity to go down to the University to work with the graduate students and post-docs. There was so much to be discovered in our burgeoning field of solid-state physics. But it was also clear, since the work of Watson and Crick on DNA, that the intersection of physics and biology might be the frontier science for the remainder of the century. I made a point of reminding the young researchers to keep on eye on opportunities in that area. Perhaps I hoped that someday this would provide the key to understanding cancer.

Just after Thanksgiving, we went to Boston to visit Jason. We walked the Freedom Trail, winding through the city past Kings Chapel, jokingly thought of as the "St. Peter's of the Unitarians," past the doorstep of Paul Revere's house, ending on the deck of Old Ironsides. In the evening we heard the Boston Symphony perform Beethoven's Ninth Symphony. During the final choral movement I reflected on the audacity of Beethoven, alone, sick, and deaf, setting to glorious music Schiller's *Ode to Joy*:

> Freude, schöner Götterfunken . . .
> Alle Menschen werden Brüder
> Wo dein sanfter Flügel weilt.

"Joy, thou source of light immortal . . . All mankind shall be as brothers beneath thy tender wings." I glanced at Rosie. In the corner of her eye there was a tear that I thought to be a tear of joy—or perhaps a tear of empathy for poor Beethoven. If, with Schiller, joy is the inspiration antithetical to strife, perhaps that idea was playing out in our lives.

Rosie had always liked to walk to work, but now I drove her part of the way and made sure she had a ride home. As the weeks went by, even with the warming days of early spring, Rosie asked to be dropped off closer and closer to the school. Now she was finding it painful to walk too much. She was easily winded. By May, I was taking her the entire way to and from work. But she loved her work and her students and refused to give up as long as she felt she was doing a worthwhile job. The principal was sympathetic. He found a little closet-like room near the storerooms where I installed a cot for Rosie to have a short nap after lunch.

I went with her to the final teacher's meeting of the school year. It had been Rosie's thirtieth year with the school. There was a sheet cake—chocolate with white icing. This was Rosie's favorite combination, but she didn't eat much. The principal gave a little speech, remarking how he was barely out of diapers when Rosie first came to his school to teach. He was careful not to sound as if this was a farewell, but almost everyone knew that she would not be back in the fall. I was asked to say a few words. I recounted how, sometimes Rosie would be so immersed in her teaching that it would take her an hour after she came home to let go of her teacher voice. I told them how much I had learned that was not in my grade school education by occasionally helping her with her lesson plans. There were a couple toasts made with punch in paper cups.

Finally, after many hugs I took Rosie home. We lay down in the double hammock I had strung between the birch tree and the rear porch. She turned on her side; her head nestled in my right arm. Her arm was across my waist. Soon she was asleep. When she awoke, she announced that she felt well enough to go out for a little supper. We went once more to the inn by the river at the edge of town for a light supper of pasta and salad. It was to be the last meal out we ate together. Before going home we took a short walk on the riverside trail.

Throughout the summer Rosie gradually declined but she refused to spend her days in bed. She insisted that she be up and dressed before taking to the chaise on the rear porch. She fretted about how this might be affecting the kids and me, but the joyous side of her personality remained with her to the end. Friends came to visit. Jon Raskin came to see her couple of times a week even though doctors now rarely made house calls. Carl Becker often stopped by, sometimes with his wife. Carl has told me that the conversations that seemed most comforting to her were those where he could tell her about the social justice and peace action work being done at the church.

Family came too—her brother Alec visiting from Chicago, brother Dave and Dolly, my kid sister Sari. Each of them arrived feeling some trepidation about how to be with someone they felt they were seeing for the last time. And each time their dread was disarmed by Rosie's matter of fact attention to the here and now, her extraordinary sense of living with the present. Despite pain, she delighted in family news and in Sari's undiminished impish ways. André came from New York. He carried with him the dual language copy of *The Little Prince* that Rosie had read to him when he was a boy. This time he read to her the part about the little prince on his home asteroid and the rose he loves. To her delight he read this in French, translating, when necessary, as he went along.

Esther moved back for the summer and Jason came as often as he could. In August, Rosie spent a couple of days in the local hospital being treated for dehydration. Upon her return, we were informed that there was little that could now be done except to make her comfortable. Jon arranged for a palliative care nurse to spend mornings and evenings at the house. Rosie now alternated between periods of morphine induced insensibility and total awareness. I placed the bird feeder where she could more easily see it during her alert periods. She was especially excited to see the finches and orioles.

"Abe, look what's here," she called to me one morning in late August, when I had turned my back to refill her glass. On the feeder a house finch was poking for seeds. This one had a bright orange patch beneath his head, a variation from the usual dull red coloring. "Show off!" she exclaimed. We both laughed.

"Just showing the possible, I guess," I said. "He thinks he is important. Well certainty the finches were important to Darwin."

"Important to us all, Abe." Rosie remained silent for a few moments, her gaze fixed upon the bird until it flew off. I had taken a seat beside the chaise. Despite the mild weather, she lay beneath the pale blue throw that Sari had knitted for us when Jason was born. She had lost weight and her complexion had taken on an unaccustomed pallor. But at this time of partial release from her chronic pain, her eyes had that radiant glow that I had always thought of as the hallmark of her beauty. No wonder, I thought, Plato asserted that vision was due to emanations flowing out from the eye.

"Abe," she went on, "thank you for sharing this life of ours."

"You needn't say that, Rosie."

"No. No, I want you to know that. It's a wondrous thing, this world. To have had this piece of it, especially with you, I feel thankful. To own that together eternally—well, I feel so privileged. I want you to know that."

I thought back to the conversation at our campfire by the edge of the lake long ago. *The eternal now.* I squeezed Rosie's hand. "I'm always with you," I finally said. "That will always be my greatest privilege."

By early September, Esther, Jason, and I were taking turns sitting with her around the clock. It was expected that the end would come in a couple of weeks. Instead, through periods of total alertness alternating with the haze of morphine, Rosie took 26 days to slip away from us. Jason was by her side when he noticed that she wasn't breathing and called the nurse. Finally then, at 11 minutes past 8 pm on the 28th of September of 1956, Rosie, source of our joy and our love, departed from us.

CHAPTER 30

These Three Abide

1956

The weeks following Rosie's death are mostly a blur. But a few disconnected recollections somehow have managed to penetrate my veil of grief. I remember my sister Sari coming to stay with me for a couple of weeks. Esther or Jason came often for a day or two, as their schedules allowed. I also recall that in a daze sometime during the first week I rearranged two of our upstairs rooms. The bedroom at the front of the house that Rosie and I had used for almost thirty years became my study. It's as if a presence of her now moves me to carry on with our life. The small room in the rear that had been my study; my solitary domain for so long, is where I sleep. It looks out on the yard and our old birch tree.

But now, a couple of months later, as winter beckons, from conversations with others I have regained a clearer idea of how those days of loss were passed. It was as if I had been living in a sate of mild amnesia, slowly reconstructing the past during long walks with the kids or with Carl Becker, who is now minister emeritus and a trusted friend. In retrospect, I am a little surprised by my relative helplessness during the first weeks. Before Rosie passed away, I felt well in control; and even as she was slipping away, she seemed still to be a wind beneath my wings. I knew that I would suffer from not having her around me. I knew that I would have to adjust to a great emptiness. But I supposed I would readily cope. Now, however, I feel almost as if I have acquired some of the resilience that was so much a part of her.

It was after the memorial service for Rosie held at Carl's old church, five weeks after she died, that I sensed my strength begin to return. Rosie's wish was for a cremation. It is not a Jewish custom, but she was adamant. She insisted that she had taken up valuable space on the earth, and she would no longer have use for it. Instead of a large funeral gathering just after she died, a service honoring Rosie was arranged for a Friday afternoon in early November. It was important to emphasize to the family that this was not a service of mourning or regret. It was to be a celebration of a life. It was not for Rosie but for us, the living; for those who knew her and loved her.

The family from New York arrived the day before. Dolly took over the kitchen in the morning, preparing a large breakfast of scrambled eggs and lox. She had brought a large sack of bagels. "New York bagels," she assured us. In midmorning Jason and Esther arrived. As usual, Sari kept the mood light and cheerful. She now refers to herself as the jolly maiden aunt. She teased Esther about her social life.

In early afternoon we went down to the church where Carl Becker waited for us. The new, young minister had enthusiastically endorsed my request that Carl conduct the service. Rosie's brother, Alec, had come in from Chicago and was with Carl in his office when we arrived. I had not seen Alec in several years. He had indeed "grown up," as I had predicted to Rosie when I had first seen him more than thirty years ago. Now he was a personable, middle-aged man working in real estate in the sprawling suburbs of the Midwest. His face had become somewhat pudgy, a bit like his father's. His hairline had receded almost to the point of baldness. Rosie sometimes joked that he was a Jewish Buddha.

In Carl's new office we had coffee while he went over the order of service with the family. Carl needed to confer very little with me about the service. Rosie had made known her thoughts about appropriate music and readings. On the regular walks that Carl and I had been taking since his retirement he had learned pretty much all that he needed to know to compose a eulogy. Carl had not met the entire family before, but he knew a great deal about most of them. He kept the conversation upbeat. He knew of the tension within me. We would rejoice that Rosie had been with us and we would strive to keep Rosie's spirit alive into the future. And that spirit was a joyful one of hope and love. Yet, a vague sense of dread was rising within me.

In the sanctuary above us the organ began playing the great Bach organ prelude *Wachet auf*—Sleepers Awake. A few years ago the student radio station had used this piece as the opening theme for its early morning music program. It was a wry choice, either ignorant or dismissive of the theological intent of the title. At the time Rosie had thought it to be an inspiring melody to start off the morning, and she set the clock radio to catch the opening bars.

At two o'clock Carl ushered the family into the sanctuary. As we took our seats in the front pews I glanced around. The room was fairly overflowing. There were teachers from Rosie's school and women from her lady's club and birding group. I could see that university colleagues of mine had come. As I turned to take my place I noticed that André was there with Cecile and Sol. He was a young man now but, as he caught my eye, I saw that he retained the boyish smile that we had known when he lived with us.

There were no flowers on the dais. Instead a splendid arrangement of autumn leaves and grasses that I supposed Rosie's lady's group had gathered was displayed beneath the pulpit. Teasel and cattails from the riverside framed the arrangement—yellow witch hazel, scarlet oak, and orange tinged red maple. A warm late autumn light seeped in from the side windows of the sanctuary, suffusing the space in a pale apricot glow. When the music ceased, Carl stepped to the podium and offered the opening words. He reminded us that we had come to both remember and honor a life and to embrace one another. We also came to give thanks for that which Rosie brought to each of us. The opening words concluded with the reflections on joy and sorrow written by Khalil Gibran:

> When you are joyous, look deep into your heart and you shall find it is only that which has given you sorrow that is giving you joy.

When you are sorrowful look again in your heart,
and you shall see that in truth you are weeping for that
which has been your delight.

Some of you say, "Joy is greater than sorrow," and
others say, "Nay, sorrow is the greater."

But I say unto you, they are inseparable.

Together they come, and when one sits alone with
you at your board, remember that the other is asleep
upon your bed.

There was an opening hymn Rosie herself had chosen from
the Unitarian hymnal. Dave and Dolly are shy about singing in a
church but Sari, always outgoing, joined with enthusiasm.

For the beauty of the earth,
For the splendor of the sky . . .
. . . we raise our voice in grateful praise.

The substance of Carl's eulogy was deeply etched in my
psyche but I found myself drawn in by Carl's telling. It was like
going through a photograph album that has been looked at many
times before, and experiencing again, for a time, the events deeply
embedded in one's life. Rosie: the child of immigrants, the student,
the young wife, the mother, the foster mother, the model teacher,
the ever-present helper and mentor. Carl remarked on her love of
nature and her love of people. I was buoyed by thoughts of all the
people she had touched with generosity and wisdom. If only, I
thought, this could have gone on. Then I suspended the thought.
I knew I should not dwell on the "ifs." We are privileged to have
shared our time with her.

A substantial portion of the service was for personal remembrances.
Dave was the first to speak. He remembered when I had introduced
him to Rosie for the first time. His initial apprehension about a girl
from the hoity-toity Upper West Side had been melted away within
minutes by her gracious warmth and unassuming manner. He spoke
of the times his twins visited their Aunt Rosie up in the wilds of

Massachusetts and how they had returned to the city bursting with stories of the birds she had spotted for them in the woods. They talked of the pond she had showed them where the deer came down to drink in early morning. Several teacher colleagues of Rosie came forward to speak. She had mentored some of them when they first came to do their student teaching. Friends from the garden club and the birding society spoke. And the several charities she had helped made comments.

Finally André came forward to speak. As I listened to him, I was struck by his complete assimilation. There was hardly a trace of an accent that was anything but a mild New York inflection. I remembered the day we picked him up at the dock and took him home at the beginning of the war. He clutched a shaggy teddy bear, looking a little fearful yet curious, under his little brimmed cap. Now, having almost finished his college studies at my old alma mater in New York, he was indistinguishable from many of the students I have seen come and go over the years.

"It was a long time ago," he explained. "and the details are shrouded in a childhood mist. But the feelings are as clear to me now as they were the day I stepped off the boat and was placed in the care of that strange lady who could hardly speak proper French. I cannot remember the trip from New York to this place except that somehow I felt safe and secure. I also remember how amazed I was by the way this lady could produce a chocolate bar from her purse."

I thought for a moment of that train ride so long ago I had made with my own mother across Europe.

André continued. "She was a protector, a nurse, a teacher, a companion. I called her Rosie or sometimes *tante,* never *mère.* She wanted me always to keep alive the hope that someday I would be with my real mother. Within months, I think, I was speaking English, but Rosie insisted that I not forget entirely how to speak French, hoping that I would somehow reunite with my family. Her own command of the French language was not especially remarkable. How could it be? She practiced it with a six year old! But what she did practice during those years I was with her was very different and very much more important to me. And that was a love that neither smothered nor demanded anything in return. And it was a love that gradually washed away the trauma of the escape from Europe, the parting from parents, the long journey over the ocean.

"I could probably tell you little stories about the time I spent here in Massachusetts. But Rosie's capacity for love is at the center of my thoughts. So, at the suggestion of Rosie's Jason and with the encouragement of Rev. Becker, I want to recite parts of that great paean to love in Paul's first letter to the Corinthians. It is from the New Testament but it is profoundly Jewish. It is the words of a devoted Jew speaking of that thing, which in his view undergirds meaningful religion. And I think it fitting that I read part of it in the French translation, in joyful and amused remembrance of how Rosie, even when she could not fully understand the meaning, might say that something sounded better in French. True enough, there are opera librettos that, while sounding good in an unfamiliar foreign language, are reduced to triviality when fully understood. Not so with this hymn from First Corinthians. I read in part:"

Supposons que je parle les langues des hommes et même celles des anges: si je n'ai pas d'amour: je ne suis rien de plus qu'un metal qui résonne ou qu'une cymbale bruyante.

Now André paused and looked up. He gazed around the room. Then he looked down again and continued.

> If I speak in the tongues of men and of angels, but have not love, I am a noisy gong or a clanging cymbal.
> And if I have prophetic powers, and understand all mysteries and all knowledge, and if I have all faith, so as to remove mountains, but have not love, I am nothing.
> If I give away all I have, and if I deliver my body that I may glory, but have not love, I gain nothing.
> Love is patient and kind; love is not jealous or boastful; it is not arrogant or rude.

Love does not insist on its own way; it is not irritable or resentful; it does not rejoice in wrong, but rejoices in the right.

Love bears all things, believes all things, endures all things . . .

. . . So faith, hope, love abide, these three, but the greatest of these is love.

André hesitated momentarily, then repeated the last line in French:

. . . *Maintenant, ces trois choses demeurent: la foi, l'esperance, et l'amour; mais la plus grande des trois est l'amour.*

After André had finished, Carl Becker rose and invited us to prayer. His words were a meditation, a call to remember the enduring things and put aside the transient, to honor the good and to strive for the better, and to learn from the examples that have come our way. The service ended with another of Rosie's favorite hymns, "Praise to the Living God." The music and the message of faith and hope is that of the *Yigdal*, so often used at the conclusion of Shabbas evening worship at synagogues. Rosie had once said it gave her a sense of kinship with all of humankind.

In the social hall below the sanctuary, Jason, Esther, and I greeted friends and colleagues. Some of them I had not seen for some time. My old friend Jacob was there with his wife. He was leaning on a cane but seemed almost as spry as the young boy who had challenged me to a race back in the old village. It was somewhat a relief to know that the old generation, having already passed on, did not have to be a part of this occasion. Hugs, handshakes, and kind words testified to the significance of Rosie in the world she had shared with me. Through these people, I realized, Rosie's presence in the world still lived on. But I was painfully aware of the empty place beside me that she had occupied.

For the past months, ever since Rosie left us, I felt myself moving slowly towards acceptance of her absence. Even within their own grieving the kids have been generous with their time and support. Gradually I have turned my energies back to work. Exciting things continue to happen in physics, and I am reengaged with my students. On a regular basis, Carl and I are taking long walks. No longer do I instinctively look around for Rosie when I enter our home. But in a way she always seems to be at my side, admonishing me to check my lapses into cynicism, and to look always for the bright side and the hopeful. The world is a beautiful and wondrous miracle still. But total closure, I know, is yet to come.

CHAPTER 31

Love's Old Sweet Song

1957

Now, more than a half-year after Rosie's passing, Jason, Esther, and I gathered on a recent Sunday morning. It was not long after the spring equinox, when the sun slips from its winter vacation back into our hemisphere and does its work of warming the earth and awakening dormant life. It was a only a short drive from home to the head of the trail leading to the summit of Wolf Mountain, the road having been improved in the more than thirty years since Rosie and I had first climbed to the top. We had then informally given a name to the place. Now, following from our initial suggestion, the name had finally been made official by the Interior Department—a place of our memories now marked on the maps.

This was to be a special expedition to honor Rosie and to commit her ashes to the earth. Jason took the lead. From a multi-colored strap around his shoulders he carried his guitar. Esther followed, with me taking up the rear. In my backpack, cradled in the plaid car rug we had bought for our first automobile, I carried the urn containing Rosie's ashes.

Along the trail, in occasional open spots the grass was heavy with dew. On the margins of these glades, where the sun cannot fully penetrate, some of last year's high grass formed mats of brown recently pressed down by the snow blanket of winter. Here and there, the remains of mouse tunnels, which had recently been covered with snow, were beginning to fade into the surrounding ground.

Where the path ascended gradually along the side of the mountain the forest pressed more closely in upon the trail.

When we reached the place where the steep switchbacks began, Jason stopped to wait until Esther and I could catch up with him. In the last few years my aerobic capacity has declined. I do not have trouble hiking these trails but both kids are measurably faster. Yet they are careful not to leave me far behind. And they know that I usually prefer to walk quietly in the rear in the company of my thoughts.

On that day I thought mostly about how life has played out in the last six months. Each of us, in our own way, has gradually adjusted to life without Rosie. It was no surprise to me to see the kids quickly resume their career paths. Jason is now finishing his second year at the divinity school and negotiating for a minister intern position in a Unitarian church for next year. Esther has developed a circle of friends in Pittsfield and will be enrolled in a couple of biology courses here at the University in the coming summer. I have accommodated slowly. No longer, returning from the University, do I feel a jarring emptiness upon entering the house. For a time, even though Rosie had slipped away gradually from us over a long period of time, her absence seemed unreal. Now she is like a comfortable presence.

After a half hour of moderately strenuous climbing, we reached the familiar place where a small stream flows out of the woods and crosses the trail. It was noontime. I wiped beads of sweat from my face as we sat down on some rocks for lunch. Esther brought out from her backpack a large loaf of crusty bread and chunks of cheddar and Swiss cheese. I remembered the first time Rosie and I came across this spot. Little seemed to have changed. Along the edge of the stream, where the water runs slack against the bank, mimulus still prospers. Rosie and I had dipped cups into this pool and drank the sweet water. But now we are constantly warned about the danger of Giardia, so Esther had brought along a plastic bottle of iced tea. I told Esther and Jason about the first time their mother and I had been to this spot, retelling the story of how the mountain got its name. Eventually a couple of gray jays came and perched in a branch above our heads, alternately swooping in to pick up the crumbs we held out for them on the palms of our hands.

When we resumed the hike, Jason suggested that I take the lead. This time we remained close to one another and walked in silence. We reached the summit about two in the afternoon. A chilly breeze swept across the open space from the west, but it was comfortable in the bright sun. To the west we could see the sweep of the valley, the silvery thread of the river braiding through it. To the east, undulating hills, faintly green in spring foliage, gave way to rolling farmland. We gathered in a circle and joined hands. We had agreed that this was not to be a solemn occasion, but a time to rejoice at Rosie's having been with us. Her greatest pleasure was with our pleasure and we would not deny her that.

Jason began with some words.

> "In this place, to which Mom gave a name, we remember that she gave to us life and love. In this place, where earth and sky meet, we know that we are of both. In this place, we have each other and we have our memories of Rosie. In this place, where the sun kisses our cheeks, we are thankful for her kisses. In this place, in which nature sings, we will sing. And let the wind bear our song to the heavens."

And sing we did. Jason sat down on a large rock with his guitar. I sat opposite him. Esther kneeled on the ground beside him and introduced her first song. "Mom was such an old-fashioned sentimentalist. I'll never forget her teaching us to sing this one on a camping trip. The words didn't mean much to me then, but now I can't think of a better way to begin."

> The ash-grove, how graceful, how plainly 'tis speaking,
> The harp through it playing has language for me;
> Whenever the light thro' its branches is breaking,
> A host of kind faces is gazing on me;
> The friends of my childhood again are before me,

Each step makes a mem'ry as freely I roam;
With soft whispers laden, its leaves rustle o'er me,
The ash grove, the ash grove alone is my home.

Esther's plain but lovely voice reminded me of Rosie's voice, a warm, mellifluous alto, not operatic, and almost conversational. On the second verse, Jason joined in with the harmony. They finished with a barely audible sigh. Then Jason played a little riff on the guitar, saying "Time to lighten up folks. You know Mom wasn't entirely a fuddy-duddy. In fact, come to think of it, I think she had a secret passion for Elvis."

"You're kidding, Jason," Esther said. "Where do you get that idea?"

"A couple of years ago I caught her in the act. She was in the kitchen making dinner. The radio was playing Elvis Presley and Mom was prancing about with a suggestive hip swivel. I swear."

"What was the song?" Esther asked.

Jason stood up. He struck a jarring chord, and began to sing.

You ain't nothin' but a hound dog,
Cryin' all the time.

Rosie leaped up, began gyrating and joined him.

Well you never caught a rabbit,
And you ain't no friend of mine.

I beat time with my hands as they finished their little dance. We all were laughing. "What did Mom say when you caught her prancing around the kitchen?" Esther wanted to know.

"She quoted from *archy and mehitabel*, as she sometimes did:"

my youth i shall never forget
but there s nothing I really regret
wotthehell wotthehell
there s a dance in the old dame yet
toujours gai toujours gai

When our laughter subsided I spoke up. "Well, most of the time your mom was a model of quiet dignity, as you know. But then there were moments. I've probably mentioned the time she had too much champagne at Uncle Alec's wedding?"

"Yes you have," Esther said. "And Mom always tried to hush you up."

"I guess she always felt embarrassed about it. Singing at the top of her lungs, kissing everyone, even the waiters," I said, feeling a little wistful. "She never overdid the champagne again. It's those little CO_2 bubbles, you know, that sneak up on you. Promotes the alcohol absorption."

"The scientist in you is untamed, Dad," Esther said, putting her arm around my shoulder and giving it a little squeeze. "That Good Ol' Mountain Dew," she sang. We joined in and sang a chorus.

There were more songs—"Tsena Tsena", "Logger Lover", "Good Night Irene." Between songs we remembered the family camping trips when we had sung together around the campfire. Finally Jason said, "I think it's time."

I took the Rosie's urn from my rucksack and unsealing it placed it on the ground in front of us. It was quiet except for the rushing breeze moving across the mountaintop. I took out our old copy of the *Rubaiyat* that Rosie had given me before we were married and read aloud.

> I sometimes think that never blows so red
> The Rose as where some buried Caesar bled;
> That every Hyacinth the Garden wears
> Dropt in its Lap from some once lovely Head.
>
> And this delightful Herb whose tender Green
> Hedges the River's Lip on which we lean—
> Ah, lean upon it lightly! For who knows
> From what once lovely Lip it springs unseen!

I picked up the urn and stepped to the edge of the rocky place where we had been sitting. Here, a carpet of mountain cranberry gave way to patches of newly rising grasses and budding witch hazel and sassafras. As I tipped the container the breeze caught the first of the ashes and carried them up and out before us. I watched as dust of our memories settled upon the ground, nestling among the roots of the grasses, settling within the folds of the shrubs. The wind bore a fine cloud aloft into the woods on the lip of the mountain and down into the valley below us.

One by one we picked up the urn and returned Rosie's ashes to the earth. None of us said a word. Every eye was moist. And I experienced a strange sensation of sadness mixed with utter relief. When the urn had been emptied, Jason and Esther, each in turn, came to me and we embraced. We stood there in silence for a while gathering our thoughts.

Eventually we gathered our belongings and turned back to where the trail enters the woods. Before it was out of sight I looked back briefly at my special garden of memories.

We descended silently until we again reached the place where the creek runs across the trail. There we sat for a short rest by the side of the water. The early spring sun was now low in the sky. Nearly horizontal shafts of light filtered through the tree branches. Jason lowered his guitar onto his lap.

"Esther and I want to do one more of Mom's sentimental favorites." I nodded approval and they sang in harmony. The chorus echoed in my head even the following day.

> Just a song at twilight, when the lights are low,
> And the flick'ring shadows softly come and go.
> Though the heart be weary, sad the day and long,
> Still to us at twilight comes love's old song,
> Comes love's old sweet song.

By the time we reached the trailhead it was nearly dusk. We drove into town and stopped at the inn by the river for supper. The waiter brought three mugs of beer while we waited for our food. We discussed our plans for the coming week. Esther would return to Pittsfield that evening to be ready for Monday morning classes.

Tomorrow Jason would take the midday train to Boston. Several important papers and a practice sermon had to be finished in the next few weeks. I planned to spend the next day at the lab working with the students. I was looking forward to the afternoon seminar on the recent confirmation at the Bureau of Standards of the idea of non-conservation of parity. I tried to briefly explain the concept.

"The bottom line is that for some phenomena Nature prefers to twist in one direction rather than another. If we could talk with those extra-terrestrials, even though they couldn't see us, we could suggest a test so that they could know what we mean by right-handedness as contrasted with left-handedness." Then I added, "Unless, perhaps, the extra-terrestrials live in a world of anti-matter, rather than our kind of matter."

"Is that possible?" Jason asked.

"So far there's no evidence for that at all. It's a great mystery. At the moment of creation, God seems to have given us a huge preponderance of ordinary matter." I paused to reflect. "You know, it's a fascinating time. A lot of answers are coming out, and every answer seems to deepen the mystery. There's hardly time to keep up."

Esther was determined to lighten the conversation. "Yes time," she said. "I think about one of Mom's favorites among archy's maxims."

> old doc einstein has abolished time
> but they haven t got the news at sing sing yet

"Here's to Einstein," she said, raising her glass.

"And here's to us." Jason lifted his mug.

"To time," I said. Our glasses clinked.

EPILOGUE

On a warm day towards the end of August 1957 Abe Roth left home in mid-morning. On the kitchen table, held in place by the sugar bowl, he left a note for Esther, who had been living there during the summer while enrolled at the University. He let her know where he would be that day. He would try not to be late returning but asked that she not wait supper for him. He placed a small rucksack on the car seat beside him and drove off to the trailhead at Wolf Mountain.

Abe had hiked quite a few trails over the years, but this one he knew intimately, like an old friend. At the watering spot before the final ascent he lunched on bread and cheese. As usual he reserved some bread for the camp robbers who seemed almost to have anticipated his coming. At the top, he paused for a few minutes to take in the view, then scanned the border of the open area in which he was standing. At last he discerned a faint deer trail that led for a short distance through the brush and into a grove of trees on its eastern edge. Making his way through the thick growth of ash and oak, once again he came upon the open grassy bench that he and Rosie had found many years before. It was poised on the lip of the mountain high above the farmland and scattered stands of forest stretching out to the horizon. On the margin of the clearing, matted grass beneath low hanging boughs was evidence of deer having bedded down in the shelter of the trees.

Abe found the oak tree under which he and Rosie lay on a summer day long ago. The tree was a husky one now, vigorous in the prime of its life, its limbs reaching high and lustily for the air and the sun. There, at its foot Abe spread a poncho. A warm breeze rustled the treetops, but beneath the overhanging branches the air was still and the ground, still cool from the nighttime chill, invited him to lie down in the shade. He looked up, hypnotized by the flickering array of sky-blue patches coming and going among the branches. Presently he fell asleep.

In his dream Rosie was with him. He knew that she had been gone almost a year, but somehow she was with him again. Her reappearance was nothing he felt compelled to question or explain. He only knew the pleasure of her being with him for a while. He was following her along the footpath by the side of the river. Now and then she stopped and pointed out a bird in the underbrush. On the opposite riverbank a mud-colored juvenile heron was motionless except for his swiveling head as he scanned the water. Abe found himself thinking about water, this miracle substance with the unusual property of floating its solid form on top of its liquid essence, thus protecting the creatures within its body, for which it is the ultimate source and sustainer. He became aware of the sounds of the water, a murmur that would be hard to duplicate except by the tumbling of drops and wavelets and ripples breaking on the shoreline.

Abe woke up suddenly. There was a rustling noise in the brush along the edge of the clearing nearby. Slowly he turned his head. About ten yards from him a doe had been nibbling at the low-growing foliage. Now she stood frozen in place, her eyes locked on his gaze, her ears raised and turned towards him. In this way they looked at one another for several minutes as the details of Abe's dream faded, leaving only the warm sense that follows a pleasurable visit. Eventually the doe resumed her foraging, as if accepting Abe as a welcome and familiar visitor to her domain. Abe sat up and looked out at the sky crowning the eastern landscape. By now the sun was riding low behind the trees at his back.

He thought about the trajectory of events that had brought him to this place at this time. It was a path that could hardly have been predicted, much less imagined. In his thoughts he likened it to the observable journey of a microscopic particle in a series of fitful movements through a fluid. At each stopping place were myriad choices for each leg of the journey: the flight from Poland, the ocean crossing to New York, the pursuit of a college degree, the war work in Washington, the graduate studies at Columbia, his lovely marriage, his academic career in New England. Like the particle in random walk the possibilities for the final location were beyond counting. But unlike an inanimate speck in a sea of jiggling molecules in thermal agitation, he knew the choices made at each halting point in his life could not have been entirely random. He was sure there was some guiding principle, some prejudice in his behavior or opinion that had always narrowed his options.

On the eastern horizon he saw the moon just beginning to rise. It occurred to him that at that moment this moon was riding high in the sky above the farms and forests of Eastern Europe. He imagined it casting ghostly shadows in the streets and alleys of the village of Wizna where his journey had begun. His recollections of that place were dim and scant, but for some reason that had always mystified him, the encounter as a small boy with a coin lying in the dust in front of the tavern remained fixed in his memory. Then, unexpectedly, he saw in that event a metaphor for his life journey. Here, expressed in a parable, was the tension between the mundane and the spiritual that had been had been the essential struggle for him: the palpable versus the ineffable, reason versus dogma, the practical versus ritual. He was startled and pleased by the epiphany, as if his life was at once laid out before him as a coherent whole. The solution he had devised as a seven year old tempted by a kopek on a Sabbath morning was no better nor worse than the joining together of worldly action and respect for the divine that he was satisfied had marked his life.

The moon hung now like a ballooning parachute three or four diameters above the fading silhouette of distant hills. Abe knew that in a few days it would be a full moon, rising above the rim of the earth at the moment that the sun is sinking below it on the opposite horizon. Then, the body of the earth would be in its twice-monthly maximum tension, stretched between the ruler of the night and the ruler of the day. The crust of the earth beneath Wizna would rise imperceptibly and the bulge would speed across Europe at a thousand miles an hour tracing the path he had journeyed more than six decades ago. On the great ocean a spring tide would rise up, crossing the waters and racing up the inlets and bays of America. Below the great mountains and basins of the West little fractures and dislocations would appear, helping prepare conditions when pent up energy in the rocks would unpredictably emerge in a catastrophic release. The great tidal bulge would now move out over the Pacific, and on its western edge certain corals would welcome the full moon at certain times of the year in a frenzy of synchronized spawning. As he thought about these things, Abe felt an abiding humility.

Presently, the sun slipped below the horizon. Abe rose and from his pack he removed a slim box that had been tucked among the folds of his spare parka. Within the box was a single crimson rose. He removed the damp tissue paper in which he had wrapped the stem and held the flower in his hands. In the diffuse light from the sky it seemed almost to glow. Abe looked at it carefully, admiring the delicacy and intricacy of this creation: fold within fold, a microcosm of an ideal world created only to inspire and delight. He raised the blossom to his lips and inhaled the delicate perfume that surrounded it. Then he bent down and gently laid the rose at the base of the young oak tree.

Gathering his belongings Abe turned back into the woods. The trail to the bottom of the mountain was sufficiently lit by the lingering summer twilight and the nearly full moon. When he reached the bottom of the mountain the western light was totally gone. Now, before making his way to his waiting car, he paused to view the star-filled sky. Tilting back his head, and with a sense of unspoken gratitude, he peered down into the great bowl of the universe.

CPSIA information can be obtained at www.ICGtesting.com
Printed in the USA
LVOW131117030613

336653LV00002B/155/P